THE LONG WAY HOME

Other Five Star Titles
by Lauraine Snelling:

Hawaiian Sunrise
Daughter of Twin Oaks
Sisters of the Confederacy
An Untamed Land

THE LONG WAY HOME

HOME

Lauraine Snelling

Five Star • Waterville, Maine

Five Star Christian Fiction Series.

Published in 2002 in conjunction with Bethany House Pub-
lishers.

The text of this edition is unabridged.

Set in 11 pt. Plantin.

Printed in the United States on permanent paper.

Library of Congress Cataloging-in-Publication Data

Snelling, Lauraine.
    The long way home / Lauraine Snelling.
      p. cm.
    ISBN 0-7862-3686-8 (hc : alk. paper)
    1. Women pioneers—Fiction. 2. Overland journeys to
the Pacific—Fiction. I. Title.
    PS3569.N39 L66 2002
    813'.54—dc21   2001050174

The Long Way Home is dedicated to
the glory of God and to the gift
He has given me in my Round Robin Circle.
These friends help keep me sane and on track.

CHAPTER ONE

WEST OF FORT LARAMIE
ON THE OREGON TRAIL
LATE JUNE 1863

Gray Wolf Torstead, long dark hair tied back with a piece of latigo, topped the hill on his blood bay Appaloosa as the sun broke the horizon. Turning to look over his shoulder, he could no longer see the smoke from the campfires of the wagon train. Looking east he knew he could make it back to the fort with some days of hard riding, gather his supplies, and head home.

Home. Would his mother's tribe's tepees feel like home, or had he lived with the white men too long? Like he'd been trailing the wagon train too long. They didn't need him. Jesselynn didn't need him. Jesselynn—a much better name than Jesse. But he'd had to make sure the new wagon master knew what he was doing. They'd camped in the right places, kept watch at night, and grazed the herd. He'd even heard the fiddle singing one evening.

He knew the scouts had seen him, but then he hadn't been trying to hide. Just making sure they were safe.

He nudged his Appaloosa into a mile-eating lope and promised himself to put Jesselynn Highwood out of his mind.

7

Out of his heart was another matter entirely. Questions that kept time with his horse's hooves circled round again. Why had he let her go? Why had he not at least asked her to stay, to marry him?

"Worryin' gots you lower den a turtle belly."

Jesselynn Highwood looked over at the smiling black face of Meshach, who used to be overseer at her home in Kentucky. Now he was a freedman and her friend. "I'm not worrying. I'm thinking." She tucked her slouch hat, which looked to have been wheel fodder, between her britches-covered knees and finger combed her shaggy hair back off her forehead. The hat kept her hair out of her eyes at least, dark blond hair now barely stained by walnut dye. Masquerading as a male to keep her people safe took a lot of sacrifices, especially for a nineteen-year-old Southern woman.

I thought you gave up lying. That little voice inside woke from a nap and, smirking, tapped her on the shoulder.

Jesselynn, her elbows propped on her knees, the reins to the two span of oxen loose in her fingers, stared out over the backs of her trudging bovines. Dust from the wagons ahead of her wore her face dry and crunched between her teeth. She'd lost the juice to swallow with, and the sun hadn't come on eleven yet.

"Whoa, son." Meshach gentled Ahab, the Thoroughbred stallion that would be the foundation of their horse farm when they made it to Oregon Territory and a new start—away from the war.

Right now, after weeks on the trail, Oregon seemed farther away than ever.

Meshach kept the horse even with the left front wheel of their lead wagon. "Looks like worryin' to me."

Jesselynn kept the bite out of her voice with great effort. "I

8

said I'm not worrying." The emphasis on the last word rang hollow even to her own ears. If this wasn't worrying, what was it? She chewed on the thoughts like a hound dog with a knucklebone.

"I don't trust Jason Cobalt." She said the words loud enough for Meshach's ears alone.

"They say he be a good man."

"I don't doubt that. I just doubt his ability to guide this wagon train through to Oregon. Last night they were talking about taking a shortcut."

"I heard."

"Wolf said that shortcut was short on water and the hills steeper." That was her *real* problem—Mr. Gray Wolf Torstead, better known as Wolf. She knew it down to the stitching on her boots. Why had he left the train and his job as wagon master? She thought she understood the answer to that too, thanks to a conversation with an Indian scout. Wolf had felt a call to return to the land of his mother, an Oglala Sioux who died when he was a youth. However, understanding and agreeing were two entirely different things. She wished she understood all the scout had said.

But if she dug deep enough, and she did that only in the still hours of the morning before the rising sun dimmed the starlight, she knew the *real* question. Why? Why had he left *her?* Thanks to that one embrace they'd shared, she'd dreamed of more. More embraces, perhaps a life together. After all, she didn't take embraces lightly, not when they made her breathless. Seemed like his had. She let her head drop forward like a heavy blossom on a slender stalk. Why had he left?

Meshach was entirely too perceptive. Aunt Agatha would be on her back next. Keeping her feelings from her nosy aunt would take some doing. Pious, upright, Southern to the

9

smallest bone, Aunt Agatha would definitely not approve of the direction her niece's thoughts were taking in regard to a half-white, half-Sioux man named Wolf. No matter how much Agatha had changed since the early days of Springfield, with these woman-man thoughts, Jesselynn was seriously transgressing.

Jesselynn forced her head upright and a smile to her lips. Wolf was a moot point anyway. He'd left the train, left her, and all she had to do was keep her sights on Oregon.

Am I not sufficient for thee?

At the gentle reminder, she shook her head. *Of course you are, Lord, but you know what I mean. I . . . I thought maybe— okay, I don't know.* The sigh came from the balls of her feet. *He's a good man, and I hope and pray he will be happy up there with his mother's people.* She glanced ahead to see that Meshach now rode beside the McPhereson wagon. Something Mrs. Mac said made him throw his head back and laugh, a hearty laugh that said more about the man than the joke. Meshach laughed a lot more on the trail than she'd ever heard him laugh at Twin Oaks. His body-shaking laugh drew in others like bees to blossoms. One would have to be carrying a huge lump of a heart to not laugh along with Meshach.

Jesselynn saw it all and tucked it away to ponder later. Is this what freedom did to a man once enslaved? He'd told her once that Christ set him free long before she did, but she knew she witnessed the change.

Do others see that joy in me? The thought made her flinch. The last three days had been particularly empty of any emotion that bore even a fleeting reminiscence of joy. "Sorry," she said aloud and shook her head as she flipped a glance heavenward. *Praise ye the Lord.* Meshach had read that in a psalm the night before. She'd heard it with only half an ear. She had a feeling God would rather she not only heard but did as He commanded.

She could hear her mother too. *"No better time to change than right now."* Oh, Mother, such wisdom you had. *What would you say to all this that's gone on?*

"Marse Jesse, you all right?" Benjamin, another of her former slaves, looked at her out of the corner of his eye, as if afraid of intruding but caring enough to want to know.

"Yes, I'm right as a June bug." Jesselynn flashed him a smile that she'd dredged up somewhere out of her middle. "You want to drive awhile?" She grinned at the rolled-eye look he gave her. She knew he'd rather ride than drive any day, just like she would.

"Yes, suh." His sigh made her smile again. "I go tell Miss Agatha." He turned his horse and rode to the wagon behind hers. Jesselynn had become Jesse instead of Jesselynn and Sir or Suh or Marse to her family to keep them all safe when they were forced to leave Twin Oaks near Midway, Kentucky. When Benjamin returned, Jesselynn whoad the oxen and leaped to the ground, her feet sending tingles up to her knees. She swung easily into the saddle and waited while Benjamin climbed up on the wagon seat and hupped the oxen forward. The wheels creaked in protest. One of the oxen bellered.

Jesselynn dropped back to the end of the wagon train and crossed to the north side. No one had reported the Indian shadowing them in the last day or so. On one hand she felt the same relief the others expressed at his supposed departure, but on the other she wished she'd known who he was and what his purpose was. When Wolf had led the wagon train, she'd not wasted time thinking on such things.

Turning Ahab, she cantered back to the herd of horses and cattle that snatched grass along the way as they trailed the train. Daniel, another of her young freedmen, and two other young men from the train kept the herd moving, watching out for danger, be it Indian or beast.

"Anyone seen the Indian that followed us?" she asked as she drew even with Daniel riding Domino, her younger stallion. The two mares along with their foals kept to the center of the herd.

"No, suh." Daniel stood in his stirrups to stretch his legs. "We ain't seen nothin', not even a coyote. This sure do be empty land."

"Getting rougher too." Jesselynn looked westward toward the undulating hills that grew ever steeper. Black clouds billowed on top of the hills like frosting piled high on a three-layer cake, the sun stenciling the rims with silver. The cooling breeze felt welcome to her dry skin, but the thought of a thunder-and-lightning storm made her squint. Heat lightning speared the blackness.

Surely Cobalt would send others back to help with the herd.

Jesselynn saw Meshach cantering back toward them, but no one else.

"Is he going to circle the wagons?"

Meshach shook his head. "He say got to make up lost time. Keep dem wagons rollin'."

Jesselynn gritted her teeth. God help them if they had a runaway. Another lightning bolt streaked the sky, this time with a thunder rumble. Several of the herd leaders raised their heads, sniffing the wind. Bellows answered restless bellows.

Oxen lowed from the wagons ahead.

Meshach dropped back to speak with one of the young men and pointed out where he should ride, then did the same for the other. With the five of them circling the herd, perhaps they had a chance.

At the first heavy crack of thunder and lightning, Wolf had

always circled the wagons with the herd inside. While restless at first, the herd had settled down, ignoring the rain, with the cattle chewing their cuds.

But now the pace picked up. More bawling. A horse whinnied.

Do I go confront Cobalt or not? Ice balled in her middle. The first drops spattered her hat brim and sprinkled her hands. Cold all right. It could turn to hail real easy.

"We need to settle the herd down in a low place. You want to take on Cobalt, or should I?" She knew better than to ask. Cobalt had already made his opinion of black men obvious. But then he'd ignored her also.

"We take care de herd first," Meshach said.

Jesselynn nodded. In a stampede her foals would be the first to go down. She turned and rode up beside one of the other young men with the herd. "Swing those ropes in front of the leaders and keep them calm. Whistle, sing, whatever you can do."

"Yes, sir." The boy—she couldn't remember his name—did as told. If only some of the others in the train were as cooperative.

"Over there!" She pointed off to what looked like a basin set among the hills. "Get the herd down there and off these hills."

Lightning lit the sky with blue light. She counted until the thunder crashed. Coming nearer. She drove Ahab into the center of the herd to cut out their mares. Daniel followed suit, and without adding turmoil to the tail-twitching, bawling herd, they each lassoed a mare and eased her and her foal out of the mass of animals. They still needed the filly and Roman the mule. Their loose ox would have to take his chances.

Meshach brought the filly out and handed his rope to

Daniel. "I'll get de mule."

"No!" Jesselynn had to shout to be heard, close as they were. "Save the herd."

Never had she wished for another rope as much as now. Lightning flashed again, thunder rolled and boomed with another crack right after. The lead cow broke into a trot. Jesselynn handed her lead rope to Daniel and pointed to an arroyo that cut off to the north. "Get the horses up in that arroyo and hold them there."

Knowing he would follow orders, she whistled for Patch, their cow dog, and broke into a canter, heading for the leaders of the trotting herd. "Swing them in a circle. Now!" Thunder and splattering rain drowned out her shout. She whipped her hat off and waved it at the still-milling cattle. *"Hai, hayup!"* Patch headed for the leaders. Ahab shook his head but obeyed her squeezing legs and edged closer to the herd. Seeing what she and Meshach were doing, the other two herders followed suit, and the herd surged over the rise and down into the depression. With Patch barking and nipping when necessary, they turned the front-runners and got them circling with the riders loping around them. Sheltered by the hills in the shallow valley, Jesselynn breathed a sigh of relief. They could catch up with the train later.

Lightning turned the darkness into day, a blue day with the smell of lightning and rain on the air. The crack near to broke her eardrums. Ahab half reared, and only Jesselynn's hands clenched on the reins and her legs clamped to his sides kept him from bolting. She fought him back to a standstill, her voice calm in spite of the terror that set her heart to racing.

"That was a strike for sure. I'm goin' to check on the wagons. Can you hold them here?"

Meshach nodded, so Jesselynn reined Ahab away from the

herd and trotted him up the rise, lightning flashes illuminating her way. Ducking her head to keep the rain from blinding her, she broke into a canter now that she was beyond the distance of panicking the herd.

This time she saw it. A forked bolt of lightning cracked the heavens, blued the world, and struck the ground up toward the front of the wagon train. The sound set the earth to ringing like an earthquake rolled through. Ahab leaped forward, his shrill whistle adding to the panic in Jesselynn's heart. She clung like a burr, her "Oh, God, oh, God" the only prayer she could offer.

Fire flared from the lead wagon. Screams rent the air. Teams broke loose from the train and drove ahead in all directions, wagons rocking and bucking over the rough ground.

Ahab slowed at her fierce hold on the reins, and they pulled even with the last of the wagons. The wagon drivers near the end of the train had gotten a strong enough hold on the reins that they were already stopping.

"Pull into a circle and unyoke!"

Aunt Agatha, white faced but able, pulled her oxen to the right, Benjamin right behind her. For once being at the rear of the train proved to be a blessing. She could hear Ophelia singing and praying loud enough to scare away thunder. The sound brought a smile to Jesselynn's face. She caught up with Nate Lyons, who waved when he saw her, and his grandson, Mark, clutching the seat beside him.

"Go on back. Benjamin and Agatha are circling."

"What we shoulda done some time ago, that . . ." Lyons, whom Agatha referred to as Brushface, cut off his sentence, but Jesselynn had a pretty good idea what he was thinking. He waved her on.

She pointed another wagon back to the circle and cantered

on. A long storage box smashed open on the ground forced Ahab into the air in a jump that sent Jesselynn clinging upon his neck. She pulled him to a stop, settled herself in the saddle again, and peered through the sheeting rain, waiting for another heavenly candle to light the sky.

When it did, she blinked, trying to dislodge the eerie sight. Broken wagons and suffering oxen littered the land. Slowly picking her way among split barrels, soaked bedding, and a splintered rocking chair, she searched for injured people. One wagon missing a rear wheel stood upright, its driver unyoking the oxen, one down, one holding up a foreleg.

"Are you folks hurt?" Jesselynn paused by the man.

"Only shook up. Better'n some of the others."

Jesselynn touched her hat and nudged Ahab forward. The next wagon lay on its side, hoops crushed like paper. A limping man struggled to release the braces that held a thrashing ox to its still mate. A child's cries caught her attention from a nearby heap of debris.

"I'll be right back," she told the man and nudged Ahab forward. He snorted and trembled as they approached the shattered wagon bed. "Hello, anyone here?"

The cries rose louder.

Jesselynn dismounted and, looping Ahab's reins over her arm, dug into the mess. Lifting a soggy sack of grain, then assorted clothing, she found a young child dressed in the shift of all small children. She knelt beside the screaming, arm-flailing little one, seeing the right leg twisted at an angle.

"Easy, child, easy." The child opened its eyes and choked on a scream, reaching for her with both arms and a plaintive wail.

"Ma-a-a. Want Ma." A hiccup followed.

Jesselynn ignored the rain pelting them both and took the child's hands in hers. "Easy, baby. I can't pick you up until I make sure there's nothing else broken." The child's hands in one of hers, Jesselynn used her other to explore the child's body, watching for any signs of pain at her probing. "Now, you lie still and let me do something about that leg, you hear?"

But the child clung like mistletoe, refusing to let loose of her hand.

Jesselynn looked up, hoping and praying someone else would come by and help her. "Father, what do I do? I've got to get this child out of the rain, or we'll have more problems than just a broken leg." She glanced back to see if her wagons were in shouting distance. Barely able to see them through the curtain of rain, she figured not. A man shouted for help from some distance.

Thunder rolled again but heading east. The rain continued unabated. She pulled a piece of material from under more debris, ripped it in strips and, taking a piece of a shattered wagon board, folded part of the cloth around the board, then laid it beside the child's leg. "All right, little one, this is going to hurt again." With infinite gentleness, she slipped the board under the twisted leg.

The child screamed. Jesselynn bit her lip and whimpered herself. "Please, Father, guide my hands. Make this work. If you're near my mother, sure wish you could send her here to help." All the while she murmured soothing sounds to the child and reiterated in her mind her mother's instructions on setting a broken bone. *"Pull steady on the joint on either side until the break slips back in."* "Now we got to wrap this all the way up your leg, and then I can carry you to Ophelia. She'll help make it better. I know she will." With the last knot tied, Jesselynn slid her arms under the child's body and, holding the leg steady with the other hand, rose to an upright position. Trying not to jar the leg, she covered the ground to her wagon as swiftly as possible.

"Oh, dear Lord, what have we here?" Aunt Agatha, oil-cloth cape over her shoulders, reached for the burden.

"No, I'll lay her down. I didn't set the leg. We'll have to do that later." She laid the child on top of a wooden box in the rear. "I've got to check on the others." She glanced up to see six wagons now in the circle and another approaching. "You seen Cobalt?"

Agatha turned from comforting the child whose weak "Ma-a" tore at Jesselynn's heart. "No, and don't say I care if'n I ever do," Agatha retorted.

"I know, me too." Jesselynn swung back on Ahab. "If Meshach comes, send him on to help me. Oh, and get my medicine box out when you can. We're going to be needing all the supplies we can find."

She made her way from wagon to wagon, assessing the damage. When she reached what had been the lead wagon, she asked one of the men what happened.

"Struck by lightning. Hit that first hoop, and the noise scattered all the critters. Never seen such a awful mess in all my born days."

"The driver's dead?"

"Umm. And the two rear oxen." He pointed to the two carcasses. "The others burnt some but alive."

Jesselynn studied the scorched wagon, burned at the bolts, the joinings, the wheels.

"The man have a family?"

"Uh, yup. Someone come and took the missus and the little boy. They was stunned bad but sittin' in the back outa the rain kept 'em alive."

"Better cut the throats of those two dead ox. Let them bleed out so they can use the meat."

"Uh, yup. That's what I come to do. Can't waste the meat

in spite of all the tragedies." The man went about his task, and Jesselynn cantered off to help wherever she could.

The downpour continued.

She'd just checked the last wagon when Meshach caught up with her. "Herd safe. Good thing Daniel brought our horses back to the herd. Gully washer come through dat arroyo not long after."

"Thank the Lord above." Jesselynn reined Ahab so they rode knee to knee to be heard over the drumming rain. "At least there will be oxen able to pull the wagons that can go on. I think at least four are totally wrecked. Not sure how many people dead, or animals. Still haven't seen that so-called wagon master."

"He's sendin' folks back to the circle. Good thing you got them wagons turnin'."

"Only about an hour late. If he'd circled them at the first thunder roll, none of this would have happened." She indicated the area with a swept arm. "The man oughta be shot."

"You can't say for certain nothin' happen."

Jesselynn sighed. "I know. Let's get on and see how we can help."

Darkness fell with two wagons unaccounted for.

Jesselynn, Ophelia, and Aunt Agatha spent the evening bandaging wounds, comforting those who'd lost family members, and wringing out their mud-heavy skirts. Jesselynn was at least spared the skirt routine, since even after the others knew she was a female in men's clothing, she had never bowed to the pressure to give up her britches. When her box ran dry of rolled bandages, she set Jane Ellen to tearing up one of their few remaining sheets.

She and Benjamin strung a tarp off the rear of one wagon, and thanks to Meshach carrying dry wood in slings under the wagon, they got a fire going to heat soup and coffee. As the wagon folk ate and warmed themselves at the fire, Jesselynn heard comments about the wagon master, none of them good.

If I'd just followed my instincts and gone after Cobalt, this whole thing might have been averted. Wolf, where are you when we need you so bad? I sure hope you're happy with your family, tribe, whatever you want to call it.

"Anyone seen Cobalt?" She kept her voice low for Agatha's ears alone.

"I heard he's searching for any lost ones. If'n he had any sense, he'd be heading for the hills."

"Where Mr. Wolf go?" Three-year-old Thaddeus Highwood wrapped an arm around his sister's leg and leaned into her warmth.

"I told you he went north to his people."

"When he comin' back?"

Jesselynn squatted down to look her little brother directly in his blue eyes. "Thaddeus, he's not coming back. I reckon we just have to get used to that." She smoothed the honey-hued curls back off his forehead. "Do you understand?"

He nodded, one forefinger making its way to his mouth. "Where Patch?" The black shepherd-type dog had adopted them after his home and family went up in flames on the road before Independence. He took his job herding Thaddeus and Sammy seriously.

"Out with the herd, he was a big help in turning those critters into a circle."

"Did he bark?"

"Yup, and bit one old ox right on the shoulder." Jesselynn stood up, taking Thaddeus with her. He hugged both arms around her neck, his legs around her waist.

"Lightnin' scared me."

"Me too." She kissed his cheek. "But you were brave so Sammy didn't cry, weren't you?"

"Uh-huh. Sammy the baby." Dark as Thaddeus was fair, Sammy came to them when they found his mother dead in the Kentucky woods.

"He was mighty brave. Like an eagle, he was." Jane Ellen patted the little boy's bottom as she passed by. "Rain's done."

Jesselynn and Thaddeus both looked up to the canvas over their heads. Sure enough, not even spatters ticked the tarp. She hugged her little brother closer, and at the same moment they turned to listen, their smiles matching.

Someone had taken out a fiddle, and the plaintive notes of "Amazing Grace" floated across the circle.

Jesselynn blinked back the tears that burned at the back of her eyes. She hummed, stopped when her throat filled, swallowed, and picked up the words. "I once was lost, but now am found. . . ."

Jane Ellen's sweet soprano joined her. "Was blind, but now I see."

"Oh, Lord, help us find those who are still lost." Jesselynn set Thaddeus down on the wagon tailgate and motioned for him to stay there. She looked upward to see one star twinkling through the ragtag drifting clouds. "I'm going for Daniel. I'll stand guard so he can go look for the other two wagons." The notes of the song sang on in her mind, even after the fiddler segued into another tune. Lost and blind, that's what they were for certain sure out here on the Oregon Trail. What she wouldn't give for the friendly lights of a town or even one house. She stopped Ahab and looked back toward the camp. Two fires glowed now and a lantern or two, and hammers already rang in repair. Meshach's blacksmithing skills would be in great demand in the morning.

Coyotes yipped a hill or so away, sounding like they were behind the nearest rock. Most likely they smelled the blood of the dead and injured. "Oh, Lord, please send us a legion of angels to guard the camp tonight. We don't need an animal or Indian attack now."

CHAPTER TWO

FORT LARAMIE, WYOMING TERRITORY

The storm broke as Wolf rode into Fort Laramie. Before he could dismount and tie his horse, he was soaked as if he'd stood under a waterfall, so he led his horse up the two steps to the porch with him. Lightning turned the evening into day in flashes close enough together to make a lamp unnecessary. The blue white light carried its own peculiar fragrance, and the ground failed to suck in the moisture quickly enough to keep from puddling.

Once under the overhang of the general store, he glanced back to the west. While he could see no farther than the water curtaining off the roof, in his mind he knew the wagons were circled in a hollow and the herd safely bedding down in the middle. Jason Cobalt surely had enough trail sense to do that, didn't he? *Of course he did,* Wolf answered his own silent question.

"Come on in out of the downpour," a man called to him from the door of the mess hall.

"Thanks, but I got to take care of my horse first."

"Down to the livery. Red'll put yer horse up, you too, if'n ye don't mind a hay pile for your bed. Then come on back. We got hot coffee in here that'll drive the damp out."

"Any food?"

"That too. Say, ain't you that wagon master called Wolf?

Thought you was takin' a train west."

"I was. Long story." Wolf clucked his horse back down the wooden stairs, mounted, and trotted to the half-rock, half-wood hulk of a barn, recognized as such by the wide rolling door across the front. Wolf dismounted, slid the door open wide enough for his horse to follow him through, and stopped to drip. The roar sounded like the rain was intent on washing the shingles clear to Kansas City.

"Anybody here?" He shouted to be heard over the onslaught. When no one answered, he flipped the reins around a post and waited for the lightning to give him an idea where a door might be, other than the one he came in by. "Halloo."

Still no answer. He listened in the interval between thunder rolls. He could hear a horse chewing off to his right and a snort to the left. Figuring on stalls on both sides, he waited and, at the lightning flicker, saw an empty box ahead and to the right. Untying his horse, he led him to the place. One didn't need light to complete such a familiar task. Stalls were much the same everywhere. Hanging his saddle over the half wall between him and the main door, he tied a latigo around his horse's neck and to the manger, already filled with hay. He felt for the water bucket in the corner. It too was full.

"That Red runs a good barn. Now if we just knew where the grain bin lay." The horse nudged his elbow and nosed around him to drag out a mouthful of hay. The familiar sound of horses chewing gave the barn a cozy feeling. If his stomach hadn't rumbled about as loud as the last clap of thunder, he might have rolled up in his bedroll and slept out the remainder of the night.

Instead, he opened the door again, just enough to slip through, and headed for the mess hall, lights from the windows a friendly beacon. He pushed open the door and paused just inside. Two tables of poker, cigar smoke writhing above the players, appealed to him about as much as stepping back outside in the downpour, so he headed down the center aisle to trestle tables toward the back. Two men were writing letters, one reading in the lamplight.

"Grub's still hot." A sergeant motioned over his shoulder to the counter.

"Thanks." Wolf nodded as he spoke.

"You Gray Wolf Torstead?"

"Yes."

"Umm. Captain stopped by, said he wanted to see you first thing." When Wolf paused, the man continued. "You can eat first. They be closing up in here soon."

Wolf took the plate of stew and biscuits offered him and made his way to the end of the table, against the wall where he could see around the entire room. Not that there was much worth seeing.

"You want coffee?" The sergeant held up a steaming pot and two mugs.

Wolf nodded. The man plunked the cups down and filled them to the brim. Setting the gray coffeepot in the center of the table, he stepped over the bench and sat down.

With grizzled hair and a face that had seen more than man wanted or needed, the man sipped his coffee and let Wolf eat. When he'd scraped up the last of the juice with his remaining biscuit, the sergeant leaned forward on his elbows.

"What made you let the train go on with Cobalt?"

Wolf looked up to see the man studying him. "Why you asking?"

"Got me curious, that's all. I've heard nothing but good on you as a wagon master. . . ."

Wolf waited. If the man continued, fine. If not, he'd head for the captain's quarters.

"Not that I need to be nosy or nothin'."

Picking up his coffee mug, Wolf drank and set the mug down. "Anything I should know before I go talk with the captain?"

The sergeant shrugged. "Guess not. You know those Jones brothers?"

Wolf paused in the act of standing up. "Yes." Been some time since he was so close to killing a man as he had that Tommy Joe Jones.

"They took off outa here sometime after your train left. Said they was gonna catch up, like maybe the new wagon master would let them travel with him."

"I thought one of them was in the guardhouse."

"He was. Captain said to let 'im go on the condition they don't show their ugly faces around this fort again."

The words Wolf thought in regard to the Jones brothers went far beyond the biblical admonition to let your yes be yes and no be no. His father had added, *"No sense embroidering on what's right."* Or wrong, as could be in this case. "I see." He almost asked if the sergeant knew what the captain wanted but stopped himself. No sense appearing concerned. After all, the army no longer held any control over him. Nor did the wagon train. Cobalt knew about the Jones brothers, and if he didn't, the men of the wagon train did. They'd keep a close eye on those scums.

"Thanks for the food—and the information." He had no idea what he'd do with that information, but he now knew what a horse felt like with a burr under the saddle. The burr was named Jesselynn Highwood, and in spite of all his efforts, she clung closer than his skin. What a fool he'd been to let her go.

He dropped his dishes off at the window and exited to the captain's office. He didn't need to ask directions, although what the captain was doing in his office instead of being home with his family only brought up more questions. Was there more going on here than it had seemed when he had brought the wagon train through?

The orderly passed him on through, and Wolf shook hands with the blue-coated officer behind the desk. Obediah Jensen had a reputation as a spit-and-polish man, and his appearance this late in the day bore that up. He also had a reputation as a fair man who believed keeping the peace between Indian and white was his primary job. And supplying wagon trains, so they kept moving on through Indian territory, was only part of that.

"Have a seat," Captain Jensen said, indicating the chair with a sweep of his hand. "Thought you were going on home—to Red Cloud's tribe, wasn't it?"

"I was and am."

The captain reached for the humidor that reigned on a corner of his desk and held it out to Wolf. Then, at Wolf's gesture of refusal, he extracted a cigar, bit the tip off, and lighted it. After two puffs he leaned back and blew the smoke at the ceiling. "How long since you been up there?"

"Too long."

"Kept in touch?"

Wolf gave him a level stare. The captain knew the Oglala did not read or write. Those were two things Wolf hoped to change.

"I see." Captain Jensen appeared to be in deep thought.

Wolf sat as still as if he were hunting, his quarry in sight but too far for an arrow to hit. He never had cared for cigar smoke. Nor the chewing of tobacco. Nor the white man's firewater. His rifle, however, was another matter.

The captain leaned forward, forearms on the desk. "I have a proposition for you."

Wolf quirked an eyebrow.

"I need to know what Red Cloud's band is planning."

So do I, if I am going to help keep them alive.

"They have got to quit attacking wagon trains—not that it's been his band raiding the trains, but the Sioux in general."

"Red Cloud can't speak for all the Sioux."

"I know that, but he is gaining in leadership. I hoped you could be an influence on him."

"And come running to you if he chooses to wage war on the whites?"

"I wouldn't put it quite thataway."

Again the raised eyebrow. "The tribes have been warring on each other since time began."

"I know, and I have no trouble with that. Just leave the white men alone."

"But when white men settle on tribal lands—"

"Or kill off the buffalo—I know all the arguments, Torstead." The captain tapped off his ash in the pewter tray on the side of the desk. "Let me reiterate. I want to keep everyone alive. If the Indians steal horses or oxen from the wagon trains, the settlers won't get through to Oregon. They might choose to stay here instead. Can you understand me?"

The look Wolf sent him said he understood all too well and didn't much care for the tone the captain was taking.

"Well, you think on it. In the meantime, I wondered if you would take a couple of men out hunting. Our meat supply is running out, and I know you can locate elk far more swiftly than my men ever could. A couple days shouldn't make a big difference in your journey north."

When he could see Wolf was about to decline, he added, "I'll pay you in blankets, grain, whatever you want from the stores. Anything but rifles and whiskey."

"Done." Wolf extended his hand as he rose. "We leave at first light. Tell your men to bring packhorses."

But when he rolled up in his bedroll in the livery, visions of Jesselynn Highwood kept Wolf awake. Maybe after he got things going in the direction he knew was necessary for his tribe, he would make a trip to Oregon. And maybe the mountains would fall flat.

Chapter Three

Richmond, Virginia
July 1863

Louisa Highwood heard them crying in her sleep.

"Dear, dear, Louisa, what is it?" Aunt Sylvania, mobcap askew, leaned over Louisa's bed. She laid a gentle hand along Louisa's cheek and patted softly.

"Wh . . . what's wrong?" Louisa shook her head and half sat up. She stared around the room into the corners that missed the light from the candle Sylvania held. Louisa flopped back on her pillows. "There's no one here. Oh, thank God." She turned to look at her aunt. "They wouldn't stop crying, the groaning . . . ah, there was nothing I could do." She rolled her head from side to side. "They're dying, Aunt. All the men are dying."

"There now. You've been having bad dreams is all. Go on back to sleep. You are doing all you can."

A groan floated up the stairs from one of the soldiers recuperating from war wounds, who were now sleeping on pallets in Sylvania's dining room and parlor. Many houses in the city of Richmond and across the South were being used for nursing homes for the soldiers, overflow from the heinously over-crowded hospitals.

Louisa started to throw back her sheet, but Sylvania laid a

hand on hers. "Reuben will take care of them. You sleep."

Louisa knew Reuben was as exhausted as she, but that thought would not enter Sylvania's head. Kind as she was to her people, and though they were no longer slaves, she expected them to do all the heavy labor and the cooking and washing, just because that was the way it had always been. The blacks took care of the whites, and the whites provided homes and necessities for *their people.*

"Thank you, Aunt, I will. I'm sorry to have disturbed you." Tired didn't begin to describe how Louisa felt. And it wasn't just muscle tired. Weariness of body and mind had crept into her soul, and no matter how diligently she read her Bible, soul weariness took more than a night's sleep to restore. During the day she covered her inner turmoil with a smile and a sprightly step, but at night, when she was asleep, they would come to her. Her boys, her friends, her fiancé—all gone on to their heavenly home.

She'd begun to think that if the war kept on much longer, there would be no one left to bar the doors against the conquering bluebellies. "Oh, Lord, how long?" Her whisper seemed trapped within the mosquito netting, unable to ascend to the throne above.

While the Union troops had yet to enter Richmond, the capital of the Confederacy bore her battle scars from the repelled attack proudly. As Louisa well knew, pride was never lacking in the South. But the war that they'd thought to win in weeks had been raging for months and into years. Perhaps Christ would come again before it was over.

"Anytime, Lord, anytime." Her mother and father would be waiting to welcome her and the rest of them home. Home, where there'd be no sorrow, no tears, and no more war. Instead of going back to sleep, Louisa rose and crossed to the white-curtained window. The elm trees in the front yard whispered to one another, a nightingale warbled, the crickets sawed. A dog barked somewhere down the street. Night sounds, emissaries of comfort and peace. At least they no longer heard the rattle of rifles and the terrible cannonading of the heavy artillery.

The breeze cooled her skin. She laid her cheek on her hands crossed on the windowsill and fell immediately back to sleep until she slipped sideways and jolted awake. Crawling back in bed, she hugged her pillow. "And, Lord, please take care of Jesselynn and all the others."

Perhaps Gilbert will come today. Always her first thought on waking was of her first suitor and almost fiancé. She turned her face into the pillow. Gilbert Lessling would never come. He'd perished in a train wreck. *Lord God, you said you would gird me up with the strength of your right hand. Jesus, Savior, I need that strength—to even get out of bed.*

Staring in the mirror a few minutes later, she shook her head. Zachary, her brother, would take one look at the smudges beneath her eyes and send her up for a nap. In spite of losing a foot, a hand, and an eye in battle, he figured *she* shouldn't be working so hard. "Ha." She combed her hair back from her face and let the curls hang down her back. Two ivory combs held the masses back and out of her way. She should be wearing her hair bound in a snood, but the men appreciated her looking young like their little sisters back home.

She pinched some color into her cheeks, dusted powder under her eyes, and brushed any loose hairs off the shoulders of her day gown, which was so badly faded one could hardly see the tiny yellow and white daisies that graced a sky-blue background. Tying her apron, she realized the bow was bigger because her waist no longer needed a corset, even if there were such to be had. She'd used all the bone stays for wrist and finger and arm supports for her boys.

Louisa did not consider a lack of corsets a terrible deprivation of war, even though her baby sister, now nearly eight months pregnant, could hardly wait to be laced up again. But then Carrie Mae always did put fashion ahead of fact, even when they were girls growing up at Twin Oaks.

Ordering herself to let the past be just that, the past, she pasted a smile on her face and tripped gaily down the stairs. "Good morning, brother dear." She peeked into his study to find him already at his desk working on improving his handwriting, since he'd been forced to learn to write with his left hand. His right lay buried somewhere on a battlefield along with myriad amputated limbs.

Zachary, dark hair falling over his broad brow, nodded and continued to dip the quill in the ink and form legible letters.

"Can I get you anything?"

"Coffee?"

"I wish. Roasted oats with chicory will have to do."

"Just so it is hot." The frown pulled at the scar on the right side of his face, a scar that ended under the black patch he wore to cover the eyeless socket.

She almost crossed to rub his shoulders but knew that he would grumble until he got his coffee. "Did you sleep well?" *Why are you dallying here? Get going before he growls at you for something else.*

"Need you ask?"

"I'll get your coffee. Breakfast should be ready soon."

After they'd fed the five guests, those who could feed themselves helping those who couldn't, Louisa cleared the table and then set out the wool pieces that were slowly forming into a uniform coat. Those with two good hands learned to sew and knit. Those who had legs and at least one hand worked in the garden. She'd learned that the men recovered much faster if they could be busy and felt like they were doing something useful. The army always needed uniforms and wool stockings. The household always needed food.

Aunt Sylvania alternately read from either the Bible or Shakespeare and corrected their sewing before they would have to rip out their painful stitches.

Louisa took up a basket and escaped out the back door to the garden. While picking feverfew and other herbs to hang to dry, she encouraged her two garden helpers.

"Ned, if you will cut the potatoes so that each piece has an eye, we can replant that section over there." She pointed to the bare spot they'd dug the day before.

"Yes, Miss Louisa, be glad to."

"You want I should clean out the chicken house and turn it into the compost pile?" Due to a throat injury, her other young man sounded more like a rasping file than a man, but he made himself understood.

"Yes, that would be wonderful. Take the eggs in to Abby, if you please. Perhaps she'll make us lemon cookies for afternoon tea."

He nodded. "That be good." As he turned to go, Louisa felt a clenching around her heart. He'd be sent back to his unit, or some other, any day now. No matter that his wound had been near mortal, he was well enough to carry a rifle again and willing to do his duty.

Duty. How she was coming to hate that word.

About midmorning she heard a carriage stop in front of the house. Dusting off her hands, she smoothed her apron, just in case it was someone for her. She glanced down. She needed a clean apron.

"Is Louisa here?" Carrie Mae's voice tinkled through the open doors.

"I most surely am," Louisa called back. "Come out here and sit in the shade." She met her sister at the door. "How ever did you get away in your condition?" she murmured in her ear while giving her a loving hug. "Mama would take a switch to you for being out in public like that."

"I'm not in public. I'm here visiting my sister who never takes time to come to me so that I don't have to go out." Carrie Mae lowered herself carefully onto the lounge. "It will take three men and a pulley to get me up again, but ah . . ." She slumped into the comfort of the cushions. The shade from the ancient magnolia tree dappled her face as she removed her wide-brimmed straw hat. The strip of pink gauze bound round its crown hung over the edge of the settee.

"Is that new?" Louisa's voice squeaked on the final word.

"Yes, Jefferson insisted that I needed something new to perk me up." She fanned her face with the hat. "He heard that doldrums aren't good for the baby."

"And you have been in the doldrums?" Louisa eyed her sister's ankles, or rather where her ankles should have been.

"This heat. Our house is still not ready, and the flat gets no breeze at all." She pulled her dimity dress away from her bosom. "Do you have any lemonade?"

Louisa patted her sister's shoulder. "I'll be right back. I'll bring some cold cloths too." While on one hand she could tell Carrie Mae was indeed in distress, on the other, her lack of concern for the suffering soldiers went so far against their mother's teachings that Louisa wanted to shake her younger sister. She'd married an attorney, Jefferson Steadly, who'd lost an arm in the war, so one could not say he had not done his part. He was now an assistant to one of the local senators, and he and his young wife had become members of the congress with all the society obligations his position entailed.

Balls, soirées, dinners, and teas kept Carrie Mae busy until lately, when one in her condition stayed home to knit booties or some such thing.

Carrie Mae never had been one for knitting. She painted lovely watercolors, played both piano and harp with wonderful skill, entertained ranking officers and politicians, and believed she was doing her best for the war.

Once in the kitchen, Louisa set the glasses on the tray with a bit more force than necessary, causing Abby, Aunt Sylvania's maid, to raise an eyebrow. "Have we any cookies left?"

"I'se got dem right here." Abby set a plate of molasses drops on the tray.

"The boys need them worse than we do." Louisa huffed one more time and lifted the tray. "Oh! Could you please bring a basin of cold water and a couple of cloths? Carrie Mae's ankles don't look good to me. But then what do I know about having babies?" *And at the rate I'm going, I might never get the opportunity to find out.*

Louisa used her hip to push open the screen door and set the tray down on a low table by the lounge. Carrie Mae lay fast asleep, her eyelashes feathered over purple shadows under her eyes. Perspiration gathered on her upper lip, and her body seemed dwarfed by the huge mound under her thin dress.

"Look like she have two in dere." Abby knelt beside the young woman and, wringing out the cloths, applied one to each swollen ankle.

Louisa brought out a collar to sew on while her sister slept. *Oh, Mother, if only I had listened more when you were trying to train us to be good wives and mothers and to care for all the people at Twin Oaks. I was so young, so terribly young.*

When Zachary came out some time later, he took a chair next to his youngest sister and picked up a fan, waving it gently. "She looks tired." His whisper made Louisa nod. "You think the baby is all right?" Another nod.

"Are you two talking about me?" Carrie Mae stretched and smiled up at her brother. "Doze off for a minute, and you get all worried."

"A minute?" Louisa smiled and shook her head. "You've been asleep for nigh unto two hours. I reckon you needed a good nap."

"It's the shade and the breeze and . . ." Carrie Mae inhaled deep. "And honeysuckle. I declare, that smells so fine." She reached for one of the glasses of lemonade and took a sip. "And this tastes even better." Her smile never quite reached her eyes. "I wish Mama were here."

Louisa gathered her close, knowing that tears were pooling in her own eyes just as they were in Carrie Mae's. "Me too, darlin', me too." She knelt by the lounger, holding her sister while she cried, and let her own tears flow unchecked.

Zachary cleared his throat when the shower started to abate. "I take it this is usual behavior for a young woman in her . . . in her . . ." He waved in the general direction of the mound.

"Oh, for mercy's sake, say the word, pregnant. As if having a baby was an embarrassment instead of a joy."

"Yes, well, I have some more correspondence to answer, so I shall leave you two to discuss female things." He beat such a hasty retreat for a man with one leg that both his sisters suffered an attack of the giggles in spite of their tears.

After Carrie Mae left, promising to send the carriage round the next day for Louisa to come visit her, Louisa ambled into Zachary's study, bedroom, meeting room, whatever he needed it to be. Ned, who shared the room at night, had gone next door to help Widow Penrod with her garden.

The new men at her house were too ill to help out yet.

"Close the door, please."

Louisa did so and took the chair he nodded to. "Something has happened." Her words were more a statement than question.

"Yes, I have located enough funds for us to make another trip north. The Quaker folks who brought me home last time are willing to assist us again. Are you sure you want to go through the lines again?"

"Quinine or morphine?"

"Quinine. The malaria is killing our men fast as the Union bullets."

CHAPTER FOUR

WEST OF FORT LARAMIE
JULY 2, 1863

"You shouldn't be out here!"

"Mr. Lyons, since my animals are part of this herd, I have as much responsibility as anyone else to ride night watch."

Nate rode up beside her. "I know that, but this ain't no place for a lady."

At least the conversation made staying awake easier. Jesselynn knew she'd never live it down if she fell off her horse for sleeping. She was so far beyond tired that her hands felt numb.

"Come on, Mr. Lyons, you know about how long it's been since I got to think and act like a lady, let alone look like one. Besides, you're not relieving me but rather that young lad over there. Did you bring a rifle?"

"Yup." He slapped the gunstock on his right side. "Why? You see anythin' suspicious?"

"No, just a feeling." She whistled for Patch and started to ride on around the herd, then stopped. "Any sign of Cobalt yet?"

"Not that I know of."

Jesselynn shook her head and continued to circle the grazing herd. While the animals would normally have bedded down by now, the storm and ensuing panic had prevented them from filling their bellies. The coyotes yipped again, their wild music bringing the hair on the back of her neck to attention.

The hoofbeats of the young man heading back to camp told where he was. A dog barked from the circled wagons. Patch growled low in his throat.

"What is it, boy?" Jesselynn kept her voice to a whisper and her ears on full alert. Crickets sang, slowed to a hush, and then picked up their notes. The only part of Patch she could see was the one white cocked ear. Otherwise, his dark fur blended into the shadows. A cloud hovered over the half-moon, a reminder of the now passed storm.

She should have taken Meshach's advice and gotten some sleep before riding the herd. Doctoring the wounded and comforting the grieving took a toll on a body, but at the time she'd been too keyed up to even think about sleeping. She'd thought of moving the herd in sight of the circled wagons, but the cattle needed rest as bad as the people.

Patch growled again and, with a yip, took off around the edge of the herd. Jesselynn wheeled Chess, the gelding they'd saved from death by bullet wounds, and followed the dog. She yanked her rifle from the scabbard as Chess leveled out. Cocking the hammer with her thumb, she heard a yip and a snarl. She eased back on the reins, Chess slid to a halt, and she raised the rifle butt to her shoulder. More yips and snarls, and then Patch's barking.

"Coyotes." She nudged her horse back to a trot and followed her ears. The moon released its hold on the cloud in time for her to see three coyotes feinting and attacking the snarling dog. She took aim, fired, and levered another bullet into the chamber before firing again. A yelp, retreating yips, and Patch streaked after the two departing coyotes, one lying dead.

"Some shot." Nate Lyons rode up to stop beside Jesselynn. "How'd you see 'im good enough to hit?"

"Pure luck or heavenly intervention. I go for the latter." She whistled, and Patch came panting back to sit beside the horse, tongue lolling and tail wagging. "Good dog." She dismounted and stooped to scuff his ears. Her nose took a licking, and Patch put his front feet on her knees. "Yeah, real good dog." She thumped him on the rib cage and swung back aboard her mount. Waving her arm, she sent the dog back to circling the herd.

"He's better'n two riders." Nate turned off in the other direction. "Think he can spot Indians like that?"

"I sure do hope he never has to." But the hair settled to where it belonged on the back of her neck, and the breeze kicked up signaling the coming day. Another rider came from the camp to tell her the camp news and take her place. She filled him in on what happened with the coyotes and headed back to her wagon—and bed.

At least the final wagon had been found, and Cobalt returned with it to camp.

Everyone spent the next day repairing what could be salvaged from the destruction. Meshach's forge ran from before sunrise to long after sunset. The dead oxen and one mule were hung and cut up, having been bled and gutted the night before. Tents of drying strips of beef hung over the fires, fueled by a couple of dead trees dragged down from the hills. The older children were set to keeping the fires smoldering to smoke the meat while it dried. The younger ones, under the supervision of Jane Ellen, were instructed to find dried cow or buffalo chips to supplement the wood supply.

Jesselynn awoke to the sound of two men arguing at

the top of their lungs.

"I say that's my barrel and I kin prove it."

"Huh, got mine in the same store, same brand burned in the bottom."

"Why, you no good, sniveling dog's belly, if'n I din't know better, I'd—" The mushy thud of fist on face kept her apprised of their continued actions.

"Gentlemen, gentlemen." Cobalt was breaking up the fight.

Jesselynn lay in her bedroll, not even bothering to look out from under the wagon bed. At least the wagon master could break up fights. Of course if he'd done his wagon mastering right, there might not have been call for an argument.

"Soon as y'all can manage, I'd like to have a meetin' over by my wagon."

She knew he was speaking to the men, but the women would be there too. They had just as great, or greater, a stake in the trip ahead. Men decided to go. Women had to make the trip happen. But then, wasn't that the way of the world? She thought to the verses Meshach had read a few days before. God told Abraham to gather up his family and flocks and head out across the desert, but Jesselynn knew who did the gathering and the packing and the saying good-bye—Sarah. And Abraham couldn't even tell her where they were going or why, other than that the Lord told him to do so. Things didn't seem to have changed much in the years since then.

Some days Jesselynn felt sure the Lord was leading them to Oregon, and other days she wondered. Like today. She hauled herself out of the quilt, slammed her feet into her boots, and wished for a pitcher, nay a tub of hot water, to wash the dust from every inch of her body and clothing. Back home at Twin Oaks there had been lazy mornings to bathe and dress, but not for her since her mother died and even less since the war began.

She'd planned on spending some time with her journal and catching up on the bookwork, but now she'd have to be at that meeting, whether Cobalt wanted her there or not.

"Thanks." She accepted the mug of hot coffee Ophelia offered her and retrieved a strip of smoked meat from the drying rack. Steam rising from the bubbling kettle told her they'd have stew for dinner, same as everyone else. She gnawed on the stringy meat as she surveyed the bustling camp. Those that weren't repairing wagons and harnesses used the unexpected break to wash clothes. Nate Lyons had a group of children gathered at his feet as he explained the times tables. Ever since he took over the schooling of the young'uns, he'd not lacked for dinner and supper invitations.

She tossed the dregs in her cup into the coals and dipped a cup of cold water out of the barrel tied to the side of the wagon. They'd poured water from the Platte River through several layers of cheesecloth to strain out the bugs that coated the surface of the water. Most likely the river was higher, too, after that rainstorm. She studied the hooped canvas above the barrel. At home they'd run downspouts from the roof right into barrels to collect the soft rainwater for using in the house and especially for washing hair. Nothing felt better than long hair washed with soft rainwater. Her head itched for just such a treatment. The walnut dye she'd used as a disguise when she donned her men's britches had mostly worn off, and her hair had grown out nearly long enough to tie back with a thong. Soon she would be able to braid it. Soon she would look like a woman again.

Shame that Wolf wouldn't be there to see the transformation. The thought brought her up short, her teeth still implanted in the stringy slice of half-dried meat. Here, she hadn't been out of bed an hour yet, and she'd already thought about him. She sighed, and fetching her hat from under her bedroll, she clapped it on her head and tucked her deer-skin-covered quilt into its customary place in the wagon. Like her mother always said, *"A place for everything, and everything in its place."*

But her place had been a plantation named Twin Oaks. The memory of the big white-pillared house caught at her chest and burned behind her eyes. No way could she think of Twin Oaks being burned to the ground. It lived on in her memory, the fine white house shaded by ancient magnolia trees, a veranda for rocking chairs and neighborly chats, green rolling fields of grass, grain, and tobacco, and barns, wonderful old barns with box stalls for the Thoroughbreds raised there.

Jesselynn swallowed a sob and turned at the sound of Cobalt's voice calling them to the meeting. With a snort, she headed across the circle. Didn't take a college professor to figure what he was going to say. If he'd thought making time so important that he'd not circled the wagons, he'd surely be pushing for the shortcut now. The man just didn't under-stand that rushing and shortcuts most always took longer in the long run.

She let the others draw in closer, fairly certain that she'd be arguing with Cobalt before too much discussion com-menced. Within moments Nate Lyons flanked her on one side, Mrs. McPhereson on the other. She could sense Meshach right behind her.

"I called you good folks here to say publicly how sorry I am we got caught in the rainstorm like that." Cobalt stood on a block of wood so he could be seen and heard by all.

Jesselynn waited for him to admit his mistake, but as he picked up his pace, she realized she'd wait until the hot place froze over. One more mark against Cobalt. He wasn't man enough to take the blame for three deaths, scores of injuries, and the destruction of wagons and goods.

Nate hawked and spat off to the side. Jesselynn knew it for the statement it was. If she were a man, she'd do the same.

"Easy now."

The whisper from behind her said she was doing something that gave Meshach a chance to read her mind. She dropped her hunched shoulders and sucked in a straightening breath. *God, help us, please, to do what's best.* Only through force of will did she keep her mouth shut and listen.

"I'm hoping we can be on the trail again by tomorrow. . . ."

Several groans met that statement, and many were shaking their heads.

"Or the next day at the latest. I know some of you disagree with me, but I think we have no choice but to take the shortcut. We can cut days off our travel time and—"

"What about water?" Jesselynn kept her voice deep in the hope he'd think someone else was talking.

"Far as I have heard, there is water shortage only in dry seasons. We all know this ain't been much for dry."

Someone snickered. Someone muttered. Another spoke up. "And the hills are steeper, the trail rougher."

"Now that's all a matter of opinion. I hear tell that there's been Indian trouble on the regular route."

Had there been? If so, how come none of the rest of them had heard that news?

"What you hear about savages?" This came from across the crowd.

"That they attacked one train. Got it from one of the soldiers at the fort."

More rumblings and mutterings, people talking with those around them.

"Now, y'all know that if you don't like what I propose, you

can head on back to Fort Laramie and wait for another train, if another one comes along, that is."

"Or we could go it on our own."

Jesselynn strained on her tiptoes to see who was talking.

"True, but I been there and back two, three times. You got to admit experience counts for something."

"If he's so experienced, why didn't he circle the wagons and prevent the stampede?" Jesselynn spoke loud enough only for her friends around her to hear, but a couple in front of them turned to see who had spoken. A man, clad in a black leather vest over a once white shirt, nodded. The sling holding his right arm gave mute testimony to the tragedy of the night before.

"Any news about Indians on the route you want to take?"

"Not that I know of."

"The land's so rough even the Indians don't want it," Jesselynn muttered under her breath. She'd heard someone talking at the fort about how hot the area could get in July and August. Hot weather, no water, steep hills—didn't add up to her.

"So let's have a show of hands. How many of you are with me on takin' the shorter route?"

Hands raised slowly, as if unsure of the decision, but it looked like about everyone signed on.

"And those wantin' to go the usual route?"

Jesselynn shot her hand in the air, followed by those around her. The couple in front raised theirs too.

"Well, since we live in a democratic country where majority rules, guess we'll be takin' the shortcut, the safe route." The look he shot her made Jesselynn clench her fists. Had she been a man, he'd have taken her comments more seriously, she was sure of it. By the mutterings and stirrings she heard, she wondered if the answer would have been the same had the women been allowed a voice. Not that they couldn't yet put some pressure on their husbands.

"I'll be around to check on the repairs tonight. If we can leave in the mornin', so much the better. 'Bout sundown we'll have a buryin' service if'n y'all want to come. I asked Mr. Lyons if he would read a few words over the graves."

With that, the meeting broke up, and everyone went back to their chores. Meshach pumped the bellows to heat up the forge again and the sound of his hammer on the anvil rang through the camp.

Jesselynn headed back to their camp and found the mother of the girl with the broken leg, with a knot on her forehead the size of a pullet's first egg, waiting at the Highwood wagon. "Kin you come look on my little girl again? She be awful hot to the touch."

"Of course. Do you have some willow bark to make tea? That will help her fever come down."

The woman shook her head and blinked in obvious pain.

"Perhaps the tea will help you too." Jesselynn dug in her medicine box for the packet of dried willow bark.

"If'n you say so."

"How is your husband doing?" As she asked her questions, Jesselynn dug through her box for more supplies, but too many of the packets were empty. If only she could have Lucinda search the woods near Twin Oaks and send the medicinal herbs on to her. Fort Bridger was the next fort she could remember, and that was some distance away. Of course she had no way to mail a letter home either, so she might as well not waste her time thinking about it. Surely, many of the same things grew out here, if she only knew where to look.

She turned to look at the woman, only to find her weaving, her eyes rolling back in her head. Jesselynn caught her just as she collapsed. "Ophelia, Aunt Agatha, come help."

Together they spread a tarp and laid the woman on it.

"What do you think it might be?" Agatha straightened and scratched the end of her chin.

"That clunk on the head." Jesselynn indicated the swelling. "She needs to be lying down herself, not running around the camp. She's the mother of that little girl with the broken leg."

"*Tsk, tsk,* more's the pity. That baby gets the croup or some such from all that cold rain, and there won't be nothin' anyone can do for her."

"Thank you, Aunt Agatha." Jesselynn shook her head. Agatha did have a morbid streak in her, but this time she could be so right. "Come along, please. Let's bring the child back here where we can watch them both." As they made their way past two wagons, one where Meshach was just resetting a wheel he'd fixed, Jesselynn thought longingly of Ahab, grazing so free. She'd been thinking of going for a ride to help sort out her thoughts on whether they should go with the train or continue on the original route. Or should they return to Fort Laramie?

Every time she thought to get away, someone else came asking for help. By evening she gave it up. As the camp settled in for the night after the burying, Jason Cobalt made his rounds.

"We'll be pulling out first light," he said when he got to their fire.

"How many you leaving behind?" Jesselynn looked up from writing in her journal.

"Depends on who don't want to go." He rocked back on his heels. "You made up your mind?"

Jesselynn shook her head. "I just wish you'd take the regular route, the route most traveled by those who've gone before."

"I know that, but in good conscience, I got to get these

people over *all* the mountains before snow flies." He nodded toward Meshach. "Sure hate to lose a good blacksmith like that if you go the other way."

"What about the Boltons?" Jesselynn now knew the name of the woman and child she'd spent the afternoon caring for.

"He says they'll be ready."

Jesselynn didn't even try to stop the snort that put paid to his comment. "You could give these people one more day of rest." She held up a hand when he started to answer. "I know, you got to get over the mountains."

Pushing against the unrest that weighed on her, she got to her feet with a sigh. "You know, I think we'll go the other way. Anyone wants to go with us, they'll be welcome." She pushed a coal back in the fire with the toe of her boot. "And you know what else? I sure do hope you learned your lesson about circling the wagons at the first roll of thunder. Might save a number of lives that way."

At his first move toward her, Meshach insinuated himself between them. "Time to be movin' on, suh." His voice, though gentle, held a flicker of steel.

"You think you know so much, I wouldn't let you come with my train if'n you paid double." His growl and scowl narrowed her eyes and drew her hand to the knife at her side.

"Good night, *Mr.* Cobalt. Go with God."

He glared again, spun on his heel, and strode away. Jesselynn wondered if he could feel the daggers she was sending him.

"You think I made the right choice?" She glanced up at Meshach.

"Yes, suh, I do."

"I sure hope so. Dear God, I hope so." *But what if I didn't?* The thought kept her staring at the stars, seeking an answer that never came.

CHAPTER FIVE

"I'm goin' back for Wolf," Jesselynn announced two days later.

"How will you ever find him?" Aunt Agatha stared at her niece with a look of utter confusion.

"Perhaps he stayed on at Fort Laramie. I know he needed to purchase supplies for his family."

"Maybe we should all go back with you. It safer'n stayin' here." Mrs. McPhereson stared around at the ridgetops, as if expecting Indians to ride down on them from all sides.

Jesselynn ignored Mrs. Mac's comment, looking instead to Meshach, who made no comment.

"But what if he ain't there?" Aunt Agatha said.

That was the hole in her bucket all right. What if Wolf had indeed gone north to only God knew where? Jesselynn looked around at her troop that had seemed adequate until the other wagons pulled out. Could they make it to Oregon with only five wagons? Surely there was safety in numbers, but this is what they had. Could they make it without a guide?

It would be hard to miss the trail.

"We could always wait for another train to come along. Could wait right here in fact." Aunt Agatha stirred the coals and moved the coffeepot back over the heat. "I can always think better over a cup of coffee. How about the rest of you?"

Meshach looked up from testing the shoes on the oxen. He'd already reset Ahab's. "You can't ride dere alone." He made the statement with a "no argument" look.

Why does everyone think they can tell me what to do? I'm supposed to be in charge here. Jesselynn looked up in time to catch a glance between Aunt Agatha and Meshach. What in tarnation did *that* mean?

"I can make better time on Ahab alone than with everyone else."

"Domino go just as fast." Meshach nodded at Benjamin. "Him too."

Jesselynn sighed. Of course he was right. But if something happened to her, the rest of them could go on, and they'd need Benjamin. But one glance at the set to Meshach's lower jaw and she knew better than to argue. When had he become their leader? She was the eldest Highwood.

She rubbed the side of her face where the mosquitoes had feasted the night before. Since no one had elected her wagon master, or mistress in her case, she realized she needed to ask everyone's opinion.

As soon as they all had cups of coffee, she cleared her throat. "Y'all know that I think I should ride back for Wolf. I need to know what you think." She looked to Nate Lyons, then to Mrs. McPhereson, and finally to the Jespersons, who were still having trouble with their wagon and had decided to join them at the last minute.

"Seems to me the choices are to wait here, head on west, all of us return to the fort, or you and Benjamin ride for help." Nate ran his tongue over his teeth and, squinting, nodded. "Guess now that you asked, I'm in favor of all of us returnin' to the fort. Just in case Wolf can't be found or, if he can, refuses to come." He looked to Mrs. McPhereson. "What say you?"

Mrs. Mac glanced over her cup at Jesselynn, then to her near-grown son. "I say wait a day and start back in the

51

mornin'. Give the Jespersons here time to work on their wagon so two oxen can pull it. Perhaps they can find another span back at the fort."

"Thankee. That would be good." The husband and wife, he with a sling and her with a limp, both of them blue with bruises, nodded to each other and then to the others.

More people, Lord. You've added to our troop again. How will I feed them all, get them to Oregon safely? Jesselynn felt the weight of the load settle about her shoulders, heavy like a buffalo cape.

"Should pray 'bout it before doin' anythin'." Meshach's words carried the simple truth of all the ages. "We be in God's hands."

"We be in God's hands." Thanks, Lord, for the reminder. I almost took it all on myself—like I used to. What do you want us to do?

Meshach stood and, with an arm about Ophelia's shoulders, drew her into the circle that formed without conscious action on anyone's part. Heads bowed, and a silence settled over the group. Even Sammy, who jabbered constantly, stuck his finger in his mouth and leaned against his father's shoulder. Thaddeus one-armed Jesselynn's leg and leaned against her, Patch next to him. Jesselynn dropped her head forward, relief stealing from the top of her head to the heels of her boots. She closed her eyes, the better to concentrate. *Father God, thank you, thank you. I know I don't have to do it all, that you will. You are right here with us. You never left. No matter how big this land is, you are bigger.* She let the tears seep without wiping them. She wanted to hug herself, to sing and dance and shout for joy, to run up the hills and throw herself down in the grass to roll back down. The black anxiety that threatened had been blown away.

"God is in His heavens and on this earth, and all will be

well. All will be well. We are His and the sheep of His pastures. He is the shepherd, and He guards the sheep. If anyone hear His voice and comes to Him, He will come in and . . ." Meshach's deep voice rose on eagle's wings.

Jesselynn sniffed and blinked hard. Music bubbled inside her, a meadowlark trilled on the breeze, the wind sang in the grasses. The sky arched above them and on forever, the deep blue of a rain-washed summer day.

" 'The Lord is my shepherd, I shall not want.' " Aunt Agatha began the psalm, and around the circle each one added a phrase.

" 'He maketh me to lie down in green pastures:' "

" 'He leadeth me beside the still waters.' "

" 'He restoreth my soul.' "

" 'He leadeth me in the paths of righteousness for his name's sake.' "

As one, their voices lifted. " 'Yea, though I walk through the valley of the shadow of death, I will fear no evil: for thou art with me; thy rod and thy staff they comfort me. Thou preparest a table before me in the presence of mine enemies: thou anointest my head with oil; my cup runneth over.' " The voices ebbed, then swelled. " 'Surely goodness and mercy shall follow me all the days of my life: and I will dwell in the house of the Lord for ever.' "

The meadowlark sang liquid notes, pouring peace over their heads and into their hearts.

"Amen." Thaddeus's voice rang out, strong and firm beyond his years.

Jesselynn picked him up and buried her face in his shirtfront. She sniffed again and used his sleeve to dry her eyes.

Thaddeus put a chubby hand on either side of her face and looked deep into her eyes. "Don't cry, Jesse. Jesus be here."

The tears burned again behind her eyes and filled her nose. "Yes, Thaddy, Jesus most certainly be here." She settled her little brother on her hip and looked to those around the circle. Everyone was either blowing or wiping, but their smiles wavered only a little. "Well, what do we do?" she asked.

"Go back to the fort. But you and Benjamin ride on ahead." Nate Lyons glanced at the others to get their nods of agreement. "If'n Wolf is leavin', you might could stop him, so's he can listen to us."

Jesselynn nodded. "We leave before sunrise, then?"

Again more nods.

Meshach tossed the dregs of his cup into the fire to sizzle and steam. "Mr. Lyons, you want I should check your oxen shoes?"

"If you would be so kind."

A humph came from Agatha, and she stuck her head in the back of the wagon, ostensibly searching for something. Jesselynn, leaning against the rear wagon wheel, could hear her muttering.

"Butter wouldn't melt in that man's mouth. 'If you would be so kind', indeed." She mimicked his rusty voice perfectly.

And here Jesselynn had thought perhaps a truce had been called, or that her aunt had finally realized what a fine man old Brushface, as she called him when he was out of earshot, really was. She'd heard Meshach and Ophelia laughing about them one night. Ophelia was sure Nate was sweet on Aunt Agatha and that all he needed was a little encouragement.

The look on Agatha's face brooked *no* encouragement. *Or doth the lady protest too much?* Jesselynn dug her knife out of the case and used the newly sharpened tip to clean her fingernails. What would happen if they threw Mr. Lyons in the creek along with a bar of soap and instructions not to come out until both he, including hair, and his clothing were scrubbed clean? Surely he had another pants and shirt in that wagon of his.

She pushed away from the wagon and went searching for Mark, Nate's thirteen-year-old grandson. Her fingers itched to use the scissors on Mr. Lyons' hair and beard. If her plan worked, Aunt Agatha would no longer be able to refer to him as Brushface.

"I ain't a'gonna! I look fine just the way I am!" Nate waved his arms, trying to grab hold of those behind him.

"Shush, you want her to hear you?" Jesselynn managed to speak around the laughter exploding around her.

"Don't care. Stop, please, I gotta get my watch out."

They let him dig his pocket watch and fob out of his leather vest, and his grandson accepted the offering with appropriate reserve. But the light dancing in his eyes earned him a sock on the shoulder from his glowering grandfather. With that taken care of, Meshach and Benjamin each grabbed an arm, Daniel pushed from behind, and Nate Lyons splashed into the waist-deep pool surrounded by drooping willows and whispering cottonwood.

"Here's the soap, Grandpa." Mark waded out to hand the spluttering man soap and a washcloth. "Your towel is up there." He motioned toward a tree limb. "Me 'n Patch, we gonna stand guard."

"Yer clean clothes are waitin' dere too." Benjamin pointed to the same tree limb.

"Bring him back here when he's dressed," Jesselynn hissed from behind the tree. They were far enough from camp to not be overheard, but she was taking no chances. She'd even found a stump for him to sit upon in her impromptu parlor. With ivory comb and sharpened scissors in her hands, she was ready to go to work.

When Lyons clumped through the brush, the look he sent her from under shaggy brows made her smile and swallow her laughter. His wet hair hung in curling locks to his shoulders, and his beard did the same on his chest.

"You sure you know how to cut hair properlike?"

"Learned at my mother's knee, just like I learned most everything else. Got so's my brothers would rather have me cut their hair than Mother, said I got it more even." Jesselynn studied the mass before her. "This is going to take some whacking."

"Whackin'! You said—"

"Just teasing." She clamped her elbows into his shoulders and pushed him back down. She leaned forward just a bit and whispered in his ear. "Don't you know I'm trying to help you?"

He cranked his head around to peer up at her. One hand came out to push back the locks that obscured his vision. "Help me what?" He huffed as he turned forward again.

Jesselynn lifted a lock and snipped, then repeated the action with the next, starting with the top of his head.

"Help me what?"

"Sit still or you're going to have a mighty funny haircut." She snipped as she spoke.

He sighed, a heavy sigh that rocked his shoulders. "Sometimes help is awful painful."

"You know, you have very nice hair, thick, and now that I can see it without the dust, a fine color." *How old are you? Maybe I shouldn't think of you as "old man."* There didn't seem to be much gray in the fox red mass.

"Thankee, I guess." His shoulders slumped. "You wouldn't mind tellin' me what kind a help I'm needin', would you?"

Now it was Jesselynn's turn to sigh. "Ophelia seems to think you are sweet on Aunt Agatha. . . ." She waited for some sort of answer. When he didn't respond, she shook her head and continued snipping. Now all the ringlets lay in a pool at her feet. With the comb she lifted the hair, held it between two fingers and cut. Slowly but surely, snip by snip, a well-shaped head appeared. "So are you?"

"Are I what?"

"Dear Lord, preserve us." She combed his damp hair back to reveal a broad forehead. The hair fell in waves, glinting in the sunlight. "Well, I'll be . . ."

"What in tarnation are we talkin' about?"

Jesselynn stopped her barbering, leaned forward, and whispered in his ear. "Are you sweet on Aunt Agatha?"

"The way she treats me? What kinda idjit you think I am?" He spun around to stare at her.

"You need your eyebrows trimmed too. I'll do them when I work on your beard."

"I kin cut my own beard."

"But you didn't, so I will." She leveled a gaze at him that would stop a charging buffalo. When he clamped his eyes shut, she tapped him on the nose. "Relax. I promise not to stab you."

" 'Sides, she don't like me."

"Maybe so, maybe no." She trimmed the sides of his face. "You want to keep the mustache?"

"Yes."

"Why? You have a well-formed mouth. You know, I think there's been a handsome man hiding behind all this hair."

His skin took on the tone of the hair and felt hot. He closed his eyes.

Jesselynn made one more pass with the comb and scissors, then stepped back. She tilted her head, studying him from all sides. Using her fingers, she fluffed the hair and combed the sides back. "Sure do wish I had a mirror here for you to see." She removed the sheet she'd tied around his neck and brushed the hair off his shoulders and shirtfront with it.

"There now, that didn't kill you, did it?"

He studied his hands before looking up at her. "You think there could be a chance for me? With Miss Agatha, I mean." His voice was so low, Jesselynn had to lean forward to hear him.

"I'm thinking there might. You read her some of that Shakespeare every night and just be your sweet self in general, and how could she not enjoy your company?" *And besides, she might have to beat off Mrs. Mac when they see what a handsome man we've been driving with.*

Nate nodded, slapped his hat against his thigh, flinched at the dust cloud that billowed, and let out a breath. "Guess I better wash the hat too. No tellin' what water might do to it." He stared at the relic that looked like mice had nibbled off nest lining from its brim.

Jesselynn stepped back. "Glad you see it thataway. Maybe a dunking would suffice. Get rid of the dust at least, though how your hat can be so dusty after that rainstorm we had—"

"Ingrained, I 'magine." He turned the hat in his hands, poking a finger through one hole. "Goin' to have to be soap." Shaking his head, he got to his feet. "Thankee, Miss Jesselynn. You done me a world a service."

Jesselynn ignored the "Miss". Nate Lyons had always called her Marse Jesse like the others. Looked like they'd become friends at last. After all, from now on, she could go by Miss Jesselynn again, britches or no britches. "Thank you, and you are most indeed welcome."

Agatha never said a word when Nate Lyons presented himself back in camp, but she poured him a cup of coffee and handed it to him without a harrumph or even that stitched look about her mouth.

Nate drank the coffee down and hung the cup back on the row of mugs.

"Where's your hat?" Agatha moved the coffeepot into the cooler coals.

"Gave it a drubbin'."

"Might be I could patch that hole in the crown." She didn't look at him as she spoke but studied the potholder twisting in her hands.

"Bein' as it's wool felt, you s'pose I could trim up that brim with a scissors?"

"Perhaps. But you might want to put it back on your head so the crown don't shrink."

"Thankee for the good advice. I'll go do that." Nate Lyons left the cook fire whistling.

Jesselynn, standing out of sight behind the wagon, used every bit of her self-control to keep from whooping and hollering. Those two had spoken more words to each other in the last five minutes than in all the rest of the trip combined.

She strolled out and, taking a mug off the rack, poured herself a cup of coffee. "Old Brushface surely is looking good."

For that she did get a humph but an exceedingly weak one.

Meshach winked at Jesselynn when she passed by his forge and anvil, and Ophelia giggled behind her fingers.

Jesselynn and Benjamin mounted up in the cool breezes before the stars left off their twinkling. The rest of the folks were just starting to shuffle around.

"God be wid you." Meshach's blessing lifted on the cool air. "We be prayin'."

"We too. See you back at the fort, if not before."

The two rode into the rising sun, watching it gild the hillcrests and paint the clouds in shades of joy. They kept the horses at a steady jog, stopping to rest midmorning, then pushing on. When they reached a wide creek, they dismounted and let the horses have a couple of gulps of water before pulling them back to graze. Jesselynn removed her boots and rolled up her pant legs before striding out in the creek. She dipped water and splashed it up her arms and over her face.

Ahab threw up his head, his nicker catching Benjamin unaware.

"Now, ain't this a purty sight." Tommy Joe Jones stepped from behind a tree, his rifle at the ready. A slouch hat shaded a face that might have been handsome had it not been mashed so many times by fists and even cut by a knife. To Jesselynn he was ugly as sin and ten times meaner, inside and out.

His laugh sent fear stampeding up Jesselynn's back. "What are you doing here?"

CHAPTER SIX

"Why, we was just stoppin' fer a drink, same as you."

"We?" Anything to buy time.

"Oh, me'n my purty little wife."

The slitting of Tommy Joe's eyes told her much about his feelings for his "purty little wife." The way he knocked her around, she'd long before lost her "purtiness" to his heavy fists.

"No hope, I suppose, that your brother's dead?"

"Nope, none."

The leer he gave her sent more chills racing up Jesselynn's spine. While she had a pistol stuck in the waistband of her pants, reaching for it would be sure death. Without moving her head, she glanced sideways to see what Benjamin was doing. He had a rifle on the other side of his horse if he could get to it.

"Well, *Mr.* Jones, if you're lookin' for a drink, I'll move out of your way. Plenty of water here for everyone." She took a step toward the bank, but the end of the rifle now pointed directly at her.

"No, you don't." He stepped out farther and leveled the rifle, the grin on his lips nowhere near matching the flames in his eyes. "Take yer hat off."

"My hat?"

"You heerd me. Don't ya understand English? Take yer hat off—now!"

Jesselynn did as he asked, clutching the worn brim at her side.

"Ah, your hair, it's done growd some. Bet you was real purty afore you cut it all off."

Jesselynn narrowed her eyes, staring directly into his. Even across the distance she could see the spittle gathering at the corner of his mouth. *Oh, dear God, I'm in real trouble now. He knows I'm a woman, and he has just one use for women, other than knocking them around. Any time you want to send some angels in would be fine with me.* "How's that leg doing that I bound up for you?" The two Jones brothers had gotten into a shooting argument, and much to her disgust, she'd been on hand to patch them up.

"Good as new. Got a little somethin' else you can do fer me now, though. Take yer shirt off."

"Sorry, can't do that. Wouldn't be at all proper." Keeping her lips or any other part of herself from quivering took intense concentration. If those angels didn't show up, she'd need every bit of backbone she'd ever had.

He stepped forward. "I said, take yer shirt off—now!"

"Now, Tommy Joe, you know what your mama would say about such goings on."

"My mama is long gone, and even if she was right here, I knowed how to handle Mama." He waved the rifle. "Yer shirt."

In looking down to the buttons, Jesselynn glanced at Benjamin from under her lashes. He needed more time too. With shaking fingers she pulled her shirt out of her pants and freed the lowest button. Raising her head to stare at Jones with all the venom she could muster, she let her shirttails flap.

He licked his lips.

She slowly pushed the next button back through the fabric and, with fingers curled under the edges, held the shirtfronts apart so he could see her waistband. As she revealed the front, the gun at her back felt heavier.

"You're going to regret this." She kept her voice conversational while her fingers fussed with the third button. *Lord, if not angels, would you send Wolf? Please, I want to see him again.*

"Sure, who's goin' ter make me? You?" His laugh made the rifle bounce.

She shuddered. His finger had been so close to the trigger, he could have fired accidentally.

"You mind if I get a drink? I'm powerful thirsty."

He wavered. "I guess that won't hurt nothin'. Just make our little game last longer, that's all." He motioned with his head. "Drink away."

Jesselynn leaned forward to scoop water up in her hand. The other still held her hat. Could she shield her arm with her hat and retrieve her pistol? She dipped another handful and let some run down the front of her shirt.

Tommy Joe Jones stared at her, took two steps forward, his gaze burning into her shirtfront.

She sighed, an audible sigh that carried directly to his ears. "Ah, this water is so fine. Nothing quenches one's thirst like a clear flowing stream on a hot day." When she stood, she drank again and patted her cheeks with her wet hand. "Aren't you thirsty, Tommy Joe Jones?" Her voice carried a lilt put there by sheer desperation. Never in her life had she behaved like this, but if wanton would save their lives, wanton she could act. *Come on, Benjamin, get the gun.*

Keeping her gaze on the man with the rifle, she undid the next button, one to go. If she weren't wearing the strips she used to bind her breasts, he'd be staring at bare flesh. The thought alone made her skin tighten. Surely maggots crawling on her body couldn't feel any worse.

Tommy Joe took another step forward. The gun barrel

pointed toward the ground.

"Ah, this water feels so good. You ever learned to swim, Tommy Joe?"

Another step. Benjamin took two and disappeared behind Domino.

She arched her back. *Lord, forgive me if actin' this way is against any of your commandments. It's not me doin' the lustin' here.* She splashed one hand in the water. The gun, if only she could get to her gun.

"Take it off!" He hawked and spat, his eyes never leaving her chest.

Jesselynn slid the final button through its hole and with both hands keeping the shirt closed, lifted the front of her shirt so that it fell back, revealing her shoulders.

Tommy Joe Jones took one more step forward. He never saw the brown arm that threw the knife, hitting him right between the shoulder blades. *"Arrrg."* His groan strangled in his throat as he pitched forward face first into the water. The barrel of his rifle smacked the edge of the stream, sending up a small spurt.

Benjamin slowly waded into the water and lifted Tommy Joe. "He be dead."

"It couldn't be helped, Benjamin. You had no choice. God knows." Jesselynn's hand shook a bit as she pulled her shirt back into place. Stuffing it in her waistband, she strode out of the creek. "I'll water the horses while you pull him back in the brush, and let's get out of here before his brother comes looking for him." While it seemed like hours since Tommy Joe Jones strolled back into their lives, she knew it had been only a matter of minutes.

Keeping her gun at the ready, she led the horses to the water. After staring across the creek for a few seconds, Ahab dropped his head and drank. Jesselynn breathed a sigh of relief. But how had the man gotten that close to them without her watchdog, or watchhorse in his case, letting them know? Unless he'd already been there and was downwind so Ahab didn't smell him.

She looked up to see Benjamin with a leafy branch brushing out the tracks the dragging heels had caused. He reset a stone that had been turned over and, standing, looked back to check his handiwork.

"Looks fine."

"I'se sorry I took so long, Marse Jesse. Had to wait till his back to me." Benjamin walked upstream and bellied down to get a drink. When he finished, he wiped his mouth and reached for the reins. "We go soon's you get your boots on."

I wonder where his no-good brother is. Not far, likely. We better get out of here. Jesselynn sat down to pull on her wool socks and then her boots, all the while checking over her shoulder in case Rufus showed up. Knowing him, he was most likely abusing his brother's wife, one way or another.

When Ahab dropped his head to snatch a few mouthfuls of grass, she breathed a sigh of relief. The thought of taking the body into the fort went out of her mind as fast as it came in. There was no way on God's green earth she was wasting any more horsepower, manpower, or even regrets on a man like Tommy Joe Jones. He'd earned the hell he'd be consigned to.

They crossed the creek and kept to the trees until they were far enough away so that Rufus Jones wouldn't see them, then picked up a lope to make up for some of the lost time. They covered five miles or so before either of them said a word.

"He were a bad'un." Benjamin finally broke the stillness.

Jesselynn could only think of one worse, Cavendar Dunlivey, who'd burned Twin Oaks to the ground and then come after her. While she hadn't pulled the trigger there, she had left him, gut shot, to die. Did war bring out the worst in men, or did they always harbor such cruelty behind a thin veneer of civility? Another one of those questions for which there were no answers.

"You all right, Marse?" Benjamin raised his voice in case she hadn't heard him before.

Jesselynn nodded. She could still hear the thunk the knife made, and she knew if she closed her eyes she would see the shock on Tommy Joe's face as he fell forward. *Lord, what if . . . How do I . . . ?* She couldn't even finish the thoughts. *Lord, am I becoming as callous as these men?* This thought gave her another case of the shakes. "Thank you for saving our hides back there," she finally responded to Benjamin.

"You done more'n me. If he hadn't been . . ." Benjamin let his words trail off. He shuddered.

Jesselynn knew that if anyone discovered who'd killed the man, Benjamin would be hung without judge or jury. *I can't let them at Benjamin. Father, I promised not to lie anymore. How? What? So many have died. Please, Father, protect us.*

"What we goin' do?"

"Nothing." Jesselynn sighed. "We're goin' to trust in God to protect us."

"Yes, suh." But the fear hadn't left his eyes.

When they finally reached Fort Laramie several days later, they heard the bugle blowing the evening call and saw the flag coming down for the night. The haunting notes floated over the valley. As they rode closer, Jesselynn searched the grazing horses to see if Wolf's Appaloosa was among them. She took in a deep breath and let it out. So much for that hope, but perhaps Wolf was within the quadrangle somewhere.

Or maybe he's long gone, and you've been building up false hopes. She ignored that reasonable sounding voice within her head and continued to hope. Just the thought of seeing Wolf again set her heart to thumping.

"What can we do for you?" The first soldier they saw wore the bars of a sergeant.

"I'm Jesse Highwood. We came through here with a wagon train, the one led by Gray Wolf Torstead, until Cobalt took over." The man nodded. "Our train met up with a terrible thunderstorm and a near stampede."

"Where's the train now?"

"Those that still trusted Jason Cobalt are on their way to Oregon Territory, taking a shortcut he talked them into."

"I take it you weren't part of that trusting group."

"No, sir. We have five wagons on their way back to the fort. We're hoping for another train." *Or for Wolf to come back to us.*

"How bad was the damage?"

"Three people killed, several wagons beyond repair, and probably half their supplies gone."

"And the oxen and horses?"

"We kept the herd safe." She noted his raised eyebrow. "The herd was some behind the wagons. Got them down in a hollow and running in a circle."

"That was good herding." He looked up at her, head turned slightly to the side. "Didn't Cobalt circle the wagons?"

"No, sir."

"Well, I'll be . . ." The man shook his head. "See any Indians?"

"Only one that trailed us for some days. I never saw him."

"Hmm. No new wagon trains shown up since you left. Nowhere near as many this year as in the past. Folks scared of the Indians, if'n you ask me."

"Have you seen Wolf?" She hardly dared look at the man

when she asked the question that had been festering like a boil.

"Cap'n sent him out elk hunting with a squad."

"So he hasn't left for the north, then?" She kept her lips pressed together with an effort. Wolf hadn't left!

"Nope, but he didn't look any too happy at the setback. He'll go north soon as he can load his ponies."

Jesselynn touched her fingers to her hat brim. "Thank you, sir, you've been most helpful."

"What we gonna do now?" Benjamin rode beside her.

"Guess we get something to eat and ask where we can bed down. I'll go on over and talk with the captain's wife, Mrs. Jensen. She was real nice when we were here." They angled their horses across the parade grounds and dismounted in front of a two-story white house with porches across the front on both levels. The green trim looked freshly painted, and lace tieback curtains graced the windows. Flipping the reins over the hitching rail in front, Jesselynn mounted the two steps to the porch.

"I stay wid de horses."

Jesselynn nodded and crossed to knock on the green door. She'd barely raised her hand when the door flew open and Rebeccah Jensen took her hand and drew her inside.

"Land sakes, child, what a wonderful surprise. I thought you'd be halfway to Fort Bridger by now." She stopped her river flow of words and looked deep into Jesselynn's eyes. "Something bad happened, didn't it, to bring you back like this? Come, come in and sit down. Supper will be ready in a little bit."

"No, I can't . . ." Jesselynn motioned to her dusty pants and pointed to Benjamin out front. "We've been riding all day. I reckon you might let us have a plate of supper out on your back stoop or something. Or you could tell us where to go to get something to eat."

"You think I'm going to waste female companionship like that? Not on your sweet smile. Why, I reckon a bath might be something you'd enjoy. Then, while Clara is washing your clothes, you can wear a dress of mine. Bet you're dying to wear a dress again after all these months in those britches. I'll send my maid out to show your boy where to put the horses."

As she spoke, Rebeccah hustled Jesselynn up the stairs and into a guest room that had a hip bath in the corner. "I'll send water right up. There's soap and towels behind that screen. Oh, I am so excited to have you back. Are you thinking of staying here? Now that would be pure delightful."

Jesselynn hated to break in on this happy daydream, but she had to set the woman straight. "No, we're not staying. I came back to see if I could talk Wolf into taking our much smaller train on to Oregon."

"Oh, I see." From a chifforobe Rebeccah pulled a white cotton dress sprigged with blue forget-me-nots and the bodice laced with blue ribbon. She held it up against Jesselynn. "This should fit about right. You and I aren't too different in size."

"But . . . but this is too nice. An old housedress would do me just fine." In spite of what her mouth was saying, her fingers had a mind of their own, and that mind said to stroke the fabric and remember what a dress feels like.

Jesselynn could feel the heat creeping up her neck. "But I don't have any undergarments either. Please, this is too much."

"Nonsense." Rebeccah turned to a chest of drawers and pulled out the necessary camisole, pantaloons, and petticoats, all made of the finest lawn and trimmed with lace and ribbons. "I don't have an extra corset, but you are too thin to lace up anyway. I heard that corsets are going out of style."

"Water's here." A voice spoke from the hall.

"Come in." Rebeccah spun away to open the door. A black woman with a bucket of water in each hand led the way, followed by another.

Just the sound of the water swishing into the tub made a smile begin in Jesselynn's heart and spread quickly to her face. A bath, a real honest-to-heaven bath, with hot water and soap.

"Enjoy yourself. When you finish, if I haven't called you yet for supper, you can stretch out on that bed for a few minutes. Might feel real good." Rebeccah shepherded the two servants out ahead of her, then peeked back around the door. "Happy bathing."

Her light laugh trailed behind her as she descended the stairs.

Jesselynn needed no second invitation. Within moments she was stripped to the skin and stepping into hot water scented with rose petals. The fragrance rose with the steam, and no matter that the air temperature was hot as the water, she sank into the froth with a sigh. Leaning back against the slanted metal, she closed her eyes and inhaled to full lung capacity. When she let it all out, she took another breath, sank under the water, and came up blowing and wiping the wet hair from her face. She soaped herself, scrubbed her hair, and sank again. A sound made her open her eyes upon rising.

"Don't pay me no nevermind. I jest set this pitcher here for rinsing." The black maid left as silently as she'd come.

Jesselynn lay back and let the water lap her chin. If she moved too quickly, water swelled over the tub edges, so she soaped the cloth and extended one foot for scrubbing. When finished with both feet, she sighed. How wonderful it would be to lie back and float for a while. Let all the troubles take care of themselves, remember back when a bath like this was taken for granted, was a woman's right.

She stood up cautiously to keep from slopping water, reached for the pitcher, and poured a stream of cool water on her head. It gushed down over her shoulders, rinsing, cooling as it flowed. She hadn't felt so clean since before her father died.

Once dried, she discovered rose-scented powder on the shelf, and so she dusted herself before stepping into the bloomers and settling the camisole around her middle. She came out from behind the screen after folding the towel and looked longingly at the bed. Crossing the room, she stroked the pale yellow coverlet, quilted in a scroll pattern with stitches too tiny to count.

Such beauty in the midst of a harsh land. The fabric felt like silk beneath her fingertips. She pulled herself away and sat at the dressing table, a triple mirror showing her every feature. Her damp hair, freed from dust and grime, feathered about her face like a cloud of golden butterflies, tipped with walnut stain. Freckles dotted her slightly turned-up nose, causing her to shake her head.

"So much for soft white skin. Mine looks like old shoe leather, with spots." She ran a brush through her curls, rose, and slid the dress over her head. Lucinda would tsk if she saw her, but what Lucinda didn't know wouldn't hurt Jesselynn. Keeping her face from the sun had been the least of her worries, and now along with her hands and arms, it glowed golden brown, as if she were an octoroon.

The dress fit as though it had been sewn just for her. Puffed sleeves, a scooped neck filled in with a shirring of lace to be proper, and a full skirt gathered to a waist that dipped in front. She smoothed her hands down her sides. And stared at her boots. She daren't go barefoot. But boots with this dress?

Whirling in place so the skirt billowed and swished around

her legs, she stretched her arms above her head.

A knock sounded on the door. "Jesselynn, I brought you some slippers."

"Come in. I'm decent." Slippers even. How would she ever repay Rebeccah for these luxuries?

Rebeccah came through the door and stopped, her eyes dancing in delight. "Oh, I knew you would be beautiful. How lovely." She crossed the room and handed Jesselynn the slippers. "I do hope they fit."

"Anything is better than those boots. Couldn't picture myself clumping down the stairs, trying to keep from stepping on the hem." She slid her feet into shoes that were a bit tight but certainly tolerable. "Thank you, dear Rebeccah. I'd almost forgotten . . ." She gestured to the dress, the hair. Further words refused to pass the lump in her throat. *If only Wolf could see me like this.*

"You are most welcome. My husband sent a note saying he was bringing company for supper, so as soon as you are ready, please join us in the parlor."

"Thank you for the invitation." Wolf leaned his rifle against the wall. "I need to wash first."

Captain Jensen pointed to the door leading to the back of the building. "There are basins and towels right out there. I'll give you five minutes. Rebeccah dislikes me being late, so when I can, I make sure I'm there early."

Wolf nodded and headed for the back of the building. While he had no clean clothes, he would wash off what dust he could. He shucked his shirt, washed, shaved, wet his hair, and combed it back for retying. With the latigo knotted in place, he shook the dust out of his shirt and pulled it back over his head. The wavy mirror only told him he had no dirt spots on his face, or razor cuts either.

Together the two men crossed the parade grounds and took the two steps as one. Captain Jensen held the door open and motioned Wolf to precede him. Just inside the door Wolf looked up to see a vision descending the stairs. The woman looked vaguely familiar, so he nodded and smiled.

He doesn't even recognize me. Jesselynn swallowed hard to get her butterflies back down to her middle. She lowered her lashes to keep him from seeing her soul. He looks, he looks . . . No words powerful enough came to mind. She trailed the banister with one hand and raised her chin just a mite.

"Hello, Mr. Torstead. How nice to see you again."

CHAPTER SEVEN

RICHMOND, VIRGINIA

"Take this note to Carrie Mae, please, Reuben, but don't let her know we're gone."

"Yessum." Reuben took the envelope, shaking his head all the while. "I knows dat what you do is good and is de Lawd's will, but dis ol' darky goin' to 'sail the gates of heaven dat He brings you back safe."

Louisa patted his arm. "I am grateful for any and all prayers. Our Father says He puts His angels in charge of us. I surely do hope He sent an entire brigade this time." Her stomach hadn't stopped fluttering since the afternoon a few days before when Zachary broke the news. Zachary nearly didn't come home the first time they went to Washington. While she'd made it straight through, his trip back had taken him three weeks. During that time, they didn't know if he was dead or alive. That after the months of not hearing from him when he was off fighting and then showing up in her hospital, wounded and unidentified.

With a black hat and veil, along with widow's weeds borrowed from a neighbor, she looked near like a spook, far as she was concerned. But there was no way to disguise Zachary's injuries, so they had capitalized on them instead. He sat hunched in a chair with wheels, his dark hair powdered white, his crutch bound to the handles, two boots in

74

place on the footrests, with a blanket covering his knees and a shawl around his shoulders. He looked like an old man, a very sick old man.

"If only we had Meshach here to push this contraption." Louisa studied the handles on the back of the chair.

"This isn't all. There will be a coffin in the back of the buggy, with a dead possum in it to smell so bad no one will open it. We will be taking our dear brother home to Washington for burial. We have passes to get through both lines."

"How will we bring back enough quinine to do any good?"

"There's a false bottom in this chair and a false bottom in the floor of the buggy. And rocks in the coffin to make it weigh out like it carries a man, though he not be overly large. I heard that if you put pepper in your handkerchief, it will make tears a natural part of your demeanor."

Louisa returned to the kitchen to fix herself a small packet of pepper, tucking it into the edge of the basket filled with food for their journey. When they had the buggy loaded, she took up the reins and clucked their horse forward.

"Lord bless and keep you," Aunt Sylvania cried as they started out.

"He must, for there is no other," Louisa muttered under her breath.

The road to Fredericksburg seemed to speed by, as the Union lines were now north of Gettysburg. While they knew of the battle fought there, little information had come down before they left Richmond. Reaching the ferry at South Point, Zachary asked what anyone had heard of the battle.

"We done took a whuppin'," the man taking the money replied. "Three days fightin'—don't know how many kilt." He shook his head and spat a wad off to the side. "Lee done his best. Bet it nigh to broke his heart losin' so many of his boys like that."

Louisa blinked to stop the burning in her eyes. How many of the men they'd nursed back to health were now lying dead or injured again? And the supplies they would get wouldn't even fill a pinhole in the need.

She looked over at her brother. Mouth lined in white, Zachary thanked the man for telling them and clucked the horse forward as they loaded onto the ferry. Too late to plead for them to go home, but she knew it would do no good anyway. If their journey helped one wounded man, it was worth it.

As they neared the shore Louisa's heart picked up the pace always caused by the sight of blue uniforms. She could feel Zachary's gaze upon her.

"You all right?"

She nodded and forced her hands to relax in her lap.

"State your business, sir." The soldier held his rifle across his chest.

"We are taking our brother to be buried in the family plot."

"And where might that be?"

"North Church Cemetery. Generations of Highwoods are buried there."

Louisa held her handkerchief to her eyes, the pepper causing instant tears. She sniffed back a sob and laid a shaking hand on her brother's arm.

"I know, dear, this will soon be over." Zachary handed the sentry his papers. "You'll find them all in order."

The sentry glanced down at the signature and seal. "Pull your buggy over there while I show this to my superior."

Oh, Lord, preserve us. Louisa had no need to fake a sob. She instead fought for control of the fear that made her want to cry out. Oblivious to the traffic passing them by, she closed her eyes against the burning from the pepper and let her head droop against the seat back.

"Sorry to keep you waiting." The sentry handed back their papers and waved them forward.

Louisa nearly collapsed from relief.

"Thank you, Jesus" became her consistent prayer.

Since the procurement of the quinine and some morphine had been arranged ahead of time with sources of whom she knew nothing, they quickly packed the carriage, used their return passes at the Union lines, and faded into the morass of defeated and retreating Confederate soldiers, several of whom rode south with them unaware of the precious cargo accompanying them. Upon returning to Richmond, the supplies were dispersed among the hospitals. Their cargo was a mere drop in the vat of unimaginable misery, but Louisa felt she'd done something of value. If only she could do more.

Whenever she could, she canvassed Richmond homes, pleading for any small delicacy to give to the soldiers in the hospitals. She and Reuben picked peaches and apricots off trees badly in need of pruning but producing in spite of the war. Her regulars baked what they could, made puddings out of precious sugar and milk and eggs, shared jams and jellies, whatever they had been able to preserve.

With the rebels retreating from Gettysburg, every hospital was filled, including floor space with the overflow of the miasma of misery spilling into the churches. Thousands were buried where they fell on the battlefields, and those not buried were picked clean by scavengers, their bones bleaching in the hot summer sun. Louisa had an entire cadre of helpers who carried water to the suffering men, read to them, wrote letters home, eased whatever they could for the living. And a few chaplains came regularly to comfort the dying.

One night Reuben came to her, calling her gently to rouse

her from sleep deeper than any well. "Missy Louisa." He touched her shoulder. "Missy Louisa."

"Yes."

"Dat young man dey brung today . . ."

Louisa threw the sheet back. "I'll be right there." She snatched her wrapper off the end of the bed and followed the old man down the stairs, tying her belt as she went. Automatically her prayers rose as she hurried into the dining room.

Zachary sat in the chair by the cot, dipping cloths into water and laying them back on the body burning with fever.

"Has he taken any tea?" Abby had steeped a tea from willow bark that usually helped with fever.

"Tried spoonin' it in, but he not swallow." The maid looked up from the bedside. "He choke."

"I tried to keep Reuben from waking you." Zachary glared at the old man.

"No, I told him to." Louisa laid a hand on the young soldier's forehead. So hot. What else could they do?

The boy's hands twitched, and his back arched in a shuddering convulsion. He went rigid, guttural sounds gagging on the humid air, with not even a breeze to ease the room. When he fell limp again, Louisa laid two fingers on the inside of his wrist to check his pulse.

"We've got to cool him down." She turned to Reuben. "Go get a clean sheet. We'll soak that and wrap him in it."

"It's not proper for you to be doin' all this." Zachary rubbed his forehead and sighed.

"Oh, dear brother, helpin' this young man live is more important than propriety. Our Lord . . ."

"Louisa, I don't much care what our *Lord* said or did." The sneer in his voice cut right to her soul. She'd known he no longer took part in church, but to say such things tore at her heart. He was her big brother, the one she looked up to.

"Zachary, how can you say such things, or even think them?"

"Look around you." Waving his hand, he tipped over the washbasin. Water sloshed over her bare feet. "You think God cares about which side wins this war?"

"I don't think He is on either side, but both sides. He doesn't want us fighting at all."

"You haven't seen the piles of dead bodies like I have. I lay on the field with a dead man across my legs for hours before help came. Two wounded men died right beside me, one callin' on his God to save him. No one saved him. No one saved him or the others. One wore a blue uniform. If God heard, He turned away."

Louisa's heart sprung a leak, and the tears flowed as she listened to his ragged voice. She put a hand on his shoulder, but he tried to shrug it off. Never before had he said anything about the time he was wounded. She'd known it had to be bad, for most men refused to talk about the battles, other than to mention where they'd been or whom they served under.

Father, help me help him. I hear him, but I don't know how to answer him.

The man on the bed convulsed again, his body bucking the cot, the legs scraping the floor. The sound of the scrapes ate into her like fingernails on a slate.

"Easy, son, easy." Zachary adopted the tone he would use with a fractious horse.

Reuben came into the room with a sheet soaked in a bucket of water, and together he and Louisa wound it around the gasping soldier. The sheet dried faster than if hung outside on a summer day with a hot wind.

"Mother?" The young man stared up at Louisa.

"No, dear, be easy now. Rest so you can get better." Louisa continued to stroke the hair back from his forehead, remembering how good her mother's hand felt when she had done the same.

"Mother . . . I . . . did . . . my . . . b-best, like . . . like you always . . ." He stared into Louisa's eyes. "Like you always . . . said." The pauses between words grew longer. "I will . . . see . . . you . . . in . . ."—Louisa bent her head to hear his fading voice—"in . . . the . . . mornin'."

Another breath. A long pause.

No, don't die like this. God, it's not fair.

But he was gone, the last gentle exhalation from lips that smiled, not a big smile but enough for Louisa to know that he saw something beyond and was no longer afraid.

Louisa and Reuben, both of them wiping away tears, nodded to each other. Again they, like him, had done their best. *My best wasn't good enough to keep him here, but how can I resent that, when I know he has gone on to a far better place? While he is in the arms of God, I am here and tired. So tired, Lord. I am so tired of the dying and the crying.* She stood and sighed. "I'll notify the hospital in the morning."

Zachary sat with his head propped on his hand, eyes closed, cheeks like carved marble. Louisa started to say something, but he waved her away, so she turned to Reuben. "You go on to bed, Reuben, you've not had a decent night's sleep in I don't know how long."

"Old man like me don' need much sleep. I cleans up here, den go to bed."

Knowing that arguing was as useless as trying to stop a rainstorm, Louisa made her way back up the stairs, each tread feeling higher than the last. At least Aunt Sylvania had slept through it all. Louisa fell across her bed, feeling the tears start again. The boy had never made it to manhood, yet had done a man's job. And died for it.

Oh, Lord, when will it all be over? She had no strength to stay awake for an answer that had yet to come.

Dusk was slipping in the window when she finally awoke. The birds twittered their good-night wishes outside her window. Not a sound came from downstairs. Up the street a mother called her son home. Louisa thought of the mother of the boy who'd died during the night. She would never call him home again.

A tear slid from the side of her eye and blotted her pillow. How many boys had she eased on their way, fighting to save them but blessing their passing? She didn't want to count. She crossed to the folding screen in the corner, stripped, and washed herself in the cool water of the pitcher. They should have wakened her earlier, but knowing her family, she imagined they decided she needed sleep more than anything. Once dressed, with her hair combed, she made her way downstairs, one hand trailing on the banister. Ignoring the dining room, knowing the body was gone and most likely another injured man in its place, she followed the sounds of laughter to the back veranda. She paused just inside the French doors that overlooked the backyard, a place now filled with laughter and teasing, perhaps trying to chase away the sorrow of the night.

She watched her brother as he told a story of their childhood, his good hand flashing to help in the descriptions. Was this the same man who hours earlier had said he no longer believed in a God who cared about the men fighting the war?

His words of the dark night felt like a vest of lead dragging at her shoulders, pulling her neck taut. Did he really believe what he'd said, or was his diatribe due to his grief at the death of the young boy and the frustrations of dealing with his own handicaps? Louisa rubbed her forehead where she could feel a headache starting. No one knew she was up yet. She could climb the stairs and sink back into oblivion, back where she had no worries about finding food for her men, or medicine, or even the simplest of comforts.

And if she felt that way, no wonder Zachary did. Perhaps he was more honest than she, admitting his doubts.

But I don't want to doubt you, Lord. All my life, you have been a part of me. If you were gone, would I not feel the amputation? I know you are here. I know you care. I know that you will see us through, for you said you would.

The ache in her head took up the cadence of a drumbeat leading the march. Turning, she headed back up the stairs and sank down on her bed. So much to do, and here she was lying down again. What would her mother say?

Oh, Mother, I need you so. You would have the wisdom to tell Zachary—to tell him what? I don't know, but . . . Louisa lay back on her pillows, the cool sheets blessing the back of her neck, her hand covering her closed eyes. The beat took up a place behind her eyes and pounded out the moments. *You would bring me peppermint tea and rub my neck and forehead. I can hear you singing. Ah, Mother dear, how I miss your singing. You sang when there was nothing to be joyful about, but you said singing and praising God made you feel joyful anyway.* A tear leaked from under her closed lashes and meandered down to the pillow. *You called it a sacrifice of praise. Is that what I need?*

Another tear joined the first. *My head hurts and I am so weary.* A tune trickled into her mind. *"Praise to the Lord, the Almighty, the King of creation."* She took a deep breath and let it all out, allowing her shoulders to sink back into the feathery softness. *"O my soul, praise Him, for He is thy health and salvation!"*

A bird twittered in the branches outside the window. A breeze lifted the once starched curtains and blew through the drape of mosquito netting. It kissed her cheeks and bathed her forehead with blessedly cool fingers, drying her tears as she drifted off to healing sleep.

There were times when Louisa almost asked Zachary if he really meant what he'd said, but courage failed her. She watched him, trying to decipher the pensive look he wore at times, the face he presented to the recuperating soldiers not matching the one she saw upon close scrutiny.

"Why are you always staring at me?" The snap in his voice lashed like the tip of a whip.

"I . . . I'm not. I . . ." She seized her courage with both hands and yanked it up to her heart where it belonged. "I'm just trying to figure you out."

"Well, don't bother. Just a waste of your time." He turned away and crutched out of the room, his stiff back sure evidence of his displeasure.

She hated people to be upset with her.

"Well, brother dear, two can play that game." With firm resolve, she kept herself from running after him.

But an hour later, he came up behind her where she sat sewing with her soldiers and dropped a kiss on the top of her head. She'd known it to be him by the sound of his crutch and stride.

"Forgiven?" he whispered.

She rolled her eyes heavenward. "Perhaps."

He proceeded to entertain the seamsters, keeping them laughing while their needles flew.

"Ouch!" One man stuck his finger in his mouth. "Now look what you did, made me laugh so hard I got blood on this coat."

Running header

I pray to God that's all the blood it ever gets! She had a bundle of coats in the other room that needed patches. Patches for the holes bullets had torn through the coat and into a body. By looking at the coats, she'd seen how the men had died or ended in a hospital. If only she could sew a lining that would withstand bullets and screaming shells.

"Mail done come." Abby brought several letters on a once-silver salver, now worn so that the lesser metal took precedence.

Louisa smiled her thanks, her mouth turning up further at the sight of Lucinda's laborious handwriting. "A letter from Twin Oaks."

Zachary looked up from his conversation, question marks all over his face, though he quickly wiped them away as he returned to his usual noncommittal expression.

With that brief glimpse of Zachary's pained expression, Louisa realized that she needed to look behind the mask on her brother's face to see his true feelings. What feelings he let himself have.

"Oh, and a letter from Jesselynn. How wonderful. Two in one day." She looked to the faces of her sewing group. "I will go over and see if any mail has come for you."

"I go see." Reuben nodded to the group before heading out the side gate.

Since black slaves were not supposed to be able to read and write, Louisa took out Jesselynn's letter first. Surely there would be parts in it she could share with all of them. She glanced down the page, wishing she were in her own room so she could savor every word.

She looked up to see expectant faces watching her, needles and thread lying idle. "My sister is on her way to Oregon in a covered wagon, along with others of our people. Much of Twin Oaks, our home in Kentucky, was burned last year. I'll read what she says.

" 'We have found a wagon train and are finally leaving Independence, Missouri. We were beginning to think we would have to remain there, but living in wagons is not my idea of a good way to spend a winter. The two foals are growing like weeds and making us all laugh at their antics. Living close to our horses, as we are now, has created a bond we didn't have before. Thaddeus is a born horseman, just like his daddy and older brothers. He has no fear around them, which can cause some of the rest of us plenty of fear at times.

'Aunt Agatha knits her way across the land. She has taken Jane Ellen under her wing, and the two of them are teaching the boys manners and correct speech, the kind of things I should be doing but have been too busy keeping us all together.

'The good news, Ahab can run as well as ever. While we lost the first race, I asked for more distance for the next one, and he did himself proud. The purse and selling the loser's horse back to him has caused our purse to swell to needed proportions again.' "

"Jesselynn raced Ahab?" Aunt Sylvania's eyes were as round as the lemon cookies on the plate near at hand. "That stallion?"

Louisa shrugged. "We all do what we must. I surely do wish I could see Thaddeus. He was just a baby, or so it seemed, when we saw him last. He won't even remember who we are." She hoped that changing the subject would derail Aunt Sylvania's horror.

"She rode sidesaddle?"

Louisa sent Zachary a pleading look that clearly cried *help*.

His noncommittal shrug made her eyes narrow, sending darts his way.

"Here, she continues. 'The train we are joining is of a good size and the wagon master has a good reputation.' "

"Louisa, I asked you a question."

Louisa laid the letter in her lap. She sighed, shook her head, and looked up at her aunt. "Jesselynn wore britches, has been wearing them since she left Twin Oaks, because that is the only way she can keep all of them safe. She is doing what she has to do, just like the rest of us."

Aunt Sylvania shook her head and kept on shaking it. "The war, always the war. Life will never be the same again." She sniffed and dabbed at her nose with a bit of cambric. "Lord, have mercy on us all."

"Amen to that," one of the men muttered.

"Supper is ready." Abby stood in the doorway. "You want I should bring it out here?"

"No, we'll come in." Louisa stood and tucked the letters into her apron pocket. "My, that surely does smell fine."

But when she read the letter from Lucinda later in Zachary's study, she felt as though she'd been slugged in the midsection.

CHAPTER EIGHT

FORT LARAMIE

"See you again?" That voice?

Wolf stopped as if he'd hit a granite face at a dead run. "Jesselynn?"

She stopped on the second from the last riser. "I do believe so." Her accent thickened. She smiled, ordering her lips to not tremble, nor the tears behind her eyes to fall. *Ah, Wolf, how . . . why . . . I cannot bear this.* All her mother's and Lucinda's coaching about how a Southern gentlewoman behaved came to her aid.

"God be praised, you have come back." His whisper drove straight to her heart.

She took another step down, her gaze never leaving his, her mouth so dry she could not have spoken, even if an arrow were pointing at her.

Father God, she is most glorious, like the sun rising above the mountains or a lake with the kiss of evening upon it. And she has come back. Please, I beg of you, let her stay. Wolf stepped forward. If there were others in the room, he had no awareness of them. He took her hand, drew it up in the crook of his arm, and pressed it against his side. Could she hear his heart thundering like a spring cascade over a cliff?

Does he know what he is doing to me? Lord, I cannot go through the leaving again. He must come with us to Oregon. Can he hear my heart? Feel me tremble? Once in his arms was not enough. I want forever.

As the two of them walked into the dining room, Jesselynn glanced up in time to see Rebeccah wipe a pleased look off her face, the kind of look a cat wore when it had been in the cream uninvited.

"If you would sit here, Jesselynn, and Mr. Wolf, there." She indicated chairs on the opposite sides of the table, directly across from each other. When they all had taken their places, she nodded to her husband. "If you will say grace, Captain Jensen."

Jesselynn bowed her head but not so far that she couldn't see Wolf from under her lashes. He bowed his head, giving her a view of his broad forehead, the thick dark hair springing from it as if it had a life of its own. His shoulders filled out the shirt, the open collar framing his throat and upper chest, the cords of his neck strong beneath the skin. His skin reminded her of the Cordova leather that once bound her father's books. Neither brown nor red but some mix of the two that made a hue all its own, the richer for the joining.

"Jesselynn, would you like your meat sliced thick or thin?" Rebeccah spoke softly. Jesselynn could feel the heat flaming up her neck. She'd not heard one word of the prayer, not even the "amen." She dared not look at Wolf in case he realized where her thoughts had been. Never in her entire life had she lost herself like this, not even after her fiancé died, or her father. She'd always kept her wits about her.

Until today.

While she took part in the conversation, she had no memory of what she had said or eaten when they rose from the table. Clara, the second maid, served their coffee in the parlor.

"So what are your plans?" Captain Jensen turned to Wolf.

"I'll leave for the Oglala lands as soon as the general issues my requisition for blankets and supplies for my people. We brought in ten elk, which should help feed the fort for a while. The men now know the elks' range, and they can hunt again."

"And you, Miss Highwood?"

Jesselynn forced her attention away from Wolf and back to the captain. "My two wagons are returning to Fort Laramie. We have three others along. We are hoping that"—she drew in a deep breath, wishing for a private place to talk with Wolf—"Wolf, er . . . Mr. Torstead will change his mind and take our train west after all." She watched the shutter drop over his eyes and the rest of his face. Clearly, that wasn't what he wanted to hear.

"Ah, then I have a feeling you two could use some time alone to discuss your—um . . ." Captain Jensen turned to his wife. "Come, dear, we can go help Clara with the dessert." The two of them exited the room, leaving a curious silence behind.

Jesselynn studied her fingers, finding bits of dirt still under her fingernails. Without her knife, it would have to stay there. She snuck glances at Wolf, who stood looking out the parlor window. He hadn't moved since the Jensens left the room.

"How much damage did your wagons suffer?" *Lord, can I convince her to come with me?*

At the sound of his voice, her heart jumped into her throat. "Ah, not much. They were at the end of the train, and the stampede started when lightning hit the lead wagon. Aunt Agatha and Benjamin kept their oxen in hand." *Please, turn and look at me.*

"Where were you?" *I know I am rushing her, but we must have a camp for winter—if she will stay.*

"With the herd." She told him of the almost stampede and the hollow. "It could have been terribly tragic."

"You were wise to not take the shortcut with the others. They will lose more oxen that way." The silence deepened again.

Wolf, we need you. Please take us on to Oregon. We'll pay you double if you'll guide our train. Practicing what to say did not make the saying of it any easier. She knit her fingers so tightly together that they cramped.

"Why are you going to Oregon?"

"For the free land, so that Meshach can start a new life. He wants to be a free man where no one will look down on him or call him 'boy' again."

"So that is why Meshach is going. What about you?" He turned to study her with his dark eyes.

"They say the land will grow anything, horse feed included." She twisted her mouth to one side, sighed, and looked straight at him. "To get away from the war. I want nothing to do with slavery and war ever again."

"Why does it have to be Oregon?" The question hung in the stillness.

"I . . . I reckon I don't really know. We tried Missouri, and Daniel nearly got lynched. Kansas was worse with Quantrill's Raiders, so we decided on Oregon and went ahead with obtaining supplies. We hope Oregon is far enough away from the South that we can build a new life."

He took two steps across the room to where the lamplight burnished his face and threw his eyes into shadow. "You could have the same in Wyoming."

"I've heard the winters can be fierce in Wyoming." She stared into his eyes. *What is it you are saying?* Her throat dried. Her heart speeded up.

"My people know how to live through the winter. And after the snow comes spring. There are wild horses to be caught. Our herd would grow quickly that way."

Was it a slip of his tongue? Had he really said 'our'? "What are you saying?" Jesselynn's fingers shook, so she hid them in her skirt.

Wolf took two more steps, reached for her hands, and pulled her to her feet. With their hands clutched between them, he stared down at her. After taking a deep breath and letting it out, he spoke so softly she was forced to lean ever closer. "I am asking you to marry me. We can homestead in the hills above the Chugwater. The grass grows rich in the spring, and there are wild flowers the blue of your dress." He fingered the puff of one sleeve.

"Milady's eyes."

"What?"

"That's what some call these forget-me-nots." She waited. Would he ever say the words she so desperately longed to hear?

"Meshach would find it good there too."

"But he wants to go on to Oregon."

"And Aunt Agatha?"

Jesselynn closed her eyes. Taking a deep breath didn't help. *Aunt Agatha. Oh, my Lord, help me here—and there. How will I deal with Aunt Agatha? I know you are my life and you have the answers, but this man, Father, I love this man. Is there anything wrong with that? And I sense that if I don't answer now, he'll be gone.*

She opened her eyes to find Wolf watching her; his hands had not loosened their grip, his thumb stroked the back of her right hand. "I . . . I will talk with Aunt Agatha." *Oh, Lord, preserve me. Put words of wisdom in my mouth.*

"It is of her I must ask for your hand in marriage?"

Jesselynn shook her head. *It should be Zachary. Now, if that wouldn't be a scene.* She tried to take a step back, but he moved with her.

"No, I make my own decisions." She looked deep into his eyes, trying to read his soul. *Do you love me? Say it!*

She swallowed hard, cleared her throat. "Wolf, in my world words are important. . . ." *No, I'm saying it all wrong. This feels like love, looks like love, and acts like love. Can I trust that it is? Father, are you blessing this? I feel that you are.*

"Yes?" Now both his thumbs were sending messages screaming up her arms, setting her skin on fire, her heart to thundering.

Her head dropped forward, her forehead resting on his chest. His heart, too, beat faster, louder. When she looked up, she smiled into his eyes that carried a shadow. "Yes, Mr. Torstead, I will marry you."

The shadow fled, and the sun burst forth. He cupped her face with his hands and kissed her waiting mouth. As if that weren't enough, he tasted her nose, her chin, and returned to her mouth. When he drew away, he cupped her cheeks again, tenderly, as if holding a great and fragile treasure. "You are sure?"

"Yes. I am sure." She sucked in another breath and laid her hands over his. "I am sure that I love you. I am sure that I want to be with you for the rest of my life." *And I am sure that the next few days will test everything I am.*

"We will be married here at the fort?"

"If you want."

"I will go with you to bring in the wagons."

She now stepped back. "No, I will do that myself."

He studied her face, then nodded. "As you wish."

I can't have you wounded by her words. She will go berserk. "Not what I wish, but what I must do." She took another step back and realized they were no longer alone.

"Here's the dessert, Clara's chocolate cake with whipped cream. You've never tasted anything so delicious west of the

Mississippi." Captain Jensen carried one tray, followed by his wife with another. When they set them on the low table, he looked up with a twinkle in his eye. "Your time was well spent, I gather?"

Wolf nodded. He took Jesselynn's hand. "She has agreed to marry me."

"A wedding! Oh, Captain, we will have it right here." Rebeccah beamed at her husband and then turned back to Jesselynn. "When? End of next week, of course. It must be soon if you are going to go north. Mr. Torstead, you *are* still going north, aren't you? This is the most wonderful news. Wait until I talk with the chaplain, I—"

Captain Jensen put his arm around his wife's waist. "You can tell we don't get a lot of opportunities to have a party here. Now, Rebeccah, you must let Miss Highwood do some of the planning." The smile on his face and in his voice brought matching smiles from the others.

"I . . . I haven't had time to think." *This is all so new. Oh, what have I let myself in for?*

Rebeccah took Jesselynn's hands in hers. "I would consider it a great honor if you would let me take care of the wedding. I have a silk dress you could wear that has been languishing in a trunk, needing just such an occasion as this. Why, wait until I announce this to the ladies here at the fort, not that there are many of us, but we will have a marvelous time."

Jesselynn could feel the warmth of Wolf standing right behind her. She leaned back just a mite to feel the solid wall of his chest holding her up. Getting control of the stampede seemed easier than this. At least those cows ran in a circle. The vibrations of a laugh in the wall behind her made a smile blossom, then bloom, and a matching laugh gurgled to the surface.

"Ah, I hate to tell you this, but when my wife gets hold of an excuse for a party, man the barricades, 'cause that party *will* happen." Jensen gave his wife the kind of look that brought a lump to Jesselynn's throat.

"Thank you." She accepted the plate Rebeccah offered and took a bite. Not since she left Twin Oaks had she tasted anything so fine. "This is wonderful."

"Thank you. Perhaps Clara will make your wedding cake from this recipe. But she makes a white cake that . . ."

Captain Jensen cleared his throat.

Rebeccah shrugged at the twinkle in his eye. "I'm doing it again?"

He nodded. She tipped her head to one side and shrugged again, the laughter in her eyes and the merry dimples on either side of her mouth mute testimony to her joy.

If planning a wedding brought such happiness to another, Jesselynn had no desire to deprive her of the privilege.

When he set his plate down, Wolf nodded to his host and hostess. "Thank you for a most enjoyable evening. Someday I hope to repay the hospitality, once our home is built."

Jesselynn hid a smile. Was this really the same man who so rarely strung more than five words together at a time? Another facet to the man called Wolf, the man she would spend her lifetime getting to know.

A tingle ran from her toes to the top of her head. After all this time, she was indeed going to be married. And at Fort Laramie—Indian territory, of all places. If God himself had told her in advance this would be happening, she would have had a hard time believing Him.

Since Wolf didn't let go of her hand, she followed him to the door and out onto the porch.

He took her in his arms and kissed her again. "That's to remind you that no matter what anyone says, you *will* be marrying me in ten days." With that, he stepped off the porch and strode away, fading quickly into the darkness.

Jesselynn leaned against the newel-post and watched him go, one fingertip resting against her lips, as if to keep the feeling intact. When she returned to the parlor a few minutes later, Rebeccah sat with the lamp pooling light on the rich colors of the tapestry she was working on, her needle flashing.

"Your bed is turned down and ready for you. Your Benjamin is sleeping out in our woodshed. Clara made him a pallet, even though he said he had his bedroll. Breakfast will be ready whenever you need to leave."

Jesselynn sank down in a chair and shook her head. "I cannot thank you enough."

"No." Rebeccah leaned forward. "It is for me to thank you. Life is plain on an outpost like this, and to be part of your life brings richness to mine. We never had any children, so this is my chance to pretend that I have a daughter who is marrying a fine man, and we will all celebrate." She took another stitch. "And to think that you will be living within two days or so of us. Why, we'll practically be neighbors."

Jesselynn hid a yawn behind her hand. With all that had gone on, sleep should be the last thing from her mind. However . . .

"Thank you again, Rebeccah, but I'm afraid I must excuse myself. This is so different from what I planned. I thought to sleep in a hay pile somewhere, and that would be a luxury after the ground all these months. Four walls and a roof, windows, and a real bed. And the bath. I can never thank you enough."

Someday, she thought. *Someday I will have a home again, a safe home with walls and children and . . .* The picture of the man who would lead that home made her face warm. She stood, bid her hostess good-night, and made her way up the stairs. A lamp on the nightstand made the room look even more welcoming than earlier. Her shirt and pants, washed and pressed, lay over the chair, and even her boots wore a shine. She hung the dress in the chifforobe, stroking down the skirt with a sigh. She pulled the nightdress that lay across the bottom of the bed over her head, and after blowing out the lamp, she slipped between sheets, real sheets, cool and crisp to the skin. Ah, such luxury. She was asleep after only three "thank-you's" to her God, and all of them concerned Wolf.

The ride back to the wagons gave Jesselynn plenty of time to stew over her upcoming discussion with Aunt Agatha. "Perhaps she has changed clear through, not just on the surface."

Ahab flicked his ears back and forth, listening to her and still keeping track of the surroundings. He snorted.

"I agree. I should have let Wolf come with me. Perhaps she will be happy for me." Now *she* snorted. Her shoulders curved forward as if to protect her heart. He loves me. The thought brought a rush of delight, like pure springwater in a dusty land. Then the gusher died. He asked her to marry him, but never had he mentioned the word *love*.

"You all right, Marse Jesse?" Benjamin rode up beside her.

"I'm fine. You get some of the prairie chickens?"

He held up a brace.

"Good. I reckon Ophelia will be right glad."

Father, this is becoming a muddle. Perhaps we should have just found the chaplain, said our vows, and presented this as a fait accompli. If only Aunt Agatha . . . She brought that line of reasoning to a screaming halt. "If only's" could drive one to distraction, and one isn't any further ahead after hours of worrying and stewing than at the beginning.

Jesselynn leaned forward and patted Ahab's arched neck. "Perhaps that is why our Father told us not to worry, you think?" How come deciding not to worry and actually not worrying were so far apart?

Ahab pulled against the bit, begging for a bit of a run. Ever since racing in Independence, he'd been begging to run again. She wanted to run all right—back the way she had come.

Jesselynn and Benjamin met the wagons late in the afternoon of the second day of hard riding. Counting the wagons, she shook her head. Who had they picked up now?

"Jesse back!" Thaddeus sang out his welcome, running ahead of Jane Ellen.

Jesselynn dismounted and knelt to meet his running welcome. He flung himself into her arms, almost knocking her over in spite of how firmly she was braced.

"Why you leave us? Where Mr. Wolf?" He looked over her shoulder as if she were hiding him, as if he might pop up like a jack-in-the-box.

Jesselynn scooped him up and set him in the saddle without answering. "Now, you hang on."

His stare of reproach made her smile up at him and jiggle his foot. "I know, you always hang on. A real Highwood you are when it comes to riding." Patch met her with a yip and a doggy grin, his teeth gleaming white against his black fur and pink tongue. Keeping a firm hand on the reins, in case something spooked Ahab, she ruffled the dog's ears, keeping her chin away from his lightning tongue. Anything to delay the coming confrontation with Aunt Agatha.

"You find 'im?" Meshach rode up on Chess.

"See me ride Ahab?" Thaddeus clutched a hank of matted mane.

"Lil Marse fine rider." Meshach answered the boy and at the same time sent Jesselynn a look pregnant with questions.

"I found him."

Meshach dismounted and fell in step beside her.

Jesselynn sucked in a deep breath. Might as well get it over with. She dropped her voice. "He wants us to go north with him. He says there is good land, two days' travel from Fort Laramie, where we could all homestead. He says there is a valley, good hunting, clear running streams, and . . ." She knew she was talking too hard and fast but couldn't seem to stop the spate.

When Meshach failed to answer her, she looked up into his face. "You would be a free man here too, with free land."

They stopped walking, the wagons drawing closer with every plodding step of the oxen.

"You don't have to decide immediately."

"What you not tellin' me?"

Jesselynn rolled her lips together. "He has asked me to marry him."

"Ahh." Meshach looked down at her, a smile splitting his ebony face. "Thank de Lawd, dat man done come to his senses." Meshach slapped his thigh with his hat, raising a dust cloud to equal that of a span of oxen. He stopped. "You did say yes?"

"I did. Mrs. Jensen is getting things ready. She's the captain's wife, my hostess for the night." *Please, Meshach, decide to stay. I don't want to lose you and the others.* Thoughts pelted around her mind like children just loosed from lessons. *Meshach, answer me.* The cry nearly broke from her heart, taking all her strength to suppress it.

"So, Jesse, how did you fare?" Agatha, driving the lead wagon, always wore her sunbonnet well forward to protect her face, so now she pushed it back the better to see her niece.

After her careful scrutiny of Jesselynn's face, a frown wrinkled her forehead. But without commenting, she nodded over her shoulder. "Mrs. Jones has asked if she can travel with us. Both her husband and his brother seem to have met with some disaster, as they never returned to their camp. Strange, wouldn't you say?"

Jesselynn shrugged. "Fine with me, so long as she is alone. Either of the men show up, and none are welcome." At least she knew one of them wouldn't.

"I said the same, but she seemed fairly positive that would not be the case."

Jesselynn looked toward the last wagon. Most likely she should go talk with Mrs. Darcy Jones. Had she found her husband's body? And what happened to Rufus? For a moment, curiosity drove thoughts of Wolf right out of her mind.

"Me ridin'!" Thaddeus couldn't resist lording it over Sammy, who wriggled on the seat by Ophelia as she drove the second wagon.

Gratefully, Jesselynn switched her attention to her little brother. "Not anymore if you cannot be more considerate than that." She reached up and dragged him off the horse.

"Jane Ellen, would you please take him back?" She glanced over at Meshach. "And if you will give Sammy a ride, perhaps the young marse will learn better manners."

Meshach did as she suggested but without the smile that would ordinarily greet such a comment.

Sammy, sitting in front of his adopted father, crowed with delight. "Go, go." With one arm around his son, Meshach walked his mount alongside the wagon, where Ophelia said something that made both man and boy wear matching smiles.

Jesselynn remounted. "Think I'll go help with the herd." She could feel her Aunt Agatha's gaze drilling into her back, unspoken questions bombarding her like a flock of small birds chasing off an offending crow.

That night when they stopped for the evening camp, Aunt Agatha handed Jesselynn a cup of coffee and sat down on the wagon tongue beside her.

"Now, are you going to tell me what transpired at the fort?"

Jesselynn sipped at her coffee. "I stayed with Captain and Mrs. Jensen, had a real bath, and slept in a bed."

Agatha sighed. "Now that does sound like a long-lost privilege. No wonder you look so fresh. Just getting this dust off a body would be pure bliss."

How do I tell her?

"So, what did he say?"

"Who say?"

Agatha looked at Jesselynn as though she thought her niece had left her senses on the trail somewhere. "Mr. Wolf, that's who you went looking for, right?"

Jesselynn sat up straighter. "He asked us to go north with him instead of going on to Oregon."

Silence fell around them, as if everyone had quit breathing.

"Why ever would he do that?" Agatha turned slowly to stare at Jesselynn. "What is it you are not telling me?"

Jesselynn felt her stomach twist into a half hitch, then a double knot. "I agreed to marry him."

"Marry him?" Aunt Agatha sucked in a breath that wheezed around the constriction of her throat. "Marry a half-breed?" Her voice deepened. "A man of color?" Thunder rumbling in the distance could not have reverberated more. "No one! No woman in our family has evah"—her chest swelled. Her face mottled—"evah had truck with a man of colah!"

Chapter Nine

Richmond, Virginia

"Taxes! Don't they know there's a war going on?" Zachary fumed.

Louisa was beginning to wish she'd never told her brother the news. What good did it do? He couldn't go back to Twin Oaks. If he entered Kentucky he'd be shot as a spy. And what did they have to pay the taxes with? Nothing. Unless he had some money stashed away, and that she very much doubted.

"I imagine they plan on financing the war with our tax money." Seeing the look on his face, Louisa wished she'd kept her mouth shut. If that were true, it would be a short war considering the state of their finances.

"We can't lose Twin Oaks." Zachary slumped in the chair as if all the air had gone out of him, or at least all the starch.

"Surely they wouldn't foreclose on someone who served in the army like you did, now wounded and not able to go home." She rose and paced to the other side of the room, her steps more agitated as she strode. "And both Daddy and Adam killed. And the place burned to the ground by a Confederate officer." She held up her hands to stop his objection. "I know we can't prove Dunlivey did that, but we all know it, sure as summer brings mosquitoes." She spun at the far wall and paced back again. "So what are we going to do?"

"*We* are going to do nothing. *I* am going to speak with our brother-in-law. Perhaps he can send a letter that will change their minds. He has high connections. He can use them for the family." Zachary levered himself out of the chair. "First thing in the morning. As for now, wasn't there some peach pie left over from supper? I think that would taste mighty fine."

"But—"

"No 'but's'. Let me at least handle this." He turned back after stumping to the doorway. "I think I will talk with Jefferson about a position with his firm. Surely they will realize their need to employ an ex-soldier who, while missing limbs, is every bit all right in his mind."

Louisa watched him leave the room. That surely did answer one of her questions, the one that asked how this recuperation time was affecting her brother. More questions buzzed in her mind like a nest of enraged hornets. How would he get to an office every day? What would he wear? Could he manage a job? And most of all, why hadn't Jefferson offered him one earlier, or at least promised something for when Zachary felt ready?

Like a hornet, she felt like stinging someone, anyone who crossed her path at the moment. If Zachary were working, how could they go on another mission?

Before going to sleep, she sat down to write Lucinda a message reassuring her that Zachary would find a way to meet the tax obligation. She only wished she felt as positive as she sounded. She'd thought earlier about the silver and other valuables buried in the rose garden. Jesselynn had written, in a roundabout way that took some deciphering, about the family treasures buried. She wanted Louisa to know about it for when the war ended. But in case someone intercepted the mail and read the letter, Louisa could think of no way to tell Lucinda to dig up and sell what she needed. And knowing

Lucinda, she would starve first. So Louisa simply filled her in on the news, closing with . . .

Carrie Mae looks to be having twins. She is so large, but perhaps it only seems that way because she is typically so slender. We all wish you could be here to care for her and the baby and thus continue family traditions. Thank you for all the work you and Joseph are doing to keep Twin Oaks going. Someday, when the war is over, we will come home, and we will all be together again.

With love and God's blessing, I remain

Again she signed her name, this time including Zachary and Aunt Sylvania.

Louisa brushed the quill back and forth under her chin. Ah, if only she could get on a train and, no matter how roundabout the trip, return to Midway, and home to Twin Oaks. To walk again between the two ancient oaks at the end of the drive and on up to the big house. There was no way she could picture the house burned, with only the brick chimneys standing, as their neighbor had written. Or no horses grazing the pastures, or no rolling sweeps of tobacco fields.

After sealing the envelope Louisa knelt by her bed and opened her Bible to Psalm 91. *Ah, Lord, I know we are safe and secure under your mighty wings, but so many of our boys believed that and were killed anyway. Not that I'm not looking forward to heaven and your presence, you understand, but the agony has gone on and continues. And now Zachary disavowing his faith. O Father, do not let him go. Please hold him under your wings and in your camp with angels round about.* She read more about fiery darts not assailing and not even snakes or young lions. She closed her eyes and repeated the words from memory, branding them into her soul for when she needed them.

★ ★ ★ ★ ★

The next day, as soon as Louisa had her men working at their assignments for the day, she took her writing case out under the magnolia tree. Shaking the ink, she set the square corked bottle back in its holder, dipped the quill, and started the first of at least two letters for the day.

Dear Mrs. She stopped and forced her brain to remember the name of the young man who had died under their care. How she hated writing letters like this.

> *. . . Benson,*
>
> *My name is Louisa Highwood, and I had the honor of knowing your son, Adam. He was brought to our house for care, but we were unable to quench the fever. He died praising you and his Lord. His last words indicated what a fine young man you raised. He said, "Mother, I did what you asked. I did my best." I am so sorry, Mrs. Benson, that our best was not good enough to save your son. Please know that he is in a far better place. The look on his face as he died made me sure of that. With this letter I am enclosing his personal effects.*
>
> *Sincerely,*

She signed her name and wiped away a wet spot from her tears. At least she had not smudged the ink.

Hearing a strange sound, she looked around her. Aunt Sylvania was reading from the local newspaper about how many Union prisoners had been exchanged for Confederate ones. Psalms would come next, and Shakespeare would be last. Yesterday one of the men had spoken the part of Petruchio that he'd memorized long before from *The Taming of the Shrew.*

After a few minutes Louisa heard the noise again. She

turned to look under the peony bushes. Surely it sounded like a kitten. But seeing nothing, she returned to her letter writing.

In the letter to Jesselynn she told about her trip to Washington with Zachary, glossing over the frightening parts and trying to make her sister laugh about the dead possum.

I am concerned about our brother though, dear sister. He confesses to no longer believing in our God and Savior, and at times a black cloud hovers over him that makes me fear for his soul. One minute he can be nice and the next nasty. I sometimes feel I am walking on eggshells with him. Please keep him and us in your prayers, as we do you. Your journey sounds exciting, and I am grateful you found a good wagon train. How I will bear having you on one side of this country and us on the other is more than I can comprehend.

There now, I am getting maudlin and I promised myself not to do that. Right now you would get a laugh here, for Aunt Sylvania is reading The Taming of the Shrew, *and one of our guests is playing Petruchio from memory. I keep looking around for a kitten that seems to be crying, but perhaps it is a mockingbird.*

Give Thaddeus a hug and plenty of kisses from all of us. He will be half grown before I see him, so tall I will not even know who he is.

She deliberately kept the "if" out of the sentence. Surely God would not be so cruel as to keep them apart forever. She signed her name, added the others, and prepared her letters for mailing.

The cry came again. This time it was so close at hand she put down her case and began to crawl on her hands and knees, the better to peek under the low-lying bushes.

"Oh, look." She parted the spirea boughs to reveal a ginger kitten, so small it could fit in her palm, hiding in the shadows.

"What is it?" One of the men stood and crossed to look down. "A kitten! Looks about six to eight weeks or so. How'd it get in here?"

"There are lots of places something so tiny could squeeze under our fence." Louisa reached to pick up the kitten, but it backed away, hissing like it were grown rather than teacup sized. One tiny paw struck, scratching her finger.

"Ouch! You little rascal." She grabbed the animal before it could strike again and cupped it in her hands.

"You want I should dispose of it?" The man beside her kept his voice to a whisper.

"No, I think not. We all need a baby around. He'll calm down, you'll see."

Louisa had to promise to scour the neighborhood looking for its owner before Aunt Sylvania agreed they could keep the kitten.

"Might help keep the mice at bay. Sure is a feisty little thing." Sylvania shook her head. "I don't cotton much to cats, but if no one claims it . . ." She shrugged. "I reckon it is yours."

While the kitten started out sleeping that night in a box in the pantry, it ended up with one of the soldiers sleeping on a pallet on the floor.

The next afternoon when Louisa petted the purring kitten on her lap, she lifted the sleepy, limp golden body and looked into the kitten's face. "I sure wonder why God brought you to us just at this time." She rubbed the kitten's pink nose with her own. "Bet He has something real important for you to do, hmm?" The little kitten yawned, his pink tongue curling, showing all the barbs that helped keep his short coat so shiny. "But you don't care, do you? Give you a nice lap, gentle hands, and you'll purr anyone to peace."

But the feeling wouldn't go away. Something was coming.

Chapter Ten

West of Fort Laramie

The burn ignited in Jesselynn's middle.

Thaddeus started to cry. Sammy added a wail.

Ophelia threw her apron over her head. "Lawd, have mercy."

Meshach gathered the sobbing Sammy into one arm and his rocking wife into the other. "Shush now, both of you."

Thaddeus threw himself against Jesselynn's knees.

Why is it that everyone feels they can tell me exactly what to do? Jesselynn held Thaddeus close, patting his back while she studied on her aunt's words. She could feel the older woman's flaming-iron gaze burning into the top of her bent head.

Lord, right now I need wisdom beyond Solomon's. And I need a good answer right now. She wanted to stalk off into the darkness. She wanted to scream at her aunt. She wanted others to share the joy that she felt inside.

"Gray Wolf Torstead is a fine man." There, that was peaceable rather than incendiary.

"That is not what we are talking about!" The lash of the whip could not crack more fiercely.

Jesselynn set Thaddeus gently away from her, waiting until Jane Ellen took the little boy into her lap. Ordering her reluctant body to obey, she rose to her feet, as if locking each joint as she stood so that her body would hold her upright.

"Aunt Agatha, I know my mama and daddy would agree with you, but they are dead and gone—"

When Agatha started to interrupt, Jesselynn held up a restraining hand. "Please allow me to have my say." Agatha clamped her arms across her heaving bosom. Jesselynn nodded and continued, her voice as calm as if discussing the weather. "We left the South, and the war, to seek a new life. Part of that new life is to no longer judge men and women by the color of their skin." She paused, letting her words sink in, but continued with her answer when Agatha appeared about to interrupt again. "I am going to say this only once. Wolf and I will be married at the fort. I want your blessing, but I don't *need* it." She turned to the rest of the folks gathered around the fire. "You are all invited, both to the wedding and to continue north with us, if you would like to. If any of you would rather wait and go on with another train heading west, that is up to you. You have about three days to decide before we make it back to the fort, unless another train comes along in the meantime."

However, since she'd not seen a westward bound wagon train on her journey back to the fort, that was unlikely.

"I got a question." Nate Lyons leaned forward.

"Of course."

"I heard rumors of Indian trouble. The Sioux don't like all of us passin' through their huntin' grounds. We'd be up in their country, right?"

Jesselynn nodded. "But Wolf isn't concerned about that. Red Cloud, one of the more well-known chiefs, is a distant relative of his. That's who he was going to go live with."

"Has he talked with Red Cloud yet?"

Jesselynn shrugged. "I'm not sure. I know he wants to help his tribe with supplies and such."

"Seems, well, perhaps they would take offense at so many of us comin' in one party."

Jesselynn scratched under the sweatband of her hat. "I wish I knew the answer to that." *Why didn't I ask Wolf some of these things? Because all you could think about was him.* The two voices in her mind argued back and forth. "You'll be able to talk with Wolf about those things when you see him."

The silence coming from Aunt Agatha screamed a thousand protests.

Mrs. McPhereson cupped her coffee mug in both hands. "Seems we'll be seein' plenty of changes comin' ahead. Like a stout tree, if'n we don't bend we'll break. And you got to admit, life out here can be one big storm after another."

"So are you thinking on returning east to your folks now that . . ." Jesselynn let her voice trail off.

"Now that I'm widowed?" Mrs. Mac shook her head. "No, me and my boys here talked it over. There ain't nothin' for us back there, but in Wyoming or Oregon we can homestead and get our land for the workin'. That was Ambrose's dream for us, the land, that is. I don't pretend to think it will be free. We'll earn every rock and tree. But we ain't afeered a hard work. So we'll go where you go. Good friends is worth more than gold, as the Good Book says, and I do believe it."

"Well said." Nate Lyons nodded with a look over to where Agatha sat, her knitting needles screaming of her displeasure. "And this way, we'll get a jump on winter. Can even put up some hay for the horses, maybe." He turned to where Meshach sat working on softening a tanned hide. "What about you?"

Meshach continued pulling the hide back and forth over a chunk of wood he'd smoothed and laid in a frame of crossed poles. The silence stretched like the hide he worked.

Jesselynn tossed a couple of twigs from the ground into the

fire, keeping her full attention on the orange-and-yellow dancing flames. She would not beg and plead. If Meshach felt going west was best for him, she would give him her blessing and one of the wagons along with the oxen to pull it. Daniel and Benjamin would have to make up their own minds too.

Meshach looked up from his handiwork. "Me and 'Phelia, we had big dreams for Oregon, but no reason why those dreams can't be here in Wyomin'. Free land is free land."

Jesselynn fought the burning at the back of her eyes, wiped her nose with the back of her hand, and cleared her throat. "Thank you, my friend. I wasn't sure how I was going to say good-bye to all of you."

"Daniel and Benjamin, dey say stay too. Be tired of travelin' wid no end in sight."

Mr. and Mrs. Jesperson looked at each other, and the mister shrugged. "We ain't made up our minds yet. Can I tell you after we get back to the fort?"

"Whatever suits you."

"Do y'all mind me comin' along? I ain't got no menfolk no more, but I can work hard. Won't be just another mouth to feed. I can sell my wagon at the fort or not, as you think." Mrs. Jones stammered over her last words.

Jesselynn kept from looking at Benjamin. Should she ask if Mrs. Jones found the body of her husband they had dragged into the bushes? And what happened to Rufus?

"I . . . I think I better tell you a little story, so's you know I . . . I'm a safe addition to the party." Darcy Jones hung her clasped hands between her knees, her ragged skirt bunched around her legs. "Few days ago Rufus, that's my husband's brother, ya know. Well, he come stormin' back into camp sayin' Tommy Joe be dead. Found his body in the bushes, been stabbed." She sniffed, but her eyes remained dry. "I could hardly believe it. I mean . . . But I"—she wiped her nose on her shirttail—"I was goin' to get him and give him a decent burial, ya know, when Rufus laughed like it were the funniest joke he ever heard. He come after me then, and I knew by the look in his eyes, he weren't goin' to stop until . . . well, you know. But afore he could throw me down, I ran. When he caught me, I grabbed the knife from the sheath at his side and . . . and . . ." She sighed and shook her head. "I hope the dear Lord can forgive me, but I couldn't go on livin' like that. I mean if'n he . . ." Her voice trailed away. "I dug one hole and buried them both." She hid her face in her hands. "C-Can I come with you?"

The snap of fire eating sticks sounded loud in the silence. They could hear the cattle grazing. Crickets sang in the grasses.

Jesselynn got to her feet, crossed the circle, and knelt down beside the woman who sat with hunched shoulders, the bones poking out like angel wings on her back. "Of course you can come with us. Why once we feed up your oxen, they'll be plenty strong enough to pull the wagon."

"Tommy Joe . . ." Darcy started and stopped, heaving a sigh that creaked her bones. She looked up to Jesselynn beside her. "He weren't bad back in the beginnin'. He just never seemed to have any luck, you know. He said the whole world was agin' him. He weren't bad unless he be drinkin'."

Jesselynn kept her thoughts to herself. Knowing how close she'd come to suffering some of Tommy Joe's rage herself, she could feel nothing but pity for the woman beside her. Maybe this just proved the old saw that true love is blind. *So, Lord, do I tell her? Wouldn't that be cruel?*

"Rufus said 'twas prob'ly Indians what killed Tommy Joe." Darcy shook her head. "An' I kilt *him*. Do you think the good Lord will ever forgive me?"

Jesselynn put her arm around the shivering shoulders. "I

do believe He will. All we need do is ask. Jesus died to save sinners, and we all sin."

"But . . . not . . . l-like I did." The shuddering sobs sounded worse as she tried to subdue them.

Jane Ellen brought a square of cotton around for a handkerchief. "Here." She tucked it in the woman's hand.

Jesselynn let Darcy cry in her arms. No matter how much she'd despised the two brothers and could find no way in her heart to feel bad they were gone, sorrow was sorrow, and she'd felt a mighty lot of it herself. She glanced up to see Aunt Agatha wipe her own eyes and return to her knitting.

When the sobbing ceased, Jesselynn eased her leg out to release the cramp that had come from sitting on her foot all this while. "How about I take you back to your wagon, so you can go to sleep. Things always look better in the morning." She more felt than saw the brief nod.

After settling the woman, who was not much bigger than Jane Ellen, in her bedroll, Jesselynn strolled back to the fire. "Let's bring the herd in for the night."

Meshach folded the now softened hide and, after handing it to Ophelia, dismantled his roller and put it all back in the wagon bed. One more skin to sew into shirts or vests or whatever was needed most. "We do it."

"All right." Jesselynn looked around their small circle. Hardly room for all the oxen and horses, but they were much safer this way, and one person could stand watch rather than two.

"I'll take first watch," Nate Lyons said from just behind her.

"Good. Keep Patch with you. And watch Ahab if he gets restless. He's the best watchdog around." She wasn't sure why she was telling him all this. He'd stood watch countless times and knew it all as well as she did.

"She'll get over it." He kept his voice soft, for her ears alone.

"Mrs. Jones?"

"Her too, but I meant Miss Agatha. Give her time, and she'll come around." He hunkered down at Jesselynn's side. "She's been through some rough changes."

"As have we all."

"True, but it's harder for us older ones to adapt than you young'uns."

Jesselynn felt a chuckle rising. "Young'uns?" She shook her head. "I'm old as those hills around us. Leastwise it feels that way."

"You been through a lot. Now perhaps God is restorin' the years of the locust for you."

"The years of the war, you mean?"

"Them too. I got me a feelin' we're goin' to see that valley where He pastures His sheep. He'll have a place just for all of us, our new home."

"Mr. Lyons, I do hope you are right."

"Can't you call me Nate, my dear?"

"I guess, but I like Nathan better." Jesselynn smiled into his eyes, which were so much easier to see now that he'd been barbered. Such a fine-looking man they had found under all that hair.

"Nathan it is, then."

"Good night and sleep well. Tomorrow will be a better day."

Since she didn't have to take watch, she did just that, waking with the first sleepy birdsong. Three more days and she would see Wolf again. Her betrothed. What a wondrous word.

In the morning Aunt Agatha looked through Jesselynn like she was invisible. Jesselynn shrugged and went to saddle

Ahab. Nathan's suggestion to give her aunt time echoed in her mind as she rode out of camp. From the way it looked, eternity might not be long enough.

The drive back to the fort passed uneventfully, just the way Jesselynn liked it. She rode much of the way, topping the crests of the hills away from the wagons, alone for the first time in what seemed like forever. Thoughts of Twin Oaks intruded at times, but mostly she thought of Wolf, of all that had happened in the time since she first saw him at the camps in Independence. They had come so close to not being allowed to join his wagon train.

That thought made her turn back to her small plodding wagon train. If only they could pick up the pace. She'd been engaged once before. But John went away to war before they could be married, and he never came back, his remains buried in some battlefield.

So many things could happen in the next few days. If only there were some way to hurry the wagons. And get Aunt Agatha speaking to her again.

Please, God, keep Wolf safe until we can be married. She thought about that prayer and shook her head. *God, please keep him safe for the rest of our lives.* Now *that* was a real faith-stretching prayer. But asking God to change Aunt Agatha's mind—that would take a miracle.

CHAPTER ELEVEN

FORT LARAMIE

Would she never return to the fort?

"Wolf, have you heard a word I said?" Rebeccah Jensen planted her hands on her hips and tapped her foot.

"I believe so." He turned back from staring out the window.

"Well, I'm sure your coffee is cold by now. Here, I shall warm it up." She extended a hand for his cup and saucer.

Instead of handing it to her, Wolf drained the cup and almost made a face. *Cold coffee, ugh. And weak enough to be tea.*

"I warned you." Rebeccah shook her head, rose, and poured him a refill. "Land sakes, you're worse'n kids nearin' recess." Rebeccah had been a schoolteacher before she married and still carried fond memories of her children. Since then she'd pretty much figured out that men were only boys grown larger.

"Sorry." Wolf sipped the new cup and nodded his approval, although it could still stand some backbone. "Now, what was it you wanted my opinion on?" His father had taught him white-man manners, along with those of the Sioux. One did not preclude the other.

"I asked if you wanted to borrow my husband's black suit for the wedding."

Wolf noted her discomposure and glanced down at the stained buckskin shirt he wore. He did have one shirt of what used to be white material. "I . . . I hadn't thought of that. Thank you for reminding me." *Do I go buy something? Or is my money better spent for supplies?* No question. "Yes, if you think it would fit me, I'd be more than pleased to borrow the captain's suit."

"It doesn't get worn much out here, so I shall have Clara brush it up." She held out the plate of cookies. "Have another. Now, regarding the food—"

"I thought we'd have the ceremony and then leave for the Chugwater."

Rebeccah shook her head. Her smile reminded Wolf of his mother's, warm and full of love.

"If you think we are goin' to miss this chance for a shindig, you, sir, are sadly mistaken. There will be supper and dancing and gifts and . . ."

Wolf held up a hand. "Whoa, slow down. When did all this come about?"

"When Jesselynn said she'd marry you. Now, how many weddings do you think we've had here at the fort?"

Wolf shrugged. Surely she didn't expect an answer.

"Two in all the years we've been stationed here. We have far more funerals than weddings, so this is an opportunity for you and your new bride to get to know more of us here at the fort. Two days' journey means we are neighbors, and neighbors do for each other. Captain Jensen says that when he leaves the military, he wants to establish a home right up the river from here. This valley and this land have snagged his heart, pure and simple."

Wolf kept one ear on the conversation and the other listening for the entry of a wagon train. He nodded. "Wyoming is a good land. Room here for both white man and Indians."

"Well, be that as it may, your wedding is what we were discussing." Rebeccah shook her head at Wolf's obvious restlessness. She clasped her hands in her lap and leaned forward. "May I make a suggestion, Mr. Torstead?"

"Wolf."

"All right, Mr. Wolf."

He shook his head but didn't stop her again.

"Would it be all right if the women here at the fort just do what we think best?" At his nod and sigh of relief, she continued. "I know Jesselynn will not be disappointed. Nor will you."

"Mrs. Jensen, I am deeply indebted to you for your thoughtfulness. I know that whatever you choose to do will be perfect and far beyond what we could have done." He set his cup and saucer on the whatnot table, sketched a bow, and with a "Thank you, ma'am" hightailed it to the door as if a pack of howling predators were on his trail.

He heard her chuckle float behind him.

He would head out to find them but for Jesselynn's admonition that this was something she had to do herself. Were they in trouble? Perhaps he should just ride out and see that they were all right. *I don't have to let them see me.* The thought flowed into the action, and within minutes he'd saddled his horse and trotted away from the fort, heading west.

Lord, what do I do about Aunt Agatha? The cold is so deep I'm afraid of frostbite. Jesselynn had insisted on taking first watch. She rode around the circled wagons, far enough off so as not to disturb those sleeping. Even Patch was curled up under the wagon, right next to where her bedroll would lie as soon as Mr. Lyons—she still had trouble calling him Nathan—came out to relieve her. With the moon in the dark phase, she had no idea of the time.

Ahab stopped, his head high, ears pricked. Patch tore past them, heading for the eastern hill. Jesselynn froze, not even breathing, in order to hear what roused the animals. Nothing. Patch hadn't even barked. She turned Ahab to follow where the dog had gone. Every few feet she stopped to listen. Was that Patch whining? He hadn't barked. Her stomach tightened, as if wrapped in drying rawhide.

She loosened the tie-down on the pistol at her hip and drew it from the holster.

Had whatever or whoever was out there killed her dog? Her mouth dried. Her scalp drew tight. She stopped Ahab again to listen. He lifted his head, nostrils flared to read the breeze. His intake of breath sounded loud as a steam whistle in the stillness.

When she heard his nostrils flutter in a soundless nicker, she glanced over her shoulder. Nothing had changed. No one had left camp, at least not that she could tell. Surely they would have told her. One did not go sneaking out of camp. They might get shot on the return. A necessary trip did not take one so far from camp either.

Short of Ahab's breathing, all was still, not even a cricket sang. Something was indeed amiss. Sure that someone was watching her, Jesselynn debated whether to rouse the camp, go get Meshach, or go look over the rise of the hill.

She'd just nudged Ahab forward when Patch came trotting up to her, tongue lolling, tail wagging. He glanced once over his shoulder, then sat by Ahab's front feet.

"So did you patrol the area and find nothing?"

Patch yipped and sat to scratch a flea. She could hear his hind foot thumping on the grass. Ahab lowered his head and snatched a few mouthfuls of grass before she tightened the reins.

"You can graze when I go to bed." She turned him back to

119

circle the camp again, no longer feeling that someone was watching her. It was indeed a puzzlement, as she told Nate Lyons when he caught his horse and rode out to meet her.

"Ahab is trustworthy. I've never seen him give a false alarm." Nate studied the hill she'd pointed out.

"Whatever it was, he saw no danger. Patch neither. Had it been a rabbit, Patch would have barked and chased." Jesselynn yawned, quicker than her hand could cover her mouth. "I'm going to bed. At least the crickets are singing again. Strange."

"Which way was the breeze blowin'?"

"Not sure. Seems to kind of switch around at times. But both animals smelled something." Jesselynn walked Ahab back to camp, removed his saddle and bridle, and tied him on a long line so he could graze outside the circle of wagons. Long as Nate was on guard, the horse was safe. She could get some sleep.

"What do you think it might have been?" Jesselynn stood looking up at Meshach a few hours later. The sun had yet to rise above the horizon, but preparations to break camp were well under way.

"Don' know. I walked around, seen grass knocked down like someone or somethin' walk through dere, den lay down. Gone now."

"Indian?"

Meshach shrugged.

Jesselynn chewed on her bottom lip. She watched Aunt Agatha finish stirring the mush that had been simmering most of the night. *Lord, what am I going to do?*

"Any suggestions?" She nodded toward the fire.

Meshach took off his hat, scratched his head, and using both hands, settled the hat back in place. "Sure wish I did.

But Bible say love those who persecute you. You be blessed dat way."

"What if she never comes around?"

"Never be long time."

"Breakfast is ready." Agatha straightened and kneaded her lower back with her fists.

Jesselynn knew that meant Agatha's back was bothering her. Sometimes chewing on willow bark helped. With that thought in mind, she turned away from the circled wagons and headed to the creek. Willow twigs she could supply in abundance. She tore off a couple of branches and brought them back to camp. Tying the bundle to the hoop right behind where Agatha sat, Jesselynn returned to the campfire. After dishing up her bowl of mush, she took a seat on the wagon tongue. Even Thaddeus ate quietly, sending furtive glances at Agatha.

Jesselynn reached over and tickled his ribs. "Hey, boy."

He giggled and squirmed.

Agatha turned away, her mouth pursed like she'd just sucked on green plums.

"I'll try talkin' with her later," Jane Ellen whispered. "We're all prayin' for her. She'll come around."

Mrs. McPhereson stopped right behind them and laid her hands on Jesselynn's shoulders, then brushed one along her cheek.

The tender gesture said more than ten minutes of talk.

After Meshach and Daniel finished hitching up the oxen, Agatha crossed around behind the wagon to climb up, so she didn't have to pass by her niece.

Mounting Ahab, Jesselynn swung out ahead of the wagons as they pulled into line.

In spite of Jesselynn's prayers for a return to the former

ease of companionship, Aunt Agatha spoke to everyone but her all the next day. The closer they drew to the fort, the more Jesselynn wanted to ride ahead, away from the dust and the creaking wagons, away from her aunt's judging face and sniffs. Never before had she realized how effective a comment a sniff could be, a prolonged series of sniffs, to be exact.

While Jesselynn tried to work up a good mad, she understood how her aunt felt and what she believed. In the South, marriage between white and colored was not only a moral issue but a legal one as well. The law forbade intermarriage.

But was the law right? And was it biblical? Were those of white skin really better than the others? Didn't the Bible say all are the same, male and female, slave and free, no matter the color of skin or hair or eyes? *God, Father, how I wish I knew your Word better. I've heard the preaching for so many years that having slaves is right according to the Word—that the Bible says for slaves not to leave their masters. But the Bible also says we who are in Jesus are free.*

So who's right? And does it matter?

Jesselynn crossed her hands on Ahab's withers, staring out over the valley below. Sod huts, smoke rising from a chimney, and grain bending in the breeze showed where someone had taken up the land to make it home. Sheets flapped on a clothesline.

She turned to watch their wagons start down the hill, angling so as not to let the wagons run over the oxen. Meshach and Benjamin had taken over the reins, and the women and children all walked, or rather the women walked and the children rolled down through the rich grass. Their shouts of laughter sang on the air, making her smile, especially when she saw Jane Ellen tumbling with the little ones.

If all of these folk decided to continue north with them, they would still be her family but no longer her responsibility alone. That thought brought a peace she hadn't felt since leaving Twin Oaks. Perhaps Aunt Agatha would choose to remain at the fort.

Jesselynn glanced up. No, there was no cloud in the sky. The cloud came from within. "Father, I don't want this cloud over my wedding. It should be a happy day for everyone." But as she well knew, "should" and "is" were not always the same.

And worrying wasn't what God wanted either. "So here it is, in your hands, and I will not think or worry on it again." Ahab flicked his ears back and forth and pulled on the reins. He hated to be left behind. "Amen, so be it. Come on, son, let's be going."

When they set up camp late that night, they were a quarter mile or so from the fort, with its lights in the windows, music and laughter, all the signs of civilization. Jesselynn planned on riding into the fort and finding Wolf as soon as the herd was set to grazing. She didn't care if she had supper or not, the desire to see him ate at her insides. She had her head in one of the boxes looking for her clean shirt and the skirt she'd packed so long ago, when Thaddeus came running.

"Jesse!" He jerked on her pant leg.

"I know I put that thing back in here. Where is it?" She pushed aside her journal, ignoring the reminder of how long since she'd written anything.

"Jesse!"

"Thaddeus Highwood, stop that. Can't you see I'm busy?"

"But Mr. Wolf . . ."

Jesselynn dropped the lid on her finger, yelped, stuck the wounded appendage in her mouth, and spun around.

"Hello, Jesselynn." The laughter in Wolf's dark eyes fueled her flurry.

"Don't you know it isn't polite to sneak up on a body like that?" Blood hammered in her smashed finger. Thaddeus looked as if she'd smacked him. Aunt Agatha harrumphed loud enough to wake a hibernating bear. Wolf continued to smile as he swung off his horse in slow motion and, locking his gaze into hers, crossed the few feet to stand in front of her. There he stood, all six feet of well-muscled, broad-shouldered, painter-lithe manhood, the man she'd been dreaming of for days, and now all she could think of was how much she wanted to smack him with a long board.

She pushed her hat back on her head, dusted off her britches, and pushed a small rock out of the way with the toe of her boot. *He's seen me all dressed up in forget-me-nots, and now look at me.* "Why couldn't you have waited?"

She's even more beautiful than I could picture. Wolf took another step forward. No, he shouldn't be seen kissing her, but her lips, now caught in a pout, begged him to. *Why are we waiting to get married? Why not tomorrow? I suppose women need time to prepare—even Jesselynn, who claims not to care about that sort of thing.*

Her question penetrated his concentration on keeping from sweeping her into his arms. "Waited? Why?"

"Because . . . because . . ." She dropped her hands to her sides. *Because I'm a mess, that's why.* She looked down at the source of the pressure on her leg and found Thaddeus staring up at her. He clung to her thigh, one finger in his mouth, staring from her to Wolf and back again. The puzzled look on his face banished her befuddlement like a breath blew away a dandelion puff. She reached down and swung her little brother up on her hip. She stuck out her other hand.

"Welcome, Mr. Wolf. You're just in time for supper." Her fingers clamped around his gave all the greeting her mind and mouth couldn't put into words.

What if Aunt Agatha treats him like she has me?

CHAPTER TWELVE

"How'd she take your news?"

Jesselynn wished Wolf hadn't asked that. She'd been so careful to not allude to it, hoping she could pretend everything was all right.

Honesty, right? Lord, please keep him from being hurt. "Not too well."

"I didn't expect anything different. Will she go on to the Chugwater with us?"

Jesselynn could feel her jaw drop. "You want her to?"

"Can you see her going on west with the Jespersons?" Was that a twinkle she saw in his eyes?

"She could stay at the fort."

"What? And become a washerwoman or some such?" Wolf shook his head. "I knew what her feelings would be when I asked you to marry me. She can't help it. She has always lived that way."

"She can change. The rest of us have had to do a mighty lot of changing." Her flat tone said as much as her words.

Wolf took Jesselynn's elbow and pulled her behind the wagon so he could take her in his arms. "If you can ignore her actions, so can I."

Jesselynn laid her head against his chest. "I'll try." She looked up again. "Who said the Jespersons were going on west?"

"I heard them talking with Meshach. I think the woman

would just as soon stay here, but he's got a burr under his saddle to see Oregon. They'll join up with the next train. I heard there's one about four days out."

"They could at least have told me."

The night before the wedding, Jesselynn woke gasping, fighting off a nightmare that threatened to strangle her. But when she tried to remember what it was, only nameless fears stirred her emotions. She crawled from under the wagon, wishing she had taken Rebeccah up on her offer of the guest bedroom.

Some insane sense of duty had kept her out here in the camp. Out of habit, she clamped her hat on her head and strolled to the perimeter of the circled wagons. Even here, within sight of the fort, she'd felt the necessity to do that. Horses had been stolen before and would be again. She preferred it not be *her* horses.

Ahab raised his head and nickered. She could hear him coming to greet her, his footfalls soft on the grazed grass.

"All's well, old son." She stroked his nose when he hung his head over her shoulder. "What's keeping you awake, hmm?" He snorted and rested his head weight on her shoulder. She scratched his cheek and rubbed up around his ears, all the while knowing what was keeping her awake.

Getting married was a big step under the best of circumstances, but thanks to Aunt Agatha . . . Jesselynn changed her thought track deliberately. It wasn't just Aunt Agatha. It was a whole world that thought the color of a man's skin of more import than his character. Would she ever be able to take her whole family back to Twin Oaks? No closer to answers, she and Ahab watched the sun break free from the horizon to announce a new day. Her wedding day.

★ ★ ★ ★ ★

"Oh, Jesse, you look so purty." Thaddeus stared at his sister, eyes round as his mouth. When he started toward her, Jane Ellen grabbed him by the shirttails.

"No, don't touch her. You don't want to get her dress dirty, do you?"

Thaddeus looked down at his hands, up at Jesselynn, then over his shoulder at Jane Ellen. "I not dirty." For safe measure he wiped his hands on his new britches.

"Come here, little brother. Look in the mirror and see how fine you look." Jesselynn took his hand, and together they stared at the reflection in the oval, oak-framed floor mirror.

The rich cream silk showed off her shoulders and nipped in at her slender waist. Tiny pearl buttons ran from the dip in the sweetheart neckline to the point of the bodice an inch or two below her natural waistline. Wide enough for hoops, but buoyed by crinolines instead, the skirt hosted swirls of lace and seed pearls. The dress might have seen balls and cotillions in its early life, but like Jesselynn, it was far from a society that had use for such a garment.

Jesselynn bent over and kissed the top of her brother's head. "Don't you look handsome?" A blousy white shirt with a navy tie was tucked into deep blue pants cut just above his knees, one scraped from a fall over the steps not an hour before.

Would that her other brother would look at Wolf with the adoration of Thaddeus.

"You ready?"

He nodded.

"Then I reckon we better head for the chapel."

"Dearly beloved, we are gathered here in the sight of God . . ."

Jesselynn ached to turn around and see if Aunt Agatha came to the wedding, but instead she looked up at Wolf. The black suit he wore made him look like any other gentleman, Southern or Northern, only more handsome. Many of the French Creoles from Louisiana were darker skinned than he. She'd met them at Keeneland, the racetrack in Lexington. She brought her attention back to the black-garbed man in front of her, his deep voice saying the words she'd so longed to hear.

Mama, Daddy, I hope you're seeing this and giving us your blessing. Surely you know answers by now to some of my questions. And God, if you could put a bug in Aunt Agatha's ear, I'd sure be appreciative.

When the minister asked if anyone opposed this marriage, Jesselynn waited with her breath in her throat. Surely this was the time, but when no one answered, she let herself breathe again.

Wolf turned and took her hands in his. Thoughts of anything other than the light in his eyes fled her mind.

"I, Gray Wolf Torstead, take thee, Jesselynn Highwood, to be my wedded wife." He repeated the words after the chaplain, his voice strong and sure, his handclasp warm and dry. He looked deep within to her very soul as he finished the age-old words.

"Now repeat after me . . ." The chaplain nodded to her.

Jesselynn spoke the words, her lips trembling, but her voice even. "I, Jesselynn Highwood, take thee . . . to have and to hold from this day forward . . . and therefore I plight thee my troth." Safe and sure, their hands bound together along with their hearts, they bowed their heads to pray, repeated the "I do's," and turned back to the chaplain for the blessing. When he pronounced them husband and wife, she went into Wolf's arms like she'd been waiting for him all of her life.

They held each other, then shared a kiss both chaste and full of promise.

"But, Jane Ellen, I got to go pee." Thaddeus's whisper carried to the front of the room.

Jesselynn could feel her face grow warm, knowing it was not due to the temperature outdoors or in the room.

As Jane Ellen scooted out the door with Thaddeus on her hip, chuckles flitted around the room like butterflies, and Jesselynn and Wolf turned to face the gathering. Mrs. McPhereson sniffed and honked into her hanky.

"Praise de Lawd and all Him handiwork," Ophelia sang from the rear.

Jesselynn smiled up at the man whose arm she held. "Well, Mr. Torstead, shall we go greet our guests?"

After shaking hands with everyone as they left the chapel, Jesselynn and Wolf followed Mrs. Jensen to the mess hall, where trestle tables groaned beneath the abundance of food. Elk haunches stood waiting to be carved, vegetables from the commissary gardens, fresh-baked bread, baked beans, and dishes of all kinds sat rim to rim so that the only tablecloth showing was that hanging down the sides. A white frosted wedding cake, decorated with wild asters, reigned on a separate table, as did the drinks next to it—coffee, tea, and lemonade. Bouquets of wild asters and daisies graced every table, and here and there nodded roses from the general's garden.

"Oh." Jesselynn stood in the doorway, gazing at it all and fighting the tears that had threatened during the ceremony. *All the work these women have done for us. What an amazing gift.*

"Right purty, isn't it?" Jane Ellen, Thaddeus in tow, squeezed in beside her.

"Me go play." Thaddeus looked up at Jesselynn. "Please?"

"We'll eat first." Wolf swung the child up into his arms.

Now that Thaddeus could see, he spotted the cake immediately.

"Look, Jesse, cake." He pointed to the white confection in the corner.

"I know. I'm surprised you remember what one is."

"Come on up here so we can have grace and serve our bride and groom. Then the line forms to the right." Captain Jensen waited until all was quiet before raising his voice for all to hear. "Heavenly Father, we come before thee this day with joyful hearts. Thank you for blessing all of us with this wedding and with the food our folks have prepared. We ask that thou will bless this union and bring health and happiness to this couple. In thy holy name we pray, amen."

By the time everyone had helped themselves, the room fairly rocked with laughter and buzzing conversation. Children ran in and out, Patch barked from the front step, and before long a fiddle tuned up out on the parade ground.

After cake and drinks, they followed the music outside for the dancing to begin. Jesselynn and Wolf danced the first waltz.

"I think I've about forgotten how to dance." Jesselynn lost herself in Wolf's dark eyes.

"Then we can stumble together. I never had much time for dancin' on the wagon trains, and my people didn't exactly dance this way when I was growing up."

Jesselynn leaned back in his arms, the better to study his face. "When will you tell me about growin' up in the tribe?"

"Someday. You will meet my relatives one day."

The thought made her pause, only a fraction of a moment, but still he caught it. "You need not fear them."

Fear wasn't a word she had applied so far, but horror stories were whispered about Indian attacks and how they hated whites. Getting her family through to Oregon had taken up too much of her time and energy to worry about something that might or might not happen. Meshach's admonition that they trust the Lord for their protection carried over to other things besides Indian attacks.

"As you say, my husband." Ah, what pleasure to say such words. *My husband.* She repeated the words several more times in her mind.

"I say so, my wife." He drew her closer and rested his chin on the top of her head. "My wife." His voice deepened, warmed, licked at her senses.

The music ended with a flourish, and those gathered around clapped, and someone whistled. Jesselynn felt the red creeping up her neck. She'd forgotten they danced in such a public place. It seemed there'd been only the two of them and that the music might go on forever.

The fiddle sang into a reel, and men and women lined up on opposite sides. Every time she passed Wolf, he winked at her. About the third time, she started to giggle, and with each additional wink, it grew worse. By the end of the dance she collapsed against a hitching post, out of breath from both the fast footwork and the giggles.

"Me dance." Thaddeus stood beside her.

"Of course." She picked him up, and they whirled away together, he with his legs locked securely around her waist, she with her arms around his middle. They dipped and swirled until Wolf tapped her shoulder and took the little boy off with him, this time riding on his tall shoulders.

Jane Ellen's gaze followed Wolf around the dancers. "He do be one fine figure of a man."

"That's for sure." Jesselynn waved her hand in front of her face to create a breeze of some sort. "But I've been noticing a certain young man looking your way."

"Who?" Jane Ellen glanced around the gathered people.

"He's wearing a blue uniform, and now that he thinks I'm looking at him, his cheeks are as red as the roses on the table." Jesselynn nodded over to a young private who doffed his visored cap and blushed even more. "You're going to dance with him now that he's coming, right?"

"I guess. Do you know his name?"

"No, but I'm sure we will in a moment." Jesselynn dropped her voice so he wouldn't hear.

The young man doffed his hat, half bowed, and in a voice that cracked only once, said, "I'm Private Henry Workman." Even his ears turned red. "And canIhavethisdance?"

Jesselynn gave Jane Ellen a nudge in the back. "This is my friend, Jane Ellen."

"Pleased to meet you, Miss." He extended his hand.

Jane Ellen shot Jesselynn a look of panic, swallowed, and stepped forward. "I don't dance too good."

"Me neither." The two started off, stiff as two porch posts.

Jesselynn glanced around the assembled folks in the hope that Aunt Agatha had changed her mind and at least enjoyed some of the festivities.

"She won't be comin'." Nate Lyons spoke softly from behind her. "I tried, Miss Jesselynn. I surely did, but that Miss Agatha is one stubborn woman."

"I know." *But I do hope she comes around.*

"She said 'twere none of my business, but it really is. I care about that woman, if you haven't already surmised that." He hung back, as if not wanting to look Jesselynn in the face. "I had me an idea."

"I'm a-fixin' to ask her to walk out with me. You think she will?"

"I'm a poor one to ask at this point. She won't even speak to me, nor come to my wedding."

"I told her that times are a-changin', and what used to be

in the South won't be in the West."

"I'm sure that made her very happy."

His chuckle turned into a snort, then a guffaw. "Not hardly, Miss Jesselynn. Not hardly a'tall. But you mark my words, she'll marry me before winter."

"Lord's blessing to you, Mr. Lyons. Now, will you look at that." She nodded to Jane Ellen and her young man. "I reckon she's growing right up." *At least perhaps this young man can help her get over her crush on Wolf.* While Jane Ellen had never said a word, the way she leaped to serve him and spoke his name with a mixture of gentleness and awe had announced her admiration of Wolf as surely as if she'd blown a trumpet.

"Ah, my dear, you make a lovely bride." Mrs. Jensen strolled up with her arm through her husband's.

"Thanks to your lovely gown." Jesselynn stroked down the sides of the creamy silk with both hands. The skirt and petticoat swished against her legs as she whirled through the dances, making her grateful that hoops weren't *de rigueur* out on the plains. And since she'd not been laced into a corset, she could enjoy the dancing without a near faint.

"No, it is not just the gown. Your face shines with happiness. We do"—she glanced up at her husband, who patted her hand on his arm—"wish you all the best in God's blessings."

"Thank you." Jesselynn sketched a curtsy. Her gaze automatically searched out Wolf, and when he smiled at her, she felt a quiver clear inside. That fine-looking man dancing with one of the officers' wives was her husband. Would that she would never get over the joy of it. She remembered her mother telling her how, even after all their years of marriage, her heart still leaped when her husband entered the room. *Oh, Father, to love like my mother and daddy is all I ask.*

"Come, Captain, surely you have the energy to dance with your wife. And, my dear"—Rebeccah leaned closer to Jesselynn—"I see a certain fine young man is coming to claim his bride for this dance."

Jesselynn and Wolf whirled away to the fast pace of a polka, their feet following the dance steps while their eyes made promises and their hands spoke only of love.

Later, when the musicians took a much needed break, Jesselynn and Wolf stood with the Jensens in the shade of one of the buildings sipping lemonade and the women fanning their faces.

"The women of the camp have prepared the guest quarters for you to spend the night. We thought, well . . ."

The captain broke in with a laugh. "Rebeccah, your cheeks are as pink as Miss Jesselynn's. I'm sure they appreciate the thought."

"Yes, I . . . we . . ." Jesselynn glanced up at Wolf, who smiled down at her and nodded. "Thank you, and please thank all the others for us. You all worked so hard to make this day one to remember." She tucked her arm in the crook of Wolf's elbow.

"I'm just sorry your aunt felt unable to attend. Do you think if one of us were to go talk with her?" Rebeccah's question was hesitant.

Since Jesselynn had made no mention of Aunt Agatha, she wondered how they knew, or if they knew the real reason. Shaking her head, Jesselynn sighed. "I don't know what will change her mind. Mr. Lyons tried, and I know Mrs. McPhereson spoke with her too." The urge to tell the entire story almost made Jesselynn continue, but she stopped, knowing that Wolf did not need to hear it all. Instead of making up an excuse for her aunt and thus adding another lie to her long list, she just said Agatha was staying in camp.

Before taking her wedding vows, Jesselynn had made a vow of another sort, this one only between God and herself. The vow to never lie again, to always tell the truth, made her feel fifty pounds lighter. Guilt was a heavy burden, one she no longer desired to carry, not that it had ever been her desire. Living the lies had been necessary to keep them safe, but no longer.

Does Wolf realize what a burden he has assumed, all these people that make up our train? Widows, black folk learning to be free, a woman who has played the role of a man and liked a great deal of that role, a small boy with a temper like the other males in his family, and all the others. Good thing this man has broad shoulders.

"Do you have all of your supplies for the Oglala?" Captain Jensen turned to Wolf.

"Those that were available. And two packhorses to carry it all." Wolf crossed his arms. "I still have more credit at the store. I'll be bringing the horses back before winter."

Jesselynn listened to the conversation. If they could catch wild horses, perhaps they would be bringing some of them in at the same time. *If.* So many "if's".

The party broke up after dark, with folks going back to their quarters or wagons and Jesselynn saying good-night to Thaddeus.

"But why you not come?" Thaddeus planted his fists on his hips, a banty rooster set to fight.

"Because Wolf and I are staying here at the fort."

"Why?"

"Because . . . because . . ." She looked up to Wolf from her kneeling position in front of Thaddeus. She could feel heat creeping up her neck. *Little brother, sometimes . . .*

"Because she is my wife and is going to stay with me." Wolf leaned over and swung the boy up to sit on his arms.

136

Thaddeus studied the man who held him. Blue eyes dueled with dark. "Tomorrow you come back?"

Wolf nodded. Thaddeus smiled and motioned to be set down. "Good." Feet again on the ground, he ran to Jane Ellen and, taking her hand, waved as they left.

As the crowd dispersed, Wolf and Jesselynn thanked everyone for coming and strolled over to the guest quarters, where a white bow hung on the door. Jesselynn could feel panic begin to bubble in her middle. Her feet didn't want to climb the steps. She stumbled on the second one, saved from a fall by Wolf's strong arm.

Lord, I hardly know this man!

CHAPTER THIRTEEN

RICHMOND, VIRGINIA

"We'll leave in the mornin'."

Louisa stared at her brother, questions rioting through her mind. How had he gotten a leave of absence when he started the position with Jefferson's firm not a week before? Where were they going, and what route would they take? And most important, what disguise would they use this time? The coffin trick had worked so well, but did they dare try it again?

She waited, trying to be patient, but her foot tapped in spite of her. Zachary did not like to be questioned or rushed.

When he resumed his writing, she cleared her throat.

"Yes?"

From the look he gave her, she knew he'd forgotten her presence. How could he do that—concentrate on what he was doing and forget the rest of the world existed?

"Have you nothing further to inform me regarding the trip?"

"I will tonight after I meet with—" He cut off the remainder of his thoughts, always careful to keep as much information to himself as possible. That way if they were ever questioned, she could say she didn't know, without lying. Though he had explained that to her, she still felt he treated her like . . . like someone too young to trust.

The entire family knew what a poor liar she was, although

she had lived another persona for several months at the hospital, playing the part of *Mrs.* Highwood, instead of Miss. When he was released to his aunt's house, Zachary had refused to play along, ordering her home as soon as he was able. His concept of what a proper young lady should be allowed to do was hopelessly outdated.

Knowing that further questioning would be futile, she turned and left the room, resisting the urge to stamp her feet just a little. Or slam the door.

Instead, Louisa picked up the kitten mewing at her heels and took herself outside to assist their newest patient in the intricacies of stitching a fine seam. He'd resisted the idea of knitting, but when she switched the focus to sewing and reminded him that men made good tailors, he'd accepted the needle and thread. After all, his lack of legs didn't take away the ability of his hands. She set the kitten down in the lap of a soldier who had not as yet smiled.

"Miss Louisa, you make this sewing look so easy, but it ain't, not in the least." The young man, who'd served as a lieutenant, pointed to his uneven stitches.

"Hmm. It could be the light."

"It could be the needle, or the thimble, or the . . ." The glare was more for the material in his hands than for her.

"When you first shot a gun, did you hit the target all the time?"

"Well, no, but—"

"When I first held a needle, I was five, maybe four, years old. My stitches were far worse than yours, and I had far less patience. But my mother refused to let me quit, no matter how hard I begged. Sometimes I near to wore out the thread, I had to take it out so many times." She held his work up to see better. "Just remember, the smaller the stitches, the less likely the seam will rip. All the difference between a soldier being warm enough or freezing in the winter."

"I understand." He made himself smile, for her sake, she knew. Learning to live without legs sent some men into such depression that they were unable to continue living. This man was trying.

Louisa wanted to hug him. Surely he was older than she, but he seemed like a baby brother. Even though she was only eighteen, she felt ancient. Ever since her Lieutenant Lessling died, she knew she'd aged years. She glanced over to see the ginger kitten purring beneath a stroking hand.

She patted the young legless man's shoulder. "You'll make it. Our Father will see you through."

He sighed. "Not so sure I believe in 'Our Father' anymore. Not after all the things I saw."

Louisa knelt beside his chair. "If we give up, Satan wins the battle. Remember, the Bible says 'If God be for us, who can be against us.' "

"I know." He looked into her eyes, searching her soul. "But do you really believe God is still for us?"

Louisa swallowed. "I believe God is for each one of us, and when we trust in Him, He never fails."

"But what if I don't trust no longer?"

"God never changes." *But please don't ask me if I believe God is on the side of the South. I can't say that any longer.* "Excuse me, I see that Abby needs me for something. You keep on practicing those stitches. You'll do fine." Before he could ask her another question she left the veranda. Thank God for Abby.

"Missy Louisa, Miss Sylvania, she don' look too good. I made her go up and take a lie-down."

"Thank you, Abby. I didn't realize she'd returned from her sewing circle."

Twice a week Aunt Sylvania attended the sewing circle at

her church. While she'd given up asking her niece to join her, she still faithfully attended. Louisa knew she enjoyed the gossip as much as the sewing. Together the group sewed for the war effort, just like they did at home.

"I'll go check on her." Louisa made her way up the stairs to her aunt's room. She tapped on the door. "Aunt Sylvania, may I come in?"

"Of course, dear."

Crossing the sunny room, Louisa stifled a gasp.

Sylvania lay against the pillows, her face nearly as white as the pillow slips. She raised a hand, trembling like a leaf in the wind.

"What happened?" Louisa took her aunt's frail hand in hers. "Your hand is freezing."

"I . . . I just felt dizzy, and now my head aches." Sylvania's voice sounded fretful, like a confused child.

Louisa felt her aunt's forehead, the skin papery beneath her fingertips. A faint sheen of perspiration had formed, but she was not hot with fever.

"I think we should call the doctor."

"Oh, pshaw, he's too busy with really sick folks. I'll just have me a lie-down for a while. I didn't sleep too well last night."

"How about if we make some willow bark tea for you?"

"I don't know." Sylvania closed her eyes and sighed. "My stomach doesn't really feel like anything. Perhaps a cold cloth would help."

"I'll get it." Louisa paused at the doorway. "Anything else?"

Sylvania fluttered her hand in dismissal.

"What you think?" Abby met her at the bottom of the stairs.

"I think we should send Reuben for the doctor. But in the

meantime, a cool cloth, some willow bark tea laced with honey, and a rest should help."

"I gets the tea made. She ain't been eatin' 'nough to keep a bitty bird alive. No wonder she done feel poorly." Abby bustled off, muttering all the while.

After sending Reuben on his way, Louisa took the cool cloth back upstairs and laid it across her aunt's forehead. Gentle snores never changed cadence with the attention. Louisa studied her aunt's slack face. Was there something wrong with the right side? Surely it was only a shadow.

Her stomach clenched. *Dear God, please let nothing be wrong with Auntie.* She crossed to the other side of the bed where the light was better. Sure enough, the right eye drooped, the skin of the cheek slacked, the mouth pulled downward like wax slightly melted. "Oh, Lord, apoplexy."

A bit of drool slipped from the right side of the older woman's mouth and pooled on the pillow slip.

Louisa darted from the room and down the stairs. "Abby, come quick."

"Tea most ready." Abby stuck her head around the doorframe.

"No, come now."

Drying her hands on her apron, the black woman hurried up the stairs, muttering, "Lawd, have mercy. Lawd, have mercy."

She knelt by the side of the bed. "Ah, Missy Louisa, look at her face."

"I know. I hoped . . ." *I hoped I was just seeing things. That's what I hoped.* "Do you know of anything to be done?" Louisa took her aunt's hand and stroked the back of it. Sylvania slept on.

"No. Nothin' to do but wait. See how bad. I helped wid a neighbor. Some get better, some get worse." Abby swiped at a tear on her cheek. "Please, Lawd, let her get better."

Louisa echoed the simple prayer. "I'll stay with her, you go send Reuben up as soon as he returns. Perhaps the doctor will have something to help her."

Abby left, shaking her turbaned head, her sniffing audible over the sound of Sylvania's breathing.

When the doctor finally came just before supper, he only shook his head. He lifted the old woman's eyelids, listened to her heart and lungs, and counted her pulse.

"Her heart is strong, but all we can do is keep her comfortable. Has she tried to speak since this happened?"

"No, she's been asleep since shortly after she lay down. We talked briefly then. She said she'd felt dizzy at church and her stomach was so upset, so she came on home early. She mentioned a headache, so I set Abby to making willow bark tea. She never woke up to drink it." Louisa stepped back from the bed and motioned to the doctor to follow. Lowering her voice, she asked, "Will she wake again?"

"Oh my, yes. Unless she gets much worse, I feel this is a minor case of apoplexy. We'll know more in the next few days how severe the damage is."

"Can you tell me what happened?"

"A blood vessel has burst in her brain. The damage depends on how large a vessel and the location. Sleep is the best thing for her right now. When she wakes up, if she has a hard time speaking, reassure her that it likely won't stay this way. She can learn to speak again. The same with the use of her hands and feet. As I said, this seems like a light one."

"Can you give her anything?"

"If she were real restless, I would suggest some laudanum, but . . ." He shrugged and raised his hands, only to drop them again at his side.

Louisa knew both the gesture and the situation. If she could find some laudanum on their next trip, she would keep some for her aunt.

The thought of the journey triggered panic to flutter her stomach. She and Zachary were supposed to leave tomorrow.

"Thank you for coming so quickly." She showed the doctor out, wishing, as he did, that the diagnosis had been different.

"I've known Miss Sylvania for twenty years or more, doctored her husband and her children, poor thing. She lost them all. She hasn't had an easy life, and now to have this happen to her. Hard to understand the Lord's will at times." He patted her arm. "You take care of yourself now, with all these folks to care for."

"Of course, and the same for you." The two of them exchanged a look of secret commiseration, both recognizing the polite deception. They'd often met each other coming and going on errands of mercy all hours of the night or day.

Before he reached the street, she thought of something and dashed out the door. "Doctor?"

He paused and turned to wait for her.

"If I have to be gone for a few days, would Abby and Reuben be able to care for my aunt?"

"Of course, my dear. I'm counting on her to be up and about as early as tomorrow. If there are any further developments, send Reuben for me immediately."

"Thank you again, Doctor." She watched as he climbed into his black buggy and clucked to his horse. Why was caring for wounded soldiers easier than for her own aunt? But as she returned to the house, she knew the answer. While she cared about the soldiers, she loved her aunt, her father's last remaining sister. And besides, the men were under orders to mind her, while Aunt Sylvania had never minded anyone, if

144

Louisa's father's stories were to be believed.

Louisa made her way out to the veranda, where the men were enjoying their afternoon lemonade and cookies.

"How is she?" The question came from all directions at once.

"We'll know more by tomorrow."

"Is there anything we can do?" The lieutenant asked for the four of them.

"Pray."

He arched an eyebrow, and from their earlier discussion, Louisa knew what he was thinking.

"Sometimes we find it easier to pray for someone other than ourselves. If I could think of anything else, I would tell you."

"Thank you, Miss Louisa. My prayers, for whatever they are worth, will be rising for Miss Sylvania. We all miss her sweet voice as she reads to us."

"I will tell her so." *Oh, Lord, let her return from her slumbers with a mind to understand how we love her and appreciate all that she does.*

Louisa ambled back inside, offering to help Abby with the supper preparations.

"You just go on up and sit by Miss Sylvania till I calls you. Reuben done taked my place. I need his old worthless hide down here to carry water to the washtubs. After supper I wash de sheets. Take dat kitten with you."

Louisa knew better than to argue. Abby felt strongly on issues of what the missies of the house were allowed to do. Washing was not one of them. She swooped up the kitten, setting him to purring when she stroked his head, and headed upstairs.

"She not move yet." Reuben rose from the chair, speaking softly, as if in a house of worship.

"We need to talk normally. Perhaps she can hear and needs to know we are here." Louisa sat in the chair and took her aunt's frail hand in her own. The little kitten snuggled down next to the sleeping woman, his purr loud in the stillness. How could her aunt look so fragile so quickly, or had this been going on for a time and none of them noticed? If only there were ways to find some answers.

Chapter Fourteen

"So what actually happened to Aunt Sylvania?"

"The doctor says she has apoplexy. We will know how severe in the next few days. He seemed to think it's fairly mild."

"And we are to leave in the morning." Zachary thumped on the desk with his only hand.

"I cannot do that, Zachary. I will not leave her."

Zachary stared at her, the intensity of his gaze burning into her mind. "You would put an old woman ahead of helping our wounded men?"

"Zachary Highwood, how can you say such a thing? Aunt Sylvania isn't some old woman we are talking about. This is our aunt, who has opened her house and heart for us all this year. She has taken us in and shared everything she has." Anger swelled at the sight of his appearance of disinterest. Had he lost all concern for his own family, all semblance of Christian love even?

Louisa squared her shoulders. "Yes, brother dear." She honeyed her words. "I would put an aunt I dearly love ahead of wounded soldiers." *And as titular head of our family, you should too.* She kept the thought from registering on her face, along with the urge to slap the supercilious look off his face. Surely he must be putting on an act to convince her to leave. "I will make this compromise. If Aunt Sylvania is much better by the morning, we can leave on Tuesday." Surely one more day wouldn't make a difference.

"But I have tickets for tomorrow's train."

"We're taking the train?"

"Yes, west."

"You'll have to find someone else or put off this trip. I'm not leaving our aunt like this." There, she'd had her say.

She waited for him to say more, but when he leaned back in his chair and closed his eyes, she realized the discussion was over. "Is there anything else I can get you?"

A headshake, so brief she'd have missed it had she not been glaring at him, sent her to the doorway. She paused. "I take it I am dismissed?"

A slight lifting of a corner of his mouth let her know he knew what she was doing.

Louisa and Abby took turns sitting with Aunt Sylvania through the night. Toward dawn, on Louisa's shift, Sylvania opened her eyes and looked around. Bewilderment etched the good side of her face. Louisa moved from the chair to the edge of the bed.

"Can I get you something?" She took her aunt's hand in hers, feeling a slight quiver.

"Thirsty, so thirsty." The words came slowly, as if Sylvania were unsure of her tongue.

"Oh, dear Aunt, you can speak, thank our good Lord."

Sylvania quirked her left eyebrow, a familiar sign that she questioned her niece's good sense.

"What is so, so . . ." A look of total confusion caused lines to deepen on the left side of her face, but little happened on the right. "I . . . I can't find the word." She tried to raise her right hand to her face, and it lay flaccid on the coverlet. She stared at the hand, and then her gaze darted to Louisa like that of a child pleading for mercy.

"What . . . what has happened?"

"You've a mild case of apoplexy." Louisa smoothed the wisps of gray hair off her aunt's forehead. "It has affected your right side, your face a bit, and now we know your right hand. Can you move your foot?"

Sylvania looked toward her feet and smiled, making Louisa more aware of the distorted face. "It moves—that's good, right?" She stared at her hand, which finally lifted off the bed but fell back limp, like wet laundry.

"Good, very good." Louisa stood and walked to the pitcher of water sitting on the commode. She closed her eyes and breathed a prayer of thanksgiving. Taking a cup of cool water back, she held it for her aunt to drink.

"My mouth . . . not workin' right." The tone became petulant, like a small child in need of a nap.

"I know, but I think it will get better again. Doctor said he would be back today when he could."

"He came?"

"Yes."

Sylvania nodded. "He would." Her eyelids drifted closed. "Sleepy, so sleepy."

"You rest now, and when you wake we'll bring some breakfast." Louisa realized her patient was already asleep.

When Louisa entered the kitchen, Abby already had the iron stove plenty hot for biscuits, grits steaming in a kettle, and syrup warming on the back of the stove. For a brief second, Louisa craved ham. How long since they'd had ham and redeye gravy for breakfast. A thick slice of ham that needed cutting with a knife. Thoughts of such a ham brought memories of home, memories salt and sweet, just like the meat. The smokehouse at Twin Oaks, the walls standing impregnated with salt and smoke and the dripping grease of untold delicacies, meat taken for granted, a smokehouse part and parcel of the ongoing life.

She sighed as she stepped out onto the veranda. Would life ever be the same again?

Silly question, she chided herself. *Of course it won't. It can't.* Another sigh. She leaned against the brick wall and gazed over what was once Aunt Sylvania's glorious rose garden. Now vegetables were planted between the few remaining roses. Where once only blossoms reigned, now green beans climbed poles and lettuces made borders, along with feathery carrot tops. Dewdrops glistened on petals and leaves, while bitty bushtits gleaned the roses of aphids. A mockingbird sang through its repertoire. A wren twitted from the magnolia.

"You're out early." Zachary spoke from behind her, startling her, since she hadn't heard his crutch step.

She waited a moment for him to ask about their aunt. And when he didn't, she felt like shaking him.

"Aunt awoke."

A cardinal sang for his mate, rich notes threading the rising humidity. Louisa rubbed her forehead with her fingertips.

"We'll talk when I return."

Zachary turned and crutch-stepped his way back through the kitchen. His position at the law office kept him away until dusk, and many times, he had meetings in the evening. He never asked a single question about Aunt Sylvania's condition. *Mama would have given him a lecture,* Louisa thought. *Not only a lecture on his lack of manners, but one on his Christian duty. If he weren't my brother, I don't think I'd even like him anymore.*

The thought made her gasp. Here she was criticizing him for lack of Christian duty, and look at her. She picked up her basket and shears from the shelf by the door and headed out to the rosebushes to cut flowers for the breakfast table and find a special bud for Aunt Sylvania. She did love her roses, and waking to the scent of roses in her room might make her feel a bit better.

When the doctor arrived after dinner, he greeted Sylvania with a broad smile.

"You are looking much better, my dear, far better than I feared." He took her hands. "Now, then, squeeze with your left. Good. Now the right. Umm." He nodded. "Now let's get you out of that bed and see how well your feet and legs work."

"But I am in my nightdress."

His smile and her consternation made Louisa smile. Here they were concerned about the lingering effects of apoplexy and her aunt was worried about a man, a doctor, for pity's sake, seeing her in her nightdress.

Together, an arm on either side of her, they helped Sylvania up on her feet.

"Oh, I'm dizzy."

They let her sit back on the edge of the bed.

"Better now?" The doctor rubbed Sylvania's hands. He glanced to Louisa. "You can help her by rubbing her hand and foot, even the side of her face, gently at first and then with more strength as she improves."

Abby nodded from her position at the foot of the bed. "We does that."

"Still dizzy?"

"No."

"Let's get you vertical then." Slowly they eased her to her feet. Louisa watched her aunt's face for any signs of faintness. They stood still, waiting for any sign from Sylvania. When she nodded, Louisa tightened her grip on her aunt's waist.

"Left foot first." The three took one step at the same time. A small step, but movement nonetheless.

"Right foot." The doctor's glance warned Louisa to be on

guard. Another small step.

"I did it." Sylvania gripped Louisa's hand with a strength born of fear.

"And another." They tottered as far as the brocade chair and settled her into it.

"I feel like I walked clear downtown." Sylvania slumped against the chair back, her left hand on the padded arm, her right lying in her lap. She looked up at the doctor standing by her side. "Now, what happened to me?"

She started to turn to the mirror, but Louisa nonchalantly stepped in front of it. The visible damage could be seen later, when Sylvania grew stronger.

Right now Louisa could believe that would happen. Memories of a neighbor at home who'd never been able to speak nor feed herself after such as this skulked back into the lair from which they came.

While Abby and Louisa changed the bed and fluffed up the pillows, Sylvania and the doctor visited, him telling her a story that brought out a chuckle.

"All right, now I reckon it's about time you walk back to bed. I expect you to get up every day. The more you walk, the stronger you will become."

After they settled Sylvania in her bed again, with a sigh of relief on her part, Louisa followed the doctor down to the front door.

"Sure you wouldn't like to stay for some lemonade?"

"No, I must get on. Fill an old sock with dried beans or rice and make her—"

At the raising of Louisa's eyebrow, he chuckled.

"I know, making Miss Sylvania do anything is a miracle in its own right, but she needs to squeeze that sock over and over if she wants to regain the use of that hand."

"We'll keep reminding her. Thank you for coming by."

She watched as he strode down the walk and climbed into his buggy. With his shoulders rounding and the slight limp, he looked to have aged ten years in the last twelve months. He was good at telling others to take care of themselves, but what about him?

Louisa looked up toward Aunt Sylvania's window. Not being able to sew or knit with only one hand would make her downright cantankerous. Or drive her to work her hand harder.

Could she leave right now? Could Abby and Reuben take care of not only their soldiers but also Miss Sylvania? Who could she find to come in and help? *Ah, if only Lucinda were here.*

CHAPTER FIFTEEN

FORT LARAMIE

There was knowing, and then there was *knowing*.

Jesselynn stretched her hands above her head and watched the dust motes dance on the sunbeams lilting in the window. Sheer white curtains billowed in the breeze, a breeze that felt cool as springwater on her arms. She glanced to the side to see the dished place where her husband's head had lain on the pillow. She stretched again, enjoying the lassitude.

Wolf had kissed her good-bye sometime after dawn, with the birds still twittering their morning wake-up call. He'd said she should sleep as long as she wanted. No one would come by to disturb her, or they would answer to him. The remembered growl in his voice made her smile again.

Smiles came easy this morning, her very first morning as Mrs. Gray Wolf Torstead.

She could hear soldiers marching out on the parade grounds where the wedding guests had danced the day before. Most likely she had danced with some of the men out there. Her feet reminded her that she'd danced with most everyone west of the Missouri. Or at least it seemed that way.

Ah, the only thing that would have made the day shine more brightly was if Louisa and Carrie Mae could have been here. And Lucinda. That thought brought an immediate dimming to the smile that echoed clear through her. They would most likely feel the same as Aunt Agatha. At least Zachary would. That was for certain sure.

She threw back the covers and reached for the dressing gown that Rebeccah had so thoughtfully provided, along with the nightdress, the pins for her hair, and the rose water she'd splashed on before retiring.

She closed her eyes. Yes, Wolf had liked the rose water. Dressing gown belted in place, she ambled out to the kitchen of the quarters, where a loaf of bread, a hunk of cheese, butter, and milk sat under cheesecloth on the counter. The coffeepot was still warm, pushed to the back of the stove. She sliced off two pieces of bread and enough cheese to cover them and poured herself a cup of milk. Who needed coffee anyway on a morning like this?

Once she'd finished eating and washed up her knife and cup, she peeked out the window, standing off to the side so no one would see her. No Appaloosa in sight. He'd said she should sleep until he came to wake her. By the angle of the sun, the morning was half gone, and she had a pile of things to do if they were to leave for the Chugwater in the morning.

Within minutes she was dressed in a shirt, britches, and boots. Clapping her sorry hat on her head, she headed out the door, smack dab into a broad chest that rumbled with laughter.

"Whoa." Wolf steadied her by grasping her upper arms. "You look to be in a real hurry, ma'am. Is there somethin' I can help you with?"

Her hat fell behind without her notice as he captured her lips with his.

"Wolf, people will see us." She murmured the words against lips that drew back only a little.

"I know. So how about we back up a couple of feet and close the door. That way . . ." Their feet obeyed. Their eyes spoke in paragraphs. The next kiss lasted longer, ending on her sigh. "You sure this is the way newly married folk behave?"

"If they can." He drew her over to a chair and pulled her down in his lap. "Now, Mrs. Torstead, where were you goin' in such a rush?"

"To find you, I think. Or was it back to my wagons? You get my head all mixed up." She clasped her hands around the back of his neck. "I like that Mrs. Torstead name."

"Good thing. It's yours now."

"I like that Mr. Torstead name too." Would it be too forward if she kissed him first? She did so without hesitating. He didn't seem to mind.

"So what have you been doing?"

"While you slept, you mean?"

"Um." She hid a yawn behind her hand. "I haven't been this lazy since . . ." The sun dimmed for her. *Since Mother died, and I had to take over the managing of Twin Oaks.* A sigh slipped out before she could catch it.

She opened her eyes to see him studying her. Laying her head on his shoulder, she picked up one of his hands and placed hers against it, palm to palm. "My mother taught me how to be a good wife. I can manage a plantation, keep the slaves busy and in order, keep up the household accounts, the entire plantation accounts if need be. I know how to cook, put up food for the entire plantation, garden, sew a fine seam, entertain the kinfolk and the men who come calling on the husband, read Greek and Latin. My father taught me to ride, along with how to shoot a gun, and raise tobacco—from field preparation to drying, shipping, and selling." She ticked off each skill on her fingertips.

"She taught you well."

She jerked up right. "How do you know?" At the look on

his face, she thumped him on the chest, a saucy grin tickling her cheeks. "Wolf! You taught me that." She nestled her cheek back into his shoulder. "Thank you for this morning."

"You are very welcome." He leaned forward. "Now, I have work to do, and Meshach has already been by to see what you wanted him to do."

"But of all those things I know to do"—she shook her head, her hair teasing his chin—"not many are needed out here in the wilderness."

"No, but you already have added many more things. You can tan hides, sew shirts out of either buckskin or cloth, cook over a campfire, drive a wagon, train horses or oxen, skin a rabbit or deer or whatever needs skinning, including a buffalo, birth foals, and while there'll be no call for harvesting tobacco"—he kissed the tips of her fingers—"you have made one man bone-deep happy and sometime, God willing, you'll be raising sons and daughters along with those foals that will pay for the things we can't raise."

Jesselynn could feel the blush start below her neck and flame its way up to her forehead.

"I declare, Mr. Torstead, the way you talk." She fingered the fringe on his buckskin shirt. "There is something I haven't told you."

"We have our entire lives to find things to tell."

"I know, but this is different." She sat up straight and looked into his eyes. "Someday, when that cursed war is finally over, I want to take breeding stock back to Twin Oaks."

"Domino?"

"Perhaps. But if the colt develops like he looks to be, him for sure, maybe the two fillies. Both mares took." She tipped her head slightly to one side. "That means fewer for sale in the next couple of years."

"We'll send all the horses we can, but keep in mind that I, you and I, cannot live in Kentucky."

"I know, and someone famous once wrote, 'You cannot go back.' The life I knew will never be there again. Even if someday Zachary can rebuild the big house, it will not be the same. The war has destroyed life as we lived it." She could feel the tears burning the backs of her throat and eyes. "I wish you could have seen it."

"Had you stayed there, you would not be here." His hand stroked the nape of her neck.

"I know." She dredged up a grin so that she would not cry. "God sure does work in mysterious ways." She leaned forward and butterfly-kissed his smiling lips. When she started to stand, he held her back.

"I am grateful every day to our God and Father that you came west."

"Even if you almost refused us passage with your wagon train?"

He groaned. "That was business."

"Bad business." She shook her head. "I will never understand why you allowed the Jones brothers to join up but almost refused us." She looked at him again, her head continuing to move from side to side.

"Me neither." He set her on her feet and rose. "Let's be on out to the wagons."

"I have to return my dresses first." She gazed at the creamy silk hanging on a hanger. "That most surely is a lovely dress." She caressed the material again. "Wolf, I do have a skirt in the wagon."

"Good. Let it stay there. You can use it when we come into the fort if you like. Britches are much more practical where we are going. Oglala women wear deerskin leggings under a deerskin shift. No skirts to get in the way." He thought a moment. "At least they used to. My mother did beautiful bead and quill designs on her clothes, and my father's too. Even moccasins testified to her love of beauty."

Jesselynn held perfectly still. For once, she had a glimmer into his life as a child. A life so foreign to her that she wondered if she would ever understand it anymore than he would understand life at Twin Oaks. After a moment she folded the garments over her arm so that nothing dragged and went out of the door ahead of him.

Someday they'd have a house too. But for now . . . She sucked in a deep breath. For now she must go back to the real world, of Aunt Agatha, slow plodding oxen, dust, and distances. "I'll hurry."

They left in the morning as planned, waving good-bye to the Jespersons, who figured on waiting for the next wagon train heading west. Scouts reported there was another train three days out. Jesselynn rode Ahab, she and Wolf at the head of their small train, the two packhorses on lines behind the last wagon, driven by Meshach. Aunt Agatha managed to lead the train without talking to either Jesselynn or Wolf. When Jesselynn gave thought to her aunt, she caught herself sighing.

This could be a long trip and a hard winter if Agatha kept her mouth pursed like that and went out of her way to avoid sitting by them or joining in conversation. But how could Jesselynn uninvite her along? There was no place for her at Fort Laramie.

Lord God, this is beyond me. I've done everything I can, short of not marrying, and she will not bend an inch. Yet I know she respected Wolf as the wagon master, thought he was fine man. Fine for everything but marrying into the Highwood family.

She knew Zachary would feel the same way, so the letters

she sent to Richmond and Twin Oaks made no mention of the wedding. She just said they had decided to go north instead of on to Oregon. Not a lie, but certainly not the whole truth either.

Riding with Wolf certainly beat riding alone or driving a wagon. He pointed out buffalo wallows, places where deer spent the daylight hours, and a slide for river otters. Benjamin fished the deep pools of the Chugwater River that snaked across a valley belly-deep in rich grass. Daniel's snares netted rabbits.

"Why don't we settle here?" Jesselynn looked back over her shoulder at grass shimmering in the sun as it turned from green to gold. "There's hay aplenty and—"

"And the river floods in wet years, and we would be forced to build all over again. There is grass also in the valley I know of. And we will be bothered less up the river."

"Bothered?"

"My tribe travels through here from summer to winter hunting. I do not want to be in their way."

"Oh."

"Other tribes too, and sometimes they war on one another."

"I see." But she didn't. The word "war" made her want to head south again to the Oregon Trail. Would she never be free of war?

The second day they left the verdant valley and traveled between hillocks as they followed the south branch of the river, now more like a creek. Willows and other brush lined the waterway, and grass grew deep on the flats, but the hills around them wore sparser blankets of golden grasses. Hawks and eagles *screed* above them, huge ravens announced their passage, grouse thrummed in the evenings. Deer and pronged antelope leaped the hills while Wolf promised elk in the mountains ahead.

The great sky arched in changing shades of such blue as to take one's breath away. They saw no other humans but themselves.

"Come, I have something to show you." Wolf mounted his Appaloosa and waited for her to mount Ahab. "Just follow along the creek," he instructed Benjamin who, mounted on Domino, scouted ahead for the wagons. "We won't be gone long. We'll be at camp before nightfall."

"Yes, suh." Benjamin touched one finger to the brim of his hat. "That be good."

Nudging the horses to a lope, the two riders edged the creek a ways before Wolf set the Appaloosa at a hill. Up and down they walked and trotted until Wolf stopped with a raised hand. "See."

Jesselynn stopped and looked ahead to where he pointed. A small valley, shaped like a bowl, lay before her, hills mounding on all four sides. On the face of the tallest hill three caves faced south. "While I hadn't planned on this many people, we can make do. Brush fences can keep the horses in the valley. See there and there." He pointed to low places, like small ravines, that led into the bowl. "We can bring logs from up in the mountains, or use rock, to build walls. This will keep us through the winter."

Jesselynn nodded. "We spent last winter in caves around Springfield, Missouri. Guess this won't be much different."

"Plenty snow here, but"—he drew a circle with his arm to encompass the area—"good protection. Game nearby. Water. We will do well."

"Will the creek freeze over?"

"Sometimes yes, sometimes no. We can cut hay and bring it back on the wagons."

Jesselynn thought to the bags of oats she had purchased at

the fort. Enough to feed the mares through their foaling? Enough to plant next summer?

"Come, I will show you more."

Not many minutes later they trotted around a corner with a rock face perhaps twenty feet high. Jesselynn felt like she'd stepped into a dream. The valley widened out, the creek deepened, lined by willows and cottonwood with deep green pine climbing the gentle sides of the hills. Grass rippled like a green lake under a breeze.

A slap echoed in the valley.

"What was that?"

"Beaver. They dammed the creek. That's why the pond. They're just announcing visitors."

"Why can't we winter here? This is beautiful."

"No caves. But here is where we build a house out of that rock we came around. You saw the square stones. Like using bricks."

Jesselynn leaned on her arms crossed over Ahab's withers. "This is some beautiful."

"When the red bark of the low brush shines through the snow or ice, then too this valley has beauty."

"You have stayed here in the past?"

"In the caves one winter, my father and I, after my mother died."

"No wonder you wanted to come back here." She looked to the west where hills covered with oak and evergreens climbed to the mountains hidden in the distance. "Let's get the others, Mr. Torstead. Our new life is about to begin."

Chapter Sixteen

Richmond, Virginia

"We'll still be going then?"

"I can put it off three more days, but no longer."

"What about disguises?"

"We're working on that."

Louisa wondered who he meant by "we." Who was providing the money for this trip, and who was getting them the quinine on the other end? Why did her brother see the need to be so secretive here at home? She could understand out in public, but at home? The "why's" could stretch on forever.

Secret missions brought up another thought. She'd heard rumors of secret missions before her lieutenant told her he had to return to his family home. Who had blown up the train that took his life? Did they ever search for or catch the fiends that did such things? Or was that a natural part of war?

The war. Everything always came back to the *war*.

"And when will I be informed as to what I am to do?" She didn't bother to keep the sarcasm from her voice.

Zachary shook his head, a smile flirting with the corners of his mouth.

"I've been a bit of a dolt, haven't I?"

"Now that I won't argue with." Louisa knew she'd forgive him anything when he turned on the Highwood charm. "You've been treating Aunt Sylvania most shabbily, and you

163

know she dotes on you."

He had the grace to look ashamed.

Thank you, Lord, there is hope for my brother yet.

"I will go up and see her."

"I know the stairs are hard for you, but—"

He interrupted her before she could finish her sentence. "But not impossible."

"That wasn't what I was going to say."

"Perhaps not, but you've thought it."

Louisa looked down. "I stand condemned."

"No, Louisa, don't ever even think such things." He reached for her hand. "Never, do you hear me?" His voice shook, the whisper cutting to her heart.

She looked into his eye, past the fire to see—what? Fear?

Zachary shrugged his shoulders and leaned back in his chair. When she looked at him again, the man she'd come to dislike gazed back at her.

"I need to go sit with Aunt Sylvania. When you come to see her, bring that charming man with you, the brother I used to know." Pivoting so her skirts swished, she sailed out the door, her teeth clenched at all the other words she would like to have said.

Dear Lord, what do I do with him? I want to strangle him one minute and hold him the next. I know he's in pain much of the time, but this cruelty—that's not my brother. And if it's not my brother, who is it? What is it?

The sharp edges that jutted and jabbed all around downstairs had not made it up the stairs. Peace, soothing and gentle, reigned in Aunt Sylvania's room. The evening breeze danced with the sheer white curtains, wafting the fragrance of the roses out through the open door.

Aunt Sylvania sat in her chair, pulled up by the window to catch the morning sun and any errant breeze. Her Bible lay open on her lap, her lips moving silently as she read.

In the three days since the incident—Louisa had had a hard time using the word apoplexy—Aunt Sylvania had regained some use of her hand, and her smile could faintly move the right side of her mouth. Louisa encouraged her to smile often. While her walking gained strength daily, she had yet to venture downstairs.

The ginger kitten with a white patch on its chest brought smiles to the faces of all who lived there. When Aunt Sylvania dragged a piece of string for the kitten to chase, Louisa said she had to use her right hand to do so. And when the kitten was played out, he snuggled in any lap available but preferred Sylvania's, his purr lion-sized. Excusing herself, Louisa returned downstairs when Zachary made his way into Sylvania's room.

One of the soldiers fashioned a lopsided ball of wood that the kitten batted around, his antics making everyone laugh.

Louisa wished she had thought of a pet sooner. She also wished the kitten would stay a kitten, since it brought such pleasure.

They had yet to choose a name for it.

"We need a name for our kitten," Louisa mentioned after grace at the supper table.

"I think Spot or Patch," one of the men said.

Another shook his head. "Too ordinary."

"Fluffy?" Everyone made a face.

"We had one we called Cat." The lieutenant shrugged. "Just a thought."

"What is Spot or White in French? That would sound exotic."

"Blanc."

"Nah, he's a cat. Blanc would embarrass him. I say we call him Bones."

165

"Bones?" Louisa wrinkled her nose. "What kind of name is that?" But looking around at the grinning faces, she couldn't help but smile back. "Bones it is, I reckon."

When the doctor came the next morning, he decreed this was the day Aunt Sylvania went downstairs.

Louisa breathed a sigh of relief. She'd been both dreading and anticipating this day and praying it would happen before she had to leave.

She had yet to tell Aunt Sylvania she would be leaving. But every evening since she and Zachary had their discussion, he had forced himself to stump-hop up the stairs to visit with his aunt, no matter how late he arrived home from his job.

He said very little about working in the law firm and even less about his evening meetings, but he made Aunt Sylvania laugh, and that was all that mattered to Louisa.

"Aunt, I have something I need to tell you." Sitting together while Aunt Sylvania read and Louisa stitched, the afternoon had passed pleasantly.

"You're leaving again, aren't you?" The accusation chased the peace to hiding in the corners.

"Yes. Zachary cannot do this alone."

Louisa looked up to see a tear leak from the down-pulled eye. Louisa fell to her knees at the side of Sylvania's chair. She laid both hands on her aunt's arm, which was already shrunk thin from the illness. If she left, would Sylvania keep on squeezing the sock and strengthening her arm?

Bones stretched and stirred in Sylvania's lap, yawning wide to show a pink tongue and tiny white teeth.

"Oh, you poor little thing. Louisa disturbed you." Sylvania stroked the kitten with her left hand until she caught Louisa's eye and switched. "See, I nee—" She cut off the word.

Louisa felt like Zachary had her by one arm and Sylvania the other, and that they were pulling her apart like medieval torturers.

Sylvania patted Louisa's hand. "Nothing is more important than helping our soldiers. You go on with Zachary. There are plenty here who will help me. By the time you g-get back, I will be my old self."

Louisa stared into her aunt's eyes. If only the sorrow-filled eyes matched the commonsense mouth.

The kitten arched his back and rubbed against Sylvania's chest. His straight-up tail tickled her under the chin. When the old lady stroked his back, his purr could be heard clear downstairs.

"Besides, I can go down and read to the boys again and encourage them in their stitching. We will keep busy until you return."

Was there a trace of the former Sylvania coming out again?

With desperation in her soul, Louisa prayed so.

When Louisa and Zachary drove off in the predawn, she looked back at the house. *Protect them, please, dear Lord.* It was all she could do to not plead with her brother to make him turn around.

No one gave a second glance to the old man with his octoroon maid when they boarded the westbound train at Richmond. One old darkie helped her with the trunk she wrestled from the back of the buggy.

"Thankee, suh," she muttered, keeping her head down in an attitude of submission. No one could see her blue eyes that way, and the white bandana tied round her hair, like any mammy or slave, hid her dark blond hair. Walnut dye changed her skin to the octoroon hue.

Again their papers took them through both lines, although

Louisa chewed the metallic taste of fear each time.

When they returned after two weeks, Aunt Sylvania greeted them at the door. While she carried her right arm closer to her body, Louisa could hardly detect the damage to her aunt's face, as the smile she welcomed them home with stretched both cheeks and her hug felt as of before.

Thank you, Lord, thank you. Louisa collapsed on her bed and slept round the clock. The trunk full of quinine and morphine disappeared like hoarfrost in the sun.

Summer dragged on under a mantle of humidity that wilted both men and beast. The wounded troops from Gettysburg still filled the hospitals, the churches commandeered as hospitals, and the homes that had taken in recovering patients.

A knock at the door early one morning sent Abby scurrying to answer and Louisa looking to see how they could accommodate another pallet.

"Come quick," a black maid pleaded. "Missy Carrie Mae done be havin' her baby. She be cryin' for you." She nodded to Louisa. "She say she be dyin'." The young woman's black eyes rolled white with fear.

"Has she called a midwife?" Louisa asked as she loaded a basket with a Bible, the layette she had stitched, and smelling salts, along with other things. She followed the maid out to the buggy waiting at the curb.

"I don' know."

"Give her our blessings," Aunt Sylvania called from the front porch.

Louisa waved back and turned to the maid. "How long has she been in labor?"

"She woke up before cockcrow sayin' her back hurt."

"Where is Mr. Jefferson?"

"Gone somewhere. I don' know."

"What is your name?" Louisa hadn't seen this particular maid before.

"I'se Becca, and I be new. I don' never seen a baby born before."

"I'm sure Carrie Mae is doing just fine. Women been having babies since time began." Louisa tried to sound as comforting as possible. After all, she remembered how Carrie Mae couldn't stand pain of any kind and would carry on until their mother lost patience. For their gentle mother to say, *"Land sakes, Carrie Mae, you carry on worse than a just-weaned calf"* sent Louisa and Jesselynn out of the house to snicker at their sister's expense.

Lord, please let that be the case here. While I attended one baby's birth with Mother, I've not helped on my own. "Why didn't Carrie Mae call for the midwife?"

"I don' know she did or din't."

And what happened to that French maid? "Is Elise still with my sister?"

"Yes'm, but she don' know nothin' 'bout birthin' no baby neither."

"Oh."

Three hours later, Carrie Mae was still carrying on, the pains coming closer and harder.

Louisa wanted to stuff a rag in her sister's mouth. "Carrie Mae, you get up here and walk with me right now!"

"I want Jefferson here."

"Mama always said the only thing men were good for at a birthing was lowering the level of whiskey in the cupboard." She hoisted Carrie Mae off the bed and, with one arm around her, forced her to keep walking.

"Now sing with me. 'O, I wish I was in the land of cotton.'

Sing, Carrie Mae, sing." They went on to "Amazing Grace" and "Rock of Ages." Each time a contraction came they stopped walking and singing for Carrie Mae to double over and cry.

"Breathe, Carrie Mae. Pain is always less if you ride it, not fight it. Now take a deep breath and let it all out."

They kept on walking.

"Oh! Oh no." Carrie Mae stared down at the puddle widening around her feet.

"Not oh no, oh good. Now we can get on with this." Louisa nodded toward the two maids alternately cowering in the corner and helping walk their mistress.

"Becca, you are going to sit on the bed with your back against the wall, and Carrie Mae will lean against you. You puff with her. Elise, tie these sheets to the end of the bed for her to pull on." Louisa handed her the sheets she'd had them knot earlier. "We're going to have a beautiful little son or daughter here by the time Jefferson returns, and that is just how it should be."

As the pains came faster and harder, she finally allowed Carrie Mae to climb on the bed, her back braced against Becca and her hands knotted into the sheets.

"Now, relax between these, and . . ."

Carrie Mae scrunched her face, gritted her teeth, and groaned as another wave rolled over her. "You give instructions . . . so well here . . . and you've never been through this." Her panting between words made Louisa smile.

"That's the way. Get angry at me if it will help you." With the next contraction that arched Carrie Mae right off the bed, Louisa checked. Sure enough, she saw a small circle that showed the baby's head.

"I can see it, dear sister. I can see the hair, dark like Jefferson's. When you feel like pushing, you just push away. We're almost there."

Another three good hard contractions, along with a scream through each, and Louisa assisted her niece into the world, turning her gently as her shoulders slipped through the opening.

"Ah, Carrie Mae, Mama would say you were made for bearing babies." She laid the already squalling infant on her mother's chest. "See, isn't she beautiful?"

Carrie Mae laid back against Becca's arms, panting, tears streaming down her cheeks, one finger tracing her daughter's cheek. "She's so tiny."

"I surely do hope so. Any bigger and you'd have had real problems."

Elise handed Louisa a warmed towel. "You want to wrap her?"

"Not yet. Mama said never cut the cord until it lays flat." Louisa used the towel to dry off her own face, including tears, and then her sister's.

"Ah, Carrie Mae, you did splendidly."

"I did, didn't I?" Her face scrunched again. "Ow."

With the cord cut and the afterbirth delivered, Louisa washed the baby, who seemed to be looking right at her.

"Look at you, already studying on the world. I can tell you are one smart little girl, going to be pretty as a daisy." She kept up the soft whispers as she swished the tiny body in a pan of warm water. She dried her and, after diapering and swaddling, laid the baby back in Carrie Mae's waiting arms.

While she'd been caring for the baby, the two other women cleaned up Carrie Mae, changed the bed, and dressed her again.

When Jefferson walked in an hour later, he saw his wife, all lovely with her hair combed, sleeping sweetly with his equally beautiful daughter asleep in her arms.

"Now, if that isn't about the prettiest picture I ever did see." He leaned over to kiss his wife on the forehead.

"What have you decided to name her?" Louisa kept her voice low so as not to disturb the sleeping pair.

"Her?"

"Yes, you have a daughter."

"Oh, well, ah . . ."

Louisa felt like smacking him. What was so all-fired important about having a son first? "Mother and baby are doing just fine."

Jefferson recovered himself and turned to Louisa. "I do believe we should name this little darlin' after her maternal grandmother. How does that sound to you?"

"Miriam Amelia, wouldn't that be lovely?" Louisa knew Jefferson's mother would want her name used too. No sense creating discord in the family. She smiled at her brother-in-law. "That's very kind of you, Jefferson. I'm sure Carrie Mae will be most happy."

"Jefferson?" The sleepy voice brought their attention back to the bed. He crossed and knelt beside his wife, his stump around her head, his hand clasping hers.

"She's beautiful, wife, just like you." He kissed her cheek and the baby's head. "I'm sorry I couldn't get here any sooner. I was out to dinner, but they told me as soon as I returned to the office."

Louisa stepped out of the room. "I'll let them be," she said to the maid. "Tell Carrie Mae that I'll come by to see her tomorrow."

"I call de buggy for you." Becca went out the door before Louisa had time to argue.

She arrived home just in time for supper being served out on the back veranda, where everyone hoped for a bit of breeze.

"We have a beautiful baby girl named Miriam Amelia. Mother and baby are both doing fine." She clasped her hands to her bosom and smiled at Sylvania. "I have now joined the exalted ranks of auntyhood."

"Does that make us honorary uncles?" The young private missing a leg and an eye smiled as he asked.

"But of course. Although as honorary uncles, you might need to hold her at times."

"I'm the oldest of eight. I've held lots of babies." He held up the knife he used to carve handy spoons. Abby used them all the time now. "Think I can do a rattle, you know, with a little ball within a sphere, with a handle. Made one for my baby brother. You know where I could get me some cherrywood? Even babies can't gnaw on that."

Louisa kept her astonishment to herself. He'd never said more than "please" and "thank you" and "yes, ma'am" up to now. "I'm sure I can find you some, or Reuben will." *If I have to turn Richmond upside down, I'll find it.*

Two days later Zachary came to her and announced another trip.

Louisa felt her heart knock around her kneecaps. Weren't they testing God's providence to try for a fourth trip?

Chapter Seventeen

On the Chugwater River
August 1863

Cave living hadn't changed much, just more people, more animals, and smaller caves.

Jesselynn stared out at the curtains of rain. Rain falling so hard she could barely see across their little valley. Sammy and Thaddeus both had a bad case of the squalls this morning, perhaps due to the weather.

"Thaddeus, give that back to Sammy." Jesselynn didn't even bother to turn around. With all she had to do, standing watching the rain fall could be called a direct waste of time.

The squall going on within her looked about as gray as the rain. They'd been in camp three weeks now, and Aunt Agatha still hadn't spoken a word to her. With the sour look on her face, even the little boys had taken to giving her a wide berth.

"Thaddeus, I said give that back to Sammy—now!" Where in heaven's name was Jane Ellen? Most likely with Mrs. Jones. For some reason the two of them had taken a shine to each other and had become the best of friends.

Patch came in from a check on the herd and shook himself, soaking Jesselynn before he sat down at her feet. Tongue lolling out one side of his mouth, he looked up for her pat or words of approval. When they didn't come, he whined.

"I know. You're a good dog. I'm surprised the mares didn't come back with you to stand here under the shelter of the cave." She leaned over to give him the expected and well-earned pat. All the animals looked as if they'd put on weight with the rest and good pasture. The rain of course would help that pasture remain green, but Jesselynn and Mrs. Mac had planned on washing clothes today. She had set water to dripping through wood ash to make lye, not that they had much fat to make soap with, but if Wolf and Benjamin brought back deer and elk with plenty of fat, she'd use that.

"Jesse, me go outside?" Thaddeus leaned against her leg.

"You'll get wet."

"Patch is wet."

"Patch was herding the cattle."

"Where Meshach?"

"Over making scythes and rakes."

"Go see?" He looked up at her, hope written all over his face.

"No. You'll get in the way." She looked down to see Sammy stuck to her other knee. "Where's Ophelia?"

Thaddeus pointed to the back of the cave. "There."

Jesselynn looked over her shoulder, but the way the cave curved around an angle, she could see nothing. "You two play with Patch. Get a stick of wood and throw for him." She snatched Thaddeus back as he headed outside. "No, get one from the woodpile."

She ignored the smoke floating out along the low ceiling and blinked in the dimness lit by the slow fire with racks of venison drying on A-frames along both sides of the shallow trench. A caldron of stew bubbled on a separate and more substantial fire. They'd decided to use this cave for all the storage, cooking and sleeping outside until the rain drove them into the other caves. Good thing they'd brought in plenty of dry wood. Daniel and Nathan, along with his grandson, Mark, and the McPhereson boys, had taken two ox teams and wagons up into the hills to bring back more wood. By winter they hoped to bring down logs to extend the fronts of the caves into a cabin or two with rock fireplaces and chimneys for cooking.

"You go help Ophelia. I need to talk with Meshach." Jesselynn gave her little brother a pat on the seat and sent him to the rear of the cave.

"Me go." Her little brother's plaintive plea tugged at her heart.

"Not this time." She settled her hat firmly on her head and, grabbing a cape off a peg, ducked out into the downpour. The gray sky looked to be sitting right on top of them, with enough rain tucked into the lowering clouds to last the proverbial forty days and nights.

Meshach sat just under the lip of the cave so he could use the available light, carving pegs for the three-foot rake he'd fashioned from slender willow saplings. A completed one leaned against the cave wall.

"What's that bar across the handle?"

"Get a better grip dat way." Meshach eyed the peg and laid it beside him, picking up another piece of wood and commencing to whittle it to the right size.

Jesselynn looked toward the rear of the cave where another fire and drying racks matched those in the storage cave. Aunt Agatha was laying strips of venison in place. *If only she would talk with me.*

Meshach raised an eyebrow and shrugged.

Jesselynn took in a deep breath. Just because her aunt was being stubborn gave her no excuse to act the same. "Good morning, Aunt Agatha. Looks to be raining forever, doesn't it?"

Agatha laid a final strip in place, wiped her hands on her apron, and strode on out of the cave without even glancing in Jesselynn's direction. She turned to the left and trotted on over to the easternmost cave where Darcy and Jane Ellen were sewing soft buckskin into shirts for the men for the winter.

"Give her time."

Jesselynn turned back to Meshach. "Not much else I can do, short of snatching her by the shoulders and shaking her." The thought brought a smile to lighten Jesselynn's outlook. That would be something all right.

"God work slow, it seem to us, but we don' see de whole picture. Bible say let de day's own trouble be sufficient for de day."

"I know, Mama used to say that so often."

"She teached me."

"But, Meshach, think what the winter will be like in these close caves if she continues to act like this."

"De winter long ways off."

"I know, today's trouble." *So what is today's trouble? Agatha didn't talk to me—that's nothing new. It's raining. So, we need the rain. I can't do the wash, so I'll do it tomorrow or when the rain stops.*

So here I am in a grumbling mood when we have so much to be thankful for. Father, forgive me.

"Thanks, Meshach. Think I'll go fishing. They should be biting good in weather like this, right?"

He nodded, giving her a slow smile that drew forth one in return. "Fried fish taste mighty fine. Take de rifle."

As she darted back out in the rain, she heard him pick up the tune he'd been humming when she arrived—"Way Down Upon the Swanee River." No, they weren't on a deep river here, but the creek sure was a welcome part of their new home.

Back in the main cave, she called to Ophelia. "I'm going fishing." She dug into one of the boxes for the fishhooks. "Should be biting good in this weather." Fishhooks and line in hand, she stopped. "You want I should take the boys over to play with Jane Ellen?"

"No, they be fine here."

Jesselynn checked her lye drip. She'd fashioned a skin to make a water bag with a slow leak and hung that above a pan of wood ashes. The pan had a hole drilled in the bottom and dripped the lye into an iron kettle. Oh, the things she'd taken for granted at Twin Oaks, useful things like soap and candles and a smokehouse and a cellar in the ground for storing the bounty they'd put by. Digging an outhouse was another thing they needed to do, and soon.

"You boys go on back in the cave." She snagged Sammy back from his dash out in the rain. "I told you to stay inside." The urge to swat his fat little bottom went down to setting him on his feet with a gentle shove pointed in the direction of his mother. "Here they come, Ophelia. I think they need to break up kindling for a while. I'll be up by the beaver pond."

Ignoring the look Thaddeus sent her, Jesselynn swung the waterproof cape over her shoulders again, pulled her hat down snug and the hood up. She'd just stepped out in the rain when Ophelia, rifle in hand, called from behind her. "You need gun."

"I have the pistol."

"You take gun." She and Meshach sure thought alike.

Jesselynn shook her head and took the rifle and the powder horn. "I'm just going fishing right around that hill."

Ophelia shrugged. "Fish be good for supper."

Rifle in the crook of her arm, Jesselynn struck off toward the creek to follow the trail that bordered it. While originally a game trail, they'd ridden back there enough now to make it more visible, even in the rain.

A pouch with worms in moist dirt hung at her belt, along with her skinning knife and the holster for the pistol. While tempted to leave the rifle propped in a tree, she carried it under the cape to keep it dry. Wet powder never did anyone any good. Of course, if she saw deer or elk coming to drink, she'd be ready. Now wouldn't that be a good joke if she got something and the men didn't. Right close to home too.

She stopped often, peering ahead, trying to see and hear if anything but fish and beaver had visited the pond or taken up residence there. Nothing. The rain splatting on the cape drowned out any sounds but itself.

Leaning her rifle against a hefty cottonwood tree trunk, she deftly cut a willow sapling, skinned off its branches, and tied her string to the tip. Knotting the hook took some concentration with wet hands, but within minutes she was seated on a rock on the bank with the worm floating on the top of the water ten feet out. She sighed. Should have tied a rock on for a sinker. Raising the tip to pull it back in, the pole bent and a flopping fish broke the surface of the rain-pecked pond. Jesselynn gave a jerk, and the fish flew through the air to land with a splat in the grass behind her.

"*Whooa-ee.* Let's do that again." Jumping to her feet, she heard a whoof, much like a big dog. She turned and froze. Her heart thundered in her ears, her mouth dry as cave dust. A black bear rose on his hind legs and whoofed again. He raised his snout, sniffing the air, forepaws relaxed against his chest. The falling rain shimmered like a gauze curtain graying the bear to apparition.

If he doesn't know human smell, he knows fish smell. Only her eyes moved as she measured the distance to the rifle. Without a sound, she pulled the pistol from the holster, all the while keeping her gaze on the bear. When she smelled a rank odor, she knew the wind was protecting her. If she could smell him, he couldn't smell her.

Dear God, keep him blind. Make him go away. Never had any animal looked so big. Surely he was taller even than Wolf.

Her hands shook so she could barely grip the pistol. She'd have to be close enough to smell his breath to kill him with that. But the rifle. One shot she'd have. Would have to be right in the eye. Keeping her mind at work on how to kill the monster freed her feet to ease her to the side. Barely moving, one foot and pause.

The bear continued sniffing, his big head moving from side to side, testing the air currents.

Jesselynn licked her dry lips.

A dog barked from the trail back to the camp. The bear swung in that direction. Jesselynn took two steps and grabbed the rifle, putting the massive tree trunk between her and the bear. The dog barked again, coming closer, growling.

"No! Patch, go back!" She might as well try to stop a waterfall. She stepped from behind the tree. The bear swung back in her direction.

A flash of black and Patch was at him, snarling like he was as big as the bear.

Jesselynn raised the rifle, sighted, and with the muzzle, followed the bear's weaving head.

The bear and dog snarled at each other. Patch dodged under the massive swinging front paws and slashed the bear's rear leg. The bear roared.

Patch danced out of reach, barking all the while.

"Patch! No!" She'd never trained him to "No." Not that she'd had to train him.

The dog charged again. The bear swiped and knocked the dog high in the air. Patch landed with a thump.

"No!"

The bear swung to face her shout. Jesselynn pulled the trigger, and the bear rocked back, half his head gone with the blast. He started toward her.

She drew her pistol and dodged behind the tree again. She listened. No sound but the rain on the leaves above her.

Then a crash. She stepped from behind the tree to see the bear fall face forward, crushing the brush, twitching but not trying to rise.

Jesselynn ran around the brush, leaping an overturned log where the bear had been digging grubs, and searched for her dog.

"Patch!" She screamed his name, listened, and called again. Nothing.

Ten feet farther, Patch lay on his side in the flattened grass, as still as the huge black bear. Jesselynn knelt beside him, tears streaming down her face. "Oh, Patch, not you too."

CHAPTER EIGHTEEN

Jesselynn laid a hand on the dog's ribs.

"Come on, Patch, you can't let a little ol' bear knock the life outa you." She knelt and laid an ear to the same place. Sure enough, though faint, the dog's heart beat on. She wiped away her tears with the back of her hand. "God, you have to save him. He was just trying to save me."

She glared at the bear, half expecting him to rise and charge her again. Back to the dog. Was that a twitch of his eye? The tip of his tail lifted also. Once, twice. She raised his lip to look at his gums. White gums meant internal bleeding, but his teeth gleamed white against pink flesh. "Thank you, Jesus." She felt his legs, looked for blood, none. Pushing gently on his rib cage, she heard a slight crackle. "Ribs. He broke your ribs." She rocked back on her heels to think. "But all we have to do is get you back to camp without poking one through a lung. Even dogs can heal of broken ribs." She kept up the soothing words, not sure who needed them most, her or the dog.

"You wait right here, Patch. I'll be right back." Taking her knife from the sheath on her belt, she rose and returned to the bear, nudging his hind foot to see if he moved. Nothing. No rise and fall of the back. Swiftly she twisted the massive head just enough to reach the neck and, with a slash, left him to bleed out. They couldn't afford to waste the meat, the hide, nor the fat.

"You'll make good soap, you fool critter. All over that measly fish." She glanced skyward to realize that the rain had let up. Now, how to carry Patch and the rifle? She pulled off her cape and laid it on the ground by the dog with the rifle beside him. She folded it over and, kneeling, slid both hands underneath the package.

Patch whimpered, so faint she wouldn't have heard it had she not started to lift him. She pushed to her feet, swaying against the weight. A rhythmic thudding caught her attention. "Horse's hooves. Ah, Patch, help is on the way." She turned to see Jane Ellen, skirts a-flying, riding astride on Dulcie, one of the mares. The colt ran right beside her.

"What happened?" Jane Ellen called over the clop of hooves.

"Bear."

At that same moment the mare scented blood and plowed to a stop. Jane Ellen kept right on going over the mare's neck and flat out to thud on the grass, water causing her to slide before coming to a halt. The colt snorted and retreated behind his dam.

But before Jesselynn could put the dog down and get to Jane Ellen, the girl groaned. She gagged and finally sucked in a breath. "Knocked . . . my . . . breath out." She shook her head and looked up at the mare snorting at the end of the reins still clenched in her fist. "Fool horse."

"Just sit there a minute." Carrying her burden carefully, Jesselynn approached the wild-eyed mare. "Come on, Dulcie, behave yourself."

The mare backed up, dragging on the reins. Jane Ellen rolled over on her belly, glared at the horse, and commanded, "Stop now, you hear me?" She tugged on the reins at the same time, then coughing again, got to her feet. "Nothin's gonna hurt you."

"Patch has broken ribs, so we got to carry him real gentlelike. Thanks for coming."

"We heard the shot, and it took me a minute to catch this stubborn horse." Jane Ellen looked around. "So what happened to the bear?"

"I shot it."

Jane Ellen's eyes widened, her jaw dropped. "Kilt it?"

Patch whimpered again, more strongly this time.

"We'll come back for it. We can use my cape as a sling. You lead the horse and carry this end. I'll take the other and the rifle."

"It weren't a mama bear with cubs, were it?"

"Never saw any." Jesselynn adjusted the sling, and they started off. "Saw the log where it had been eating. Think the blood smell from the fish is what caught its attention."

"You ever eat bear?"

Jesselynn shook her head. "Not a lot of them left in Kentucky, leastways not around Twin Oaks."

"It be right good. Greasy. Good for makin' soap like you started with the lye. My pap used to grease his boots with it too. Kept out the wet real good."

"All I know was it looked like a mountain, standing up sniffing the wind like it did. Then Patch came running and tore off a strip of his hide. That bear near went crazy." Jesselynn stopped walking to shift hands. "When he walloped Patch like he did, why, that dog flew through the air like a rag doll."

Jesselynn shuddered again. "Thank the good Lord he's still alive. He was trying to save me." She swiped at her eyes again and sniffed. "Fool dog."

They stopped several times to rest, and unconcerned now, Dulcie snatched mouthfuls of rich grass. The colt danced around them, inspecting flowers and brush, snorting at something on a branch.

Jane Ellen laughed heartily at the colt's antics. "We got to name him. He can't be called Colt forever."

"He'll be registered as Ahab, with the second name beginning with J—since he's the tenth colt. Ahab's been throwing mostly fillies."

"What about Joker? He is one, you know. Makes us all laugh."

Jesselynn stopped to switch hands again. "Ahab's Joker of Twin Oaks. I like that. A good handle for such a strong colt."

"That the way your daddy kept track of the get?"

"Umm. Long time tradition at Twin Oaks. Haven't used Domino for stud yet. Had planned to be racing him this year. He did all right as a three year old but was a late bloomer. Not much chance for him to race now."

"What they gonna do about the books for registerin' the Thoroughbreds?"

Jesselynn shook her head. "No idea. Not too many Thoroughbreds left in the South, that's for sure. Lot of the Northern studs were stripped too, I imagine. Those officers like fine horses to ride on." The thought of all the slaughtered horseflesh made her skin crawl. Men at least had a choice. The poor animals had no option but to go where their rider wanted. She watched Joker leap in the air and take off, his brush tail a flag in the breeze. *Thank God, I got you all out of there. We at least have something to start over with when that vile war does finally cease.*

"It can't go on forever, can it?"

"What?"

"The war. Seems they're going on until all the men and horses are dead, nothing left to fight with."

"Jesse comin'." Thaddeus yelled loud enough to be heard across the meadow.

"He can call you Jesselynn now, can't he?" Jane Ellen stopped to get her breath. "Never thought this dog could weigh so much. He ain't that big."

"Got a mighty big heart, though."

"Easy now." Jesselynn cautioned Thaddeus as he ran up to them. "Patch is hurt right bad."

"What happen?" Thaddeus eyed the sling. "He alive?"

"Yes, a bear took a swipe at him. You go get Ophelia."

Thaddeus took off as fast as his legs would pump. " 'Phelia, come help." He stumbled over something, got back up, and kept on running.

By the time they reached the entrance to the cave, Ophelia, waddling behind her big belly, met them, shaking her turbaned head. "A bear? Thaddeus say a bear."

"He's dead. Let's lay Patch on a pallet by the fire. Bear broke his ribs, or hitting the ground did."

Ophelia reached for Jane Ellen's side of the sling. "Go ask Aunt Agatha for strips to wrap him ribs. Bestest way to help."

"Thaddeus, where's Meshach?"

"Gone."

"Where?"

Thaddeus pointed up toward the hills. "To woods."

"Him went lookin' for wood for de rake. Need hardwood, him say."

"Wonderful." All the men were gone.

Jane Ellen came back with a roll of narrow strips of cloth.

After telling them all what happened, Jesselynn and Ophelia knelt on the sandy cave floor, and with gentle fingers, wrapped the strips around the dog's rib cage, tight enough to hold broken ribs in place but not so tight he couldn't breathe.

"Thaddeus, get Patch a bowl of warm water."

Someone dipped for him, and Thaddeus carried the bowl back, both hands cupped firmly on the side, his tongue firmly clamped between his teeth. The water sloshed as he set it down by the dog's muzzle.

"Drink, Patch." He stroked the white ear. "Please, Patch, drink."

"Here, like this." Jesselynn dripped some of the water on the side of Patch's muzzle. He licked it away. Thaddeus repeated her action.

"Look, he likes it." He drizzled more and giggled when Patch quickly licked his fingers.

"Good. Let off awhile and let him sleep, then do the same again until he can drink from the bowl." Jesselynn stood and stretched. "We've got to get that bear back here before some varmint comes in and takes it." But how to get the carcass up on a wagon?

"We could use one of the canvases to drag it on." Jane Ellen followed Jesselynn toward the mouth of the cave.

"Good idea. Let's yoke up a span of oxen. They won't be so flighty with the smell. You go get them, and I'll get the canvas. We'll set the yoke together."

"You need some more help?" Mrs. McPhereson met them in front of the cave. "I can get Mrs. Jones too."

Jesselynn noticed the omission of Aunt Agatha. Far as she knew or seemed to care, the bear might have gotten her. "Thanks, I'd appreciate that." When the others left to do their part, Jesselynn stood shaking her head. *What will it take, Lord? We can't go on like this forever. You say to forgive as we have been forgiven. How do I forgive someone who won't even look me in the eye, let alone talk with me? This is beyond me. You're going to have to fix it. And I'd appreciate it done soon. Life's too short to carry noxious things like this.* At the remembered sight of the bear standing upright, its heavy head swinging from side to side testing the air for scents, her mouth dried again. If that didn't bring on nightmares, not much else would anymore.

Within minutes they were striding out across the meadow to the creek and around the rock face to the pond.

Jesselynn had to tell her story one more time, since Darcy Jones hadn't heard it. Ophelia pronounced, "De Lawd done take good care of her."

"Wait until the men hear about this. They'll never let us go beyond the creek." Mrs. Jones hefted the saw over her shoulder.

"Just make sure you don't go without a gun. And don't let it get out of arm's reach. That's where I made a big mistake. I leaned it up against the tree behind me. Never again, no matter how cumbersome."

Three turkey vultures, their red heads naked of feathers, lifted off from where the carcass lay in the grass and low brush. Ravens scattered, their hoarse voices scolding at the intrusion.

"Good thing we didn't wait. They've announced the kill to the entire forest." Jesselynn stopped the oxen a ways away. "Let them graze while we dress the bear out."

Knives and saw in hand, the women approached the bear.

"He's so big." Jane Ellen stopped, her eyes as big as her voice sounded small.

"You should have seen him standing." Jesselynn stood over the carcass. "Let's roll him over. Can't be much different than dressing an elk."

"Look at his claws." Mrs. Mac hefted a forepaw.

"And teeth." Jane Ellen stepped backwards. "I never seen anythin' so fierce."

"Can we eat him?" Mrs. Jones wrinkled her nose. "He smells rank."

"Bear meat is good. My pa brought some home." Jane Ellen ran her hand over the fur. "Be a good hide."

Jesselynn sharpened her skinning knife on the whetstone she'd brought along, yet still, sawing through the hide took time, even on the tender underbelly. As soon as she'd slit the belly, the others dug in to help her. By the time they'd gutted the beast, they were all dripping wet, though the rain had stopped and a breeze now swept across the pond.

"The wind is keeping the mosquitoes down at least." Mrs. Mac sat back on her heels and wiped her forehead with the back of her hand, leaving a streak of blood across it. Her bleached calico sunbonnet hung down her back out of the way.

"Do we want to wash these intestines like we do a pig for sausage?"

"I don't know. Might be different for meat eaters. We used them from the buffalo and the elk." Jesselynn turned her head away to get a breath of fresh air. "And to think that all I wanted was fresh fish for supper."

"You got a nice perch over there." Jane Ellen nodded toward the bank where Jesselynn had been fishing. "You want I should try for some more?"

"Why not." Jesselynn untied the pouch with worms from her belt and handed it to her. "No sense letting the worms go to waste. The pole I cut is right there too."

The three women finished cleaning up the carcass and, leaving the hide on to protect the meat, rolled the bear onto the canvas. They lashed the two sides together and across the end to form a pouch, tied the open end to the single tree, and started the oxen back to camp.

"Come on, Jane Ellen, no one is staying out here alone again."

"Just one more? They're biting like . . . like . . ."

"Come on." Jesselynn turned to Mrs. Mac. "You start on back, and I reckon we'll catch up before you get to the caves."

Taking the rifle with her, Jesselynn strolled on over to lean against the tree. Jane Ellen jerked the pole, and a fish flew back. Jesselynn ducked.

"You nearly got me."

"Sorry. I never had so much fun fishin' in my entire life." Jane Ellen dug in the pouch, turned it inside out, and shook her head. "Out of worms." She sighed and crossed her arms on her knees. "Right purty place, isn't it?"

"Sure enough is. No wonder Wolf remembered it."

"He and his daddy stayed here one winter, right?" Jane Ellen wrapped the string around the pole, then leaned forward and pulled her forked branch lined with fish out of the water. She held it up for Jesselynn to see. "You want to help carry 'em?"

Meshach was the only man in camp when they returned; he'd just come back with several cottonwood trunks and branches, which were now leaning against the cave wall. He helped unwrap the bear and whistled his surprise. Looking up at Jesselynn, he shook his head slowly, as if he couldn't believe what he saw.

"I be thinkin' you got some story to tell. Wait till Wolf see dis."

For a second Jesselynn froze. Would Wolf be angry? After all, it wasn't like she'd gone hunting; she'd just done what he'd always told her. Be prepared to shoot, and when you shoot, shoot to kill.

"We better hang dis in back of de cave where it's cooler."

"How?"

"Put up a bar, I be thinkin'."

"Have we anything strong enough to hold 'im?" While she talked, Jesselynn disengaged the oxen and loosed them to rejoin the herd.

"Mebbe one trunk I bring in." He ducked into the cave and brought out a stout trunk. "I get de brace up."

"Good, and we'll skin him and cut off the head and paws."

They all set to their jobs, and by the time the hunters returned, the bear was hanging in the back of the cave. Aunt Agatha was frying fish for supper, and Mrs. Mac was making corn pones from cornmeal, flour, bacon fat, and water. She patted them together and laid them in the frying pan to sizzle in more bacon grease.

Wolf had a deer thrown across the back of his horse, as did Benjamin.

"*More* skinnin'." Jane Ellen and Mrs. Jones looked at each other and shook their heads.

"More skinnin'?" Wolf turned from untying the deer.

Jesselynn kept from smiling. "Nice deer." She touched the four prongs on the antlers. "These will come in handy."

Benjamin looked at Wolf, then around the circle of women and back to Wolf. Meshach turned away.

"Need more bars."

Wolf narrowed his eyes and, after lowering the deer to the ground, looked full at his wife. "What is goin' on?"

Jesselynn shrugged. "Nothing now."

"Now?"

She shrugged. "Well, we got him all skinned and hung. And just in time, looks like, since you brought in more. I reckon we're going to be doing a lot of smoking, that's for certain sure."

"Keep those little boys breakin' kindlin'." Jane Ellen kept a straight face too. Mrs. Mac turned away, a cough covering her laughter.

"Think I'll go help Ophelia." Mrs. Jones scurried into the cave like something was after her.

"Jesselynn, I got me a feeling . . ." Wolf took one step toward her.

"Well, Mr. Wolf, he's only a little bear." Jesselynn rolled her lips together.

"A bear. Meshach shot a bear?"

"No, sir." She stuck her hands in her pockets and studied the design her boot toe sketched in the dirt.

"Who shot the bear?" His voice deepened.

"Me." She shrugged and looked up at him from under her lashes.

His face wore that cut-granite look she knew meant trouble.

"I had the rifle along, and the bear smelt the fish, I think, and Patch came charging to the rescue, and I shot the bear before he could finish off Patch, and so we"—she indicated the women with a sweep of her hand—"gutted him and Meshach hung him, and . . ." She felt impaled to the cave wall by his stare.

"Supper ready," Thaddeus called from the mouth of the cooking cave. "Wolf, you back."

"The rest of you go on and eat. We'll be there in a moment."

"Should we wait grace?" Meshach shoved the stick he'd been carving through the tendons on the rear legs of one of the deer and threw it over his shoulder with a grunt. "I hang dis."

"No, yes . . ." Wolf shook his head. "Show me the bear, Mrs. Torstead. Perhaps we should name you She Who Kills Bear." He slung his arm over her shoulder, and they entered the cave. "Thank God, you are safe. Shooting a bear. And here I thought I left you safe in camp."

"All I did was go fishing."

Chapter Nineteen

Richmond, Virginia

Dear Jesselynn, Thaddeus, and all the others,

I am writing a quick letter so you can be aware of what is going on here. I'm sure Carrie Mae has written to tell of her beautiful little daughter. They named her after our mother and Jefferson's, Miriam Amelia. Carrie Mae had a fairly easy birthing, even though to hear her you'd think she was in labor for all of August instead of only hours. But little Miriam is precious, and I go to see her as often as I can. Would that it were more so, but we had a major crisis here. Aunt Sylvania suffered a minor apoplexy that scared us all, especially her. But she is recovering well, and we are all grateful. Our new kitten, named Bones by one of our guests, is her delight.

I must tell you that I am concerned about Zachary. Please pray that he not turn his back on his Christian upbringing. I know Mama and Daddy are beseeching our Father before the throne, but I covet all earthly prayers too. He has become so cynical, I hardly recognize him any longer. Yet, every so often he's as nice as can be. I just don't know what to do about him.

Our boys here at the house are sewing and knitting for those still on the march.

I must tell you that Zachary and I are making another trip. Each one stretches my faith as I pray for our Father's protection, both for us and for those at home.

Oh, sister, I want this despicable war over and done with, so we may get on with our lives. I want to go home, no matter how damaged Twin Oaks is. We received a letter from Lucinda saying the taxes are due. How can they levy taxes on those who have given so much for the cause of the South? I struggle with this like the straw that broke this woman's back. Zachary has said he will take care of it, but since he has said nothing further, I have my doubts there too. The thought of losing Twin Oaks is intolerable. My heart bleeds again and again, until I fear I shall have nothing left to give. How much can our Lord expect of us? I know the answer—He has said we will never be tried beyond our strength. But, enough of my whining.

How are all of you? Where are you? I am so anxious for a letter from you. How big is Thaddeus now? I pray you tell him about us and our lives at Twin Oaks, so he knows whereof he came.

We all send our love and our prayers, as I know you pray for us. Someday we will all live together again at Twin Oaks in dear Kentucky. Lord bless and keep you, my dear sister and brother.

I know I am including love from all the others here.

A tear just missed blotting the page as she signed her name and let the ink dry while she addressed the envelope.

With the letter ready to send, she blew out the lamp and climbed into bed. Any day now and she and Zachary would be on the road.

"We'll do a grieving mother and father this time, using a coffin again and that false-bottomed buggy. I've had a foot carved to fit in a boot so it won't be so obvious I've lost mine." Zachary had made plans for another trip to the North.

"Where will we be going?"

"Washington."

Louisa flinched inside. She still had nightmares about the time Zachary was missing. All alone in that hotel, not knowing if he were alive or dead, captured or shot for treason.

She hadn't heard from her friend Mrs. Hinklen, who'd come south to retrieve her husband's body. He'd died of injuries during one of the battles. Talking with her had made Louisa realize that Northern women and Southern women suffered the same thing in losing their men to the war. Mrs. Hinklen hated the war as much as Louisa.

But her husband had done his duty, just as had Louisa's father and brothers.

If only it were over, and they could all go home.

"Zachary, have you heard anything regarding the taxes on Twin Oaks?" The question popped out before she had time to think it through.

The look he gave her said quite clearly that she should stay out of men's affairs. She'd learned to read that look well.

"You know what?" She leaned forward, staring him right in the eye. "Twin Oaks is my home too, and I have every right to inquire about it." She made each word distinct and forced herself to not draw back.

"You know, dear sister . . ."

She refused to flinch at the sarcasm.

"You are sounding more like Jesselynn every day. Mother would chide you for becoming so unfeminine."

Louisa stared him right back. "Be that as it may, dear brother . . ." Two could play at that game. "But if I waited around for men to do for me, we would starve here, along with our guests." She kept her voice low so their guests wouldn't hear them. *And considering you have not contributed one dollar to the upkeep of this house, you do not have a lot you can say.* Surely they were paying him for working in the law office, but he had never mentioned how much or when. Another very unchristian thought flitted through her head, made a hairpin turn, and returned to roost.

What was he doing with his money? Had he paid the taxes? Had he even written a letter in response to the one Lucinda had sent them? When he said he would deal with it, she had trusted him to do so. No longer was she so certain that was wise.

Lord, if I can't trust my own brother, whom can I trust? But she knew the answer there too. As her mother always said, *"In God alone do I put my trust."*

Now the real question. *Do I?* She heard herself arguing, or rather remonstrating, with herself as if she were another person standing back and eavesdropping on a conversation.

"You will be ready?" Zachary's question stopped her internal discussion. His voice had softened.

"Yes."

"Making you look old enough will be difficult."

A compliment. Zachary had paid her a compliment. Veiled or not, one had to take compliments when offered.

"Thank you, dear, I will manage." Now how would she tell Carrie Mae that she would be gone?

"But where are you going? I need you here." Carrie Mae stared at her sister as if she had left a portion of her mind at home.

"Carrie Mae Highwood, er, Steadly, some of us have more important things to do than wait on you hand and foot."

Carrie Mae slumped as though she'd been slugged in her still-tender midsection. Tears sprung from her eyes like downspouts after a rainstorm.

Even though Louisa knew Carrie Mae could put on tears

as easily as she put on a shawl, she felt as if she'd tried to drown a kitten.

"I'm sorry, dear, but I must do this. I'll be back as soon as I can, and—"

"It's that dumb old war again, I just know it. I am so sick and tired of hearing about the war I could throw up." The baby let out a wail. "Now see what you've done."

Louisa hid a smile. While she wasn't the one who'd been shouting, she knew her sister well enough to know who would get the blame. "I'm sorry." Louisa walked through the archway and picked her niece up from the basket where she slept. "There now, sugar, you don't need to cry. How long since you fed her?"

"Two hours or so. She's like a little pig, eating constantly. That's all I do, feed the baby, change the baby, feed the baby. I feel like an old milk cow." Carrie Mae threw herself down on the sofa.

Louisa nuzzled the now quiet infant. "Ah, you precious little one, if only your grandmother were alive to see you. She loved babies so." She looked up to see her sister mop away tears. At the bereft look on Carrie Mae's face, Louisa knew they were thinking the same thing. Some days, even after these years she'd been gone, the ache to see their mother again cut clear to the heart.

Louisa crossed the polished floor to sit beside her sister. "I'd stay home if I could."

"I know that. Forgive my childish tantrum. I . . . I just didn't realize babies took so much time, and I'm tired clear to the bone. Jefferson suggested a wet nurse, and now I'm beginning to think I made a mistake in refusing him." She glanced at her daughter, who was now engaged in conversation with her aunt. She watched in silence. "You are so good with her."

Louisa turned to look at her sister. "So are you."

"I get impatient."

"I didn't have to get up with her every two hours during the night. Why don't you feed her and go take a nap? I'll stay awhile."

"No, I'd rather visit with you." When the baby screwed up her face, Carrie Mae picked up a blanket to throw over her shoulder and unbuttoned her waist. "Can Elise get you anything?"

"No thanks." Louisa watched as Carrie Mae set her daughter to nursing, all the while smiling and whispering to the baby.

"Lucinda would say she's sweet as sugar and pretty as a rose."

"I know. I always thought I would have my babies at Twin Oaks. Funny, I never thought I would have to go with my husband wherever he lived. Just never entered my mind." She smiled at Louisa. "Life certainly is different than we dreamed, isn't it?"

Back at Aunt Sylvania's, working on her disguise, Louisa kept thinking about Carrie Mae's comment. Sometimes the only thing that kept her going was the thought that God knew what was happening and was not surprised. No matter how severely her world was torn apart, He was still in control. *Lord, help me to remember that, no matter what.*

Louisa reminded herself that God was in control when she and Zachary climbed into their rather odoriferous buggy.

She reminded herself again when the Union officer studied their papers. One of her prayers had been answered. He wasn't the same man who had passed them through on the earlier trip.

Union uniforms painted Washington blue. From the troops camped to the south of the city to the officers who took part in the life of the capital, one could not step out the door without seeing uniforms.

As Zachary and Louisa drove to a house in the northern outskirts, heads turned away at the putrid effluence of their coffin. Riding with the foul odor so long had deadened their sensitivities, so they could look suitably grief stricken. Pepper in her handkerchief helped as before. Red eyes only added to her appearance of age.

"Zachary, dear, I keep getting the feeling someone is watching us." Louisa had hesitated to say anything, for due to the stench, many watched them.

"I think not. I've been observing carefully." Zachary tied the reins to the whip handle, and using the armrest and his crutch, carefully lowered himself to the ground.

"Don't go lookin' around like you are frightened or some such." He barely moved his lips while giving instructions.

"I know." She climbed from her side of the buggy and followed her brother up the walk. Staying at a hotel had been hard enough but with strangers would be worse.

Zachary knocked at the door that had missed a few paint jobs, as had the porch. A curtain dropped back into place, the only indication someone was home. Within moments the door opened, and a man in a black coat and trousers invited them in.

"Were you followed?" His first words sent ripples chilling up Louisa's back.

"No, at least not that I could detect. Why would anyone follow me?"

"Just bein' careful. We have the box ready to transfer. I will take your buggy inside my barn and do so while the two of you have a bite to eat. Then you must be on your way again."

Without even a night's sleep? Louisa wished her brother would look at her so she could question him. But he ignored her, keeping his attention on their host.

"That will be fine. Perhaps you have a place my wife could rest and wash a bit?"

"Of course, follow me."

Louisa did as asked and was shown into a bedroom with a pitcher of water set on the commode. When their host left the room, she sank gratefully down on the bed and removed her hat. After using the necessary, she washed her hands and face, brushed her hair, and wound it back in a bun. Lying down on the bed, she closed her eyes, sinking into the softness of the feather bed. The night before had been spent at an inn where the only available bed had been boards with a thin pallet. Her shoulder still ached.

"Mrs. Highwood, are you ready?" The voice came far too soon, but Louisa answered yes. She rose, tucked stray wisps of hair into the bun, donned her hat, and after straightening the bed, left the room.

Zachary met her at the front door, their host beside him with a basket over his arm.

"I dislike hurrying you off like this, but we have been informed we must leave this house and find another immediately."

Louisa took the basket. Chills raced each other up and down her spine like a hawk after chickens. One look at her brother's face and the mask covering it, and she knew he was as edgy about the situation as she. Why, then, had they been sent here?

"I'm sorry there was no time to inform you of any changes." The man hustled them out the door and into the buggy. "If I were you, I would go further north and west before heading south."

"Thank you. All is loaded as needed?"

"Yes, and Godspeed."

Louisa climbed into the buggy and waited for Zachary to accomplish the same. But when he clucked the horse into a trot down the street with no difficulty, she let herself rest against the back of the seat.

The odor seemed even more pervasive.

Zachary threaded their way among the wagons, buggies, and riders clogging the streets, making Louisa wonder how he could possibly find their way.

They spent the night at an inn and left again early in the morning. A drizzle grayed the road and set the trees to dripping. At one point they pulled off the road and watched a battalion of Union soldiers pass with fully loaded provision wagons and wagons with red crosses painted on their sideboards. If only they could appropriate the supplies therein, but instead she kept her head down, handkerchief to her nose. Since no one gave them a second glance, they followed some distance behind until they met the Union lines.

"Halt!" A young soldier, rifle across his chest, stepped into the roadway.

Zachary dug in his breast coat pocket and held out his papers. "We are taking our son home to be buried." He enunciated clearly, sounding as Northern as possible.

"And where is that?" The man folded the papers and handed them back.

"Not far down the road, at Manassas."

"I've been instructed to have all civilians vetted by my superior officer. You will have to come with me."

Louisa felt her stomach tighten, then loosen, like a snake preparing to strike. *Please, God.* She looked up with tear-filled eyes.

"Please, as you can smell, we must get him home, or we

will have to bury him along the road." One sniff of her hand-kerchief and the tears ran.

"I'm sorry, ma'am, orders is orders." He beckoned to another to take his place at guard and motioned them forward.

They stopped in front of an officer's tent.

"Please leave your buggy and come inside."

"My poor husband has a difficult time getting out of the buggy. Is it possible for us to talk out here?"

"One moment." He disappeared in the tent.

"Do not say any more than necessary." Zachary spoke without moving his lips.

The young man returned. "Sorry, ma'am. Follow me, please."

Louisa controlled the shaking of her hands with the greatest effort. She stumbled as she stepped down, but the soldier caught her arm before she fell.

"Easy there, ma'am."

She recognized the discomfort in his face and voice at forcing them to do this. Knowing how old and frail they appeared, she let herself lean on his arm, then rounded the buggy to assist Zachary.

As they hobbled into the tent, the officer behind a desk looked up and commanded, "Search their buggy."

Chapter Twenty

"Sir, the body . . ." Louisa dabbed at her eyes with her handkerchief and the tears rose immediately. "Our son . . ." Her sniff was as genuine as her fear. "The smell is . . . is bad. Has . . . has he not been through enough?"

"Ma'am, we've seen enough war that the sight of one more decomposing body won't be a shock."

No, but what isn't in that box may be. She turned and hid her face on her brother's shoulder, the sobs real.

"Now, dear, please, don't carry on so." Zachary patted her back with the stump of his arm. "Now see what you've done." He shook his head sadly. "Too much. This has all been too much." His voice sounded old and feeble, as if the very life were being drained from him also.

"Here, both of you, have a seat. This won't take but a few moments, and you can be on your way." The officer, who wore the maple leaf of his rank, motioned to two chairs to the side of his field desk.

Oh, God, please make them blind or willing to accept the coffin for what it is. Please help us. Louisa could hardly sit for the shaking, her prayers skittering through her mind like desiccated cottonwood leaves before a winter wind.

"Sir." One of the men beckoned the major from the tent door. He nodded to the two of them and left.

Louisa closed her eyes. They were discovered. She knew it with every bone in her body.

When the major reentered the tent, the look on his face said it all. No longer a hint of apology, but now the steel of accusation.

"Put these two under arrest for running contraband. And bury that raccoon. He has more than served his purpose."

Zachary sat straight in his chair, one arm resting on his crutch.

The major took his seat and leaned slightly forward, his voice soft but laced with steel. "Now, would you like to tell me who you *really* are?" He glanced down at their papers on the desk in front of him. "I believe Mr. and Mrs. Tyler to be as false as that body out there."

"Captain Zachary Highwood, Confederate States of America, discharged due to war injuries. This is my sister, Miss Louisa Highwood. The contraband, as you call it, is quinine and morphine, not for resale, not for pleasure, but to ease the suffering of men who fought nobly."

"I see." The major leaned back in his folding chair, one arm cocked over the leather back. "So after fighting you Southerns for every hill and valley, I should now alleviate your suffering?"

"Some of them are your men too. Cannonballs show no partiality."

"So you can send them to rot in Libby Prison or Andersonville?" Narrowed eyes glared across the distance.

Zachary shrugged. "If we have nothing to care for our own, how can we care for yours? Besides, many prisoners are paroled almost as soon as they arrive."

"Take them away." The major waved at the young man standing at attention at the open tent flaps. "And put them in separate quarters. Manacled wrists."

"For both?" The rosy-cheeked young man raised an eyebrow.

"Both."

204

He used his rifle to indicate they should precede him.

Louisa went out first, followed by Zachary, the young soldier, and another who fell in beside them. Both soldiers held their rifles at the ready.

What? They think we shall run? Zachary hardly able to walk and me looking like a woman far beyond her prime, older even than Aunt Sylvania? Louisa tottered some for good effect, not that anything they said or did would make any difference.

Spies were shot. She would argue they weren't spies, only angels of mercy, but she had a feeling the major would hardly accept that.

Shame such a fine-looking man had been so harsh.

As if it would be easier were he ugly? The little voice snickered. *What are you doing noticing he is a fine-looking man? He's the enemy.*

Louisa turned into the tent indicated and sat down on the cot.

"Sorry, ma'am." Another soldier entered. "Please hold out your hands."

Louisa did as requested, a knot forming in her stomach as the iron manacles were snapped about her slender wrists. The sound of it sent waves of horror rolling through her body. She stared up at the blue-clad man in front of her. "Is this really necessary?" Her voice cracked, her throat so dry she couldn't have spit if ordered.

"Only obeying orders, ma'am." He dipped his head, a mere sketch of good manners, and left, dropping the tent flap behind him.

Any semblance of breeze died with the dimness. And with the heat trapped in the tent, her fear rose from a mewling kitten to a roaring tiger.

Oh, Lord, no matter how much I look forward to heaven, I'm not ready to leave this earth yet. What about those at Aunt Syl-

vania's, and Jesselynn? Please, Lord, I want to see her again. I want to see Twin Oaks. I want to be married and have babies. God help me, I don't want to be shot. I can't do this, Lord, I can't. The manacles weighted her hands like the fear weighted her heart. She curled up on the coarse blanket that covered the cot into a shivering ball in spite of the heat.

What have they done with Zachary? The thought brought the tears from her heart to her face. He'd already been through so much. Why should he have to face a firing squad? *Why, God, why? He says he is only doing his duty. And Lord, I was trying to follow your precepts, caring for the wounded.* She didn't need to use her peppered handkerchief; the tears flowed no matter how much she tried to staunch them.

A soldier with brushy whiskers brought her food on a tray but said not a word and refused to look her in the eye. When she held out her hands so he could take off the manacles, he looked the other way and left the tent.

"At least they gave me a fork." Louisa eyed the bowl, then the distance between her hands. No room for manners here, no napkin, nothing to drink. *So I won't eat,* she thought, then canceled that immediately. If there was to be any chance of escaping, she would need every bit of strength she could summon.

Escape, what a silly thought. Zachary cannot escape, and I surely won't go without him. But the stew caught in her throat, making her gag and wish for a drink.

By dark, her stomach growled and twisted. The smell of cooking fires and food teased her nostrils. *If you want something, get off this bed and go ask for it, you ninny.* Food she could do without but not water.

She tried arranging her hair, but the chain caught in a wayward tress, and she flinched. She finally pulled her hands free, stifling a yelp in the process. Instead of neatening her hair, she brushed off the front of her black skirt and aged yellowing waist and forced herself to not lie back down and hide.

When she opened the tent flap, the length of a rifle stopped her from moving farther. "Excuse me, but would it be possible for me to have a drink of water, please?" She almost neglected the please but reminded herself that she was a lady, no matter the treatment she received. Her mother's voice had comforted her in the long hours of her confinement. She could hear her quoting Scripture clear as if she were right here in the tent with her. *"Blessed are they which are persecuted for righteousness' sake: for theirs is the kingdom of heaven."*

In her case, righteousness was a matter of point of view.

"Let me ask the major."

"For water?" Her voice squeaked. She heard him move off, but the clearing of a throat made her aware someone else had taken his place.

A few minutes later a water jug was slipped through the tent flaps.

"Thank you. You are most kind." Ah, how sweet she could speak, honey more sweet than sugar in her tone.

No answer.

Had they been ordered not to talk with her, or was this normal for captives?

After drinking, another need became obvious.

"I'm sorry to bother you again." She almost choked on the words. Anger was fast replacing fear. If she was condemned after all, what was the need for civility? "But the afternoon has been long, and I sincerely need to use the . . . the facilities." How more specific could she be?

"I'll ask the major." A different voice, more gruff.

A few minutes later a chamber pot appeared at the tent door.

"Thank you."

No response.

The next day passed much the same. By the time the sun hit the zenith, her temper had reached the boiling point.

"Excuse me, but I demand to see the major or whoever is in charge."

A mumbled discussion followed, and again she could hear someone walk away.

Oh, Mama, my mouth has gotten me in trouble again. You would not be proud of me now. She looked down at her clothing, wanting nothing more than a cloth and water to wash with, a brush for her hair, and a breeze. *Oh, dear Lord, what I would give for a bit of breeze.*

The tent opened, and a hand beckoned her out. Feeling all eyes were on her, she followed the pole-straight back to the major's tent.

"Good afternoon, Miss Highwood." The major pointed to a chair.

Louisa elected to stand. Knowing how shabby she appeared, she straightened her spine and raised her chin. "Major . . ." She paused, hoping he would fill in his name. Referring to him as "Major" seemed in her mind to give him more importance than she desired he be given.

He cocked an eyebrow, waited, then finally supplied his name. "Major James Dorsey."

Insolent, bluebellied . . . She cut off the string of names, fearing she may say more than she should.

"Major Dorsey, is there some reason you are treating me with such contempt? Surely there are rules for dealing with prisoners."

"Yes, there are. Spies may be shot at will."

She tried to breathe around the punch to her stomach and sought the chair instead.

"Then I believe we are having a problem with semantics. I am not a spy. My brother is not a spy. We are not carrying messages of any sort, only succor for injured men."

"Miss Highwood, did you or did you not pick up your contraband at . . ." He named the address of the house they'd been to.

"Why, yes, but only morphine and quinine." She kept her head high.

"You are certain no messages were passed on to your brother?"

Louisa thought to the time she'd spent lying down. Zachary had not been with her.

He fingered a piece of paper on the desk before him. An envelope lay beside it. "Does this look at all familiar?" He held it up.

Louisa shook her head. "No, not at all."

"This is not a letter from your sister?"

Louisa knew she'd been trapped. "How can I tell? I have not read the letter."

He handed it across the desk.

She let the chain of her manacles clank on the wooden desk top as she reached for the letter. Her gaze dropped to the bottom. The signature read, "Your loving sister." No way was this Jesselynn's handwriting. And glancing quickly through the message, it didn't make any sense.

She looked at the envelope. No return address. No, this was not from Jesselynn, and who the writer was, Louisa had no idea.

"You don't recognize it, do you?" Was there a note of sadness in his voice?

Louisa looked up, tried to come up with a lie, and shook her head.

"We'll be leaving for Washington in the morning. Corporal, show Miss Highwood to her quarters."

Louisa held her head high until the tent flap dropped behind her.

Zachary, what have you done now? She collapsed on the cot. *Oh, Lord, how will you get us out of this one?*

CHAPTER TWENTY-ONE

Zachary wasn't really a spy, was he?

Riding in the back of a wagon with a soldier between them kept Louisa from questioning her brother.

Tarnation. If only she could ask him about the letter. Surely there was a reasonable explanation.

The gray look Louisa saw on Zachary's face as she was helped into the wagon let her know his accommodations had been no better than hers, most likely more severe. Not shaving for three days added to his disheveled appearance, and she was certain he thought much the same of her. While they'd attempted to look old, now they looked dirty along with it. She'd never worn the same underthings this long in her life, and picking a flea off her skin this morning told her what made her itch. All over. She most likely had picked up a few lice too.

The thought made her shudder.

If only I could have a bath. Hot water had never before seemed so precious. And soap. *All those things you've taken for granted,* she scolded herself. *If nothing else comes of this, perhaps you will be more grateful.* Keeping her mind on such mundane matters kept her from thinking the darker thoughts that sent her mind into a black hole of fear, peopled with specters of despair.

Her shin itched. Her mother would have said a lady never, ever, scratched in public. Right at that moment, Louisa was no longer sure she cared what her mother had said. If only she could talk with Zachary. She shifted on the hard boards. The wagon hit a bump, and she figured she now had a bruise that would only get worse on the trip to Washington, considering the state of the roads.

A tune ran through her mind, "My Old Kentucky Home." She leaned back against the boards with a slight smile. *Ah, Kentucky home. Lord, please help us make it that long.* All she'd ever heard about how spies were treated made release doubtful. *But I will not doubt, Lord. I believe you can protect us. I believe you will protect us. I don't know how, but you kept Daniel from burning in the lions' den.* She stopped. No, He kept Daniel from burning in the fiery furnace and from being eaten in the lions' den. She sighed, shaking her head. *Keep your stories right,* she chided herself, then sighed again. Here she was on a prison wagon to Washington, trying to keep track of Bible stories she learned at her mother's knee. If only she could talk with Jesselynn. *Lord, I want to see my sister again. Father, how do I keep the fear from eating me alive? Jesus. Jesus. Jesus.* Only repeating his name kept the terror at bay.

Another bump, strong enough to throw her against the guard. The leer he gave her shuddered up her spine. She pulled as far away as her manacles would allow. Besides, he smelled riper than their discarded raccoon.

She wished she could melt into a puddle when they entered Washington. She kept her gaze on the tailgate of the wagon, looking neither to the right nor left.

When they pulled up in front of the prison, the major climbed over the wagon wheel and stepped to the ground, signaling the driver to take the wagon on through the heavily barred gate that swung open just for them. The look he gave her made her skin ripple, much like the thought of lice had.

I was just doing what needed to be done, she wanted to tell him. *Just like you are.*

The gate clanged behind them, sending a scream of despair echoing through her mind. *Lord, save us!*

The guard leaned closer to her. "You'll like it here, missy. They takes good care of female prisoners." His chuckle made her want to shrivel up and disappear. Would she be thrown in a cell with all the men, or was there a separate place for women? Surely there would be. *Oh, Lord, surely.* She gritted her teeth. *I will trust you, O Lord. I am trusting you, Jesus, in your precious name.* Only repeating those words kept her from screaming.

The driver wrapped the reins around the brake handle and leaped to the ground, coming around to let down the tailgate.

"Come on, you two vermin." The guard they were manacled to scooted to the end of the wagon, dragging them along with him.

Louisa sneaked a peek at her brother only to see his mouth set in a straight line, bracketed by commas of pain. She reared back against the pressure on her wrist, dragging the guard off-balance.

He cursed at her, turning with tobacco juice spitting from his snarl.

But her stunt took the pressure off Zachary, allowing him to move more at his own crablike pace.

She reached over with her free hand and grabbed his crutch, dragging it behind her. Her wrist felt as though she'd held it above a flame.

The driver took Zachary by the arm, and between the two men, they jerked him to his feet where he sagged between them.

"Give him his crutch, you sorry excuses for men!" Louisa deliberately rammed the handle of the crutch into her tormentor's side as she reached around him to hand it to Zachary.

A slight grunt helped her endure the savage jerk on her wrist that sent her to her knees.

The driver snarled at both of them and dug in his pocket for the key. "You take her. I'll keep this'un."

"My pleasure."

Louisa read the full meaning of the word *lascivious* in the look her guard gave her. She felt stripped, as if she stood shivering in her bloomers, or less. She stared around, searching, pleading for someone to come to her rescue. Two men leaning against a wall laughed. A prisoner shouted from a barred window above them.

Another answered.

The guard jerked her in front of him wrapping his free arm around her chest.

"Keep it up, girlie, I likes it when you squirm." If his words hadn't frozen her, his breath would have.

Louisa willed herself to hold perfectly still. The pressure across her breast made her want to scream, but she swallowed the horror.

"Little, that's enough!" The major's order cut through the air.

Little released Louisa with a curse, muttering softly so that his commanding officer couldn't hear him.

"We are not animals, Little, so don't act like one."

Louisa sucked in a breath and then another, anything to deny the blackness hovering near the edge of her mind. She clutched her dignity like a staff, sketched a nod of appreciation to the major, and shivered in spite of air so thick with humidity she could scarcely breathe.

Thank you, Lord, thank you. She wanted to shout the words, but her lips were so clamped against the roiling in her stomach, she didn't dare move them.

"Unlock her."

"Yes, sir."

Even during the unlocking, Little managed to rub his upper arm against her breast. Without thought, Louisa stamped her heel down on his toes and flinched back as he raised his hand to strike her.

"Little!"

The order stopped the guard in midswing. He jerked the manacle off her wrist with a snarl, drawing blood.

Louisa wrapped her fingers around the deep scratch to staunch the bleeding. She took two steps back to get out of his breathing range and swallowed hard again. The blackness hovered, leering as wickedly as Little.

"Come with me." Major Dorsey touched her elbow.

Louisa blinked and clamped her arm against her side, her other hand still protecting her wrist. What in the world was the matter with her now? One man ripped her wrist, and a touch from the major made her elbow burn.

"Wh-what have you done with my brother?"

The major nodded to a soldier who opened another door for them, then let it clang shut after they passed through. The sound echoed and reechoed through her bones. With each clang, she felt diminished, as though the sound sliced off another strip of flesh.

Men waved and whistled from cells on either side as she followed at the major's side. When he showed her into a small room, empty but for a cot and a commode, she kept the tears of relief at bay by biting her lip.

"Thank you."

"Someone will come with your supper." He glanced around the room, nodded, and left, closing the door behind him, the sound of a key turning in the lock reverberating in the stillness.

Quiet, such a blessed relief after the din of her march through purgatory. She sank down onto the cot, releasing her fingers from her wrist to inspect the damage. Dirt crusted the blood, promising infection if she didn't get it cleaned, and soon. The sight of the wound reminded her of Corporal Little. She needed far more than water to wash away the horror of that man.

Lord, I thank you for your care. I know you can see through prison walls. Please, could you remind someone to bring me water? She crossed the short space to the window and, resting her forehead against the glass, stared out through steel bars to the yard below. Men paced along the cut block wall, others played cards in the shade, some slept, others talked in small groups. She wished she could hear what they said. While the noisy gauntlet she had traversed as she was led to this room had made her ears ring, now she wished for any voice. A fly landed on her wrist. Before brushing it away, she watched as it nibbled on the crusted blood. Another landed. And another. Three blue black creatures crawling on her wrist. When one deposited an egg, she shuddered and brushed them away. *Oh, Lord, I know you made the flies too, but what is becoming of me when I watch them feasting on my blood?* She walked back to the cot and lay down. The smell of rot and mildew filled her nostrils as she fell asleep, her opposite hand protecting the wound from the persistent flies.

When a rattle of keys woke her, Louisa noticed the room had dimmed. The door swung open, and a man entered carrying a tray with food and a pail of water.

She blinked. Was he an apparition? He looked gray enough to be so.

"Th-thank you." Her throat rasped so dry she could barely talk. His nod would have been missed had she not been staring at him. "Don't tell me. Let me guess—you've been ordered not to talk with me." Again that millisecond nod. "Well, there's nothing that says I cannot talk to you."

Was that a twitch of the sides of his mouth?

A bit of encouragement, all that she needed.

"Is there the smallest chance you could bring me a bit of bandaging?" She held up her wrist. "I really need to clean this and wrap it. Place like this must breed infection." She held out a hand. "Not that I'm criticizing, mind you."

An eyebrow twitched this time. How could the man say so much with such tiny motions? Or was she reading more into him than was there?

He set the tray on the end of her bed, reached into his pocket and drew out a small roll of bandage, set it on the tray, and pointed at a smear of ointment on a bit of paper.

Louisa clasped her hands at the base of her neck. Fighting back the tears that clogged her throat faster than she could think, she whispered, "Thank you." It had to be the major. No one else knew of the slice on her wrist. "And thank Major Dorsey for me also. And tell him you never said a word, for you haven't. Our Lord will bless you for this kindness."

He sketched a sign of the cross on his chest, dipped his head in the briefest of bows, and left the room, shutting the door with a click behind him, not a clang. She heard the key turn, but at the moment, it mattered not.

Bread, stew with meat, even a cup of coffee. Soap, small but real. She sniffed the tiny sliver, inhaling the sharp fragrance of clean. And a bucket of water.

Lord, O Lord, I am the most blessed of women. Thank you. How can I thank you enough? She tore a bit of the bandage off, dipped it in the water, and then with caution born of need scrubbed at the dirt around the wound. She could hear her mother's admonition, *"Use plenty of water to cleanse an open wound, the hotter the better.* " Hot she had no control of, but a bucketful was plenty. Quickly she drank the lukewarm coffee and used the tin cup to dip out more water. Finally she rubbed the soap on the rag and scrubbed all over the cut, causing red to well up again.

"Good. Bleed. That will help." Finally she smeared the ointment on the cut and wrapped the cloth around it with her other hand. She used her free hand and her teeth to rip the end of the bandage to create two tails, wrapping them in each direction. Knotting took teeth and fingers working together, but she made it.

Eating cold stew was worth every minute of the time she took to ward off infection. *Thank you, Father, thank you* repeated through her mind like the metronome that counted time for her piano lessons in that life long ago at Twin Oaks.

Louisa paced her cell in the darkness, the stink from the chamber pot mingling with all the stenches that seemed to permeate the very walls. Unwashed bodies, sicknesses of both body and soul, vermin, mildew, hate, all imbedded in the stones and carried on the air. Mosquitoes droned and hummed in her ears, a scratching from a corner was surely a mouse, or more likely a rat. A squeak.

Her heart leaped into a pace used for running. But where could she run? She paced back again, this time banging her shin on the cot.

All her life she feared being alone in the dark. Her brothers had teased her, leaped out at her often enough. Now with no effort on their part, terrifying creatures haunted the corners and under the cot. Fear sucked her mouth dry.

She crept onto the cot, drawing her legs to her chest, leaning her back into the corner walls so nothing could reach her. *Mother, I need you.* She chewed the knuckle of the bent finger she kept at her mouth to still the screams that threatened to erupt.

Like a gentle breath, verses came into her mind. *"I will never leave thee, nor forsake thee . . . and, lo, I am with you alway. . . . Thou shalt not be afraid for the terror by night; nor for the arrow that flieth by day. . . ."*

Louisa lay down. *"I will never leave thee, nor forsake thee. I will never leave thee, nor forsake thee."*

Lord, please go to Zachary as you have come to me. Please keep him safe, and I pray they fed him as well as they have me. If he is alone . . . a song came into her mind as she drifted off to sleep.

A scream woke her sometime later. Could that be Zachary? Would they be interrogating him? She'd heard of brutality being used to get answers. *Oh, Lord, please—not Zachary.*

Chapter Twenty-Two

On the Chugwater River
August 1863

"You be careful now." Jesselynn knew she sounded like a worrying wife, but, oh, how she wanted to go along.

Wolf looked down at her, shaking his head. "I've trapped wild horses before."

"I know." Sure he'd trapped horses before, but his helpers hadn't and neither had she. "Why don't you trade some of those goods with your people"—she nodded toward the laden packhorses—"for horses." She stroked the bloodred neck of his Appaloosa. *I don't want you to go off without me.*

"Because all the blankets and supplies are my gift to them." His voice wore the longsuffering tone of one who had said all this before.

"Will Red Cloud know where the wild horses are?"

"Perhaps. Now it is my turn to say be careful. Don't go off hunting or fishing by yourself." He added a "please" when her jaw squared off.

"We're going to cut hay."

"I know." His dark eyes twinkled. "But you seem to have an uncanny ability to find trouble."

"I think trouble finds me. I don't go looking for it." *How long will you be gone? Will Red Cloud be glad to see you? What if he isn't?* The questions piled on top of each other in her mind. She'd known since Fort Laramie that he would be going, but the knowing and the doing were two separate things. "God bless, and we'll all be praying for you." She squared her shoulders and lifted her chin, forcing a smile to lips that would rather tremble.

After giving Thaddeus a hug and whispered instructions, Wolf mounted, without using the stirrups, and checked out his helpers. Benjamin, Daniel, and Mark Lyons stood by their horses, their bedrolls with supplies rolled up inside and tow sacks hanging behind their saddles and at their horses' shoulders. Each had a rope of braided latigo and hobbles tied to his saddle also. They'd spent the last days making hobbles and ropes, and practicing their throwing skills.

While she and Wolf had said their good-byes privately before rising, Jesselynn felt an ache the size of Wyoming in her heart as they rode out of camp. Something could happen to them so easily, just like the near tragedy with the bear. Feeling an arm around her leg, she looked down to see Thaddeus, one hand on Patch's head, the other around her knee, staring out after the riders.

"Come home soon." His whisper brought forth the rush of tears she'd been holding back all morning. She picked him up and used his shirt to wipe her eyes.

"Yes, Thaddy, please God, they come home soon." *All in one piece and with plenty of horses.*

"How soon you be ready?" Meshach stood right behind her, Ophelia at his side.

"Whenever you are."

"I still think I should go with Meshach." Nate Lyons spoke around the stem of the pipe he chewed on more often than smoked. "I could cut more hay."

"You heard the man." Jesselynn indicated the disappearing Wolf with a nod of her head. "A man stays in camp at all times." The slightly sarcastic tone of her voice implied more than she said. The bear incident had made Wolf far more cautious than before, and he had always been extra careful. But the bear story had a happy ending after all. They'd made plenty of soap, kept grease for waterproofing boots and leather jackets, eaten and dried the meat, kept the hide to make a robe, and she'd saved the claws and teeth to trim buckskin shirts and moccasins. The porcupine quills she had kept after killing a four-footed scavenger added to her stash of trimmings. They'd found the porcupine chewing a pair of leather gloves someone had left lying on a log. Wolf had said the porcupine had chewed them for the salt.

Killing the bear had made Jesselynn truly aware that no matter how civilized the caves were becoming, they still lived in the wilderness. And many of the other wilderness dwellers were bigger, faster, and perhaps hungrier than they.

She set Thaddeus back down and patted his rear. "You and Patch stay right by the cave, you hear? No going to the creek or anywhere else by yourself." She knelt in front of him so he would see how serious she was. When his lower lip came out, she poked at it with a loving finger. "No, don't you go getting in a huff, or we'll put you on a long line like we do the horses sometimes."

Thaddeus cocked his head to one side. "Put Sammy on long line."

Chuckling, Jesselynn hugged him and stood. "Now, Darcy, you and Jane Ellen will bring the other wagon out in three days. We'll turn the hay then."

"Yes'm." Since they'd left the fort, Darcy Jones seemed to be getting younger every day. She laughed with Jane Ellen and played with the two little boys, and was once even heard singing when off doing the wash down at the creek.

Jesselynn smiled in return. What a difference.

Now if only the same miracle could happen to Aunt Agatha.

As soon as Nate and Meshach finished removing the sides of the wagons, the two McPhereson boys helped load up the supplies needed in the hay camp. They yoked the oxen and hitched them to the wagons.

"Me come?" Thaddeus wore a look of hope.

"No, you need to stay here and take care of Aunt Agatha."

The look Thaddeus gave his sister said very clearly what he thought of that idea. Jesselynn hugged him again and handed him to Jane Ellen.

"We'll see you soon, I reckon." Without another backwards look, her haying party headed out the curving creek to the Chugwater basin. Jesselynn studied the lay of the land more this time, searching out small valleys where they would be able to graze the herd in the winter so as to not use up their hay. That would be saved for the mares in foal and for emergency rations in case of a blizzard. Wolf's stories of blizzards that kept everyone in camp for days at a time made her dread the coming winter.

She eyed the thickets along the creek. If deer and elk could winter on the branches when the snow got too deep for foraging, so could their cattle and horses.

They arrived at the valley on the afternoon of the second day. While Jesselynn set up camp, Meshach and the boys started directly on cutting grass. With Meshach's height and long arms, wide swaths of grass fell before him and the scythe that he stopped to sharpen regularly. After hobbling the oxen, finding wood for the fire, and setting a trotline baited with bits of smoked bear in the creek, Jesselynn took up the shorter scythe and started her own swath.

Meshach made it look a lot easier than it was. Getting the

223

correct angle of the blade took practice. Convincing her arms to continue swinging after the first hour took sheer teeth-clenching guts, and resisting the urge to slap mosquitoes was harder than anything. No wonder animals rolled in the mud to keep bug free.

Her shoulders ached, her hands—in spite of wearing leather gloves—sported a blister or two, and her back screamed as though she'd been stuck with a hot poker. Meshach kept on swinging, the grass falling in smooth sweeps with nary a blade missed. She looked back at her own rows—and sighed. But when she looked at those of Aaron and Lester McPhereson, she didn't feel quite as bad. Height and experience seemed to play a big part.

When dusk sneaked across the land and the red-winged blackbirds began their evening arias, Jesselynn leaned the scythe against a wagon wheel and staggered to the banks of the Chugwater. Kneeling, she splashed her face, shook her head, and after removing her boots, waded out in the gentle current. When even that wasn't enough, she dove in and flipped over on her back. Floating with the eddies, she felt every screaming muscle in her body begin to relax. Ducks flew overhead and quacked somewhere in the near distance. For the first time since she couldn't remember when, she was alone, and her responsibilities floated on along with the river.

Walking back to find her boots was a combination of swimming and slipping on the mossy rocks in the riverbed. The water weighed down her clothing, but she resisted the urge to strip to her undergarments. The fellas would be wanting a bath or a swim too.

" 'Bout to come lookin' for you." Meshach sat with his feet in the water where she had left her boots and gloves. He nodded upriver to the trotline. "Plenty fish for supper."

"Good. Where are the boys?" She plunked herself down

on a rock with her feet still in the water.

"They be gettin' the oxen."

"Go on and take a swim. The water is lovely." Swallows and flycatchers dipped and skimmed above the water, making their meal on the flying insects. The setting sun washed the water in gold leaf and tipped the grasses pure gold.

One of the oxen bellowed.

"I better get the fire going." Jesselynn waited a minute or two longer before drying her feet with her wool socks and putting her boots back on. "This sure is one pretty place."

"That it be." Meshach lowered himself into the water with a sigh.

While the boys cleaned up after their supper of fried fish, Jesselynn took out her journal to catch up on the happenings. The last entry concerned the bear. She wrote of Wolf leaving, of camp details, and of cutting hay. She prayed for wisdom in dealing with Aunt Agatha. Meshach took out his Bible and hunkered down by the firelight to read. When Jesselynn closed her journal, she looked across the fire. "Read aloud, please."

His deep voice awoke the beauty of the psalms as he read one after another. Jesselynn marveled at how many he read with his eyes closed. He finished with the twenty-third, so they all said it together. " 'The Lord is my shepherd . . .' " Jesselynn sure felt cared for. " 'I shall not want.' " *Please take care of Wolf.* " '. . . beside the still waters.' " *Just like here.* " '. . . and I will dwell in the house of the Lord forever.' " A hush fell. Jesselynn looked up at the stars embroidered like French knots across the deep velvet sky. Crickets sang, a bullfrog harrumphed. *The house of the Lord"—I'm in it. Thank you, Father.*

Picking up the scythe again in the morning, even though

she hadn't shared the watch with Meshach and the boys, took strength of both body and character. She couldn't remember ever aching so much. Cutting tobacco was far easier than this, as was the walking plow when they turned the tobacco fields.

The August sun beat down, mosquitoes sucked blood, and the swaths from the day before were already drying. Only looking toward winter and knowing she would save her horses through her sweat and screaming muscles kept her going.

By the time the others rode up on the fifth day, Jesselynn and the scythe had become intimate friends instead of screaming enemies. While her swaths were nowhere near the width of Meshach's, the grass lay smooth, she honed her blade with ease, and by evening she could still stand up fairly straight.

Several days later, after Meshach laid a frame of willow trunks across the wagon beds to extend them to hold more hay, they loaded what was dry, and Jane Ellen and Darcy Jones headed the wagon westward. By the time they returned, Meshach and his helpers had the second wagon loaded, with more cut.

"Wait till you see our haystack back at the caves." Jane Ellen, looking more boy than girl since she, too, switched to britches, dashed across the field, leaping the rows of grass raked and turned for drying. "Mr. Nate and Aunt Agatha are fencin' it off."

Jesselynn leaned on her scythe handle. "Well, I'll be. She's working with Nathaniel Lyons."

Jane Ellen pulled a piece of grass and nibbled on the tender stalk. "I think he's winnin' her over." Her eyes danced at sharing the news.

"You got to admit, the man is persistent." Jane Ellen stepped closer, her eyes sparkling like the sun kissing the river ripples. "We brought you a present, a real surprise."

Knowing how much Jane Ellen enjoyed surprises, both gotten and given, Jesselynn widened her eyes. "All right, what is it?" Hands on hips added to the fun.

"We brought bread. Ophelia baked bread."

"Real, yeast-risen, wonderful bread?"

Jane Ellen nodded.

"Not biscuits?"

Jane Ellen shook her head. "We can have it for supper. Ophelia started sourdough from milk and flour she got at the fort. It bubbles in a crock like nobody's business. Now that it is going good, she can use flour and water to keep it goin'. Ain't, I mean, isn't that just . . . just . . ." Jane Ellen threw her hands in the air, the best word not coming.

"When did all this come about?"

"Oh, when you was moonin' after Mr. Wolf."

"I wasn't mooning."

"Sure was, just like a lovesick cow." Jane Ellen dodged the swat Jesselynn sent in her general direction.

"What lovesick cow?" Darcy pushed her sunbonnet back to wipe her forehead. She'd hobbled the oxen before joining Jesselynn and Jane Ellen. "Whooee, be hotter here than up at our place."

Jesselynn noted the "our place." She was willing to wager that Darcy Jones had never had a place to call home in her entire life. When Wolf returned he planned on staking out property lines for each of the settlers, so when the day came that they could file on their homesteads, they'd be ready.

She hoped when they returned to the fort for winter supplies, they would have horses to sell, the first of many.

The bread was all Jane Ellen had promised, even though a couple days old. That along with boiled cattail tubers and wild onion made the fried fish a banquet.

★ ★ ★ ★ ★

Wolf had no idea leaving camp would be so difficult. How he'd wanted to bring Jesselynn along, both to meet his relatives in Red Cloud's tribe and to see the beauty of the country. She, who thought it wonderful where they camped, would be amazed at the mountains to the north. Besides, he wanted to show her off to his friends. If they were still his friends. Ten years was a long time to be gone, and much had happened in the meantime.

While they saw several Indian camps, none of them were Red Cloud's. He asked if the tribes knew where Red Cloud was, but the answer was always a shaking of the head. Some said Wind River country, others said Powder, and some said he'd gone south.

No one had horses to trade either.

As he and his helpers climbed higher, the trees grew larger, the creeks dashed more swiftly, and herds of elk grazed in the valleys. Scouting ahead one afternoon, Wolf found traces of another Indian band. He secreted his three young helpers, along with the packhorses, in a dense forest.

"Wait here until I return. If I don't come back in four days, head on home."

"We can make a fire?" Benjamin leaned his crossed arms on the pommel of his saddle. "And hunt?"

"Snares yes, but no guns. And keep the fire smokeless." Along the way he'd taught them how to cook over a small, nearly smokeless fire, how to shoot with a bow and arrows, and how to identify wild things that were edible. The bow he'd made during camp at night needed more arrows, which was their job when on watch during the wee hours. So far they'd sharpened, burned, and sharpened again the ends of the arrows to make them hard as flint since they'd not had time to make arrowheads.

"If you are found, they will steal our horses and the goods, so be on guard." Wolf looked each of them directly in the eyes, extracting their promises.

He rode slowly, following the trace, checking over each crest of the hill on foot before proceeding. When he finally looked down into a valley deep in grass, with tepees spaced between the trees and the sparkling creek, the familiarity of it all stabbed him in the chest. How he'd missed this simple way of life. He'd been gone far too long.

He hoped not too long.

Wolf watched the camp for several hours, realizing most of the braves were gone. He was too far away to recognize faces, but the longer he watched the more certain he was that this was Red Cloud's band. When a hunting party rode back into camp from the opposite direction, he continued to watch. Finally he mounted his horse and rode down into camp.

Chapter Twenty-Three

Oglala Camp

Gray Wolf kept his horse to a slow walk as he entered the Oglala camp.

Two dogs barked around his horse's leg. One of the pack-horses kicked back and snorted. Two braves, rifles across their chests, stepped in front of him. Wolf stopped his horse and nodded a greeting.

"I am Gray Wolf, son of Laughing Girl. Red Cloud is my uncle." He sat on his horse without moving, waiting for them to acknowledge his greeting. Speaking the language of his mother felt good and proper.

At a grunt from one of the braves, the dogs slunk off.

"You have been gone a long time."

"Yes. Too long. Is it you, Dark Horse?"

The brave on the right nodded, a smile starting in his eyes. "I did not expect to see you again." The two had been best friends from the time they tumbled in the grass together as babies.

"I said I would return." Wolf glanced around the camp. Children peeked from the entrances to tepees, and some of the women had joined the men standing at attention throughout the camp. Cooking fires with racks of meat drying looked just like those at the caves.

"You were but a boy, and the white man's ways are different from the Oglala."

More than you would ever know. "Is Red Cloud here?"

"Yes. He is head chief now." Dark Horse turned to a young brave behind him and ordered him to announce the visitor to the chief. He crossed to stand at Wolf's knee. "You are indeed welcome, my brother." He looked at the Appaloosa. "One fine horse. You want to trade?"

Wolf shook his head. Leave it to Dark Horse. "No, but I brought gifts." He swung to the ground and indicated the two packhorses.

"Come, Red Cloud is waiting."

Wolf knew that another youth, a bit older than he, had taken the name of Red Cloud when he earned the position as chief of the Oglala. There had been chiefs named Red Cloud before him, but he was winning a place in the Sioux nation as both a warrior chief and one with wisdom. Braves followed him into battle because he always won. His camp was strong because he was adept at stealing horses from other tribes. So far he counseled peace with the white man.

So far. One of the reasons Wolf wanted to talk with him. One of the reasons the general at Fort Laramie wanted to talk with him.

A woman came running from a tepee set across the camp from him and stopped at his side, staring up with a smile that lit her entire face. "Gray Wolf, is this really you?"

"Yes, Little Squirrel, my mother's sister, I have come back."

"To stay?"

Leave it to her to ask the questions right in the beginning. Wolf shook his head. "No, but I will come again. I have a wife. We live on the Chugwater."

"A white man's house?" She patted his arm. "You married a white woman?"

"Yes. You will like her. She can tan a deer hide almost as soft as you do."

"You go now. Red Cloud is waiting."

The celebration of his return lasted far into the night, with feasting, singing, and dancing. He dispensed the goods from his packs, making sure that his aunt received both a red-and-black striped wool blanket and lengths of red print calico. When the packs were empty, he joined Red Cloud in his tepee.

"We need more guns." Red Cloud sat cross-legged on a pile of skins on the other side of the fire.

"I cannot help you there. The general refused to sell me guns and whiskey."

"We all eat better because of the rifles. Hunting is easier."

"So is war." Gray Wolf studied the flickering flames. Should he mention letting the white man pass through on their way to Oregon without attacking them?

"Buffalo are becoming scarce. Not like in the days when we were young."

"I know." Gray Wolf also knew that battles between tribes had been going on for as long as the Indian roamed the land.

"Rifles bring down the buffalo."

"And the elk and deer. But I cannot help you there. I'm sorry."

Red Cloud nodded, smoke circling his head from the pipe he smoked. He raised the bowl in a salute. "Good tobacco. Very good." He nodded again and studied the fire. The silence in the tepee made the drums sound distant.

Wolf waited, knowing the manners of his people.

"You have a camp on the Chugwater?"

"No. Homesteading." Wolf knew none of his people would think of declaring ownership of land. "White men have laws about land. To farm, raise horses, cattle, and food, I must seek to own the land."

Red Cloud shook his head, indicating his opinion of such foolishness.

"Do you have any horses to sell?" Wolf broke another long silence.

"Some to trade for guns."

Wolf smiled at his old friend. "You never give up, do you?"

Red Cloud shook his head, and his smile acknowledged the joke. "Why?"

"My wife brought Thoroughbred horses to our marriage. We will raise horses to sell." He didn't mention their plan to sell the horses to the military. "I need good mares."

"When we raid again, I will find you some."

The cessation of the drums announced the end of the entertainment. Not long after that, Wolf made his way to the tepee of his aunt, where he would spend the night. He fell asleep remembering times from his childhood. Perhaps bringing Jesselynn to meet his people would help her understand more about him.

The next two days were spent recalling both ancient tales and those from their youth, as all the men had gathered to talk. They watched the boys trying to be men and the girls trying to attract the boys. The men agreed that things didn't change much except for the inroads the white men made. Talk always came back to the white man.

"You come again and bring your wife." His aunt's words sounded more like an order than a request.

"I will. And her little brother." Wolf nodded before mounting his horse, the packhorses now carrying a buffalo robe, a present from Red Cloud, a necklace of dyed quills for Jesselynn from another aunt, Swims Like a Beaver, and a small bow and arrows for Thaddeus.

"You teach him to hunt," Dark Horse said when he handed Wolf the bow. "Then he will never be hungry."

"Unless the white man chases away all the game."

Wolf heard the subdued growl of one of the younger braves. Wolf hoped Red Cloud could keep them calm as he'd said he would.

"Thank you." He grasped Dark Cloud's hand, then waved to his aunt, now standing back with the women. Several of the young boys ran alongside as he rode out of camp, shouting their farewells as he trotted off.

When he returned to his own encampment, he found the three young men roasting prairie chickens over the near smokeless fire.

"One more day and we would have headed on home. Say de Indians got you." Benjamin took the lines to the pack-horses and prepared to hobble them to graze.

"I'm here now. We head for horse country in the mornin'."

Chapter Twenty-Four

Washington Prison

Only the gray ghost, as Louisa came to call him, appeared for the next three days. Never did he say a word as he delivered food and water and removed the chamber pot, bringing it back rinsed clean.

But she gleaned plenty of information from him just the same. It all depended upon her skill in asking questions. To some, like "When will I be released?" he only shrugged. He knew no more than she.

But of "Zachary, my brother, have you seen him?" the right eyebrow rose. She'd learned that meant yes. "Is he well?" Slight shrug.

"Ah, is someone mistreating him?" She scoured her brain, frantically searching for a way to learn what she needed.

Nothing. Either he didn't know or couldn't answer.

"Has he been moved to a cell of his own yet?" His gaze roved around her walls. "I take it that means yes." The eyebrow rose.

He ducked his head and backed out the door. The interview was over.

Louisa paced the floor again as dusk grayed the window and darkness, along with the rats, crept into the room. No matter how carefully she ate her bread, crumbs would still fall to the floor for her nighttime visitors to squeak over. She'd learned to wrap her skirt up around her head and tuck her petticoats around her legs. Bare flesh was an open invitation to both rats and mosquitoes.

Forcing herself to wake with the daylight grew harder. At least in sleep she worried about neither those in Richmond nor Zachary in prison. Day after day passed much the same. Rising, eating, pacing, praying, singing, only to repeat it over and over. She tried to keep track of the passing of days by scratching a line on the wall, as many others had done before her. When August passed into September she began to despair. *Oh, God, where are you? I know you will deliver us, but when?*

"Miss, they be ready for you." Gray Ghost could talk. Louisa snapped her mouth closed.

"They who?"

"The military court."

"And I am to go before them looking like this?" She gestured to her filthy clothes.

He shrugged. "I wouldn't make 'em mad, if'n I was you." The longest sentence he'd spoken yet made good sense.

But after two weeks of solitary confinement, rather than breaking Louisa, their summons sent her into a fury.

"There must be some kind of a law against such behavior."

"They *is* the law."

Louisa's starch left her in a whoosh. With shaking hands, she tried to give some semblance of order to her hair and brush out her skirt.

"Please, miss. Don't want the sojers to come."

She nodded. *"I will never leave you nor forsake you."* She repeated the verse in cadence to her steps following the slightly stooped man.

Silence greeted her as she walked between the cells on both sides.

"God bless," a voice called, others echoed. Someone started clapping in time to her steps. Others picked it up, a cadence of respect and good wishes.

"Why are they doing that?" she asked as they passed through another slamming door.

"You a hero to the men, once they learned who you were. You and your brother."

Louisa took a deeper breath and straightened her shoulders. *Father, give me strength.*

Three men in blue, with an abundance of gold bars and braid, sat behind a long table. Major James Dorsey sat apart from them, off to the side. While he stood when she entered the room, the others didn't.

"State your name, please." The officer in the middle, the one with the most gold, wore the mask of power.

Louisa wanted to melt into a puddle and trickle out the door, but instead she ordered iron into her backbone, straightened her shoulders, and answered with all the assurance she could muster.

"Miss Louisa Marie Highwood."

"Your home is where?"

"Richmond at the time."

"And before that?"

"Twin Oaks near Midway, Kentucky." Her lips quivered, but her speech held steady.

"The charge before us is treason. How do you answer to that?"

At the horrifying word, her stomach lurched and bile rose in her throat. She swallowed hard to settle it back, then coughed into her handkerchief at the burning. She swallowed again, but the coughing refused to be pacified.

"I . . . ah . . ." Another coughing spell.

The interrogator waved at a soldier near the door. "Get her some water."

After a drink, she wiped her mouth. "Thank you." She cleared her throat again, sending pleas heavenward all the while.

"General, if trying to alleviate the suffering of wounded men is treason, then I believe you would have to convict me. I'd rather have you convict me of treason than have our Lord convict me of not caring for his sons."

"Answer only the question."

"I did." A slight narrowing of his eyes let her know she'd hit home.

"Miss Highwood." He leaned slightly forward, his hands clasped on the table in front of him. "Do you realize I can have you shot to death?"

"Yes, I do." No way was she going to call him sir, no matter what her mother had drilled into her all those years earlier.

One eyebrow twitched and settled back into a straight line with the other.

"But that will only serve to send me home to my Father." Where had that come from? She kept herself from licking her dry lips and reached again for the cup of water that had been left for her. She observed her shaking fingers as if they belonged to someone else.

He leaned back, his eyes drilling into hers. "Did you know your brother was carrying a letter that confirms our suspicions that he spied for the Confederate army?"

Her head shook before she could stop it. "N-no." *Stand straight, don't you buckle now. Why, Zachary, you promised me we were only coming for medicines.* But even while asking it, she knew the answer. He would do anything to assist the Confederacy, anything to feel he was still of use, still a man.

The general nodded to the man at the door. "Take her away."

At the look on her face, he added, "You'll be informed of our decision."

"Sir, what about my brother?"

"You are dismissed."

She shot a glance at the major, who returned it without as much as a blink.

Louisa squeezed her hands shut until she could feel the pain of her fingernails digging into her palms. *Lord, hold me up until I get to my cell.* But as she walked between rows of well-wishers, it was all she could do to keep from stumbling. She nodded, tried to smile.

"Hang in there, missy. They won't never shoot a lady."

Oh, God, make him right. "Thank you."

"I be prayin'." With that Gray Ghost shut the door behind him, and she heard the lock turn.

She just made it to the chamber pot before the bile erupted, burning her throat, searing her heart. She rinsed her mouth from the water bucket and collapsed on the cot. *Lord, I cannot take any more. I cannot.*

Though her eyes burned as though she'd been in smoke, she could not cry. She could not lie still either and paced the cell until darkness wrapped her like a shroud. Sinking onto the cot, she performed her nightly ritual, including, with no thought or will on her part, her evening prayers. *Unto thee, O Lord, do I lift up my heart, my gratitude for all thy mercies. . . .* A trickle of a song, so faint she had to strain to hear it, seeped into her despair. *I thank thee for sending thy dear son to die for me. . . .* The song swelled like a tiny creek after rain. *I thank thee that . . .* Tears broke from their dam, washed her cheeks, and cleansed her soul. She hummed the tune, the words building to be sung. "O God, our help in ages past." A whisper, but a song. "Our hope for years to come." She sat up, wiped the tears, swallowed, and continued. "Our shelter from the stormy blast, and our eternal home." She sang it again, pacing to the window and shouting it out the bars. An echo, no, someone else was singing. She started again. "O God, our help . . ." The music swelled as voice after voice from around the quadrangle picked it up. "Before the hills in order stood, or earth received her frame, from everlasting thou art God, to endless years the same." When she reached the final line of the last verse, her throat clogged. "Be thou our guide while life shall last, and our eternal home."

"Thank you," she called when the song died away, hoping the men couldn't hear the quiver in her voice.

"And you," echoed around the brick walls.

The next morning a key turned in the lock after Gray Ghost had already brought her breakfast. She watched as the door swung inward to reveal the major standing there.

"C-come in." As if he needed an invitation.

"The decision has been made. You are free to go."

"Free?" She stared at him, unable to believe it. Reality fell like a log on her shoulders. "What about Zachary, my brother?"

"He will be shot at dawn."

CHAPTER TWENTY-FIVE

SEPTEMBER 1863

"Would they take me and let him go?"

The major shook his head. "You weren't the courier."

"But what if he didn't know what he carried?" Her mind raced, banging from reason to reason like a wild thing in a cage.

"He knew."

Somehow she believed the major wished things could be different. She stared at him, willing him to look at her face instead of her hands. Hands that knit together, snarled like bad yarn. When he finally looked up, she saw anguish puddling his eyes.

"Is there anything . . . anything I can do?" Louisa swallowed the pending tears.

"Pray for his soul."

"His soul is not what is in jeopardy. Is there anything I can do in this life?"

The man hesitated, then lowered his voice, so she had to strain to hear him. "You could appeal to President Lincoln."

"Could the execution be postponed long enough for me to get an interview with him? If he would see me, that is?" Hope glimmered, an infinitesimal flame down a long tunnel.

"I'll see what I can do." He breathed what sounded like a sigh of relief.

At least she'd be off his hands. Why did that make her feel a pang of regret? If only they had met at another time, another place.

"Why, Major? Why do you care?"

He studied her, as if unsure he should answer. "You grew up at Twin Oaks, a Thoroughbred stud farm near Lexington, Kentucky."

She could tell it wasn't a question. "Yes. What do you know of Twin Oaks?"

"You have a sister named Miss Jesselynn?"

"Yes." Her heart picked up the pace.

"I was there the day of your father's funeral. Someone had told us there were horses hidden there, so I was ordered to verify the rumor."

Louisa closed her eyes. She could see a few men in blue trotting up the long avenue of oak trees that led to the big house, a house that no longer lived but in her heart.

"Miss Jesselynn, she is one fine woman. She let me know that we were intruding, and yet she served us lemonade on the front porch. A big black, shoulders this broad"—the major held out his hands to demonstrate—"he stood by the door, and an older black woman let us know we were in no wise welcome but served us anyway. Your sister made her."

"Did you find any horses?"

He shook his head. "Nary a one. Only two mules, but Miss Jesselynn made me feel so guilty, I didn't dare requisition them. We weren't in the habit of depriving citizens of their livelihood then."

And you are now? No longer is there room for feelings and manners. On either side. Lord, please keep me from losing the heritage my mother taught me, from losing the grace you taught me. "I'm glad you were treated well at my home." *Oh, God, how I wish I were there right now.* She looked up. The major had schooled his face back to officer lines. His jaw looked to be chiseled from stone.

She tried anyway. "Can you tell me any more about getting an appointment with Mr. Lincoln?"

A shake of his head so brief as to be nearly nonexistent.

"Can you promise—" She cut off the sentence. She knew he couldn't. Only the general could give stay of execution orders. To stand before that man again . . . Her hands clenched automatically. But for Zachary? She rose, hiding her now shaking hands in her skirt folds.

"Could you please take me to see the general?"

One raised eyebrow told her he questioned her sanity, but he nodded. "Follow me."

"Tole ya so," a prisoner called as she traversed the long walk between cells full of butternut-clad men. The cadence of clapping picked up again, buoying her spirits. "God bless you all." She nodded at the faces crammed between bars, hands reaching toward her. Their well-wishes followed her past the slamming door.

If only Zachary had been one of them so she could see his dear face. *But he's better off in a cell like mine,* she reminded herself. Thinking of him kept her from dwelling on her own predicament. Where would she stay? How could she force an appointment with the president? How would she get home to Richmond?

She didn't have to wait long for the audience.

"I take it you are not pleased with my decision." The general sat behind a walnut desk, campaign maps on the walls, brocade curtains at the tall windows. She thought to the tents of the men in the field. Some had it harder in war than others, that was for sure.

"Regarding myself, I am most grateful, but I have a favor of mercy to ask for my brother."

"Don't even bother asking me to pardon him. Military law states that spies are to be executed."

"I understand that. I plead for a few days' grace. That is all."

"Even heaven cannot save him now." The general narrowed his eyes, eyes that glittered like blue ice.

"Then what would hurt with putting it off for a week even?"

He thumped the desk. "I don't know what you hope to gain, but I will give you three days, no more."

"Thank you."

"Did Major Dorsey give you the money from your brother yet?"

"No, sir."

He nodded to the major who stood off to the side. "Do so and show her out." He waved a hand as if shooing a bothersome fly.

Louisa dipped her head in a semblance of a nod, turned, and followed the straight back of the major from the room. *Thank you, God* warred in her mind with *that insufferable pig.* She wanted to fall to her knees in gratitude. She wanted to shoot the general between the eyes. Instead, she thanked the major politely when he gave her Zachary's leather money pouch.

"I have something further for you." He stepped behind a shelf and brought out her satchel.

"Oh, Major." She looked up at him, at a loss for words in her delight.

"We removed the bottom."

"Oh." She shrugged. "All that money down the river."

"Oh, the quinine will be put to a useful purpose, as will the morphine. My men don't always get enough either."

Louisa refused to let his words bother her. She'd done her

best, and God didn't require more. "Thank you, Major, both for this and the other."

"Good luck." He opened the door for her.

She stepped outside and, when the door closed behind her, stood in the sunshine, letting it soak in and begin to burn out the dregs of prison. Wishing she'd asked him which way to a boardinghouse or hotel or some place where she could scrub herself clean before making her way to the White House, she glanced up the street, then the other way. Which way?

She looked down at her satchel. While she had to brush and scrub at her skirt, she now had a clean waist and drawers, a gift beyond measure.

Feeling as though she'd been granted a new life, she set out up the street. Three days, that's all. What could she say to the president of the United States to make him take pity on her and release her brother?

At a hotel she located, a maid brushed her skirt while she scrubbed from head to toenails, rinsed, and scrubbed again. Her skin burned when she finished, wondering if she would ever feel really clean again. But dressing in clean clothes helped, and fashioning her still damp hair into a bun, so she looked neat and womanly again, helped even more. After asking directions from the man at the desk in what could almost be called a lobby, she set out for the White House nearby.

She knew she'd seen it before. Officers in blue and men and women in street clothes flowed in and out the wide double doors guarded by tall white pillars. She took a seat in a room full of chairs, wishing for her knitting. If she had something to do with her hands, the time would pass more swiftly. Studying the gilded wallpaper, the heavy velvet drapes, and the walnut moldings failed to occupy even a fraction of the many hours.

One after another, the people seated around her rose when their names were called and disappeared through one door or another, and others took their places. By the time she was the only one left, dusk was falling and the man in charge shook his head.

"I'm sorry, miss, but the president will not be seeing any others today."

"So then I can make an appointment for tomorrow?"

The man glanced down at a book in front of him. "You can come again, and I will try to fit you in, but his appointments are all taken."

"I see." Louisa sighed. "And the next day?"

"The same."

"Sir, I don't think you understand the urgency of my visit. A man's life is at stake." *My brother's life.* But she had a feeling that telling the entire story to this tight-lipped minion would only earn her a hasty exit. And no return.

The second day passed as the first. Louisa trudged back to her bare room at the hotel with a heart so heavy as to tip her into the sewer drain running alongside the street. She barely missed being run over by four brawny horses pulling a dray. Ignoring the shouts of the driver, she mounted the hotel steps.

Lord, what do I do? What am I doing wrong? Please, is it your will that my brother should die? But you say to ask for what we desire, and above all else on this earth, I desire my brother's freedom. Hoarding her few remaining coins, she spent the evening on her knees pleading before the throne of grace, rather than eating.

Trusting for everything, including her daily bread, was an unusual predicament. Never in her life had she gone hungry.

Never in her life had she pleaded so for another.

Striding along the streets in the morning, she could think of nothing but that this was Zachary's last day on earth if something didn't happen to stay the execution.

The hours passed like the tolling of the bells for a funeral. People came and went. She only got up to use the necessary.

"Have you even told Mr. Lincoln that I have spent three days here waiting?" She asked the man for the third time.

"He's busy."

"I know that, but surely there are two minutes that he could spare."

"I will do what I can."

That hasn't been very much. But she returned to her seat, praying all the while.

Oh, Lord, have you turned your face away from me? Have you closed your ears? I have trusted you all my life, but I am left hanging here. Is there something else I could do? Oh, Lord, hear my prayer.

As the afternoon waned, her spirits faded with it.

Three people, including her, remained in the room. One by one the other two were admitted to the place they desired. She sat alone again.

When the man at the desk left the room on some errand, Louisa sucked in a deep breath, rose, and slipped through the door the others had used. Down the hall, peeking into each room, she prayed no one would see her and bodily throw her out. Just as Louisa was about to give up, she heard two men talking, and one said, "President Lincoln . . ." She heard no more but was certain she knew which room was the president's office. Hovering around a corner, she waited until the man left, then opened the door and slipped inside.

The president sat in a swivel chair behind an immense

desk covered in papers. He was turned facing the tall narrow window. Brocade drapes were gathered to the sides with gold cord and a heavy tassel. She heard a sigh, but all she could see was a head of dark hair, struck every which way by hands that had plundered it. After a few moments long-fingered hands smoothed the hair down, and the president turned the chair back to face the desk.

Weariness dragged at the skin of his face, and dark eyes held a sorrow that didn't lighten when he saw her standing just inside the door.

"I thought I was finished for the day."

"I wish you were, but I need to talk with you, but only for a moment, for you can save a man's life today."

He beckoned to the chair by his desk. "And this man is your husband?"

"No, my brother." She sat on the edge of the seat, her shaking hands clenched in her lap.

Lincoln leaned back in his chair. "Tell me."

"My brother is to be shot at dawn as a spy." She swallowed, tried to clear her throat.

"And is he a spy?"

"My father did everything he could to keep Kentucky in the Union, but too few would listen. He and my other brother both died in battle. Zachary is my only brother . . ." She paused. "Other than my baby brother who is out west somewhere." *Stay with the story,* one side of her mind screamed. *Get on with it.*

"I see."

How can you see? "Zachary was wounded terribly—he's lost a hand, a foot, and an eye. We thought we would lose him too." Her throat clogged up again.

Mr. Lincoln poured a glass of water from a carafe on his desk and handed it to her.

"Thank you." Her stomach growled so loudly she was sure he could hear it. She blinked back the blackness that lurked at the edges of her mind like vultures waiting for the death rattle.

"How long since you've eaten?"

"Ahh." She had to think. Was it the day before yesterday? "Some time ago, I believe, but that is not what is important. Our family has lost everything, and while I know others have given all too, I beg of you, please spare my brother's life."

"Was he spying?"

She paused. Something in his face told her only the most simple truth would be tolerated.

"I . . . we came to Washington for quinine and morphine. Mr. President, sir, I volunteer at the hospital, and we are treating wounded men in our home. I cannot bear to see and hear them suffer—if there is something I can do. So many of them young boys, boys like my brothers. I didn't know he carried a letter."

"Did he?"

She looked at him, questions in her eyes.

"Did he know?"

"I . . . I believe so."

"Why should I spare him?"

"Because he is my brother." Despair loosened the starch in her neck and spine. Her head fell forward. There was no reason he should spare Zachary. This was all a waste of her time and that of the man with whom she spoke.

"Thank you, sir, for the water and for listening to me."

A servant entered with a tray of bread and cheese, cookies, and an apple. He set it on the edge of the desk.

"Anything else, sir?"

"No, that is all."

When he left, the president leaned forward, moved the

tray to in front of her, and nodded. "Help yourself."

With hands shaking so badly she could hardly hold the knife, she buttered a piece of bread, laid slices of cheese on it, and took a bite.

As if no longer aware of her presence, the man before her took a paper and pen and began writing.

"What prison is your brother in? And what is his name?"

Did she dare hope?

Chapter Twenty-Six

The White House

"Do you promise not to spy again?"

"I wasn't spying, sir, I was . . ."

He waved a hand. "I know, I know. But your brother was. Can you speak for him?"

"An oath by any member of the Highwood family is honored by all." Louisa brushed crumbs from her skirt, her heart leaping with hope.

President Lincoln signed the paper, dusted it with sand, and leaned forward. "Miss Highwood, this letter will release your brother into your keeping. I abhor this war more than you can know, and this is perhaps not the wisest thing I can do, but . . ." He paused. "Would that we all had women like you to plead our cause." He nodded to the remaining food on the tray. "Wrap that up in a napkin and take it with you. It wouldn't help if you were to faint on the way to set him free."

"Y-yes, sir. Th-thank you." She looked into the president's sad, dark eyes and couldn't help reaching a hand to touch him. "I will pray for you, sir, and flood the floors of our Lord's throne room with my gratitude. I think I could not have gone on any longer had you not had the grace to save my brother."

"You are welcome." A smile tugged at the corner of his mouth and lightened his eyes. "Just keep that brother of yours out of Washington and be strong to rebuild our land when this heinous war is over."

"Yes, sir." Louisa settled the remainder of the food in her bag and rose, extending her hand. "Thank you again."

Her hand disappeared in his, and he tucked it in his arm as he walked her to the door. "Go this way and no one will bother you." He indicated a door in the opposite direction of the way she had come.

Louisa squeezed his hand again. "God bless you, Mr. President."

Her feet never touched the cobblestones as Louisa hurried along the now gaslit streets. She looked to neither side, her mind focused on another meeting with the general. Any thoughts of "what if" she banished with a snort. "Deceiver, you have no hold over me. God himself has set my brother free." When she finally arrived at the prison, a light rain had begun to fall. But she ignored the chill and pounded on the heavy wooden gate.

A sentry opened a square port and peered out. "Who do you wish to see?"

"The general."

"He is not here."

"Then I will wait in his office." She paused. "Where is he?"

"That is none of your business, ma'am. Come back in the morning." He shut the portal.

Louisa staggered, leaning against the wet wall for support. *Now what? Lord, where are you? Surely you wouldn't let all this happen and not free Zachary?*

She pounded on the door again.

The portal opened.

"I have an order from President Lincoln to give to the general."

A hand came out. "Let me see it."

Did she dare let go of the lifesaving piece of paper?

"It is only for the general." *Please, God, please.*

The portal slammed shut, and the door swung open.

Fear gripped her by the throat and made her gag. What if she never came out again? What if they took the paper and threw it away? What if, what if?

Lightning couldn't strike faster and more severe than fear. *God, help!* The door began to close.

She stepped through the portal, clutching her bag, and her faith, like a shield.

The man in blue pants and shirt, no jacket, led her into a small room. "Wait here." He left a lamp on the table and exited the room.

Louisa shivered in the dampness of both clothes and room. No one would ever know if she disappeared now. Like two pieces of flotsam on a river, she and Zachary could be swept out to sea and never heard from again.

CHAPTER TWENTY-SEVEN

WASHINGTON

Praying and shivering, Louisa waited out the hours. Every time footfalls sounded outside the door, she sat up straighter, only to slump again as they passed on by. Her head ached, her stomach grumbled. She dug out the bread and cheese to nibble on, but her stomach rebelled, roiling and threatening to erupt.

Thirsty. Lord, how can I be so thirsty? She felt as though she'd been trapped in the room for days rather than hours when the door finally opened.

"Come with me."

She followed the stiff back up the stairs and into the general's office.

"You have something for me?" The general held out his hand.

She laid the paper in it and fought off the shivers, of fear or freezing, she knew not which.

"I see." The look he sent her over the edge of the letter made her take a step back. Malevolent. She'd never understood that word before, but now she even felt it. When she looked again, his face had assumed a look devoid of any emotion.

His words came softly. "You had better pray that I never see either one of you again." He rang a handbell on the side of his desk. An aide entered.

"Release Highwood and show both him and his sister out."

"Thank you."

The general did not respond.

Louisa nodded, turned, and followed the aide to the hall and back to the room she'd memorized before.

Within a few minutes she heard Zachary's crutch-and-thump gait. She met him in the hall, faced his icy stare, and in moments the two of them stood outside the gate, the door thundering shut behind them.

How could Zachary walk as far as her hotel? Why didn't he say something?

"This way." She pointed up the street. "Perhaps we can find a buggy."

He stumped beside her, his false foot swinging in the peculiar gait he had developed.

"I have a hotel room. In the morning you can get a bath before we leave for home."

Still no answer. She tried to see his face in the lamplight as they passed another lamppost. The light threw shadows that made her shiver.

She paced her steps to his. Did he not care to know what had happened?

The rain picked up again, but at least now they were free. The drops fell like a warm, cleansing shower.

At one corner, Zachary stopped and raised his face to the downpour. The streetlight showed his good eye closed. He took a deep breath, and they started off again.

Louisa could endure his silence no longer. "Zachary, dear brother, what is it? Why are you not rejoicing to be freed from that . . . that"—she shuddered—"that terrible place?"

He stopped with a turn. "Would that you had let me die

there." He swung his crutch and clumped onward.

Would she ever forget the look in his eye? The gargoyle sneer on his dear face? The scar from eyebrow to chin glittered like a lightning strike in the lamplight.

Sometime later, when Louisa felt sure Zachary could go no further, as his steps had grown slower and slower, she touched his arm and pointed at the hotel where she'd been staying. "In here."

Without even a nod, he staggered up the steps. She sprang ahead of him to open the door, receiving only a glare for her efforts. Instead of following her to the stairs, he arrowed for the desk.

"Send up a bottle of Kentucky bourbon, and make sure you don't water it down." Zachary stared at the desk clerk as if daring him to argue.

"But . . . but we have no . . ." The young man with mutton-chop whiskers gestured to the single room furnished with the desk, one chair under a gaslit lamp, and a brass spittoon badly in need of a polishing.

Zachary leaned forward. "Am I to understand you don't know how to buy a bottle?"

"N-no, sir, that's not it." The man took a step backwards. "But I . . . I cannot leave my post, sir."

Louisa thought to stick up for the clerk, even so far as to take a step forward, but she restrained herself. If her brother chose to act like an overbearing boor, so be it. She turned instead and started up the stairs. *Lord, what has gotten into him?* At the scowl on his face, even she had not wanted to cross him, let alone a poor desk clerk who was only doing his job.

The sound of a fist slamming on wood made her look back over her shoulder.

The clerk scurried out from behind the desk and headed

out the door they'd entered. Louisa knew he would be back within minutes, for there was a saloon only two doors down.

Zachary crossed the room and started up the stairs, left hand on the railing pulling himself up, while his right arm clutched the crutch to his side. He hopped to each step on his good leg.

"Shame you couldn't get a room on the first floor."

Louisa ignored his comment and made her way down the hall to the room she'd stayed in for the last few nights. The single bed would not do for the two of them, certainly, but she'd ask for another quilt and make up a pallet on the floor. Every time the question arose in her mind as to how they would get home, she shoved it aside. *Let Zachary worry about that,* she commanded herself. *He's the one spending money like the bag will never run empty. God took care of the widow with the oil, but I think liquor doesn't count.* She felt like slamming the door and locking it before he could get there, but with the mood he was in, he'd pound on every door in the building.

The bottle arrived shortly after he did.

"Pay him!" His order cut through her tender skin.

Without a word, Louisa removed the leather pouch from her reticule. "How much is it?" She gasped at the price.

Zachary thumped his cane on the floor. "You suffering mess of a man. What kind of fool do you take me for? You doubled the price. Now, how much did you really pay?"

Louisa stood with her eyes closed. *How can I bear even being in the same room with him?*

"A-a dollar, ma'am. I'm sorry, but the boss says that other is what to charge."

"I understand." Louisa gave him the dollar bill. "However, this is the best I can do."

"Don't just stand there, bring it here." Again the crutch thumped.

The clerk thrust the bottle at Zachary and scuttled from the room.

Louisa shut the door behind him. *I will not open the bottle for him.* She leaned her forehead against the door, listening to him curse the cork, the clerk, and life in general.

The pop of the cork and the glugging of the liquid told her he'd succeeded without her help.

Moving to the window, she studied the street below, the pools of yellow light from the gas lamps glittering the rain. *How will we get home?* Without other distractions, the question took over. The few remaining coins wouldn't buy two good meals, let alone two train tickets or rental for a horse and buggy. *Lord, you have said you will provide, that you will take care of our needs.*

The bottle glugged again. She clenched her teeth at the sound. Sure, the booze would give Zachary momentary solace, but it wouldn't do anything for their situation. He needed a clear mind to figure what they should do next. Her stomach rumbled. Thank God for President Lincoln. Without his concern, she'd have fainted from lack of food. Taking the napkin-wrapped bread and cheese out of the reticule hanging from her wrist, she nibbled it while keeping her concentration on the street below. Anything rather than turning to face her brother. Time dragged at her like her wet skirt. The bread gone, she leaned her forehead against the cool windowpane.

"Louisa?" His words had already started to slur.

"Yes."

"How much money is left?"

At least he was still thinking.

"A couple of dollars in coins."

"They give it all to you?" He coughed, spluttered, and took another swallow.

"How should I know? You were very careful to keep from telling me anything. I was grateful to get any money back. Thanks to that pouch, I've at least had a roof over my head for the last few days."

"You could have gone to dear cousin Arlington."

"I could have. And if I were starving, I might have." She ground her teeth again, fighting the eruption pushing at her control. "I had the audacity to think it important to do all I could to keep you alive."

He lifted the half-empty bottle, drank, and lowered it to stare at her across the chasm yawning between them. "I'd be better off dead."

"Yes, you informed me of that already. Pray, come up with something new." She clamped her arms across her chest to hold in the shivering.

"You think I want to live like this?" He gestured to his leg, then raised his stump and turned his head to show his patch.

"Others do. You can be a man about it."

"What do you know?" His voice cracked. "Everything I do takes ten times as long. I can hardly dress by myself. I can no longer ride a horse—how will I manage Twin Oaks when the day comes we can return? I slave in that office on the grace of my brother-in-law, Steadly—what a misbegotten name."

"Other men would be grateful to have a place to work."

"But I'm not other men! I'm not even a man anymore. I'm a caricature! I thought I could at least be a courier, but I couldn't even do that." He stared at her out of his reddening eye. "What did you have to promise to keep me from the firin' squad?"

"That we would not make another trip like this."

"How *could* you do that?" He leaned on his crutch. "How could you take away the one thing I can contribute to the cause?" He lifted the bottle to his mouth again.

Louisa knew she should just keep her mouth shut. He wouldn't remember what he'd said in the morning anyway. "Haven't you had enough?"

He held up the bottle, shook it, and took another swig. "There's still some left." He wiped his mouth with the sleeve that covered the stump of his arm. "Worthless, that's what I am."

Louisa watched him, anger warring with pity. Might as well ask the question, or rather *one* of the questions that had been bothering her. "Zachary, did you pay the taxes on Twin Oaks?"

He looked up at her from under his eyebrows. "With what?"

Louisa closed her eyes. *Lord, please, don't . . .*

"Rest easy, dear sister. Steadly took care of the matter. One more thing we owe to dear Jefferson."

His words slurred even more, coming in bursts punctuated with silences. The scar gleamed against the deepening red of his face. Jaw slack, head back, drool slipping out the side of a mouth no longer flattened with rage.

"Twin Oaks, all for you . . ." Silence and a snore.

Louisa brushed at the tears she'd not realized were trickling down her cheeks. Zachary had been the best looking of the two brothers, the laughing, dashing brother who charmed the acorns off the trees and cookies from Lucinda. The brother who fetched kittens from trees and bonbons from the confectionary, who assisted his mother in teaching the slaves to read and write, who first promised Louisa she would be beautiful when she felt ugly with the chicken pox. While their mother insisted she had no favorites among her children, Zachary was the one who wrote her letters from college and made her smile.

Ah, Mother, I hope you cannot see him now. It would break

your heart as it has mine. So what to do, leave him in the chair or try to get him to bed? She eyed the distance she would all but have to carry him.

She knelt beside him and took the bottle from his lap, easing it out from under fingers that clutched the bottle's neck like a life preserver.

"Zachary, dear brother, let's get you to bed."

"No, no. Leave me—no more." He cringed back as though she'd struck him. "I . . . I don't know. Can't you . . . understand? I don't know."

She could barely hear his words. She studied the back of his hand, realizing that what she thought to be dirt was instead a festering sore. She pushed his sleeve up to reveal more sores crusted with dried blood.

Had they beaten him? She pulled up the pant leg on his good leg only to find the same. "Those . . . those vermin from hell." The other words that marched through her mind were beyond even thinking. She didn't mean the four-footed kind, although they must have done their share.

She smoothed back the hair that fell over his forehead. A snore flapped his lips, and the smell of both unwashed flesh and booze-burdened breath made her gag, swallow hard, and nearly gag again.

"Zachary." She shook his shoulder, then dodged back as he flailed a hand in her direction. "All right, sleep in the chair." Surely he would rest better there than he'd done at the prison.

Dear Lord, make this night like a lanced boil. Let the pus flow out and the healing begin. She unbuttoned the top two buttons of his shirt and left him to sleep off the alcohol. Worn beyond endurance herself, Louisa crawled into bed and fell asleep halfway through "Our Father, who . . ."

When she woke, Zachary was gone.

CHAPTER TWENTY-EIGHT

RETURNING FROM THE HARVEST

Jesselynn, Meshach, and the boys cut hay for ten days. By the time the last cutting was dry and loaded, they were exhausted and more than ready to head home.

Jesselynn glanced up at the thunderclouds looming over the western foothills. "The rain held off right well, wouldn't you say?"

Meshach leaned on his three-pronged pitchfork. After Jesselynn finally convinced him he could sell them at the fort, he and his students had quickly carved four of them and were working on others. Finding the perfectly pronged branches was half the battle, but Aaron and Lester were getting adept at spotting them.

"Dis load done be topped as much as I can. Rain run right off it. We should have brought de canvas."

Jesselynn studied the hay load. Both it and the two piles they'd stacked to come back for later looked like golden bread loaves with combed hair, all the strands lying curved toward the sides so the water would run off. She'd seen pictures of thatch-roofed cottages in England that looked much like these. And England was a wet country, so the thatching must work.

"Looks mighty fine to me. We could cover some miles before dark."

Meshach slid to the ground and forked back up the hay that slid off with him. He stuck his fork in behind the wagon front where they'd built a vertical frame like the wide flat one they'd built for the bed. The oxen looked dwarfed in comparison to the load.

Clouds scudded overhead as the westerly wind picked up. The oxen leaned into their yokes, and with a creak the wagon started forward. Jesselynn and Meshach walked beside. The boys were scouting good rake trees and fishing for supper. Jesselynn took out the mitten she was knitting and, other than watching for holes, continued to knit one row and purl the next. Mittens were easier to do while walking than gloves.

While the sky looked ominous, the rain held off but for a spatter or two. They covered about five miles before dark and set up camp within minutes. While Jesselynn hobbled the oxen and started the fire, Meshach tossed out a grasshopper on the hook where the river eddied and whispered in the deep dusk. Fireflies dipped and twinkled, and bats swooped for their evening meals.

Jesselynn dug out of her pocket the rose hips she'd picked as they passed a patch of pink roses. Using her knife handle and a flat rock, she pounded them into bitty pieces. She mixed them with the last of their cornmeal and water, then patted the mixture into flat cakes and laid them in the pan to bake. When the water boiled in the deep pot, she poured in the grains she'd pulled off marsh grasses. Wolf had shown her which ones tasted the best. After they cooked, she would add the greens she'd picked as they walked—dandelion, pigweed, and watercress from the river.

Her heart said Wolf had been gone forever. *Father God, please take good care of him. I know getting horses and meeting with his people are important to him, but his coming back is more important to me. I don't want to be a pest, but can you help him hurry? We have a mighty lot to do before winter.* As the wind tugged at her shirt she shivered and laid a couple more sticks on the fire.

A stick cracked, and Meshach stepped into the ring of light with enough fish for supper and breakfast hanging from a forked stick.

"Dis land got food enough for de grabbin'. Never seed such good fishin'."

Jesselynn stirred her gently boiling pot and set the cover back in place. "Wolf says the Indians use far more that the land offers than the whites do. All we have to do is learn what's good and what isn't. I think I saw a plum tree on the way down. Might be ripe enough to pick on our way home. He said something about chokecherries, but I don't know what the tree looks like." As she talked, she pulled back the frying pan and slid the cakes out onto the tin plates.

Meshach scaled the fish he'd already gutted at the river and, along with the last of their grease, laid them in the frying pan. The smell of frying fish rose with the smoke, the sound of sizzling pleasing as well.

"Seems strange, doesn't it, to be out here all this time, and to have no one else come by? Like we're the only ones on the earth." Jesselynn poked another stick into the coals so the kettle would continue to simmer. Watching the flames held the usual fascination.

"De Good Book say who be man dat God be mindful of him."

"I know. And under skies as big as these, I feel pretty small."

"But He hold us in de palm of Him hand." Meshach cupped his big hands, hands that could swing a scythe for hours or bend metal at the forge, yet also be gentle and still enough to let a gold and black butterfly, wings fanning, sit on his brown fingers. Sammy and Thaddeus had been delighted speechless when Meshach showed them the butterfly.

Now he held his cupped hands out to her. She peeked inside to see a firefly winking at her. He opened his hands, and the bitty blob of light flew off. "Dat what we do."

"But we can come back." Jesselynn turned the fish to brown on the other side.

"I know. Thank de good Lawd we can come back."

Lifting the lid of the kettle, she gave the grains a stir, then added the greens. "Supper be ready in a minute." With future rake handles on their shoulders, the boys caught up just as she was ready to serve the supper. Aaron pulled a wild onion from one pocket and tubers of cattails from the other. Together they enjoyed a feast granted them by the generous land.

The closer they drew to home, the more Jesselynn felt like that firefly that flew away. No matter how hard she tried to push them from her mind, thoughts of Aunt Agatha shoved aside concerns about Wolf. Jesselynn didn't want to call them worries, but they sure made for an unhappy state of mind. Meshach walked along whistling. She felt like telling him to shut up. The thicket of plums hung purple, still hard, but she knew they'd ripen once picked.

But she had nothing to carry them in.

Meshach studied the plums, then pulled his shirt over his head. "We knot de sleeves . . ." His hands followed his words, and within moments they had a bag of sorts. By the time they'd filled that and the kettle, she knew what to do. Tomorrow she'd send Jane Ellen and Darcy back down on the mares. The foals were old enough to be weaned anyway. She stopped picking and turned to Meshach.

"We could come here to have a picnic. How far are we from home?"

"By horseback, two hours. By wagon, four. About in dere somewhere."

"Oh." Another idea shot down before flight.

"Leave early in de mornin' and get home late. 'Phelia love a picnic."

As they prodded the oxen to lean into the yokes again, Jesselynn remembered picnics at Twin Oaks. Lucinda would load the wicker baskets, starting with a white-and-red checkered cloth. Fried chicken, biscuits, her lemon cake, sweet pickles, corn relish, bean salad. Ah, the good things that came out of Lucinda's kitchen. There'd be a jug of lemonade or cold buttermilk, blankets to sit on, and parasols to keep the sun off. Dimity dresses with ribbon sashes, broad straw bonnets, and laughter. Darkies singing and the buggy wheels spiraling behind the high-stepping bay team.

She stumbled into a hole and fell nearly to her knees, one knitting needle stabbing into the heel of her hand. "Oh!" *So much for dreaming, you silly thing. Pay attention to life now, and don't get all weepy.* She sucked on the red spot from the needle. At least it hadn't broken the skin, and she didn't break a leg or something walking along daydreaming like that.

"You all right?"

She nodded. The oxen kept plodding along.

Oh, if only Wolf would be in camp when they got there. *Now, don't go wasting your time on stupid "if only's." That'll only get you bad feelings, and yours are too close to that already.*

If only the talking to herself would work. If only Meshach would quit whistling.

Chapter Twenty-Nine

Horse Hunting on the
Powder River Range
September 1863

"There they are."

Mark looked where Wolf pointed. "I don't see anything."

"Look in that thicket of aspen, the trees with the silver trunks. The stallion is off to the left, higher up. You can see his head above the rocks."

Benjamin and Daniel chuckled. "You got to look close if you want to see wild things."

"You can be sure he sees us." Wolf backed his horse under the shade of a grandfather cottonwood. "Study the trees until you see shapes that don't fit."

"If'n they're there, they ain't movin' much."

"They're there. We're downwind of them or that stallion would have them moving already."

"How many you think?" Benjamin kept his attention on the wild horses.

"Not sure. Perhaps twenty head."

"Including young?"

"No, that would be the cream. Remember, we're looking for mares, yearlings of either sex. Might be some two- or three-year-old young bucks the stallion hasn't driven out of the herd yet. Those are the ones we can break and sell this fall." Wolf studied the lay of the land.

"Benjamin, you head on up the north rim. Daniel, go to the south. See if there are any box canyons heading off this main one that we can run them into. I doubt this one here is a box. That old stallion would be too wily to be trapped that easily."

"Do the Indians catch the wild horses?"

"Not usually. They find stealing them from another tribe easier. Besides, the horse is totem for many."

"And yours is the wolf?"

"Um." Wolf concentrated on the horses. "He knows something is here."

The stallion whistled, and the horses dozing in the thicket shifted and trotted out. A buckskin mare loped off toward the mouth of the wide canyon, followed by the rest of the herd, the stallion charging off the cliff above and nipping at the rumps of any stragglers.

"Oh, I never saw anything so purty in all my life." Mark's eyes shown, the smile near to cracked his ears.

"Thirty anyway. Some nice lookin' horses in that bunch. That stallion throws good colts."

"Where'd they come from?"

"The Spanish brought them into Mexico when they came to conquer the New World. They traded some to the Indians, gave some away, and many ran away, and when they got back on their ships to leave, the horses stayed here. Changed the life of the Indian from dogs and people as pack animals to the horse. Been in the last hundred years or so.

"We'll make camp over this ridge while you two go on and scout. If we're lucky, this valley is that stallion's favorite grazin' grounds."

As the other two trotted off, Wolf took Mark to the place he'd chosen for camping, left him there to build camp, and returned to scout the valley floor. A small lake mirrored the rocky cliff above and the aspen leaves already touched by gold. This high in the mountains, winter would come soon. *Ah, Jesselynn, how you would love to see this. One day I'll bring you back here.*

An eagle *screed* from high against the blue, and another answered. As a young boy he had found eagle nests in the cliffs above the valley floors. He'd known where the elk wintered and where the mountain sheep with the curly horns raised their young. His father had trapped all over these mountains in the years before he loved Laughing Girl. Then her tepee became his, and he lived with Red Cloud's tribe, the uncle of the Red Cloud who now led the Oglala band, selling his trappings to the white man and making sure they were not cheated by the fur traders.

Visiting the tribe made Wolf feel that he'd come home, the language rippling music to his ears, the laughter, the smells. But especially the laughter. He knew white men thought the Indian stoic, hard of face and heart. But none enjoyed a good joke like an Indian, often playing pranks to make the entire tribe laugh. He had yet to meet a storyteller better than his uncle, Brown Bear Who Limps. Not even Nathan Lyons, who could spin a good yarn.

Lord, make Jesselynn see these people as I do. Let her not be afraid, nor angry and hateful like some. He stopped and studied the grazing area. From the varied heights of the grass, the horses had been here some time, or left and returned.

That night around the campfire, Benjamin drew a picture in the dirt with a stick. Up the canyon about a mile, a box canyon led off to the right. "It about half mile long, narrowing, den cliffs, waterfall dat be big in spring, now not."

"How wide is the main canyon beyond the one you mean?"

"Narrower, gettin' wider further up. Like big landslide sometime fill in part way." He drew that in too.

"Could we fence it off?"

Benjamin nodded. "Take some work."

"But they can't get out of the box canyon?"

"Not dat I see. Go tomorrow and ride up it."

By the time they laid out their bedrolls, with Wolf taking the first watch, they'd detailed out their plan. Now if only the horses would cooperate.

Building a brush fence across the main canyon took them two days, working from before dawn until well past moonrise. They cut poles to drag across the mouth of the small canyon as soon as the horses galloped into it. When finished, the hunters headed for the lake and fell into the water.

The next morning they set out in search of the herd again. Following their trail took little skill. When they located them again a day later, Wolf reminded them of the plan.

"Remember, we want to move them slowly, but keep them on the move. No time to graze or drink until they get to the canyon." He looked to Mark. "You'll take the far side, Benjamin next, then me and Daniel closest to the other rim. Just showing yourselves will be enough to keep them moving."

They swung into position. The stallion discovered them, and the buckskin mare took the lead. When she tried to head a different direction, one of the four men appeared and sent her back toward the canyon shaking her head and snorting. By taking turns watering and grazing their own horses, they kept the herd on the move. All day, all night. In the morning they reached the canyon and took up their places. The wild horses headed for the lake, took a few swallows, and the riders showed up again, moving them on.

When she reached the brush fence, the lead mare stopped, trotted first one way, then the other. The riders held their mounts, still in view. The horse herd tried to turn around, but the stallion nipped rumps and drove them back away from the riders. The mare saw the open canyon and headed for freedom.

"Got 'em." Wolf reached down for one of the poles and dragged it into place, as did the others. Some of the poles they bound to tree trunks, others to posts they dropped into already dug holes. Within an hour, the fence was up and sturdy enough to corral the horses.

Benjamin removed his hat and wiped the sweat from his forehead. "Dat some slick herdin'."

"There's even water and grass in there for them, though that spring isn't very big." Mark climbed up on the fence to better see the herd, screened now by brush and rock faces.

"What next?" Benjamin glanced skyward. "I get fish for supper?"

"Good idea. Dried venison and canteen water puckers your mouth after a while." Wolf watched as the horses, but for the stallion, settled down to grazing. The big bay trotted to the end of the canyon, checked all the walls and returned to stand on a mound of rubble and trumpet his displeasure. The challenge ricocheted round the walls of the box canyon.

"Him know he trapped."

"But he'll fight to the death." Wolf chewed on a stem of grass. "We'll let him go as soon as we choose which horses to keep."

"Him keep de lead mare?"

"I think so. She's most likely beyond foaling anyway."

Early the next morning they started roping the horses they

wanted to keep and tying them tight to tree trunks. Five young stallions were the first, five mounts for the army. The stallion seemed not to mind so much as they were led out of the gate, but when the men began taking the mares, he lunged at Wolf on his Appaloosa, giving the horse a vicious bite on the rump.

"*Haiya!*" Wolf swung his coiled rope and slashed the stallion across the nose, sending him running off shaking his head.

"We get 'im outa here?" Benjamin rode up to check the bite. "He near to got you!"

"I know. You got to admire him. He's fightin' for his life." Wolf knew by the thudding of his own heart how close he had come to disaster.

When the stallion screamed again, they heard an answering trumpet from Ahab, tied high up the hillside in the trees.

"All we need is a stallion fight. Ahab be dead in no time." Benjamin shook his head.

"Those Thoroughbreds have done well, as Jesselynn said they would. I didn't think they'd make it to Fort Kearney, let alone up here."

"They be strong. Mostly heart, no, all heart."

"Well, let's get the mares and fillies out of there. Do we have enough rope?"

Before nightfall they had eight mares, five with foals, and three fillies snubbed to more trees and the fence posts. With the setting of the sun, they took down the bars and freed the stallion and his greatly reduced band. He drove them out of the enclosure, the buckskin mare leading the way, her ears laid back as if she, too, would tear anyone who touched her limb from limb. The stallion stopped a hundred yards out and trumpeted his challenge, but this time Benjamin had a hand over Ahab's nostrils to keep him quiet.

After they released the captured horses back into the corral so they could eat and drink during the night, Wolf had Mark build camp right outside the bars to the enclosure.

"This way that stallion can't come and steal his horses back."

"He would do that?" Mark turned from dumping a load of dead branches for firewood on the ground.

"Oh yes. Wild stallions have been known to steal horses from tame herds and drive them off. We'll have to pay close attention on the way home for both thieving Indians and a thieving stallion."

"But you met your people."

"I know, but there are other tribes in the region, and stealing horses is a good way to prove your manhood." Wolf pulled the saddle off his own horse and tied the hobbles around his front legs.

"You don't usually hobble him."

"I know, but like I said, tonight is different. Hey, Benjamin, put the others in the corral with the wild ones. That way they'll all be safe."

By the time they reached the banks of Chugwater Creek, Wolf was able to ride three of the young stallions, and Benjamin could ride two of the mares. Daniel sported a black eye, and young Mark was favoring his left wrist. But all the horses had been haltered and led part of the way, so they were ready for training.

Jane Ellen, who'd been assigned watch, scrambled down from the highest hill and ran yelling into camp. So out of breath, she could hardly talk, she yelled again, "They're coming! With the horses. They're almost here!"

"How many did you see?" Jesselynn grabbed Jane Ellen by the shoulders. "How far out are they?"

"Lots of horses and maybe half a mile." Jane Ellen hugged Jesselynn. "Wait till you see 'em."

"You're sure it's our men?" At the look on Jane Ellen's face, Jesselynn shook her head. "Sorry, I apologize. I'm just so . . . so—oh my, I've got to comb my hair." She looked down at her shirt, streaked with dirt from helping dig postholes for the corral. While it wasn't finished yet, another day's work, and it would be.

"You look fine. You think Wolf would care about your shirt?"

"No, I guess not." But Jesselynn darted into the cave anyway and returned with hair combed and a clean shirt buttoned and tucked into her britches.

Thaddeus and Sammy ran back and forth below the caves, from post to post of the corral, out to the haystack and back.

"You two stay back from the horses now, you hear?" Jesselynn put an extra dose of command into her voice, which only upped the giggles.

Meshach strode after them, snatched one boy under each arm, and returned to plunk them on the ground next to Ophelia. "Now, don' you move."

Jesselynn wanted to run just like the little ones. Run to show Wolf the three stacks of hay, the fenced draw, the corral, and the stack of poles where Mrs. Mac had been stripping off bark. She glanced around. Sure enough, Aunt Agatha hadn't come to join the party.

"Don't fuss about her. She's comin' around." Nathan Lyons had read her mind again.

"I hope so. I miss her something fierce." *If someone had told me back in Springfield that I'd be feeling like this, I would have had a laughing fit. Lord, please convince Agatha that the color of*

*a man's skin is not the judge of his heart. I don't know why I think
she should change. The whole war is being fought over just that
principle.* She looked around at the folks who'd become closer
than family. Together they were carving a home out of this
new land.

She heard Ahab whinny and could wait no longer. She
tore her hat from her head and ran across the grazed land
toward the creek, where they would come around the curve of
the hill. She reached the shade of a grand old cottonwood just
as Benjamin on Ahab led in the herd.

"We done it, Marse Jesse, we done brung home de
horses." He leaped to the ground and gave her a leg up.
"Marse Wolf, he be back dere." Benjamin flipped a loop over
the nose of the horse he'd been leading, swung aboard, and
used the lead rope as a rein. "You go on and find 'im. He be
right glad to see you."

Jesselynn allowed the stream of horses to pass, saluting
both Daniel and Mark as they waved, her attention on the
man bringing up the rear. As always, he and his horse moved
as one while keeping the new stock moving ahead. She could
feel his eyes on her. Shivers ran up her arms and down her
back. Her belly warmed. She leaned forward to pat Ahab's
neck. He shifted, sensing her tension.

"Hello, wife." Wolf's voice sent shivers chasing the others.
Thank you, God, for bringing him home safe. She searched
him for the war wounds she'd seen on the others. None.
"Hello, husband. Looks like you've been busy." *So how did
Red Cloud treat you? Was the country as wonderful as you
remember?* She noticed that his medicine pouch now hung
outside his shirt. Was there a reason for that?

Chapter Thirty

Richmond, Virginia

Louisa found him. That's all that mattered.

"Lemme go." The man on the buggy seat beside her thrashed at his invisible demons. Obviously he'd tried to drown them in whiskey and failed.

So, Lord, what do I do now? How do I pay for this conveyance even? Zachary must have been on his way back to the hotel. That's all she could figure.

The driver stopped at the hotel she'd indicated and peered over his shoulder.

"Could you help me, please?" She gritted her teeth. How was she to haul this sorry heap of humanity up to their room?

"Yes ma'am." The man climbed down and came around to Zachary's side. "Here, sir, let me help you."

"Are we there?"

"Yes." She blinked. How had he sobered up so quickly?

Zachary dug in his watch pocket and handed the driver a dollar. "Keep the change."

"Yes, sir." With the driver assisting, Zachary gained his balance. Louisa followed as the two men made their way up the steps, through the lobby, and up to the room. With Zachary in the chair again, the driver tipped his hat and closed the door on his way out.

"A driver will be here for us in the morning. Make sure you

are ready," Louisa said to her brother.

He closed his eyes and refused to answer the questions that boiled within her.

The Quakers had come to their assistance again.

If Zachary remembered any of his dark nights of raving, he never alluded to them. And other than curt orders, he didn't speak to Louisa again. Though taciturn, he was at least polite to those who assisted them.

Louisa swung from anger to fury to hurt, clear to her deep insides. Over and over she pleaded with the Lord to repair the rent in their family, but Zachary refused to even look at her, as if she were a pariah or had leprosy.

Throughout the trip home, while often she felt like hitting him with his crutch, she kept a gentle smile on her face and prayed for love and patience. Never was she happier to see Aunt Sylvania's house and to crawl into her own clean bed.

When Louisa woke after sleeping round the clock, she washed and washed again, dressed in clean clothes, and wandered out to the back veranda to visit with those gathered there.

After returning the greetings, she asked her aunt, "Where's Zachary?"

"Gone to work. He will be staying with Carrie Mae and her family now that they have moved into their new house. That way the poor boy won't have to travel so far."

Poor boy, my liver. Good thing Aunt Sylvania wasn't a mind reader.

But at the sweet smile on her aunt's face, Louisa knew Zachary had said nothing about their ordeal.

"I was getting so worried when you didn't return as soon as you said you would."

The statement obviously needed a reply. What should she say? Louisa cleared her throat and leaned close to her aunt's chair. "We ran into some difficulties, but as you can see, we are all right now." *Or at least I am. Lord, only you know what's on my brother's heart.*

"I feared that. We all prayed for you, even our soldiers here. You haven't met Charles, Corporal Saunderson yet." She took Louisa by the arm. "Come meet him. He's such a sweet boy."

Louisa stopped at the chair where a man, all bones and angles, sat staring straight ahead. A lock of dark hair fell over his forehead. Tall and thin as he was, he reminded her of Lieutenant Lessling. Louisa couldn't help thinking that a sweet *boy* he was not, as a deep, resonant voice answered her aunt's question.

"I am doing well, ma'am. You are not to worry."

"I'd like you to meet my niece, just back from . . ." Aunt Sylvania glanced at Louisa, who stepped forward and touched the man on the shoulder.

"I'm glad to welcome you to our home. I was . . . I mean, the trip took longer than I expected, or I would have been here to greet you." She glanced over his body, looking for injuries but found none except that it appeared he couldn't see. He held out a hand in her direction, but his eyes never tracked her nor showed emotion. He held his head still, as though he thought it might fall off if he moved too fast.

"The surgeon general thought perhaps, since you have helped others who lost their sight, you could help me." The tone of his voice told her what the words cost him, for his face registered nothing. Blank like a freshly washed blackboard was all she could think of.

"I'll be glad to help you. Where is your home?" She settled herself on a chair that Reuben set behind her.

"It was in Fredericksburg but no longer stands. So far I have not been able to locate any of my family." He lifted a hand to his face. "This, this has made everything impossible." He dropped his voice as he did his hand.

"I could write letters for you."

"I would be most grateful." Louisa gave the corporal as much attention as she could in the next few days, teaching him how to feed himself, shave, and find his way around the house. They moved him into Zachary's room, along with one of the men who'd been at the house for some time. He had no legs and was fashioning himself a low cart that he could ride in and propel with his hands.

"Better'n draggin' meself along the floor. Can't abide feelin' sorry fer meself. Bad 'un that."

Louisa smiled at her legless friend. "Thanks, Homer, you always brighten my day." As she left the two together in the room, Louisa paused in the hall at the sound of Corporal Saunderson's voice.

"Describe Miss Louisa for me, please."

She could feel the heat flame her face as she headed for the kitchen. Now, what had brought that on?

That evening she was putting away the sewing supplies when Reuben brought an envelope on the once-silver tray.

"This comed to de door. For you." The grizzled black man wore an air of curiosity as he glanced back over his shoulder to the front of the house.

"Who brought it?" Louisa took the letter and studied the handwriting. Only her name. She looked up to see Reuben shaking his head.

"Don' know who brought it. Knock on de door, I goes to answer, no one dere, but dis on de mat."

Louisa slit the flap open with her fingernail and withdrew a single sheet of paper. She leaned closer to the lamp.

Dear Miss Highwood. She glanced to the bottom of the

sheet and caught her breath. It was signed by Major James Dorsey.

"Who's it from?" Aunt Sylvania glanced up from her knitting.

"A-a man who assisted me on . . . on this last trip."

Sylvania cocked her head to the side. "You know, both you and Zachary have been most evasive about details of this last trip."

"Someday I'll tell you." Louisa drew in a breath to slow her thudding heart and read the remainder of the letter.

I hope and pray this not only finds you, but finds you well and recovered from your experience. I have been transferred back to my company in the field and am grateful, as I'm sure you were, to leave Washington behind. Please know that I do not bear you and your brother the rancor that the general does. We were all just doing our duty. Please remember me to your sister when you write to her.

I am proud to know two such fine Southern ladies. May our loving Lord bring you safely through this abominable war and home again to your beautiful plantation.

Sincerely,
Major James Dorsey

Louisa folded the letter and tucked it back into the envelope, shaking her head all the while. What a surprise! Nay, what a shock.

Several nights later, after she'd visited Carrie Mae, she wrote to Jesselynn, telling her not only of their escape and all that happened but also of the major, reminding her sister where and when she had met the man.

It seems a shame to me that we should meet under such rep-

rehensible circumstances. If only it had been another time and another place, not on opposite sides of this abominable war. I am eternally grateful God brought us safely back to Richmond, but I have not seen Zachary since I returned.

She told Jesselynn about the new men in the house and then continued with news of the family.

Carrie Mae and the baby are settled into their new home, or as settled as anyone can be at this point. Her house is lovely, and our baby is a bright spot, like a nodding daisy in a field of thistle. The war colors everything. Sister, dear, I hate this war with such a passion. And fear strikes clear to the bottom of my heart for our brother, who is bitter and angry beyond description. I do not know what to do but pray for him. I know that God can bring our brother back to himself, but will Zachary allow that to happen?

Forgive my rantings here and give Thaddeus hugs and kisses for me. He is growing up without knowing his sister Louisa, who loves him dearly. One day we will meet again at Twin Oaks, God willing.

She signed her letter, then added a postscript. *Aunt Sylvania is back to being her old self but for a slight limp, and her eye droops when she gets tired, which also happens more easily.*

She didn't tell her sister about the rush of joy she'd felt when she saw the major's signature.

If only James Dorsey were not in the Union army.

CHAPTER THIRTY-ONE

ON THE CHUGWATER RIVER

"Fall is on the way."

Jesselynn stopped beside her husband at the mouth of the cave and leaned against him. He put his arm around her shoulders so she could fit right next to his heart. "How do you know?" she asked.

"Smell the air, and the geese are flying south."

Jesselynn inhaled, sorting the smells as she became aware. Horse manure, dust, skunk, the grasses down by the water. She inhaled again. Her husband's special scent, woodsmoke, meat drying over a low fire. Nothing else.

"So what does fall smell like?"

"That bite in the air, turning leaves—there's a difference between growing and turning—you can smell the pine. . . ." He glanced down at her. "Maybe after a few more years here, you'll know what I mean."

Jesselynn sniffed again. "Guess I haven't been paying enough attention to the smells."

"Do you know that to the Indian, the white man has a peculiar odor? Can smell one coming if the wind is right."

"And if your Indian family uses bear grease, I know what they'd smell like." At the flash of something, she wasn't sure what, across his face, she wished she'd not brought that up. However, moccasins soaked in bear grease really did repel water, as did boots soaked in bear grease.

"So you want another lesson in training horses today?" Wolf looked down at her. "You have a talent along that line."

"Lesson?" She cocked an eyebrow. "I gentle 'em. You and Benjamin train 'em."

"Works well. Another couple of weeks and we can take them to the fort. That'll give us seven horses to sell. What about selling some of the oxen too? They could use them for beef, if nothing else."

"I've been thinking. What if we give one or two of ours to Red Cloud's people?"

Wolf nodded and smiled down at her. "Guess we better ask everyone else what they want to do. Can't see how we can winter over this many oxen though. They can't dig down to the grass like buffalo and elk, or eat the willow tips."

"And yet we'll need them for breaking ground in the spring. Some of this bottom land ought to grow oats real well." She slipped her arm around Wolf's waist. They so seldom had time alone together without sixteen interruptions. She treasured moments like these, perhaps more so because they were rare.

"This is why the Indian bands keep on the move. Graze off one patch and move to the next. Summer near the rivers and winter where the trees protect the tepees and the snow is not so deep the horses can't dig through to graze. Easier, I think."

"Some of the tribes are raising gardens down along the river, I heard someone talking about that at the fort. Then the other tribes come trade for pumpkins and squash and such."

Wolf sighed. "I know. Times sure are changing."

"Will being a farmer be hard for you?" She bit her lower lip, waiting for his answer.

"Not as long as we raise horses. If training horses is my work, I'll play all my life."

Jesselynn smiled up at him. "We have to feed them too."

"Ah, wife, ever practical." He tipped her chin to share a kiss when they heard from the cave behind them, "Jesse, I got to pee."

"Today we'll put those young pups to diggin' an outhouse." Wolf sighed. "Civilization has indeed come to the high country."

"So we'll have the first latrine. Will that make us famous?" Jesselynn reached up and kissed him quick. "I'm coming, Thaddeus."

As soon as they'd eaten, Jesselynn brought another mare into the corral and began her training. She followed the mare around the circle for a time to keep her moving. When the mare lowered her head and turned to face her, Jesselynn stopped and waited. When she took a couple steps backward, the mare came toward her. They continued the dance until the mare came right up to her, head lowered, acknowledging Jesselynn as leader of the herd. Jesselynn stroked her ears and rubbed down the dark neck. If only she'd learned this easy way of working a horse years ago, although the Thoroughbreds at Twin Oaks were handled from the day they were foaled and never had to be broken.

She slipped the loop around the mare's neck and walked her around the circle, then turned the other way and walked figure eights. Always the mare followed. The only time she hesitated was when she heard her colt cry. They'd weaned the babies as soon as they arrived in camp, much to the consternation of both mares and offspring. Some were being more stubborn than others.

Stroking the mare, rubbing her with a cloth, then putting the saddle blanket in place—nothing bothered the mare, as long as Jesselynn stopped and backed up a step as soon as the horse began to tighten up.

Wolf leaned against the top bar of the corral. "You sure do have the touch."

"Thank you. You can probably ride her tomorrow." She crossed the corral, the mare following. "How are the geldings doing?" They'd gelded the five young stallions two days earlier. "You'd hardly know they'd been cut. Meshach is a man of many talents."

"He says all you need is a sharp knife and someone to hold the horse down."

"Benjamin sitting on their heads did that trick. No bleeders, no infection." Wolf stepped back from the rail. "Ahab took care of the mare that came in heat. She's good and sturdy, should make a good colt." Since they had no idea how many of the wild mares were already bred, they were watching them carefully. They couldn't afford to winter over a mare that hadn't taken.

"Think I'll go up and see how Nate and Daniel are doing with the loggin'. You want to ride along?"

"Oh yes." Jesselynn stopped. "No, I can't. I promised Jane Ellen that we'd go looking for hazelnuts, herbs, and such as soon as I finished with the mare. She works so hard, she deserves a treat like that."

"You're riding?"

"Dulcie and Sunshine."

"Agatha rode up with Nate and Daniel. Nate said she can snake a tree out good as any man. Those oxen do just what she tells them."

Jesselynn smiled up at him. "Is that what he says? I think he just wants to spend time with her away from all the prying eyes."

"Up loggin'?"

"Heard tell she fixed a special basket for dinner. Even

some molasses to spread on the corn bread."

"Well, I knew he was sweet on her, but looks like it goes both ways."

I just hope her happiness spills out on the rest of us. Jesselynn knew she particularly meant on her and Wolf, but others in the party had borne the brunt of Agatha's displeasure too.

She'd just turned back to the mare when two rifle shots echoed down from the tree line. Two shots were a signal for help.

Wolf whistled. His Appaloosa broke free from the herd and galloped toward him. He swung aboard and galloped on around the bend up toward the hill.

"Get my medicine kit!" Jesselynn called into the cave. "Something's wrong up on the hill." Benjamin had Domino saddled and ready for her, along with Dulcie for himself, by the time she had grabbed her small kit with extra bandages and had run back out to the corral.

"Dear God, take care of them, whoever's hurt." She muttered the prayer over and over, both inside and out, as she galloped up the hill.

"This way!" Nate hollered down the hill, waving his arm at the same time.

Jesselynn urged her horse straight up the incline rather than following the zigzags used to skid the logs down. Domino was heaving by the time they got to the site, but Jesselynn ignored that, dismounting and running for the body she saw lying on the ground. Aunt Agatha. Something had happened to Aunt Agatha.

"The chain slipped and caught her hand." Wolf kept his voice low. "She's lost some fingers and fainted, I think from the pain."

Jesselynn dropped to her knees beside the pasty-faced woman. Blood everywhere told a story all its own.

"I done de best I can." Daniel had clamped his fingers over the blood vessel in her wrist so that the bleeding had stopped. He looked up at her with tears in his eyes. "I shouldn't a let her do de chain."

"Hush, Daniel, no one *lets* Aunt Agatha do anything. She does what she thinks best."

"But she saved my life in dat town."

"Thanks to your quick thinking, she's not goin' to die. So you returned the favor." As Jesselynn spoke, she inspected the mangled hand. Two fingers gone, another might have to go by the looks of the shredded flesh, a deep gash at the base of the thumb. She looked up to Nate, who now cradled the woman's head in his lap. "How long she been out?"

"Since before Wolf got here." He sniffed, his thumb stroking Agatha's cheek.

Jesselynn bound the hand, tying a tight knot over the wrist. "You can let go now." She glanced up at Daniel, who sat with closed eyes and mouth moving without sound. She knew he was praying. "Daniel."

The young man slowly opened his eyes. "You sure, Marse?"

"I'm sure." She watched her aunt's hand as he released his thumb. No gusher. She sighed, relief evident in every line of her body. "Aunt Agatha." She patted the woman's cheek. "Aunt Agatha, can you hear me?"

A slight nod of the head. Nate leaned over and laid his cheek against her forehead.

"You'll be all right, my dear Agatha. You'll be all right."

Agatha murmured something and turned her face into the cupping hand, her eyes slowly opening. "Hurts some bad."

Jesselynn uncorked the small flask of whiskey she kept for emergencies. "Here, drink some of this. It will help."

"I don't drink spirits."

"Today you do." A note of command in Nate's voice caused Jesselynn to look up to Wolf, who smiled back at her.

A slight nod and Agatha swallowed several times. Her eyes flew open and her good hand went to her throat. "Oh! You are tryin' to kill me!" She coughed and gagged. "Water." Wolf held the canteen to her mouth for several more swallows.

"We can dilute that with this."

Agatha shuddered. "No, thank you. I'm done with fainting now." She tried to sit up, but before she could do more than make a motion, Nate had her propped against his knees and leaning back against his chest. Agatha looked at the bound hand and closed her eyes for only a moment. "How bad is it?"

"We'll know more after we get you to camp and clean it up."

"Then we better go."

"Do you think you can ride?"

"If I must."

"If you will ride in front of me, I can hold you secure." Wolf looked her directly in the eyes when he offered. "Otherwise we will go for a wagon."

Agatha looked up to Nate, and at his nod, she did the same. "Th-thank you. I will ride."

Jesselynn knew her aunt well enough to know what this was costing her. "Daniel, switch my saddle to the Appaloosa." She turned back to her aunt. "I'm going to bind that hand up to your shoulder, so you can't bump it. All right?"

Agatha nodded, her face still white from the pain, her lower lip quivering the slightest bit.

Jesselynn wanted to wrap her arms around her aunt and hold her close, but now was not the time for that.

"I'll go ahead and get things ready."

Agatha reached for Jesselynn's hand with her free one. "Be careful."

Fighting the tears that threatened to flood her, Jesselynn raised her aunt's hand and kissed the fingers. "I will."

By the time Wolf made his way down the hill and into camp, Agatha was near to fainting again. Her eyes fluttered open when they stopped, and she slumped into Meshach's waiting arms.

"God be takin' good care of you," he whispered as he carried her to a pallet laid by the outside fire pit. "Me 'n 'Phelia been prayin'."

Jesselynn had water boiling with her needle, thread, and scissors in it. Jane Ellen stood with the bottle of laudanum in one hand and the whiskey in the other, fighting the tears that seeped in spite of her efforts.

"We takes good care of you." Her smile wavered, but her words held firm.

"I know." Agatha lay down with a sigh. "Such a bother I am. But I wasn't bein' careless." A trace of her normal asperity flavored her words.

"I want you to drink some more of that whiskey. We can dilute it with water if you like." Jesselynn shook her head. "Wish I had some honey for it to make it more palatable, but—"

"I can drink it if I must." Agatha glared at the silver flask. "Let's get this over with." She held it in her own hand, swigged as much as she could before her eyes watered so bad she had to sniff, and her throat closed. She choked and coughed. "More?"

Jesselynn nodded. "Just think, Daddy and Uncle Hiram thought this the best sipping whiskey anywhere."

"Well, Joshua and Hiram weren't always known to

have the best of sense." Agatha took another swallow and sucked in a lungful of air. "Huh." She blinked and closed her eyes. "I burn so bad inside, I won't feel you work on my hand."

Jane Ellen chuckled and rocked back on her heels. "You one fine, strong woman, Agatha Highwood."

"I'm ready." Agatha lay back and closed her eyes. "Don't worry about gentle. Just get it done."

Jesselynn handed her a bit of clean rag. "Bite down on this if you have to. It can help."

With Nathan Lyons holding Aunt Agatha's other hand and Wolf and Meshach ready to hold her down if necessary, Jesselynn unwrapped the mangled hand. Carefully she cleaned all the dirt and debris away and washed it with whiskey. She then sewed flaps of skin over the severed fingers and stitched up the slash on the thumb. While the third finger looked bad, once it was cleaned, she was able to set the broken bone, grateful to not see bone splinters. It didn't look like the tendons had been severed either. When finished, Jesselynn poured more whiskey over the entire hand, took the thin wrapped board that Meshach handed her, and bound the hand to the splint.

"Please, God, make this heal with no infection, so Agatha can have full use of her hand again. Thank you, this wasn't worse."

"Amen," Agatha murmured from between clenched teeth. "Now, if I can have some of that laudanum, I will gladly and gratefully go to sleep. Thank you, all."

Jesselynn stumbled when she stood, for her feet had gone to sleep. Wolf caught her and held her against his chest.

"You did a fine job. No doctor could have done better, and most of them not as well."

Jesselynn leaned against him. "That was a close one."

"Yes, but as Agatha said, 'tweren't her fault. She was bein' careful."

She could hear his chuckle down in his chest. What a miracle that this man could still care for Aunt Agatha in spite of the way she'd treated him and his wife. She looked up into his eyes. "You know, Mr. Torstead, you are one fine Christian man, and I am right proud to know you."

"Thank you, Mrs. Torstead," he whispered in her ear. "And I'm glad to *know* you, and the more often the better."

She could feel the heat start low and race to engulf her face. "I better see to my patient." She poked him in the chest. "And you, sir, mind your thoughts." Her whisper was for him alone. His chuckle made her warm all over.

Several days later Jesselynn walked into the cave and stopped, placing her hands on her hips. "Aunt Agatha, what happened to your sling?"

Agatha straightened from laying strips of venison across the drying racks. "It was in my way." She poked her board-bound hand back into the sling of white muslin tied behind her neck. "There. Now are you happy?"

"Yes, although I'd be happier if you were to take it easy for a few more days."

"I *am* takin' it easy. If I went any slower, I'd be sittin' down, and since I can't knit or sew, I won't sit."

"As you wish. But the more you bump it, the longer it might take to heal." Jesselynn left the cave before her aunt could have the last word. At least she was talking to them, oh happy day. And there was no sign of infection. *Ah, Lord, you are so good to us.*

Sunday, after Meshach read the Scriptures and they'd sung several songs, Nathan spoke. "I would like to say somethin', if'n you don't mind."

Agatha, sitting beside him, tugged on his shirt sleeve. "I'd like to speak first."

Nate patted her hand. "If you want."

Agatha stood up. "I have a confession to make, since the Bible says that we must confess our sins to one another so that we might be healed." She held her wounded hand to her breast with the other. "All of you know how hateful I have been to Jesselynn"—she nodded toward Jesselynn—"and to Wolf." Another nod. "In my own defense, I have to say that I only believed what I was born and raised in. But Meshach, with his wisdom of the Word, and Na—ah, Mr. Lyons, with his persuasive tongue, have forced me to look at other parts of Scripture. Jesus said to forgive as we are forgiven and to love like He loves, with no mention of skin color or anything else, just to love our neighbor as ourselves." She paused and looked skyward, a ploy that helped fight unwanted tears. Taking a deep breath, she continued. "I want to love God with all my heart, strength, and mind and my neighbor as myself. Therefore, Jesselynn and Wolf and each of you that I have wronged with my self-righteous ways, please . . . forgive me?"

Jesselynn stood and crossed to her aunt. "I forgive you if you will forgive me for being so angry at your bullheadedness." The two hugged and sniffed together. Jesselynn took a square of calico from her pocket and wiped her aunt's eyes. "I'm so glad to have you back. I've missed you terribly."

"And I you." Agatha turned to Wolf, who stood right behind Jesselynn. "And you, nephew, will you forgive an old lady blinded by color?"

"Most certainly. And I am honored to hear you call me nephew."

Sitting back down, Jesselynn felt as if she were so light she could hover above the block of wood on which she sat. It seemed that if Wolf didn't hold on to her, she might float away and go dancing with the breeze.

Mr. Lyons stood beside Agatha. "And now I get to speak." He took Agatha's left hand in his. "I have asked Miss Agatha to be my wife, and she has said yes. We thought perhaps we could be married at the fort when we go for supplies."

Jesselynn flashed an I-told-you-so kind of grin at her husband and rose to be the first to wish the couple well. Everyone crowded around, shaking hands, hugging, and laughing at one another's teasing.

"Where's Ophelia?"

Jesselynn looked around. When had Ophelia left their gathering?

CHAPTER THIRTY-TWO

RICHMOND, VIRGINIA

"Has Zachary said anything to you about our trip north?"

Carrie Mae shook her head. "Not to me. I just know he is real unhappy."

Unhappy doesn't begin to describe our brother. But Louisa just nodded. No sense making Carrie Mae worry. It was unlikely they could do anything about Zachary, anyway, other than pray for him, of course. Why did that lately feel like such an exercise in futility?

Louisa cocked her head. "Think I hear the baby crying." She rose before Carrie Mae could move. "I'll get her."

Louisa admired the silk damask wall coverings and the walnut wainscoting as she made her way down the hall to the nursery. After the one cry Miriam had chosen to play with her fingers instead of setting up her "I'm hungry" howl.

"You sweet thing." Louisa lifted the baby from her crib and kissed the side of her smile. "Miriam, what will we do with you? You get prettier every day." Laying her down on the padded dresser, she changed the baby's diapers, dusting the little bottom with cornstarch and blowing on her rounded belly.

Miriam cooed and waved her fists, legs pumping like she was ready to run.

*I wonder what my baby would look like if I—*She stopped the thought in shock. *Why, Louisa Highwood, you were going to add the major's name. Whatever has come over you?* She could feel the heat rising up her neck.

"You won't tell anyone, will you, sugar?" She patted the baby's hands together and tickled her toes. "Ah, baby dear, I hope and pray you never have to go though a war like we've been having. Lord, please, please bring peace. I want a baby like this, a husband, a home. I want to go home to Twin Oaks."

"So do I." Carrie Mae stood in the doorway. "Not fair sharin' secrets with her. She can't pass them on."

How long has she been standing there? A moment of concern about what Carrie Mae might have heard flickered through Louisa's mind, but she brushed it away. Cuddling Miriam to her cheek, she turned to her sister. "Who better to share with?"

"Me." Carrie Mae leaned against the doorjamb. "I feel like I live all alone in this big old house."

"You have a brand-new house, servants, and a husband, and—"

"A husband who is never home, a brother likewise, and a baby who, sweet as she is, doesn't carry on much of a conversation yet."

Louisa studied her younger sister. Frown lines aged her forehead. While she'd regained her figure, her bounce had yet to return.

"You know what, Carrie Mae?" *Oh, Lord, here I go again. Give me the right words, please.*

"No, but I have a feeling I'm about to learn." She crossed the room and pulled at the cord in the corner. "I'll order tea so we have the sustenance to continue."

"I'm not joking."

"Neither am I. You take the baby. She's going to want to

295

eat any minute now." Carrie Mae gave the maid who appeared at the door her instructions and motioned her sister down the hall. "You know, sometimes you sound so much like Jesselynn that I have to stop and remind myself you aren't."

"I think I'll take that as a compliment."

"And then I remember that she is clear off in the wilderness somewhere, and I prob'ly won't see her again in this lifetime, and I get sorry for all the mean things I said to her."

"She was just trying her best, like all the rest of us." *If only our best were good enough.*

When they were settled back in the parlor, with tea poured and Miriam making her little pig noises at her mother's breast, Louisa stirred sugar into her tea with a silver spoon, wondering where such things came from anymore. She laid the spoon on the china saucer and, propping her elbows on her knees in a decidedly unladylike manner, sipped from her cup and studied her sister.

Might as well say what she was thinking.

"Carrie Mae, I reckon your trouble is this. You have entirely too much time on your hands."

"Why, Louisa Marie Highwood, however can you say that? You have no idea how much time this baby takes. I'm just an old milk cow far as she's concerned, and running a house like this—you know how hard Mama worked at Twin Oaks."

Louisa sighed. "I know Mama worked hard. She ran an entire plantation along with the big house and made sure close to fifty people had food in their bellies and clothes on their backs."

"Well, I have to entertain too, you know. Jefferson is always bringing home friends for supper, sometimes without even having the grace to let me know beforehand."

"And how often have you cooked supper for these guests or cleaned up afterward?"

"My word, why would I do that? We have servants—and let me remind you they are not slaves—to do those things. Jefferson says we are doing our part giving these people a place to work, and"—her voice rose—"I think you are just horrid to talk to me like this."

"You could knit, sew uniforms, and roll bandages like the rest of us." Louisa cringed inside at the tone of her own voice. *Whatever happened to "A soft answer turneth away wrath"?*

"Is that all? Why, you silly, I sent an entire box of rolled bandages over to the hospital just yesterday."

And who did the rolling? But Louisa had a notion that those who worked in the Steadly home did the rolling in order to make their mistress look good and thus keep their positions. She'd not taken time to count the number of personal maids Carrie Mae had employed in the time since she and Jefferson had been married.

Louisa sighed. "I'm sorry, dear sister. You just look unhappy, and I hoped to help that sad look go away."

Carrie Mae put the baby to her shoulder and patted her back. A big burp made both women smile.

"There now, sweet thing. That's what we think of your mean old auntie's ideas. We work real hard for the cause, don't we?" In spite of the sugar-sweet words, the glare Carrie Mae sent around her daughter's head could have ignited coal.

"I'm sorry, Carrie Mae, I don't know what's gotten into me lately." But Louisa knew that was an untruth. She did know what had gotten into her. She was sick of the war, sick of Zachary acting like he was, sick of being so far from home. When would it ever end?

"You needn't look so sad yourself." Carrie Mae handed Louisa the baby. "Look at that smile and tell me anything in this whole wide world is more precious than that."

Louisa cupped the baby with her hands and lower arms, elbows propped on her knees. Miriam smiled, her full, rounded mouth open, her eyes intent on her auntie's. Rosy lips thinned as she struggled to make a sound, not a scream, but an answer to Louisa's gentle baby murmurings.

"That's right now. You can talk with me, of course you can." She nodded slowly, smiling and cooing back.

"You two certainly can carry on some kind of conversation. Why, I'd think you knew exactly what she was sayin'."

"She's saying 'I love you, Auntie Louisa.' Can there be any doubt of that?"

Carrie Mae sat down on the horsehair sofa beside her sister and, leaning her chin on Louisa's shoulder, watched her baby's efforts. "Isn't she the smartest, most beautiful baby you ever did see? Why, Mama would bust her buttons over this baby, and can you think what Lucinda would say?"

"I reckon Daddy would have been carrying her out to the barn already to make sure she loves the horses from the beginning."

"Carrying, my right foot! He'd have had her up in the saddle with him." Carrie Mae traced the outline of her daughter's cheek with a gentle fingertip. "Sometimes I want to go home and see Mama and Daddy again so bad that I near to run out that door and call for the carriage."

"I know." Louisa sniffed back the tears. No matter that their parents had gone ahead to heaven, when she thought of home, they were still there. The big house and all the barns, the slaves' quarters, the trees, the rose garden, all were still there.

"Miss Carrie Mae, message from Mr. Jefferson." The maid paused in the doorway, waiting to be acknowledged.

"Thank you." Carrie Mae took the envelope, and with a

slight shrug to her sister, slit it open.

"Oh, bother." She heaved a sigh. "Is he waitin' for an answer?"

"Yes, ma'am."

"Tell him I'll be ready." Carrie Mae turned to Louisa. "Jefferson says I have to accompany him to a soirée tonight. President Davis and General Lee will be the guests of honor." She tapped the envelope on the edge of her finger. "How would you like to come with us?"

Louisa shook her head. "No, I wasn't invited. And besides, I have nothing to wear to something like that. I'll just go on home and—"

"And you'll do nothing of the kind." Carrie Mae studied her sister. "You've lost so much weight we might have to take in one of my dresses. I'll have Lettie do your hair. She is the best with a hot iron and pins. Come on, we haven't played dress-up in years."

Louisa looked down at the baby now blinking her eyes to stay awake.

"I'd much rather stay here and take care of Miriam. She and I can have a fine time."

"No, we'll put her down to sleep, and you and I are going to get ready."

"But Aunt Sylvania is expecting me." Louisa now had a pretty good idea what a drowning victim felt like. Getting enough air in the face of Carrie Mae's whirlwind tactics took extra doing.

"I'll send her a note." Carrie Mae picked up the baby. "Besides, maybe you'll meet the man of your dreams there."

I think maybe I've already met the man of my dreams, but no one will ever know that.

Chapter Thirty-Three

"Is that really me?" Louisa stared at the figure in the full-length mirror.

"It most surely is. I knew there was a beauty hiding under that mouse look of yours. I know you do good works, but you don't always have to look so . . . so . . ." Carrie Mae made a face.

"Should I take that as a compliment?" Louisa touched one of the springy curls that lay over her shoulder. Lettie had gathered the curls up in back with diamanté clips and waved the hair on top of her head. The clips caught the light every time Louisa moved her head. She touched the strands of gold and sapphires around her slender neck and smoothed down the sides of the blue silk overskirt that flared from her narrow waist and was gathered into scallops by small nosegays of single roses. The pleated underskirt of cream lace was threaded by matching narrow ribbon.

"Here." Carrie Mae handed her a silk fan. She stepped back and studied her sister. "You look lovely."

"So do you." Louisa turned from her image. "Wouldn't Daddy be proud of his girls?"

"The cab is here, ma'am."

"Do you need a shawl?" Carrie Mae held out a diaphanous drape.

"Maybe I should." Louisa looked again at the amount of flesh showing above the low cut of the bodice.

Carrie Mae draped the shawl around her sister's shoulders, stood for Lettie to do the same for her, and the two of them sailed out the door.

Louisa swallowed the butterflies that threatened to take wing. What on earth was she doing all dressed up like this when she should be home taking care of her boys? What if something happened to Aunt Sylvania? What if—

"Now you just quit your worryin' and have a good time. You deserve a good time for a change. You've been workin' like a servant ever since we left home. And before then."

But Louisa knew better—it was Jesselynn who had worked so hard to keep Twin Oaks going. While she and Carrie Mae could be excused because they were young, she knew they could have been more help. Should have been more help.

The driver halted the cab under the portico of the Ambergine Mansion, and a doorman stepped forward to assist the two women. Louisa shook out her skirt, reminded herself to quit chewing on her lower lip and, head held high, followed her sister through the doors. *Oh, Lord, here we go. Are you sure this is where I belong?*

Light danced among the crystals on the chandeliers as they waited in the receiving line. Within moments Jefferson Steadly joined them, kissing his wife on the cheek and smiling at Louisa.

"What a pleasure to have two such beautiful women to introduce around this evening. I'm glad you could join us, sister Louisa." He bowed over her hand and led the two sisters forward.

"Is that who I think it is?" Louisa tried to hang back.

"Of course." Jefferson stepped forward again. "President Davis, may I introduce you to my sister-in-law, Miss Louisa Highwood?"

"Why, most certainly. I am delighted." Jefferson Davis,

president of the Confederate States of America, took Louisa's hand and bowed, his neatly trimmed beard brushing the back of her hand.

"I-I'm honored, Mr. President." Louisa tried swallowing, but her words still sounded breathless.

"No, I am the one honored. I have heard tales of a lovely young woman who, with her brother, dons various disguises and ventures north to bring back medical supplies for our suffering men. Someone even told me of a nefarious raccoon. . . ."

Louisa couldn't contain the smile. "The poor creature who gave its life to assist us was a possum, sir."

"Ah." He nodded, eyes twinkling. "So it is you." He turned. "And that is your brother over there?"

"Yes, sir."

"Besides these mercy trips, Zachary has proven a great help since he came to work for me."

As if sensing he was being spoken of, Zachary turned. At the sight of his sisters, he straightened, then ordered his face into a semblance of a smile and nodded.

"Thank you, sir. I am truly grateful that we could help our wounded." *But please make this war stop.* But she kept the smile on her face as they were handed to the next man in line.

"I heartily concur with our president's comments." General Robert E. Lee, hair now fully white, bowed over her hand.

Louisa glanced at Carrie Mae, seeking support. "Th-thank you, General. I-I never . . ." She swallowed and sucked in a breath of air, air now grown sultry with perfume and cigar smoke.

The general leaned closer, speaking more softly for her ears alone. "In spite of what a certain young man believes, I am grateful for your efforts to keep him alive. We need his talents to help bring our country through this war and out on the other side."

I cannot believe these men know about what we did. "Thank you, sir."

With a hand at her back, Jefferson eased the sisters through those trying to talk with the two famous men and on toward the table set up with food that far surpassed anything Louisa had dreamed of in the past years. Hams and roasts of beef, salads, bite-sized vegetables, hors d'oeuvres of delectable colors and shapes. Young men in white jackets walked about the room with trays of fluted glasses that Louisa knew contained spirits.

She declined a beverage and allowed herself to be propelled to the end of the table where the serving began. Full plate in hand, she seated herself at the table Jefferson indicated, all with the feeling she was up high in one of the corners looking down on some stranger who had assumed her name.

She studied the food on her plate. If only she could take these delicacies home to her boys, how they would delight in the tempting fare.

"Now don't you go thinkin' of others right now. Just enjoy what you have before you, now hear?" Carrie Mae leaned close enough to whisper in Louisa's ear.

"Are you a mind reader or what?"

"Never you mind, but I was right, wasn't I?"

Louisa nodded. Since she was sitting with her back to the damask draperies, she could watch the room, or what she could see of it between groups of people. Zachary remained on the other side of the ballroom, one man staying by his side. The two of them were in deep discussion, interrupted by brief interludes of conversation with other men and women. She could tell by watching him that he greeted these interruptions out of necessity but would rather have talked only with the one man.

And that man looked familiar. Where had she seen him before? Trying to figure that out, Louisa ate most of her supper without much attention to the conversations around her.

"Sister, come back. Where are you?" Carrie Mae tapped Louisa's arm with her fan.

Louisa started, nearly dropping a bite of ham. "Why? What?" She dabbed at the corner of her mouth with her napkin. "Did you say something?"

Carrie Mae giggled behind her fan. "I wondered if you noticed."

"Noticed what?"

"That man over there with Zachary. He keeps lookin' our way. Do you know who he is?"

"No, but he does look familiar."

"Well, I thought sure you must know him, the way he's been starin' at you."

"Well, if he's a friend of Zachary's, he—"

"Look, he's comin' this way. Jefferson, dear, do you know who he is?"

"Who?" He followed his wife's gaze. "Oh, of course, that is Wilson Scott, recently recovered from his war injuries. He was a year or two ahead of Zachary at college." Steadly stood to extend his hand. "Welcome back to Richmond, Wilson. Glad to see you are looking so well."

"Thank you, good evening." He stopped in front of the table. "Miss Highwood, Mrs. Steadly, I'm sure you don't remember me."

Louisa felt like someone was cracking open a door in her mind but wouldn't open it to reveal the secret hiding there. Then the door swung wider.

"Willy?" Louisa laughed in delight. "You visited Twin Oaks one summer with Zachary. I remember that—"

"Oh, please. I know what you are going to say. I fell off one of your horses, smack dab into a slough. Your older sister laughed so hard I thought she might fall off, but—"

"It would take more than laughter to unseat Jesselynn."

"Join us. Please sit down." Jefferson swung a chair next to the table. He waved to a waiter. "Bring this man a drink."

Louisa watched as Wilson sank into the chair with a sigh of relief that she knew she wasn't supposed to notice. By the way he moved, she guessed he'd suffered a back injury.

While he answered Jefferson's questions, she noticed other things, like well-cut lips that smiled so readily, hazel eyes with creases at the edges that spoke of either laughter or lots of time in the sun. A patch of hair on the right side of his head had turned white, stark against the rich cordovan of the rest. A slight bead of sweat on his clean-shaven upper lip made her think he might be in pain, even now. While he wasn't a tall man, his broad shoulders filled out the dark coat and gave him an imposing air.

Louisa brought herself back into the moment. "And what rank will you return as?"

"Major."

Ah, another major in my life. The thought made her sigh. And from the sounds of things, this one would be gone as soon as the other. She felt her sister's foot nudge hers under the table.

"Can I get you anything, Major?" She nodded toward the table of food.

"No, thank you, but I'd best be going on." He looked Louisa directly in the eyes. "But I would like to call on you tomorrow, Miss Highwood. If that is not too forward. I mean . . . I know . . . if times were different . . ."

Louisa smiled. Now would be the time to use her fan, to open it and fan herself oh so delicately. But she kept her fan closed on the cord about her wrist.

"That would be fine." She could hear the squeal that Carrie Mae didn't utter. Had this all been a setup? She wouldn't put such a thing past her baby sister, not for one minute.

Chapter Thirty-Four

On the Chugwater River

Jesselynn found Ophelia kneeling by the drying racks.

"Are you all right?"

"Soon be." She laid more strips in place as the smoke shrank the former. She groaned and clutched her belly.

"The baby is coming?" Jesselynn knelt beside her.

"Yessum. Be soon now, I be thinkin'."

"I'll get Mrs. Mac." Jesselynn could feel her heart speed up already. While she'd helped at many birthings, she'd never done one herself.

"Not yet."

"You'll tell me when?"

Ophelia's laugh turned into another groan. She got up and walked around the fire to move more strips around. "Dis baby in a hurry to be borned."

"I'll have Jane Ellen take the boys to play in the other cave and get Mrs. Mac. My medicine box is . . ." She glanced up at the shelf. "Right here." Jesselynn laid a hand on Ophelia's shoulder. "Do we have time for that?"

Ophelia nodded and started slicing more strips off the elk haunch.

Jesselynn headed back outside to the gathering and, drawing Meshach aside, whispered the news to him. Then she made her way to Jane Ellen.

"Please watch the two little ones. Ophelia is having her baby."

Jane Ellen jumped to her feet. "You want I should help?"

"You will be by keeping them out of the way. I'm getting Mrs. Mac."

Jesselynn stood just behind Mrs. McPhereson, who was talking with Aunt Agatha. "Mrs. Mac, Ophelia is having her baby," she whispered. "Come when you can."

"I'll be right there. Let me get my things."

"Is she all right?" Aunt Agatha had obviously overheard.

"I hope so. She keeps working at the drying rack."

"You want to take her to one of the other caves and let the rest of us see to dinner?"

Jesselynn stopped. Aunt Agatha had indeed spoken to her, just like she used to. *Thank you, Lord.* The forgiveness was a reality.

"How far along is she?"

"No idea."

Though Jesselynn hadn't been gone more than five minutes, when they returned they found Ophelia lying on a pallet, pushed up against the wall so she had a backrest.

"It comin'," she groaned, panting between contractions.

Mrs. Mac dashed to her side, and Jesselynn fetched her medical kit off the shelf. At least she had scissors and tincture of iodine in it. The baby had slipped out and lay in Mrs. Mac's hands by the time she returned.

"A girl. You have a baby girl." Mrs. Mac sniffled between the words. "She is so perfect." The baby let out a squall loud enough to be heard over thunder, making all three women chuckle. "She sure has a healthy set of lungs." She laid the baby on Ophelia's chest and turned to Jesselynn. "You can cut the cord after we tie it off. You brought some string?"

"No, but a fine piece of latigo should work." Jesselynn

knelt at Ophelia's side. "You did fine, 'Phelia, just fine. And now we got a little girl in camp. Just think, she's the firstborn of our new life." She kept up the comforting words as she waited for the cord to cease pulsing, knotted the latigo, and cut the cord.

"De baby borned already?" Meshach stopped just inside the curve of the wall.

"You have a baby girl, and she is not happy with any of us at the moment." Jesselynn smiled up at the big man. "We'll get things cleaned up here, and you can come visit."

Ophelia held out her hand. "Come see our baby."

Within minutes, Ophelia was sitting propped against Meshach's chest, their daughter tugging on a nipple like she'd been nursing for weeks.

"She just like a little pig." Meshach traced his daughter's skull with a gentle forefinger. "What shall we name her?"

"Lucinda."

"Ah, such a fine name. Lucinda be pleased she have a namesake."

"And what name will you use for your surname, now that you are free?" Jesselynn knelt beside the family and offered a cup of water for Ophelia to drink. "You must drink lots now to make milk for the baby." She glanced back to Meshach to see a look of pure fear masking his usual smile.

"You don' want us to be Highwood?"

"Oh, Meshach. That's not what I meant at all." She shook her head and held out her hand. "No, Meshach, I would be proud if you want to keep the family name. But some . . . some . . ." She turned her slightly cupped hands palm up. "Some freedmen never want to hear their old name again."

"But some freedmen had massahs what beat dem. Marse Joshua was one fine Christian genneman. He more like a father to me den my own father."

Thank you, Lord, for giving me a father like mine. Times like this I miss him so much I could bawl like a baby. Daddy, if you can hear, be proud of us. Be glad for us, for our new life out here.

"Thank you, Meshach, we will never mention this again." Jesselynn cupped the baby's head. "Do we call you Lucy, for Lucinda is such a big name?"

One by one the others tiptoed in and admired the baby. Sammy and Thaddeus stood back until Ophelia beckoned them to her.

"See our baby girl?"

"Can she run?" Thaddeus leaned closer to Jesselynn.

Ophelia shook her head. "No."

"Can she go fishin'?" The day before Thaddeus had been fishing with Daniel and caught five fish.

"No. But someday."

"Can she play with sticks?"

"No. Not yet."

He looked up at Jesselynn. "Is she broke?"

Jesselynn stooped down beside him. "She's not broken. She was just born, Thaddeus. She has to grow some."

He shook his head, disgust in every line of his sturdy body. "We eat now?"

"Yes, dinner will be ready very soon. You two go on out and help Mrs. Mac."

Meshach chuckled and laid his cheek against Ophelia's head. "I reckon dey don' think much of de baby." He looked down to see his wife and daughter both sound asleep.

Two nights later, Jesselynn and Wolf were just falling asleep in the tent they'd pitched down in the meadow near the grazing herd, when Jesselynn heard a voice. She crawled out of the tent and, looking up the hill, saw Meshach standing with something in his hands. She paused in the shadow while moonlight outlined him in silver.

He raised his cupped hands and looked heavenward, his arms strong and unwavering, his face radiant with glory.

"Lord God, see my daughter, my daughter who is free. No slave but free!" His voice rolled over the land, his words ringing like cathedral bells. Like the angels who came to the shepherds, his voice spoke of freedom from fear. "My daughter, Lord, who is born free, named Lucinda after your servant, Faith after you, Highwood after our family, she be yours. She be yours."

The baby cried once but stopped as soon as her father gathered her to his bosom.

Jesselynn crept back to lie beside her sleeping husband, the tears continuing to wet her pillow long after she fell asleep.

Getting ready for the trip to the fort took weeks. October stayed warm with chilly nights as they all worked toward winter preparations. The horses to be sold were well trained and groomed to look their best. Trade goods, such as carved pitchforks, willow baskets, knitted stockings, buckskin shirts, braided rawhide bridles, and ropes took up wagon space. The three fattest oxen were chosen to sell for beef, and seven horses formed the herd to be sold.

The night before they left, the temperature plummeted, leaving the ground white for their early morning departure.

Nate and Aunt Agatha drove one wagon, Benjamin another, and Jesselynn the third. Wolf rode his Appaloosa, and Mark Lyons mounted one of the new mares. Daniel and Meshach stayed in camp with the others.

Jesselynn laughed at the sight of her breath in the air. The rising sun sprinkled the ground with gemstones, glittering every color of the rainbow.

"Lord bless and keep thee." Meshach raised his hand in benediction.

"And you, also." Jesselynn raised her gloved hand in return. "Be watching for our return in a week." If it weren't for the wagons, the trip would take two days each way, but because they needed to haul so much back, it would take longer.

"We'll throw a wedding party when you return," Mrs. Mac promised.

Aunt Agatha laughed and ducked her head against Nathan's shoulder.

As the wagons creaked out of the meadow, Jesselynn looked back over her shoulder. What a beautiful valley. Now to just keep it peaceful.

The closer they drew to the fort, the more traffic they encountered—army patrols, fort Indians, and other settlers who occupied land near the fort.

"Sakes alive, never saw so many people," Agatha said loud enough for Jesselynn to hear as she rode the mare alongside the wagons.

Jesselynn laughed. "We used to see twenty wagons all day every day."

"I know, but that seems in another life. Like Springfield is a dreamland that I made up."

"At least everyone will be reminded we are still alive." Jesselynn patted her saddlebag that carried the letters she and the others had written. The next stagecoach would take them all east, and hopefully there would be letters with news from Richmond and Twin Oaks to collect at the post office.

Jesselynn paused for a moment. She'd started to think *home* in reference to Chugwater, but her mind often changed it to Twin Oaks. It was confusing. Had this outpost already become home to her? She pondered the question. *Maybe it is that wherever Wolf is, is where my heart now calls home.*

She looked across the herd to Wolf, who rode so effort-lessly. As if he felt her gaze, he turned to look at her. Her stomach clenched, and her cheeks grew warm. Always his look had that power over her. She touched the brim of her hat with one finger. He touched his brim in return, a signal of love across the bobbing heads of horses. In her second saddlebag were rolled her skirt and a new waist sewn by Aunt Agatha. Wolf had yet to see her in her new finery. She'd been saving it for Aunt Agatha's wedding.

Since the sun was about to set, they made camp a quarter mile from the fort, and Jesselynn and Wolf rode on in to make arrangements for the wedding and the trading. Bugle notes floated on the air as they rode into the parade ground. They stopped their horses and watched the Stars and Stripes ripple in the breeze as the soldiers brought it down for the night.

After folding the flag, the detail tied down the halyard and stepped back. They saluted, pivoted, and marched off in pre-cise time with their officer's orders.

As one, Jesselynn and Wolf signaled their horses forward, then stopped in front of the store and tied their horses to the hitching rail.

"I'll go see when the captain would like to inspect the horses while you place our order. Meet you at the Jensens'." At her nod, he strode off to the quartermaster's office, and she climbed the two narrow risers to the roofed porch. The bell tinkled over the door when she pushed it open, and the cornucopia of smells that said "store" greeted her entrance.

"Why, Mrs. Torstead, good to see you. Y'all makin' out all right up in that Chugwater country?" Sam Waters came from behind the counter to greet her.

"We most certainly are." She handed him her list. "Takes a lot to feed and care for all those people."

"Like a village all your own, ain't it?" He read down her order. "Why, looks like we got about everything. You need it all tomorrow?"

"Yes, thanks. There's something else, though. You know anyone who has a milk cow for sale? I'd like a couple of chickens too."

"Hmm." Sam scratched his chin. "You might could ask out at the Breckenridge place. He raises and sells oxen to the folks goin' west."

"Where is that?"

"Off east of the fort. Cross back over the river and head due east about a mile or so—no, more like two. Tell 'im I sent you." Sam looked down at her list again. "He and his family live in a sod house and dugout."

"Thanks. Sure would like to have milk for the little ones."

"You might could use a goat if he don't have no milk cow. Goats is cleaner and don't take so much feed. My wife runs goats out back. You could talk with her."

Jesselynn nodded, then swung her saddlebags off her shoulder. "I got mail to go out. Anything come for us?"

He took her letters with a smile. "You goin' to be right pleased." Moving behind his counter, he pulled a thick packet of letters out of a cubbyhole. "I put McPheresons' in with this too, along with Mr. Lyon's. If'n you let me know about where you live, I could sometimes send mail out with an army patrol, if they're goin' thataway."

"Thank you, we'll do that. Oh, and I have a lot to trade too. We'll bring the wagons in early in the morning."

"Fine by me." He walked her to the door. "You might want to take time to look through our new shipment of cloth too. Just came in t'other day."

Jesselynn slid the packet of letters into her saddlebag as she left the store. She'd wait until they could all hear them together. But the temptation to peek dogged her all the way to the Jensens' home.

Aunt Agatha and Nathan Lyons stood before the chaplain the next morning, with Jesselynn standing up for her aunt, and Wolf for Nate. As they said their vows, Jesselynn leaned forward enough to see Wolf, only to find him doing the same. The smile he gave her sealed their own vows all over again.

Strange, Jesselynn thought as she heard her aunt making the same vows she'd repeated so recently. *A month ago she wouldn't speak to us, and now we're standing up for them. Lord, you sure do have a sense of humor.* The word "cherish" leaped out at her. To cherish one another. Love, honor, and cherish. *Lord, please show me how to cherish Wolf. I get so busy that I overlook things, things that might be important to him. How am I to know them?*

She brought herself back to the matter at hand.

"And now, may the Lord, who gives us so abundantly more than we think to ask, bless and keep thee in the way everlasting."

So all I have to do is ask?

"I now pronounce you husband and wife." The chaplain smiled at the newlyweds. "You may kiss your bride."

Jesselynn turned enough to see the red creeping up Aunt Agatha's neck. Turning further, she caught Wolf's wink at her. Now her own neck was heating up.

"The guesthouse is ready for you," Mrs. Jensen said after congratulating the couple. "I made sure there is food for your supper all ready."

"Land sakes, you didn't have to go to all that trouble." Aunt Agatha shook her head. "It's not as if we're young like—"

"Agatha, let us thank these wonderful friends of ours and

be on our way." Nathan took her by the arm, thanked them all, and away they went.

Jesselynn looked at Wolf, then at Mrs. Jensen. "Well, I'll be. Did I really hear a 'Yes, dear'?"

They swung by the guesthouse shortly after dawn with the wagons loaded, including a pair of gray goats and a trio of chickens, the young rooster missing the stewpot by only a day. The way home didn't seem so long when they had so many wonderful surprises to share.

Jesselynn was pretty sure her secret would get told soon. Each day made her more certain. She hugged her midsection with joy, hoping Wolf would be as delighted as she.

CHAPTER THIRTY-FIVE

RICHMOND, VIRGINIA

October 1863

Dear Jesselynn,
Thank you so much for your letter. I was beginning to think you had fallen off the face of the earth. The poor mail service is frustrating at times, but I suppose it is one more thing for which we can blame the war.
Thank you for telling me such wonderful things about Thaddeus. It sounds like he has his uncle Zachary's sense of humor. At least the way our brother Zachary used to be. Since our return from our last mission north—I wrote you about that time when Zachary was saved by a pardon from Mr. Lincoln—our stubborn, hardheaded brother cannot seem to get over the experience. When I revealed our angel in disguise to be President Lincoln, I thought Zachary was going to explode right then and there. At times I think he hates me for getting him released. He doesn't seem to want to live anymore, at least that's what he told me. Please help me pray that the brother we once knew will come back to us.
My news here is that I have met a man, thanks to the conniving of our sneaky little sister. She dressed me up one evening in a dress the likes of which I haven't seen since before the war, and off we went to a soirée, where I was introduced to President

Jefferson Davis and my hero, General Lee. My heart nearly jumped out of my chest when they both commended me for helping Zachary on our missions. I hoped their approbation would please Zachary too, since he received the brunt of it, but I wouldn't know, because he hasn't spoken to me since. The glares he sent my way gave me an indication of his feelings, however.

But in spite of all that, Major Wilson Scott asked to be introduced to me and then asked if he could call on me. We met him years ago, when Zachary brought him home from college to visit Twin Oaks. Carrie Mae was so excited she couldn't quit talking about him.

He did come to call and charmed Aunt Sylvania all a-twitter. He is recuperating from a back injury and hopes to be rejoining his company soon.

Isn't that the way of it? He seems a fine man, the kind Daddy would be proud to have come calling. Major Scott is from Tennessee. His father raised Tennessee Walking Horses, and like most of our horses, they were sacrificed to the war.

Louisa reread what she had written. *Hmm, sounds like I'm enamored of Major Scott, and here I've only seen him three times.* She continued her letter with bits about the men staying at Aunt Sylvania's, Miriam's antics, and her hopes for them to all be together again.

We miss you, and think of you every day. It pains me to think of how quickly life is changing. We have so little control. Therefore I commend you to the keeping of our Lord and Savior, who is far more able to keep you safe than I ever could.

Be assured that I pray for you all every day and always look forward to seeing your dear faces again.

Your loving sister

She signed her name and caught the tear that would have blotted the paper. If only she could share good news about their brother. If only the distance were not so great as to be impossible.

No, she reminded herself, *with God all things are possible. Even bringing this family back together again. Even bringing Zachary back.*

Somehow the latter seemed far more difficult than the former.

"Miss Louisa, dat genneman be here to see you," Abby announced from the French door leading out to the veranda where Louisa had escaped in hopes of finding a bit of breeze.

"Show him out here." Louisa looked down at her waist. Should she change? She shook her head. Perhaps it was time for Major Scott to see her as she really was, not all groomed and polished like a horse readied for auction. She tucked a strand of hair back in the chignon she wore most of the time, since it was cooler, and wiped beads of perspiration from her upper lip. "Please bring out a pitcher of lemonade when you can."

"He talkin' wid de sojers."

"Good. Perhaps he can cheer them up. Tell the men that lemonade will be served out here shortly."

Abby shook her head. "I don' think dat a good idea. Why, de major come all dis way to be wid you, not all de others."

"Oh." Louisa sighed. "All right. I will show him the roses or something. I can't keep the entire backyard for myself, now can I?"

"Not every day a fine genneman come callin'." Having stated her obvious disagreement with Louisa, Abby spun fast enough to make her skirt swirl and returned to the house.

Louisa shifted her gaze from outer to inner. Was her heart beating just a mite faster? Her cheeks warmer? Unbidden,

Major Dorsey strolled into her mind.

Lord, I cannot pay attention to that man. After all, he's a Northerner, he's military, and besides, I'll never see him again. I loved Gilbert and he died. That's what the war does—kills the good men. She amended the thought to men in general.

I don't want to fall in love with an army man again.

But when Major Scott walked through the door, she had to admit he was a fine-looking man, with a voice deep enough to send shivers up her back.

"I'm sorry to intrude like this, but I cannot stay more than a few minutes."

"You are in no way intruding. I've just finished a letter to my sister who now lives in Indian territory not too far from Fort Laramie." Louisa knew she was babbling. She took a deep breath. "I take it you have news?"

"Yes, both good and bad, depending on how you look at it." He tucked her hand through his arm. "Shall we walk and talk?"

Louisa started to draw her hand away, but at the look of supplication on his face, she kept it on his arm. She hoped he couldn't feel the way her heartbeat picked up.

Under the magnolia tree in the far corner of the garden he turned to look down at her. "My good news is that I've been reassigned to my regiment."

"Oh." What more to say? "I'm glad" would be a lie. "How sad" would hurt his feelings.

"The sad news is that right now I'd rather stay in Richmond. I never thought I'd feel this way." He took her hands in his. "Miss Louisa, would it be all right if I wrote to you?"

"Of course, sir, I'd be right honored."

"And . . . and would you write back?"

Louisa nodded. "I would. I know there is no guarantee my letters would get to you, but I will do my best."

"That is all one can ask." His eyes said far more than his lips, and the gentle pressure on her fingers added a third dimension.

"Thank you, Miss Louisa, you have made me a happy man." He sighed. "I leave as soon as I can get packed. Say a prayer for me, please. I feel I need all the prayers I can get."

"Of course. Let me wrap some cookies for you to take along."

The two strode swiftly back to the house, and within minutes he was gone, a package of lemon cookies tucked under his arm.

Louisa leaned against the pillar post on the front porch. Was she always destined to send men off to battle?

November 1863

Dear Jesselynn,

You are married? Tell me more! How? When? And you must tell me more about your husband. You have been rather enigmatic concerning this great event in your life. How did he come to be called Wolf?

I am so glad to hear that you had horses to sell to the quartermaster at Fort Laramie. I am not at all surprised that you have become a trainer of horses and the methods you described make such good sense. I still have a hard time picturing you in britches and Daddy's old felt hat.

I love your descriptions of Wyoming and of those you claim have become like family. I am jealous, you realize, that others can visit with you and enjoy your company when I cannot. But I am coming to realize that loss is a part of life, and we just need to do our best to weather the changes.

I am glad you were able to write good news, but I am not so fortunate. Remember the man I met at the soirée with Carrie

Mae? Major Wilson Scott called on me several times and then announced that he was being sent back to his regiment and asked if he could write to me and would I return the favor. Of course I said yes, but after three letters I heard no more from him. Jefferson told me last evening that Major Scott had been killed in the line of duty. Such barren words. Please don't ask me if I loved him, for I am no longer sure I know what that means. I was beginning to care for him, however, and I now am grieving for what might have been.

She didn't mention another letter she had received only two days earlier, this one signed *Major James Dorsey.* She told no one about the letter that Reuben again found on the mat at the front door.

I am beginning to believe that I am destined to be an old maid, caring for my sister's children. And yes, that means what you think. Our Carrie Mae is in the family way again, and Jefferson is sure it will be a boy this time. As if any boy could be more lovable than our baby Miriam. I must close and go assist with the sewing bee. Two of our men were released to return home, so I must train others. May God hold you close and protect you and those you love from all harm.

Your loving, but sad, sister

Louisa picked up Bones and cuddled him under her chin. When he began to purr, she sank down in a chair and let her tears dampen his fur. Major Dorsey had written that he thought of her often and prayed that God was keeping her safe. Wishing she could write back, she shivered in the cold. They had no coal nor wood to heat the house, so all their work was done in the kitchen where the cooking fire devoured any sticks they could find. Some folks were cutting down the big old trees that lined the streets and provided shade in backyards. Another sacrifice to this wretched war. Louisa shivered again. When would it end?

CHAPTER THIRTY-SIX

RICHMOND, VIRGINIA

April 1865

Dear Jesselynn,

The war is over. I cannot begin to describe my feeling of relief that there will be no more killing. While I know some in the Confederate government were eager to fight on, all I can think of is that we can go home. Home to Twin Oaks, if I have to walk all the way. Though that is such wondrous good news, I have news of the other kind, which brings me to frequent tears. Aunt Sylvania went home to be with our Lord a week before the surrender. She went to sleep one evening and never woke up. I know she is happy, for there was a look of such peace on her face that Jesus must have met her right there himself, instead of sending any angels.

Louisa wiped away the tears that still fell when she thought about her aunt who'd become so frail in the final months of the war.

We will be leaving for home soon. Zachary has not given me a specific date, but I have our things all packed, and tomorrow will go to say good-bye to Carrie Mae. Little Miriam is the one I shall miss the most. She is such a delight, chattering

*away. Though I cannot always understand her, she has a
large vocabulary for one so young. I shall miss her dreadfully.
Please write to us at Twin Oaks. Perhaps now that the war is
over, the mail will go through on a regular basis. I do so love to
hear from you. Is there any chance at all that you will come
back to Kentucky? I can tell that you love Wyoming and your
life there, but along with seeing you and Thaddeus, I want to
meet the husband you speak so highly of, and my other niece
and nephew also.*

With love always from your sister,
Louisa

As she sat rereading the letter, Zachary strode into the
room.

"If you want to go along, be ready in the mornin'." He
turned away without waiting for her answer.

"But what about. . . ?" Louisa didn't bother to finish her
question. Zachary didn't care one whit what happened to
Reuben and Abby, or Aunt Sylvania's house. Should she
deed them the house? After all, it had been their home for
much of their lives. But what would they live on? Reuben was
far too old to find a position easily, and while Abby might find
one as a cook or maid . . . Louisa shook her head. Should she
take them with her? Or at least ask them if they wanted to go?
Oh, Lord, what am I to do? What will they eat if they stay here?

Why do I have to be the one to make these decisions? This
thought ignited a spark of anger. If Zachary was head of the
Highwood family, why didn't he act like it? *Daddy, you would
never have made Mama handle all of this.*

Her sigh came from so deep inside that it took all her
strength out with it. *Lord, I cannot handle this. What am I to
do?* She wondered if her mother had felt the same way, and
now that she reconsidered, she realized the Highwood

women always made the major decisions, even long before the war, when the men were off trying to either start it or keep it from happening.

Louisa wandered out to the back veranda where their remaining two guests were enjoying the sun, weak as it was. Actually, the air felt warmer outside than in.

"Y'all want a cup of coffee?" Louisa asked as she stopped between their chairs. Since they had no more sewing to do, Louisa had finished the last jacket and given it to one of the men to wear home. They were talking about what they'd do when they got home.

Samuel looked up, his smile creasing a face too young to have seen all he had. "That sounds mighty fine, Miss Louisa. Looks like we'll be headin' out tomorrow. I do thank you for keepin' us as long as you have."

"You're more than welcome. Coffee coming right up." She returned to the house in time to meet Abby carrying a tray out to the veranda.

"You read my mind."

"You gonna sit a spell and drink wid dem?"

"No, I think not. Could you and Reuben meet me in the parlor as soon as you've served them?"

Abby gave a brief nod and continued on out the French doors.

Louisa stood by the lace-draped windows, fingering a hole where the sun-rotted threads had separated. Who would have money to buy a house like this one? And what was it worth? She heard movement behind her and turned to find Reuben entering the room right behind Abby.

"What you be needin', Miss Louisa?"

"Nothing, thank you, but we need to talk." She laced her fingers together, then unwound them. "Abby, Reuben, Zachary and I will be leaving for Twin Oaks in the morning."

"So soon?" The two in front of her exchanged glances.

"I know. He's not giving me any time to make arrangements."

"You don' need to worry none about us." Abby took a step forward. "We gots kin to go to."

"You're sure?" Louisa felt like a smashing weight had just lifted.

"We be all right." Reuben nodded.

"Then I shall ask Mr. Steadly if he can sell this house for me. I would be grateful if the two of you could live here until that happened, if you wouldn't mind."

"Makes no nevermind. I keep up de yard, Abby de house. We keep it lookin' nice."

"Is . . . is there anything here you would like to take with you when you go?" Louisa looked around at the walnut highboy on one wall and the carved arms of the horsehair sofa. They could use all of these things at Twin Oaks if . . . She knew the "if" didn't mean a thing. The big house at Twin Oaks was no longer, and that was that. No matter how much she dreamed it to be different. They would need furniture eventually, but there was no way to transport these furnishings from here to there, nor any place for proper storage.

"Well, if you think of anything, let me know, and I will not include that in the list I shall make up for Jefferson." She sighed again and straightened her spine, squaring her shoulders as if for battle. "I need to go say good-bye to Carrie Mae and the babies. Perhaps Zachary has told them more than he has me." Keeping the bitterness from her voice was hard, and from her thoughts even more difficult.

"You want I should borry Miss Julie's buggy?"

"Thank you, Reuben, but I need the walk." As she strode toward the doorway, she caught the sheen of tears in their eyes, and instantly tears ran down her own cheeks. "I . . . I am so sorry it has to be like this, so rushed and—" She wrapped an arm around each of them, and the three stood in the embrace, wiping their eyes and reassuring one another that all would be well.

When Louisa left the house, she had one more stick she wished to beat her brother with, his hurting those two gentle people who had worked so hard caring for them all, including all the soldier guests they had helped bring back to health.

"Zachary Highwood, if Mother could see you now, she would take a willow switch to your bare legs." Another sob caught in her throat. He only had one leg to switch. The old Zachary would have made a joke about it all and had everyone laughing.

By the time Carrie Mae's buggy had returned her home, Louisa felt like she had no more tears to shed. Or at least hoped so.

Carrie Mae had promised to come visit as soon as the trains were rolling regularly again.

Louisa hadn't added the "if." Somehow she doubted life would ever again be what it used to be.

But when Zachary and the buggy stopped in front of the house in the predawn stillness, she was ready, her clothing packed in one bag, bedding in another, and a basket of food that Abby prepared, salted with her tears.

"God be wid you," Reuben whispered as he placed her things in the lidded box in the rear of the buggy.

"And with you." Louisa gave Abby and Reuben each a hug and, with the old man's hand assisting, climbed up in the seat.

"Did you bring water?" Zachary asked, voice abrupt as ever.

"Yes." She settled her skirt and wrapped her shawl more

closely around her shoulders. She wasn't sure if the chill came from the air or from the agony of leaving. But either way, it crept into her bones, setting her teeth to chattering.

The buggy started forward, and Louisa waved once more to her two old friends. As long as it remained in sight, Louisa gazed at the house that had been her home for five years. *Dear Lord, keep them safe, please.* She fought the tears that clogged her throat, knowing that if Zachary heard her, she would receive one of his looks that stripped flesh off her bones. Maybe she should have stayed in Richmond, at least until . . . at least until what? She knew there were no good answers to any of her questions.

Zachary never looked back.

The trip passed in a morass of despair, with soldiers clumping their way home, stepping back off the road to let the buggy by. More than once she was grateful for the rifle Zachary had prominently displayed. Hungry men would do whatever was needed to eat.

Any time she tried to start a conversation, Zachary acted like he didn't hear her, only giving orders—to get down or to hand him whatever he needed at the moment. At least the harness was light, and she was adept at backing the horse into the shafts and hooking the traces. Every time she had to do something he would have been doing had he been able, she made sure not to look at his face. Icy or flaming, rage was rage.

The contents of the silver flask seemed to be his only antidote. She came to think on it as a friend.

Trees were donning new leaves as they drew close to Lexington. And the rolling green hills looked no worse for the war, except for the burned-out shells of houses in some areas and the battlefield at Richmond, Kentucky. As they drew closer to home, places looked much the same, but they didn't stop to talk with anyone. When they turned on Home Road, Louisa could hardly swallow, her throat was so dry. The Marshes' house and barns stood, needing paint and general fixing up, but smoke rose from the chimney. If she squinted, she could make herself believe it looked no different.

Ahead she saw the two ancient oaks at the end of their lane. *Oh, Lord, we are home. Thank you, thank you, we are home.*

Zachary turned the horse in between the green-furred sentinels and stopped.

No white house with green shutters and welcoming portico beckoned from the slight rise at the end of the lane. No big barns that had once looked to have been placed there when God created the earth. The brick chimneys poked skyward like skeletal fingers.

Louisa crumbled within, her heart faltering. No matter that she'd known this to be true, still some small part of her had hoped, dreamed, that Twin Oaks still stood.

She sneaked a peek at Zachary. He sat frozen, like a bronzed statue, a single tear sliding down his cheek.

CHAPTER THIRTY-SEVEN

TWIN OAKS

May 1865

Dear Miss Highwood,

I have been assigned to Kentucky to assist in the reparations now that this horrible war is over. I hope that I might call on you at Twin Oaks, as I am hoping you have returned there. I called at the house in Richmond, only to learn of your loss. Please accept my condolences on the death of your aunt.

Yours truly,
Colonel James Dorsey

Louisa read the letter for the third time. James Dorsey, a Union colonel, was coming to Twin Oaks. Of course she had seen blue uniforms in Midway, and rumor had it that Frankfort and Lexington were well populated with blue-and-gold soldiers, along with their wives and families. While shopkeepers disdained serving them, the truth was, they were the only ones with money to spend.

What will Zachary say? More important, what will he do? Louisa climbed back up in the buggy and clucked the horse homeward. At least they had a horse and buggy, thanks to Jefferson, or she, like most of the area folk, would be walking to town. She'd stopped by the neighbors to see what they needed, but with Confederate money being worthless and a frightening shortage of gold coin, everyone was getting along with what they had or going without.

The knot in her stomach that tightened whenever her brother raised his voice twisted now. When would Colonel Dorsey call? Should she warn Zachary? She glanced down at her faded and well-patched skirt. She had one dress in less deplorable condition. Thoughts of all the lovely garments that Carrie Mae took so for granted roused the little demon of jealousy. Perhaps if she had asked, Carrie Mae would have shared some of her things, but pride had kept her quiet. Her sister should have volunteered. Carrie Mae wasn't intentionally selfish, just thoughtless.

Once out of town, she clucked the horse to a trot. Perhaps the mail addressed to Zachary would lift his mood. While she'd been hoping for letters from Jesselynn and Carrie Mae, she couldn't deny the tingling joy brought by the one she received.

"I will see him again and have a chance to thank him properly." The horse flicked his ears, listening to her and keeping track of all around him.

When she returned to the log cabin that Lucinda and Joseph had built behind where the summer kitchen used to stand, she tucked the letter away in the box where she kept her writing things. Zachary never came up in the loft where she had a pallet, as climbing the ladder would be next to impossible for him. She hung her bonnet on a peg in the wall and donned her apron. Best get to hoeing. Dreaming over a handsome man never did put victuals on the table.

As each day passed and the warmth of May caused the tobacco plants to shoot up, along with the corn and beans in the garden, Louisa kept one eye on the long drive, waiting for a man in blue to ride up. She trimmed the roses back and weeded the rose garden, in between hoeing the tobacco. In spite of the wide-brimmed straw hat, ventilated by mice, that she had found in the cabin, her face and arms took on the golden hue of one who worked outside.

Two of their former slaves returned, and as they hoed and mended fences, the place took on a more kept appearance.

Everyone walked on tiptoe around Zachary, for no one ever knew what might ignite him in a roaring rage.

"I don' know what to do wid dat boy." Lucinda watched Zachary's back as he stomped and stumbled back down to the shed where he kept his bottle under his sleeping pallet. If he slept at all.

"Wish I knew. I'd sure enough tell you." Louisa kneaded her aching back. The weeds in the garden grew far more quickly than the carrots. Before that she'd been out hunting greens so they would have a noon meal. She eyed the rose garden, knowing what still lay deep beneath the soil. Zachary had no idea that the family silver and their mother's jewelry lay boxed and safe. She had no intention of telling him until the day they could be used again or were needed to save Twin Oaks.

Some days it was harder than others to be thankful for what they did have—food to eat, a roof over their heads, and work that would pay off in the fall. All Zachary could see was what was gone, not what they had. And it was eating him alive.

"You gon' write to Jesselynn and ask her to bring de horses back?" Lucinda sank down on a stool, rubbing her gnarled fingers.

"No. She will do so when she can. Besides, what use would stallions be when we have no mares?"

"Dey be runnin' at Keeneland dis year?"

"I don't think so. At least I've not heard of it. But then, if Zachary knew, he wouldn't tell me anyway." Keeping the bitterness out of her mind and voice took real gumption at times. *Lord, forgive my judging spirit. You sure have to love this brother of mine for me, 'cause at times like this, all I want to do is haul off and smack him with that crutch—or something heavier.*

She turned to wash her greens when movement down the lane caught her attention. The sun glinted on gold buttons and bars on a blue uniform.

"Oh!" She looked down at her skirt, knees dirty from grubbing in the dirt. "I have to change clothes. We have company coming." She dashed inside, disappeared behind the screen in the corner, and whipped off her skirt and waist. She'd hung her remaining dress on a hook, just in case, and now pulled it over her head. Her fingers shook as she fastened the buttons, while her mind told her it could be someone else coming down the road.

But her heart knew differently.

She stepped out the door as he dismounted from a horse that looked as if it could have been bred and raised at Twin Oaks. Reins over his arm, he removed his gray felt hat. The smile that carved his cheeks seemed only for her. He was more handsome than she remembered.

"Miss Highwood, good day."

"Yes, it is a fine day." Her tongue adhered itself to the roof of her mouth. She knotted her shaking hands in her skirt. *Say something, you ninny.*

"I'm sorry for all your losses."

Was he having as much trouble talking as she?

"Yes, thank you."

Lucinda cleared her throat behind her. "Ah . . ." What could she offer him? "Would you like a drink of fresh spring-water?"

"Yes, thank you." A smile tugged at the side of his mouth.

"Ah, good. Have a seat, please."

Lucinda harrumphed. "Here he come." While a whisper, the shock of it sent Louisa into a panic. Why did Zachary have to see this? Why couldn't he be sleeping off his drunk like he so often did?

"Louisa, get in the house!" The war injuries hadn't affected her brother's voice. It cut like glass.

Louisa tucked her chin, forced a smile to her trembling lips, and nodded to the bench beside the house. "I'll get that drink for you."

"You needn't, you know."

"Yes, but I do." She lifted the cheesecloth from the drinking bucket they kept in the shade and dipped him out a cupful, handing it to him with a steadier smile.

"What are you doin' here, you—?"

Louisa's ears turned hot at the name he'd used. "Forgive my brother, sir, he knows not what he does."

"Oh, I think he does." Dorsey handed the empty cup back to her. "I had to make sure you were all right."

"We are doing the best we can."

"Get off my land, you—" More epithets.

Louisa tightened her jaw and straightened her spine. "Zachary, I ask you to be polite to a guest here. Mama would—"

"Our mother is dead and gone, and I won't have any murderin', thievin' bluebelly contaminatin' this soil." Zachary stumbled and caught himself. "Get out of here before I get my gun, and you'll never leave." His words slurred, and spittle flew in front of him. Unshaven, hair sticking every whichway, he looked as deranged as he acted.

"Zachary Highwood, Colonel Dorsey only came to inquire as to how we are. If you can't keep a civil tongue in your head, just return to your room until this visit is over." Louisa couldn't believe those words had come out of her own mouth.

But when Zachary raised his crutch as if to strike her, she stepped back, only to find herself staring into a blue-clad back.

"You strike her, and cripple or not, I'll see you don't strike anyone ever again."

Zachary caught himself and propped his crutch firmly back under his arm. "Get off my land."

"The war is over. I'm here to help you Southerns—"

"You're not here to help nobody. You bled us on the battlefield, and now you'll bleed us again." Zachary took two steps forward.

Louisa stepped from behind the blue wall and looked up at the man beside her. "You had better go. As you can see, we are doing as well as can be expected."

"May I call on you again?" The look in his eyes set her heart to fluttering.

"No, you may not!" Zachary screamed the words. If he'd been a cottonmouth, he would have struck.

"Yes!" She swallowed hard.

"You lyin' witch. You see this man again, and I'll kill you."

"Would he?"

"No." But the uncertainty must have shown on her face.

"I can get you protection in town."

"Go with him, then. Who needs you here, anyway?" Zachary swayed on his feet and lurched forward. "I'll kill you both."

"I cannot leave you like this."

"Just go. We'll be all right."

Dorsey turned toward his horse, then back. "No, come with me now."

"I . . . I can't. Please, don't ask me to."

"This wasn't the way I hoped to do this, but Louisa, I love you. Come with me, and we will be married in the morning."

Louisa felt her jaw drop. Her clasped hands flew to her throat. Her heart raced as though she'd been running for hours. "M-marry you?"

"Go with him, then. And don't ever come back. You are dead to me. Get out!"

Oh, Lord . . . She took one more look at her brother, nodded, and met the warm gaze of James Dorsey. "I'll get my things."

"You take nothin'. Just get."

Louisa turned to Lucinda, whose tear-tracked face wore the sorrows of forever. "Please get my Bible for me and the packet of letters." She lowered her voice. "I will keep in touch."

They rode out the long lane with Zachary shouting imprecations after them. By the time they reached the ancient oaks, Louisa could no longer hold back the tears. Up the road a piece, James Dorsey swung his leg over the pommel and dropped to the ground, reaching up to lift Louisa into his arms. Murmuring comfort and endearments, he stroked her hair until her sobs lessened. She nestled against his chest, hearing his strong heartbeat against her ear.

"You know that every man I've become attached to has been killed in the war?"

"No, I didn't know that. But now that I have you, I'll be sure to watch my back."

"How about your front?" She drew back to see a water stain the size of a dinner plate on his uniform. "Good thing this is wool, so my tears won't show." She looked up to see his eyes crinkle in a smile so tender, she caught her breath. "You were really serious about loving me? That wasn't just to chase off Zachary?"

"Oh, no, ma'am. I've been wanting to come find you since that day at the prison. I figured any woman who would offer to give her life for her brother's would make a wonderful wife and mother. That you are so beautiful and sweet and caring and—"

She laid a finger against his lips. "I believe you."

"Do you think . . . ah, that perhaps . . . ah . . . ."

She watched red heat travel up his neck and face. "Why, Colonel, you're blushing." Her laughter tinkled like wind chimes on the breeze.

He sighed. "What I want to say is . . ." He paused again. "Do you think you could learn to love me?"

"Oh, I think the learning has already begun, some time ago, in fact. When your letters made my heart go pitty-pat, I told myself to stay away from military men, because they always get shot. Made me begin to think I was the kiss of death, not that all of them kissed me, mind you, but it's the thought." She sighed and in the sigh let go of all the fears she'd been holding in. "Could you hold me close again, sir? Your arms are indeed most comforting."

They were married late that afternoon by a chaplain known to Colonel Dorsey.

June 1865

Dear Sister,

I have both wonderful news and terrible news. In fact there is much to be thankful for. We planted five acres of tobacco, thanks to some seed Zachary was able to find. And thanks to Jefferson and Carrie Mae, the taxes are paid. So we will be able to keep our home.

Or rather, Zachary will. I'm sorry to say that he has banished me from Twin Oaks. When Colonel Dorsey came calling, Zachary threw him off the place. And when I stood up for the man who helped save our brother's life on that horrible trip to Washington, our dear brother, and I say this with great sorrow, threw me off the place too. James and I were married that afternoon, and now I shall accompany him west where he will be stationed at Fort Kearney, Nebraska. His orders were changed so quickly. I can't help but believe God's hand is directing us. How far is Fort Kearney from where you live? Is there some way we can meet together? I would so love to see your family. As I said, I am both sad and happy.

Please pray for Zachary, as he is drinking far more than is good for him, and he is so bitter that he is driving all his friends away.

> *Love from your married sister,*
> *Louisa*

P.S. I cannot wait for you to meet James again. He speaks so well of you, and sometimes I tease him that he married the wrong sister. Isn't it strange the directions our lives have taken, and all because of the war.

> *Your loving sister,*
> *Mrs. James Dorsey*

July 1865

Dear Louisa,

I am so glad for your joy and happiness. Reading a letter from you reminds me so much of Mama that I can scarce read for the tears. At Fort Kearney you are half of Nebraska and part of Wyoming away. Should you ever be quartered at Fort

Laramie, I could ride there in two days. That is how long it takes us to deliver the horses we sell to the army and to get supplies.

Things are tense here due to the battles between the army and the Indians. I pray that your colonel will be safe and not have to fight again. This war, like the other I believe, could be stopped if men would learn to sit down and talk instead of shooting off both their mouths and their guns. Wolf does what he can to help our Sioux friends and family have enough to eat and adapt to the white man's ways. I know that God made us all equal, none better than another because of skin color or family, but all loved by our Father in heaven.

I have not received any letters from Carrie Mae since the war ended, not that she was a regular correspondent before then, either.

Thaddeus has grown so big, and Peter John, at fifteen months, follows him everywhere, on unsteady little legs. Mary Louisa is three months old and such a joy. Wolf dotes so on her. I am busy training horses when I get the chance. You would be amazed at the things I have learned about horses since I married Wolf.

We have our own little community here. Jane Ellen is married to Henry Arsdale, a fine young man she met at the fort. He joined her here on the piece she had homesteaded, so they are our neighbors to the north. Meshach and Ophelia send their love. He has pretty much taken over as our pastor and to some of the members of Red Cloud's tribe also. I do hope and pray that we will be together one of these days. Always remember that I love you.

Jesselynn

Epilogue

Wyoming Territory
Spring 1867

"Now, Thaddeus, you have to sit still."

"I know. I'm tryin'." Thaddeus blew the hair off his face and sneezed as some tickled his nose.

Jesselynn lifted another curl with the comb and snipped it off. Since they would soon be leaving for Cheyenne to catch the train east on their journey to Twin Oaks, she wanted him to look his best. While the letter from Zachary had demanded she bring Thaddeus back to Twin Oaks to live, she had no intention of leaving him there, not unless he really wanted to stay. She knew that would break her heart, but right was right.

"The horses are ready." Wolf stopped in the doorway of their stone house, built three summers before.

"Thaddeus, if you keep squirming like that, it'll be tomorrow before we leave." Jesselynn ran the comb through his hair again and trimmed another spot. "There." She untied the towel from around his neck. "Go outside to brush off." She reached down to pick up Mary Louisa, who'd been playing with the curls of hair on the floor. Jesselynn brushed her off and kissed her freckled cheek. "Whatever will we do with you?" She kissed her daughter again.

"Now don't you go worryin' about the young'uns. They'll be fine with me." Mrs. Mac swung Peter John up on her hip. "Won't you, honey?" When he screwed up his round face readying to wail, she handed him a cookie. Sunshine returned.

Jesselynn had knit a sweater for Wolf and started a matching one for Peter John by the time the train pulled into Frankfort, Kentucky. What they thought would take three or four days took more than a week. They'd changed trains so many times, she'd come to the point she wasn't sure where they were going. At times she envied Wolf and Daniel in the boxcars with the horses. Thaddeus had alternated between the horses and sitting with her. As they drew further east, he'd chosen the men and horses over the boring sitting. When the train finally screeched to a stop, they unloaded the horses, and Wolf went to find a buggy. *I'd rather ride in on horseback than a buggy,* Jesselyn thought, but here in civilization she had to be proper. No britches and no riding astride.

She chewed on her bottom lip. *Lord, what are we heading into this time? Has that brother of mine improved any?* Not according to Lucinda's last letter, but they'd all been praying for a miracle. And miracles did still happen, did they not?

She answered that question with a smile. After all, she and Louisa had seen each other not once but twice. Surely that counted as miraculous.

A tall shadow brought her out of her reverie. She looked up to see Wolf blocking the sun. "We're ready then?" she asked.

"The bags are loaded." He held out his arm, and when she put her hand through the crook of his elbow, he patted her hand. The smile he gave her warmed her heart and put starch in her backbone.

The nearer they drew to Twin Oaks, the more Jesselynn's heart speeded up.

"The trees are still here." She pointed to the two ancient oaks that held sentinel on either side of the drive. But when they trotted the rented buggy between them, she had to shut her eyes. No white house stood at the end. While she'd been preparing herself, still the pain caught in her throat. The big house of Twin Oaks really was gone.

Wolf stopped the buggy to give her time to recover. "Even though the house is not there, I can see it clearly, thanks to your descriptions."

"Don' look de same, do it?" Daniel leaned on his horse's withers. "But dere's tobacco growin' green."

"Zachary must have more help now." Jesselynn tucked her handkerchief back in her bag. "Let's go."

Wolf clucked the horse, and they trotted between the trees that still lined the drive, grown some bigger since she left.

A dog ran out to bark at their arrival. Smoke rose from a log cabin set back behind where the summer kitchen used to stand. But while Louisa had told of the brick chimneys remaining upright, they were now only piles of bricks.

A thin black woman came to the door of the cabin, shaded her eyes, then threw her apron over her head.

"Lucinda, we've come home." Jesselynn didn't wait for the buggy to come to a full halt before leaping to the ground and running to throw her arms around the turbaned woman. Together they laughed and cried, hugging, stepping back, and then hugging again.

"I din't think dis day would ever come." Lucinda wiped her eyes with the edge of her apron as Thaddeus and Wolf came to stand beside Jesselynn. "And is dis big boy my baby, Thaddeus?" She put her hands up to her cheeks. "Lawd above, he near to grown."

"Lucinda, this is my husband, Gray Wolf Torstead." Jesselynn slipped her arm through her husband's and finished the introductions. Then looking around, she asked, "Where's Zachary? Didn't he get the telegram?"

"Oh, he did." Lucinda's face lost its smile.

"Has he a place ready for the horses?"

"He do." She nodded to where the barns used to be. "Down dere."

Something's sure wrong here. Jesselynn turned to Wolf. "You and Daniel want to take the horses down there?"

Wolf looked from Lucinda to the pole building he took to be the barn.

"You better go wid." Lucinda shook her head. "I have supper ready when you comes back."

"I'm comin' too." Thaddeus kept within touching range of Jesselynn's arm, as if sensing things weren't quite what she had promised him.

Each of them leading one of the horses, they walked on down the track to what looked more like sheds than barns. Rosebushes so overgrown they were hardly recognizable still bloomed pink and white in what had been the rose garden. *Louisa said she trimmed them back before she left. Looks like Zachary cares not a whit for beauty.*

"Perhaps I can take some cuttings back with me. How I would love to have one of Mama's roses growin' by our house. See that old burnt tree there by the house, Thaddy? That's a magnolia. I used to climb out my window and down that tree when I wanted to be at the barn."

"Why not use the door?"

"Because my mother didn't want me down riding Ahab or the other Thoroughbreds. She said that wasn't ladylike, and Lucinda was worse than Mama." Jesselynn started to laugh but stopped when she saw a man leaning on a crutch step out of the pole building.

"Zachary?" *Oh, dear Lord, can that really be my handsome brother?* She forced a smile to lips that quivered and ran forward to greet him.

Hugging him was like hugging a stone. She stepped back. Lines crevassed his face, his eye bloodshot, the black patch slightly askew. He smelled like he'd taken a bath in a whiskey barrel.

"We brought you pure Thoroughbreds, no crossbreeding."

"Only four?"

"The two mares are bred to Domino. I couldn't come until we weaned their babies, and those two fillies were too young to have made the trip well. Joker is the older stallion. He's by Ahab, Dulcie's foal when we were traveling west. Their papers are up in my bag."

"Tie 'em in there." He turned to look down at Thaddeus. "Can you ride?"

"Yes, sir."

"Like all the Highwoods, he is a natural horseman." Jesselynn nodded to Thaddeus. "Come tie your horse in that stall."

After settling the horses, the four of them stepped back out into the soft air of late afternoon. One of the horses whinnied.

"I'll feed and water them if you like." Wolf nodded to the man still standing in the same place as though the post might fall over if he moved.

"Why? You think I can't?"

"Just being neighborly." Wolf took a step closer to Jesselynn.

"So you a breed, then?"

"Zachary!" Jesselynn only stopped because of Wolf's hand on her arm.

345

The one eye burned into her. "I had three sisters, and now I got one. One married a Northerner; one a breed. I ain't got no truck with Northerners nor breeds. You can leave Thaddeus. He belongs here."

Jesselynn squeezed the small hand that had crept into hers. "We'll be up at the cabin if you have any questions about the horses." She turned and, taking Wolf's arm, led the way back to the cabin. "Daniel, if you want, you can stay here."

"No, not to work for the likes of him. I got land in Wyomin', free land."

"For a free man." Jesselynn finished the quote they all used from Meshach. She imagined daggers assaulting her shoulder blades but kept on walking. In spite of all Louisa had said, she'd hoped and prayed the return of the horses would melt the anger her brother carried. After all their work to bring the horses back, he didn't even say thank-you or comment on how wonderful they looked.

"I don't have to stay here, do I?" Thaddeus tugged on her hand.

"No, darlin', you don't have to stay here."

She stopped to gaze over the growing tobacco fields and the green, shimmering pasture. Tears made her sniff. "I . . . I'm sorry, Wolf."

"Not your fault. Nothing to apologize for. Like Meshach warned us, we got to pray for our brother Zachary, pray that someone or something will help him see what he's doing. We've got room in our hearts for that."

Jesselynn looked up at the man beside her. "How come I am so blessed to be married to you?"

"Because you had the foresight to hook up with a wagon train going to Oregon, whether the fool wagon master wanted you to or not."

Thaddeus giggled beside her. The story had been told many times, always to his delight.

Jesselynn glanced over her shoulder to see that Zachary no longer leaned against the post. "How will he handle those horses, take care of them?" She'd seen his hands shaking in spite of the tough show he put on. And the look of despair that flashed across his face so quickly she almost missed it spoke louder than his words. Northerners and breeds, eh? She sighed, this time for him. She and Louisa were both so happy, and Carrie Mae too, still in Richmond.

"Someday we'll be back. God says He answers the prayers of His people. Zachary will come out of this. We must believe it," Wolf said, taking her arm.

"God willing," she responded.

"Yes, God willing."

After eating the meal Lucinda prepared, they gathered their things. "I do wish you would consider coming with us. We have plenty of room for you, Lucinda," Jesselynn entreated.

"I stay here in my home. 'Sides, dese old bones need warmin', not cold winters like you tole me."

"Write to me and tell me if you need anything, promise?"

Lucinda nodded, and the two women hugged as if they'd never let go. Lucinda stood waving as they climbed back in the buggy. Daniel and Thaddeus squeezed in between the bags in the rear.

Jesselynn waved again, then looked toward the barns. Sure enough, Zachary stood there watching them leave. "I love you, brother, no matter what. We all do." She sighed. "Please, Lord, heal my brother." She wiped her eyes and blew her nose.

"It's a long way home." Thaddeus leaned on the seat back in front of him.

"Not really. With the fine trains and all, we'll be there before you know it." Wolf slapped the reins on the horse's rump. "Get up there, horse. We got to get on home."